D1586343

This is the contrasting story of two professional hunters of entirely different schools and origins, each one critical and suspicious of the other's professionalism to the point of enmity. Their desperately dangerous forays and ultimate mortal clash with *El Jefe Politico*, the bitter, scheming enemy of Ramirez, who covets the hunter's fortune—and his daughter—make *Viva Ramirez!* a compelling reading experience.

'Sheer encyclopaedic gusto of the descriptive writing in his straight tale of the beasts and beauties hunted by his hero in the cities, rain forests and savannahs of Central America.'—*Daily Telegraph*

Also by James S. Rand
RUN FOR THE TREES
and published by Corgi Books

James S. Rand

Viva Ramirez!

CORGI BOOKS
TRANSWORLD PUBLISHERS LTD
A National General Company

VIVA RAMIREZ!
A CORGI BOOK 0 552 08887 0

Originally published in Great Britain
by Michael Joseph Ltd.

PRINTING HISTORY
Michael Joseph edition published 1970
Corgi edition published 1972

© 1970 by Bernard Attenborough

This book is set in Plantin 10/11 pt.

Corgi Books are published by Transworld Publishers, Ltd.,
Cavendish House, 57–59 Uxbridge Road, Ealing,
London, W.5.

Made and Printed in Great Britain by
Richard Clay (The Chaucer Press), Ltd., Bungay, Suffolk.

To a *cazador* of tigrés
who looked like 'Juan Ramirez'.

And to 'El Viejo'.

And to Mike Legat
for his enthusiasm and encouragement

CONTENTS

ACKNOWLEDGEMENTS

This is not a conventional *Foreword*. It is currently the only way I can express my thanks and gratitude for a great mound of correspondence which came, and still comes my way as a result of a book called *Run for the Trees*.

In the *Foreword* to that book I mentioned a hunch I had long harboured. Namely, that there might still be *'a formidable number of readers who like their escapism bounded by an open sky'*.

It turned out to be, internationally, a considerable understatement. Of course there were strong objectors, too. A Public Librarian and some Criticasters—I distinguish from professional Critics doing a professional job—deduced that, like a highly successful contemporary American author, I write to some kind of formula. In my case that of 'hunting and sex'.

Well, I know a little about hunting and I remain, basically, a Reporter. I am also a Square.

Most Squares, I think, subscribe to the belief that sex is a true part of life. And most Reporters worth a damn believe in Ernest Hemingway's dictum of 'writing truly'.

But I know of no 'formula' of application, nor have I ever thought to invent one.

I also testified that through 'fiction based on fact', *Run for the Trees* was as accurate as research and some personal experience had enabled me to make it.

So, also, is *Viva Ramirez!* I hope it may be of some interest to some of those I have come to feel of as a kind of Brotherhood—of hunters. Both kinds.

James S. Rand

'Green Meadows',
Heads of Ayr,
Scotland.

PROLOGUE

EL VIEJO

1

When the old man came from the hut the white *halcon* immediately took off from the great matopolo tree at the edge of the compound. He flew steeply. Into the red-gold dawn light washing the roof of the jungle.

It was the fourth time in five successive mornings that El Viejo had seen him. The second time the hawk had tried to take a humming bird from the *neto*. But his talons had fouled the mesh, panicking him. Clearly, he came now to the matapolo each day to puzzle over the young jungle hens in the coop of woven *chiquihuite*.

Go hawk, El Viejo thought, for there is nothing for you here! Not that I wish you ill, a fellow hunter, he said inwardly. But the forest is full of parrot and macaw, and the *gallinas* are part of my tools.

He went down on his knees and began to rekindle the fire, using sticks that did not need to be broken so as not to wake the child in the hut.

Paradoxically, he had been known as El Viejo ... the Old One ... since his teens; because of his precocious knowledge of the jungle. Whereas his real name, that which his father had bestowed upon him, was Diego.

Now, indeed, his dialectal name was fully appropriate. For he *was* now, assuredly, an old man. Yet still, *es muy hombré*! Which, loosely, means that he was still formidable. Despite the fact that he held one arm somewhat unnaturally, as if hampered with arthritis. Though it was not arthritis that had caused it, and it no longer gave him pain when not in heavy use.

He looked over his shoulder, but the old woman and the child were still sleeping in the hut. The hut, and the adjacent one, which was his store, were isolated from the derelict cabanas farther long the compound. Except for the periodic re-

12

thatching of the roofs with plaited pandanus leaves, they had required little repairing since they had first been built by his father.

According to the recollections that he had of his father, from when he was a boy, he bore strong resemblances to him. The same shortish powerful frame, straight nose, wide-set eyes and mahogany-coloured skin.

His father had been a logger and, in the bad times, an itinerant hunter, of mixed Spanish and Indian descent. His mother a full-blooded Mayan.

It was during one of the bad times that his father had been killed by a Bushmaster when he, Diego, had been nine years old. Which had been a double sadness for him. For as well as the great anguish it had destroyed his ambition of learning the business of hunting from his own flesh.

Even before the time of the tragedy the demand for the fine woods of the forest had been becoming less and less. Each time, after a shipment, more of the loggers had followed it. Or subsequently drifted away to seek more suppositive living in the Capital, or the few citrus and cane plantations of the south. Soon, only a handful of peón families had remained in the camp. They had lived on the meagre produce of plots laboriously hacked from the fringes of the jungle, and save for the rare times when a demand had come from the Capital, their poverty had been complete. Even so, that so often they had gone hungry when the jungle offered so much had always amazed Diego. Indeed, as he had grown older he had come to think of the jungle as, *La Hermosura*, a woman, a bountiful woman, and not, *El Peligro*, a place of dread and danger, as they had done.

At the time of his father's death there had been nothing left for his mother, an Indian woman, unwanted and now destitute. They had taken the only course, and the headman of his mother's native village had taken them in.

The boy had not actively rebelled against the change though he had felt it to be humiliation, and, covertly, he had never accepted the Indians as his kin. For it had seemed to him that to have done so would have been to dishonour the memory of

13

his father.

In the five years that he had lived as an Indian, Diego had become attached to the hunters of the village. Principally, as the custom still remains, they had been an élite of half a dozen. Three younger men chosen by the three most experienced hunters. The meat providers. Not that meat for all, save in the form of fish, had been a regular, still less a staple food.

They had hunted with bows and spears of various types and uses, and by the time he was twelve Diego had been expert with the small and medium bow. By the time he was fourteen his father's strength was growing fast within him. He could then nearly manage the great bow and, of greater importance, his bushcraft was almost entire. He could cut trail through virgin bush for days, and then return with little hesitation. Pausing only to confirm his course by the sun or the stars, by the flow of a creek, the stem of a tree fern, the other things of hunter's lore. Most of the ways and treacheries of the forest were known to him then. Those that remained could only be learnt by personal encounter, rather than exposition.

Then it had been, feeling himself complete, that he had actively rebelled. Cast off from the Indian village, though with mutual amity, and returned to the polyglot people of the logging camp who, perhaps irrationally, he had always felt to be his true kindred.

The quasi-slave labourers of the camp, ever since the decline of their working use, had fought an endless battle with hunger. Their own, and that of their families. The peón who had sponsored Diego's return, helped him to make a bed in his father's cabin and encouraged him in other small ways, had done so with grave misgivings that had not been lessened by his wife's passionate forebodings.

But in the shortest space Diego had established his worth. Turkey, laaba, capybara, peccary, iguana had fallen regularly to his bow and sometimes he had brought turtle, fish or the greatly prized giant river tortoises from the creeks and lakes. Never had his adopted family eaten so well, and at times there had been surplus enough to make barter at the trading store of

14

the Chinese mulatto a few miles distant, where the track from the Capital ended. For knives, real coffee, sometimes even cigarillos or tequila for his 'step father'.

The cigarillos had been a great advantage because he had used to bring wild tobacco from the jungle, and, indeed, it had been typical of the ineptitude of almost all the loggers that, even when the camp had been fully habited, none had ever thought to grow their own.

At sixteen Diego had still not yet fully mastered the great seven-foot bow. For he had still lacked quite the strength to enable total concentration on accuracy. But with his medium bow he had already excelled, and with his near-maximum six-foot bow his aim had been scarcely less effective. It had been at sixteen that he had discovered a more profitable and exciting but dangerous way of earning. Unintentionally. *Tigré*.

Though they were almost wholly noctural creatures he had occasionally seen the great spotted cats during his seasons of hunting with the Indians. There was no great danger from them, save by chance you had approached too closely, and although there were rare ones who would attack a man without provocation. Certainly if they had tasted human flesh before and, thereby, lost all apprehension. But usually it sufficed to shout, the raised human voices defeating them. Nevertheless, the Indians had never attempted them, singly, or in a group, and he had known only one man who had killed a *tigré*. In self-defence.

With the Indians the taboo had been, and remained, a practical interdict. Specifically, their large bows were used only for infrequent tapir hunts. (The big lumbering bush cows could be stalked with relative impunity, then overcome with heavy arrows from three sides.) Accordingly, their skill was largely confined to the smaller bows they habitually carried, and to attack *tigré* with those, to provoke the charge by wounding, was to court disaster. Suicidal. Even given a lucky arrow piercing the hide to reach the vital spot. Even given three or four arrows that had found their mark. For a big cat could still charge, rip a man to shreds and then run three or four hundred yards pierced by an arrow that had not been

15

powerful enough to transfix, to *pulverise* his heart.

From the Indian who had survived the *tigré*'s attack Diego had learned that long before, in the time of the man's forbears, there had been some, a few, who had hunted the cats. He had learned also the only way in which it could be done. With the crucifix spear. To provoke the charge and then receive the beast, impale him, on the crucifix!

With Diego it had happened through impulse, and then in desperate defence. In this way. He had been hunting for peccary, trailing a small herd of the hogs through heavy bush, and at a sudden turn of the *camino*, the deer trail, he had come upon the jaguar eating an armadillo. It had been a *tigré* of medium size, not fully grown, and his arrow had been already notched in readiness. Instinctively, he had shot, taking the cat in the shoulder. Then the cat had screamed and charged. In the fraction of time left he had remembered, had known, above all, not to run. The boy had received the *tigré* crouched on one knee behind his inclined stabbing spear. Luck had been with him.

The force and impact of the charge had knocked him sprawling. But the blade had gone clean through the cat's body, protruding from his back, splitting his heart. Then, ironically, Diego had panicked, springing for a liana and hauling himself into the tree from which he had watched the *tigré*'s death convulsions.

When the feeling of shock and tension had begun to leave him he had skinned the beast, and all the long day back to the campo he had thought of nothing but the combat. For the germ of an idea had entered his mind, and he had become aware of an element in himself that some call self-pride, and others courage. That he possessed the essential quality of the complete hunter. The will power. He had not run!

He had sold the pelt of the jaguar at the store for three dollars. But from the demeanour of the Chinese he had afterwards suspected that he, himself, had not done well. Still, he had been so-to-speak in business; a business which had none of the restrictions of barter. Which paid real money. Of course, jaguar, puma and ocelot were not easily taken. But he

16

had rarely returned from his deeper, two–three-day forays without the skin of at least one good cat. Or two or three of the small *tlalocelotls* which, ridiculously, as it seemed, were of greater aggregate value.

Also it had transpired that the hides of *acayouman*, the great saurian reptiles of the lakes and the rivers, were of money value; though at times, according to the mulatto Chinese, the price of these seemed to vary.

He had always supposed that the Chinese had sent his skins to the Capital on the truck which came each month. But then, one day, he had discovered otherwise. This time the sun had already set when he had reached the post, and there had been a mule train there. He had never seen one before. Each of three *vaqueros*, mounted on horses, had led two mules piled with rolled pelts and a miscellany of trading ware. The kind of junk goods for which the Indians brought in tapir hides, ocelot and caiman skins from a radius of many miles west and south.

But from the inflexions of their speech he had known they were different. Foreigners. It had been then that he had first met the men of the Jefe Politico, from the other country across the Border.

He had overheard the conversation between the leader of the strange Facciosos ... which was the name his father had used for them, though it had had no meaning for Diego ... and the hybrid Chinese, from outside the store. The storekeeper had been declaring that in all the time since the Feast of Los Dolorosos ... for though he had no religion himself he pretended the Christian nonsenses ... there had been only four skins of *tigré*, two puma and a few of ocelot and caiman.

It had not only been the lie which had angered Diego. In payment the Chinese had never seemed to acknowledge the risks which he took for many, if not most of his skins, and when the *vaquero* had come outside he had addressed him directly.

'It is not true that there were only those few skins,' he had said.

'*Come qué no?* What do *you* know of it?' the big Faccioso had said derogatively.

17

'I am the hunter!' the boy had answered simply.

For a moment the *vaquero* had stared at him incredulously, then he had taken his sleeve and led him inside. 'This child claims to be a *cazador* ... of *tigrés*. Is it true?'

The Chinaman's eyes had widened, and he had tried to shrug if off. But the big *vaquero* had banged his fist upon the counter. '*Is it true?*'

'Ai, it is true,' the storekeeper had said reluctantly. Then he had tried to regain the goodwill of both, smiling obsequiously, '*Es muy vivo*, he is much smart.'

'I will return to talk further with you ... *Hijo*,' the Faccioso had said. Then he had turned to Diego, grinning, the look of incredulity returned. 'Come, *compadre*, we will talk business.'

That had been over forty years ago, though he still remembered the conversation exactly. Could even recall the precise smell of the *vaquero*'s cigarro. And for more than forty of those years Diego had, thereafter, dealt directly with the Facciosos, whom the Chinese had not dared to betray to the Government. First with the old Jefe, whom he had never seen, then with his heir, the new Jefe, who had once travelled in person with the mule train. It had been the time that the Jefecito had come himself that the break had occurred. Through the catastrophe of the arm. Which had happened in a moment of carelessness, in the taking of an ocelot.

Ironically, it had been but a small one too. But the half-grown fury had ripped the muscles of his right arm, his important arm, tearing into the biceps. Unable, then, to use the great *tigré* bow, scarcely even the little bow, there had been a long period of persisting inactivity. It had been then, after the *calamidad*, that they had come, bringing with them the new Jefe.

The Mestizo Chinese, successor to his father's store, had received the new Jefe with great deference. Calling him Excellency, and other meaningless occidental extravagances learned from his father. But after the paucity of Diego's cache had been seen the hunter had been treated with assurgent coldness. Without commiseration or even civility. Moreover, the Jefe, the open-handed *Excellency* himself, had reviled him

18

more than any of the others.

Surprised and chagrined he had recalled to them the great number of years that he had served them. The few times ... in all that time ... when his hunting had fallen short. That this happening of the arm was the first and only time he had fallen victim to any of the natural hazards of his calling.

The Jefe had listened in stony silence, then had cut him short. They had not been interested in his explanations. *Que te importe?* Unless there were good results next time there would be nothing more. Nor, it seemed, would the Mestizo advance a cent of goods or money meantime. More than that. This time the bag of meal and flagon of alcohol ... the alcohol was as important as his bow ... would be a loan. The cost to be taken from the next cache. Further still. That the price for the few hides now, and hereafter, would be lower because, they had said, of lowered city prices.

But despite his resentment and humiliation Diego had not been greatly perturbed. For he had never doubted that things would right themselves. Just as scythed grass grew again. And then they would see. Maybe he could come to agreement with the driver of the truck which came from the city. Or even, he told himself, in his brooding anger ... not that he really believed such madness ... he might go to the Capital himself.

But then, when at last his arm had seemed better, less painful, he had found that he could still no longer pull the seven-foot bow. The safe bow. The realisation had first saddened and then scared him. Of course, he could still take fish and turtle. Use the small bow. No one would go hungry. But he had been, was still, he insisted to himself, El Viejo, a *cazador de tigrés*! A man able to earn more, by his arm, his knowledge and his courage, than mere subsistence. To earn money. Even sometimes city-made cigarillos or tequila, though he had no real liking for liquor.

At first he had prayed often and profusely for the restoration of his arm. Saying ten Hail Mary's before he went to sleep, and at times in the day. And then for a time, in his bitterness, he had begun to renounce Her. Recalling that She had failed to save his father. That until he had never asked

19

help for himself, and surely this had not been a great thing to ask. Merely for the strength to take up again the bow which had become as vital as the arm that wielded it. The great bow, with which he could transfix a caiman at thirty paces. Which had the force to drive its arrow right through a *tigré*. So that, thus smitten with its shock power, few cats were still able to charge the spear, and those that sought flight could never travel far because of the big arrowhead, copiously poisoned, deep in them.

It was true that he had inherited an ancient single-barrelled gun from his father. But in those days he had mistrusted guns, and with good cause. For both of the times he had tried to use it had almost ended in disasters. The first time the shell had failed to fire and the second time the effect had merely been to sting the enraged beast into an immediate charge.

He had not known that the shells were much affected by damp. Nor that those dearly bought from the *vaqueros* were suitable only for birds. But more than that, if you failed with the bow there was always the chance of calling another *tigré* with the gourd. Whereas with the frightening din of the gun there was no possibility. Also, regular use of the gun, he had reckoned, would have driven whole tracts clear in quite a short time.

Yet despite the great handicap in the first period of his travail he had still managed to gather a small cache using the little bow. Mostly of the smaller creatures. But also two caimen, speared before they could reach the water, a red *suassoran*, a small *tigré* and one of eight feet. The red puma had not been difficult. Two arrows and the spear. Great climbers, and great cowards, as all the *suassorans* were, the cat had treed itself. But with the *tigré* it had been even more a happening of luck. Oddly, the cat had not seemed to see him, and he had placed two arrows in him from the deep shadows of a hardwood. Even then the raging beast had seemed unaware of the whereabouts of his assailant, and, in the passing minutes, the doubled poison dose had begun to take effect, bringing him down just a hundred yards along the *camino*.

The jaguar had been blinded in one eye with a porcupine

20

quill. But he had been a good cat which, El Viejo had thought, would help to bridge the gap with them. Remind them of his worth once the arm was strong again.

Yet when they had come again the Facciosos had cursed and reviled him even more than the first time. Declaring that he had caused them a long ride from the frontier for an obscenity of nothing. Which had, in any event, been a lie. For, as he had known, they had always had some kind of trading business with the Mestizo.

There had been worse treatment to follow. They had refused him even the meal and the alcohol, and had then taken his few skins without payment, claiming that he had been fore-paid by the previous loan.

El Viejo had spread his hands in perplexity and disbelief. 'But,' he had said, 'you cannot do this. You do not understand, amigos. The meal is for my woman and the child. Sometimes, according to the moon, I must stay in the *manigua* for three or four days. Then, I can eat meat or fruit, but they have nothing. Equally with the alcohol. Without it a man could die from even a small wound.'

The big *vaquero* had merely shrugged. 'Of your concern, *tonto*. Besides, you are finished, do you not *yet* understand that?'

'No, no. *Por favor!*' the old man had said, 'I assure you very soon all will be well again. *Como siempre*, as always!' He had smiled his assurance, truly believing it himself. Still the leader had only laughed derisively, pointing to El Viejo's arm.

'*Nada! Nada por nada*, old man! Nothing for nothing. You are finished, I tell you.' Then the old man, feeling the anger within him, had gone for his bow and would have fought. But they had also threatened the woman and the child with their guns.

In the weeks that followed it had gone hard. Spearing with his good arm he had got iguana at times, and some fish. Though seven or eight times the stalks had been wasted because his strange arm had lacked the accuracy. And then another misfortune had befallen him. Again, ironically, with a

21

comparatively unformidable creature. A young capybara. In his over-anxiety to secure the struggling *hass*, in his awkwardness, the rodent had bitten him. The bite itself had been nothing. But without the alcohol, festering and then fever had followed.

Hunger had never troubled him for himself. Often in the jungle he would not recollect food until he was ready for sleep, and then, like as not, would ignore it. Even sometimes make a breakfast of fruit, rather than wait to boil turtle eggs, roast iguana or bake a fish.

But when he had lain, weak and ague-ridden, watching the small *chino*, his granddaughter, and the old woman, it had troubled him greatly. For in his moments of clear-headedness he had known that the ache was heavily upon them, and at these times, remembering also the affliction of the arm, it had seemed to him that the Virgin had finally deserted him. She, he had believed, who had blessed and preserved his strength and courage for almost a lifetime.

Juan Ramirez had come, in the extremity of the old man's despair. Twice before the younger hunter and his men had made camp for a night at the old settlement. This time they had stayed two weeks. Until he had been well enough to fish, to use the small bow again. And they had left him a bag of meal, obtained from the Mestizo, a smoked haunch of tapir, dried fish and wood alcohol. But before that the younger hunter had taught him almost a new way of life.

From the beginning there had been the mutual respect of hunters between them. But Ramirez was a cazador of new ways, though still using some of the old ones too. Clearly a man of wealth, with strange equipment besides guns. And strange ideas beyond pelts and caiman hides. The times he had come before it had been more than a week before he had returned. Save that he had gone north and west the old man had not known which 'country' they had hunted. But they had brought back many orchids and live birds, *guainambis*, even some snakes, as well as pelts of *tigré* and *tlalocelotl*. Obviously, the plants and the humming birds must have had city value though it had been beyond his comprehension.

22

Their friendship had first become solidly established when Ramirez had begun to teach him the significance of the birds and the plants and, more particularly, the new business of the gins, the *trampas*.

At first he had been sceptical of the iron devices. Until he had witnessed the strength of the jaws: which had had more force than those of the greatest caiman. Which, indeed, resembled the jaw structure of a caiman. Even the smaller ones had the snap and grip of the big reptiles. Those you lightly buried, without bait, chiefly along the *caminos* leading to drinking places of the creeks. For ocelot and capybara. With the big *tigré* gins you used bait, live bait, and they were so strong that you needed leverage to set them. Vicious devices. As vicious as the *tlalocelotls*, with which, as with all, much care was needed in the setting and the concealing.

As soon as he had sufficiently recovered Ramirez had begun to teach him. The first two nights the traps had held only a capybara and the gnawned and severed leg of a wild dog. But the third time they had gone at night. They had settled themselves in the fork of a big mahogany, and the old man, impatient to observe the performance of the gin, had called with the gourd until a *tigré* had answered.

Once the jaguar had come through on to the deer path some fifty yards from them, the clucking of the tied fowl had immediately drawn him. In the dim moonlight the spectacle of the big cat moving on to the bird perched above the *trampa* had been of interest to both men. For it had been the actual stalking of a quarry, which you rarely chanced to see.

Immediately the jaws had taken the *tigré*'s hind-leg the cat had screamed. Both hunters had long been familiar with all the *tigré* sounds. The aggression roar, the hunting cough, the pain scream, the deep purring of a female with cubs. But the mad threshing of the cat, held fast, had been something to remember. More fearsome in a way than the roar and charge of a wounded one.

The cat had been an adolescent male, in fair condition, and it had been a very satisfying beginning though less because of the medium pelt than in the proving of the *trampa*, the iron

23

quijada thing.

But after he had mastered the art of the gins there had still been the business of the birds. Chiefly, the tiny *guainambis*, whose wings hummed as they hung in the air taking the nectar of flowers, though also a small green and gold parrot of rare species.

With the birds it had only been necessary to go to the edge of the compound. At the first glade Ramirez had spread the *neto* between two palmettoes standing some seven or eight paces apart. The mesh was soft and fine. No wider than a thumb. It was about one metro deep, and they had hung it two metros above the ground because the *guainambis* rarely flew higher across the clearings.

At first, though he had offered no comment, it had seemed to the old man a foolishness. For how would you snare such sharp-eyed *chicos* with a contrivance that, unlike the gins, had no grip to it? And even if you did, of what use were such morsels? So small that barely a dozen had total flesh enough to feed one man. But then Ramirez had assured him that each bird, alive, was worth the half of a dollar to him, and he had explained that he sent them to many places overseas. Usually by the American airplane which came each week to the Capital.

It had been hard for Diego to understand what the foreigners had wanted with the birds. But he had known that all Norte-americanos were rich, and perhaps it was that, although some *guainambis* flew far north at one time of year, they had no birds of their own that could hum and stand still in the air.

His scepticism of the *netos* had been shortlived. Surprisingly, they were quite effective, and usually without harming the birds. Not, however, that the business was entirely one of easy earnings. For apart from the few who choked themselves in the mesh there was a more common drawback. Less than half of them survived to become reconciled to captivity.

24

2

When the fire was burning well he mixed the meal and hung the pot of grey gruel over it. Then he took the square *chiquihuite* basket which hung by the door and began to walk towards the edge of the jungle. About a hundred metros beyond the fringe he came to the clearing. There were three birds in the *neto*. One was dead. It had entwined its head through a second interstice of the net and strangled itself. But one of the others was a small golden parakeet. Worth seventy-five cents.

He put the two live birds in the basket and disentangled the dead one. For a moment he supported it in his palm. *Tonto*. Foolish one!

The two repositories for the birds stood beside the hut. Basket-work boxes on bamboo stilts, fronted with mesh. Capacious cages so as to enable the half-tamed ones to hover, or hop between the perches. One contained four birds which had become reconciled. Of the three in the other cage, one had given up to the claustrophobic thing and lay on its side, eyes closed. The other two had survived the *camisado* stage and looked well enough. They scuttled along the perch without undue flutterings as the old man took out the dead one.

He removed the *camisa*, the shirt, from the small corpse and slipped it over the head of one of the new captives. Carefully, because the *camisas* had not to be tight, though well-enough fitting to stay in place. Next he took the threaded needle from the tin on top of the cage. He held the bird far enough away for his eyesight, and then made three painstaking stitches through the thin cloth of the *camisa*, the last reducing the aperture through which the small tail fan protruded.

The shirts allowed the birds to hop. But they prevented them from opening their wings. From dashing themselves against the sides of the cage and breaking their necks, or strangling themselves in the mesh.

When Ramirez had first shown him the performance of the

25

camisas he had been astonished, and then greatly amused at the sight of the tiny creatures in their shirts.

After he had clothed the *guainambi* he took the small gourds, adding a little palm syrup to the tin lid in one corner of the cage, and water to the other. While he was stirring the gruel he heard the child come out of the hut. The small girl stood by the door, rubbing the sleep from her eyes with her little brown fists.

'*Mama?*' he asked.

'*Mama sta dormido.*' Still asleep. He took the melon gourds which the child held out and poured some gruel in each. He was not very hungry himself. But it was unlikely that he would eat again before sunset, and it would be afternoon before he reached the place of the big *trampa*.

He went into the hut and for a moment he stood still. The old woman made no movement and he began quietly to gather his equipage. He carried his things outside and laid them on the ground. The bag of plaited rush, fashioned like a haversack, the leather *bota* of alcohol, the *cordel*. He went next to the store hut and got out his medium spear, the light bow and the three new arrows he had freshly treated with *curare*. As an afterthought he found his fishing box and transferred a length of line and two or three hooks to a small tin. If the hunger really came on him he would take a fish in the evening. The spear and the bow were much the same length, the height of his chin, and easily carried in one hand. For a time he had used to take the big crucifix spear, with the crossbar which prevented an impaled beast from bearing you down. But when he had grown used to the pattern of things with the *trampas* it had seemed to be superfluous, and the fewer things to be carried the better. For the same reason he did not take a machete, since there were *caminos* over most of the way he was going, and there would be little need of diverging through thick jungle.

When he had wound the *cordel* around his waist he went to where the child was sitting on the ground. He put his hand on her head, ruffling the untypically ringleted hair.

'There are two new birds, *chino*, curly one. How many days

26

have the others worn their shirts?' The child held up a hand, spreading fingers and thumb. 'Good. That is long enough. You can take off their shirts today and put them in the cage of the *descamisados*.'

'Will you bring back more frogs?' the small girl asked. 'The big *ranas* ... green like the grass with the yellow spots. The first ones are lost.'

'If you promise to tend the birds then,' he said.

He heard a sound and turned. The woman stood in the door of the hut. For a second or two she regarded them impassively, then she went to the fire and poured herself a little of the gruel. Once she had been slim and agile, though always of a somewhat taciturn demeanour. But now she, too, was old. Her skin was even darker than his or the child's. Yet it had not wrinkled, which was unusual for an Indian, and perhaps because, until the catastrophe, they had fed well on meat and turtle, eggs and fish. Whereas before El Viejo had taken her for wife, meat had been occasional and her staple diet the grey maize gruel.

He had taken her as much for companionship as for the pleasure of her body when his adopted family had eventually followed the last of the *campo* people, and she had borne him a daughter and two sons. Both of the sons had brought great sadnesses upon them, especially the second one. The first child had died in infancy and the second, Alvaro, had repeated the tragedy of the old man's own father. Playing in the fringe of the jungle the little lad had been killed by a Bushmaster when he had been seven years old.

At the time Diego had been hunting. She had run to the boy when she had heard his scream, seizing the reptile's jaws and tearing the great fangs from his arm and hurling the eight-foot writhing *demonio* into the brush. But within two or three minutes the child had lain dead in her arms.

She straightened herself from the fire, slowly, because of the stiffness and to avoid spilling from the gourd. She began to sup the gruel, using one of the *cucharas*, the hardwood spoons which Diego had first carved and explained to her when he had been a young man.

27

The old man gathered up his tools and weapons, glancing towards the small girl. 'Take much care of the child.'

'*Como siempre ... juramentado*,' the woman swore. It was an announcement of departure which had become a ritual exchange between them since the death of the boy, though there was no rancour nor condemnation in it. She had been very young and had not thought the child would stray, unheeding of her warnings.

'This time tomorrow, I think,' the old man said. 'Perhaps even before the *salida*, the sunrise. But if not tomorrow, go to the *neto* and if there are birds let the little one take them.' The child's small hands were gentle, whereas once or twice the old woman had accidentally crushed the bones of the fragile creatures.

'La Santo Virgen go with you,' she said, using another of the phrases she had learned from him.

'And with thee,' he answered. He walked the twenty paces to the larger coop. Beside the white cock there were five speckled jungle hens, and one in a corner, closed off with a reed hurdle, on a clutch of six eggs. The hens were the tamed descendants of nestlings he had originally brought from the jungle, but the cock had come from the Capital. The fowl were of little account for eggs, but that was not the real reason for them. One of the birds was almost half white. He let himself into the pen and caught it, then put the hen in his bag. Mostly he used acuris, the greeny brown jungle rabbits, or young capybara. But when there had been evidence of a very big cat a bird made the best lure because, fortuitously, the lesser preditors tended to shy at the perch, and the man smell, as a common fox will pass even a deer carcase tied with a handkerchief.

When he reached the small stream which ran across the cleared ground and into the jungle he turned. The woman was not to be seen, but the child standing beside the fire raised her hand to him. Carmela, her mother, had brought her to them two years ago, on the truck from the Capital, but she had never returned to reclaim her. Neither he nor his wife had really understood the difficulty of the child. Even given that

28

Carmela had no husband. For were there not, in the Capital, opportunities of schooling? And then to earn money in *departimentos*, the big stores or offices? And then, eventually, having become educated, to gain a good husband?

Not, indeed, that they had been unwilling. To the contrary, they had been pleased to have the little one, and would, now, have been much saddened to lose her, though, had they known, there was little likelihood of it. For Carmela was too committed to her trade in the backstreet brothel which, unversed and illiterate, had been the only employment she had ever found.

For a time he followed the stream until he broke through on to a *camino* which, linking with other deer trails, enabled good progress for some miles. This time of early morning, before the sun began to probe through the canopy of the trees, was the best time for walking. Perhaps the best for thinking also. He moved steadily, though without hurrying even despite that this time his sense of anticipation was quickened because of the spoor he had found a few days before. To move hurriedly, disregarding the respect that *La Hermosura* demanded, was always unwise, and sometimes it could be disastrous.

Automatically, as he walked, he read the sign on the forest floor. The spoor of capybara, the smaller imprint of a *laaba*'s rat-like toes, the pug-marks of an adult tapir, and a young one, in a patch of mould. And, passing through *akalche* bush, skirting palmetto groves, he watched the head fronds as a matter of habit for jumping tommy-goff. The bite of the vicious yellow-jawed ones rarely killed a healthy man. Usually, only a child or infirm adult succumbed to their venom. But the pain and sickness lasted for three days, and the fer-de-lances were always liable and able to propel themselves at a man's head.

He reached the river in the blistering heat of midday. It was not a big river. About eighteen or twenty paces wide, and there were many places where it was no more than waist deep. But even the shallower stretches sometimes harboured piranha or caimen. Both the murder fish and the saurians were lightning swift. So that it was always wise first to stone a crossing place thoroughly; which made a tedious delay.

He moved downstream along the bank until he came to the great dead mahogany that formed a natural bridge. The lesson of the rivers had been first impressed upon him as a boy when he had been with an Indian hunting party. Suddenly, the man wading ahead of him had disappeared in a brief swirling turmoil, almost before he could cry out. Taken, in water less than breast high, by a *fangoso*, an anaconda.

The bank on the other side was steep and difficult, and the heat was intense. When he got to the top of the slope he was breathing hard and sweating heavily. He moved a little way into the trees, wiping the sweat drops from his eyes, and sat down against the bole of a nargusta. After a moment or two he felt easier and stretched himself out at full length. A flicker of colour above his head, red and yellow, caught his eye. The bird edged along the bough and cocked its head, indulging its curiosity, studying the man.

That this time the big one has found the white fowl, the old man thought. *That the trampa has gripped him fast!*

When he had first come upon the big *tigré*'s sign it had given him a sensation of excitement that he had not experienced since his youth. For unless there was some abnormality, some disproportion of the feet, this was a *tigré* of remarkable size.

Once, as a young man, he had experienced a freak thing. A beast of medium size which had had the forefeet commensurate with a cat of far larger proportions. But he had been deceived then because only the pugs of the forelegs had been clear, whereas this time it had been a complete set of prints that he had found in the softer moist soil of the watering place at the edge of the creek. And the pug marks had confirmed a *tigré* of nearer three metros than two. Truly a *campeon*. Of the size and strength able to take cattle over the wall of a corral.

He felt convinced. And why not, after all? For though they were rare, though it was ten seasons since he had killed a comparable beast . . . and then it had not really been comparable with the promise of this once . . . they were not unknown.

That the trampa has taken him, he said again inwardly. *A*

30

compensacion, a recompense for the long lean time! He crossed himself to fortify the wish and opened his eyes.

The bird had not moved. It was still cocking its head now and then to stare down at him. It was a young bird, he saw. Perhaps only a week or two from the nest. And manifestly inexperienced. Separated from the other mature ones of its kind, from whose behaviour pattern the young ones had to learn the subtler dangers. Which was why it had not yet seen the black thing that had slowly grown on the branch behind it. The black obscenity, which was as big as a man's fist, ran suddenly a foot nearer to the bird and froze again. Then the old man abruptly clapped his hands and the bird took wing.

El Viejo rolled on to his side and scooped up a handful of earth. He flung it in a shower at the unspeakable thing and the tarantula scuttled back along the bough to its place of ambush.

Ofensivo! Filthiest of the filthy *ofensivos*, poison stabber, bloodsucker of little birds and nestlings, more hideous than any of the other loathsomes, the crab armies, the reptiles, the scorpions, the warriticks. He had never been able to understand why God had created the *ofensivos*, nor why the Virgin allowed them to perpetuate their vile and evil crimes. 'Fly, bird,' he soliloquised, 'and learn about the tarantulas, the tree snakes and the hawks if you would survive.'

For an hour he skirted an area of high razor grass and spiky bamboo, which you could not traverse because of the cutting edges of the grass and the wicked three-inch spikes of the bambusa. There was no protection here from the fierce blaze of the sun, and when he finally reached the parasol of the big timber again he sat down to rest for the time of a cigarillo.

He was getting near, now, to the *camino* that wound into the heart of the 'country' which the big cat had appropriated. Of those which he hunted to a form of rota ... leaving each in turn for three or four weeks ... it had always been one of the surer *tigré* territories because of the creeks and, accordingly, the plentitude of pig, deer and armadillo. Staple diet of the cats. Until now the cats he had taken from it had all been of average size and, as a consequence of such fortuitous parity of strength between them a kind of neutrality, reluctant toler-

31

ance, had existed. Which was auspicious because it was a reproductive situation.

But, as he knew, when it happened that an unchallengeable invader came to a 'country', a beast of exceptional size bent on conquest, ready to attack any other, to rob of kills, the habitual felines gradually forsook the territory to seek other enclaves. For, strangely, unlike some others of the great cats, African leopard, Indian tiger, the kingdoms of the *tigrés* were rarely of any great magnitude. And they rarely roamed widely unless, for some natural endemic reason, such as if the creeks had dried up and the game had migrated. So that where the indigenous *tigrés* of a 'country' had been driven from it by the usurpation of some overload beast, or a mated pair of them, that was another reason why the situation should be ended.

He reflected on it as he walked. *That this day may end thy rule here, then, El Campeon! Though that thy loins may many times have ensured thy rebirth before I kill thee*, he thought.

He turned a bend in the trail and saw the trio of ceiba trees. A natural landmark, which was even more definite than his blazings because of their grouping, and because one, having twin boles joined by a lateral bough, was a vagary growth like a letter H.

Now, turning aside and beginning the rising ground through the trees, he felt increasingly the agamic sensation of anticipation in his genitals and the pit of his stomach. He was on the last stage now. When he reached the top of the ridge he could look down into the clearing where he had set the big *quijada*.

He halted for a moment to let his breathing slacken. He could even feel the nerve tingles in his hand against the tree. In the dim light the new scar of the capybara bite on his wrist stood out, livid and shining, against the walnut mat of his skin and the lustreless marks of old scars. His free hand trembled. He felt that if it was failure this time, if *La Hermosura* denied him now, he would not be able to accept it, that it would be the sign to quit.

Then he heard the scolding chorusing of the birds and a tremor ran through him, dismissing despondency, changing his

32

mood to tension and excitement.

That it was not a suassoran, or any of the smaller carnivores, or even a commonplace tigré! He put the thought from him like a bad omen, willing it otherwise. *I am coming now, El Campeon,* he said to himself. *That the iron has held you. For if not I must stay here in the manigua until I have you.*

He began to climb the remainder of the slope, moving more stealthily now, because if it was the beast he had predicted for himself he wished to study the situation before disclosing himself. He had no fear of his scent for their powers of smell were very poor, and what movement of the limpid air there was was favourable.

When he was a few yards short of the crest he went down on to his knees and crawled forward. He sidled eagerly, brushing away the grasses until he found a clear view down through the trees to the pool of dappled shade beneath the cherimoya, and as soon as saw he sucked in a breath.

The great spotted cat lay on his side, his flanks dilating. Even at the distance of perhaps fifty paces he was big. Impressively big. The froth around his jaws told of frenzied, repeated effort, but he was resting now. Temporarily exhausted. Where the mottlings of sunlight touched his coat, filtering down through the foliage of the tree which held him, it glinted irridescently. A small crumpled lump of white and crimsoned feathers lay at the edge of the shade and the sunlight. The bird and its perch had probably been destroyed by the first swipe of a great paw when the iron jaws clove home and the malefactor whirled screaming.

The old man lay still.

Dios! What a *tigré.* There was a confusion of wonder and elation in his mind. Apprehension too. Lest somehow this *monarca,* this *campeon* of *campeons* should still escape him. For the first time in many years his resolution was disturbed.

He licked his dry lips, tasting the salt tang, forcing away the danger thought. Obviously, the beast was held by his extended hind leg, which was unusual, because the way he made his callejóns ... vee-shaped with piled brush funnelling to the anchor tree ... it was nearly always a foreleg. An advantage,

33

because a cat held by his forepaw was more hampered. Easier.

The cacophonous scolding chorus of the birds rose and fell, lifting each time another jackdaw flew in, or another fellow of the lurid jay species. Then, as he watched, a shadow floated across the yellow pool of the clearing.

The King Vulture made his leisurely landing on a branch above the smaller carrion eaters, and those other birds who were only gathered to voice their instinctive hate. The bald orange head and neck of the big vulture, with his yellow comb, black collar and white body, contrasted even more starkly with the green-grey backcloth of the foliage than the small colour blobs of the jays and the parrots.

When the great cat saw the vulture he came alive again, apprehending the portent of the bird, rage transcending his pain.

He rose on his three unfettered legs, displaying the majestic depth and span of his chest, the great length of his heavy tapering body. The anger rumblings in his throat deepened to a snarl, then to a great roar of fury and frustration. Even in their safety the sound dispersed a number of the birds in a cloud of colour. But the King Vulture, the harbinger, remained unmoved. Staring dispassionately down at the magnificent fury below without emotion or affront. Rather with the cold unruffled consideration of the *empresario de funebres*, the mortician. For there was no instinct or urgency in him, nor any necessity. At any time now the common, smaller assembly of his kind would arrive to keep sporadic vigil for days, for a week if necessary. When he was satisfied that death was assured, and only the time of it uncertain, he would depart. Though he would return from time to time to observe progress, or, of course, if he heard the raucous feasting sounds of his resentful subject species, the commoners who mostly preceded his own kind.

The old man watched the primordial tableau avidly. Now that the *tigré* was risen he could see the heavy chain which harnessed the *trampa* to the tree. The beast was unquestionable held fast. A fox or a wild dog would have chewed and bitten through his own leg. But that was something the cat

34

tribe, lacking similar fortitude, never did.

Even so, the iron teeth would be through hide and flesh and into the bone. And the pain and ache in the cat's leg must be intense. For the first time, paradoxically, his imagination extended to the agonising power of the great gin.

Perhaps it was wicked to kill this way, he thought. But then he dismissed the idea. For when you considered it there was much justice in it. All the felines themselves were the embodiment of cruelty. Even down to tame cats with mice. Once he had seen a female jaguar tear to living shreds an ant-bear cub which she could have killed with a single blow, or bite. The *suassorans*, the pumas, were even more diabolically disposed. Always killing first a mother and then, purring with satisfaction, all the defenceless young. Killing every creature that they could for pleasure, not food.

But, even if it were sinful he had no choice. For he was a hunter and, now, he had no other way.

For a few seconds more he lay supine. One arrow, he thought, at five paces. Truly directed, into the neck, then await the poison. The small arrows made little damage to the pelt. Still, one was always better than two. Given a true neck shot, which with a raging beast required precision of timing, the poison would paralyse an ordinary beast in ten minutes, or less.

But not you *Señor Campeon*, he said inwardly. Of such size and virility, a monarch in your prime! Perhaps twice as long before the spear thrust through your throat. He rose to his feet, sliding the bow from his back and taking an arrow. The vulture saw him at once and, as he began to descend the slope, the great bird launched itself and flapped away over the treetops.

For a moment the big cat stood frozen, staring at the man approaching. His lips drew back in an increasing snarl and then the great jaws opened, issuing the crashing threat roar, the proclamation which reverberated through the twisting corridors of the forest. He launched himself in an attempted charge, terminated by the iron pull which sent him rearing on to his side again. Twice more he tried to bound forward and was thrown again as the man drew nearer.

35

The old man moved forward steadily, resolutely. Ever since he had begun to descend the slope he had felt the fear in him, as he always did. As all honest hunters did. Did any man live who could look into that yellow-eyed, flat-eared, huge-fanged mask, the essence of malevolence and berserk fury, and not feel fear? Lack the imagination to sensitise the searing pain-capacity of those great hooks? Only liars professed no fear and only fools believed them.

But his fear was controlled fear. Over the years his command of it had increased involuntarily. He had grown used to it, disciplined it. It was not the panic which petrified. And he was unaware of the sweat beads on his brow, scarcely conscious of the anxiety sensation in his belly as he walked.

When he was within fifteen paces of the terror his mouth clamped tightly, and his eyes narrowed, straining to ward off the intimidation of the harrowing din envelopment. He halted. Without shifting his gaze he thrust the spear into the ground beside him and notched the arrow. Then he began to move nearer. Now the beast's ferocity had grown to madness. Again and again, tail lashing against his pinioned leg, he hurled himself forward, heedless of the leg agony.

The old man drew the arrow against his cheek. Then, suddenly, he saw the stretched link and halted the pull. Holy Mother of God! The curve of it was almost straightened. He continued the pull again, not daring to wait another instant now. For a fraction he held the bow-string fully tautened, then, as the great cat reared again, he released the shaft.

The arrow stuck, quivering, in the thick column of the *tigré*'s neck. Intuitively, as he backed away, he knew that it was too high to have entered the jugular, but the long barb was fully buried. The poison was home. For an instant the cat seemed benumbed with the new pain stab, then he reared again and fell forward, tumbling, into the sunlight beyond the shadow.

The old man whirled and ran the few yards for the spear. He wrenched it from the ground and spun around to face the charge. In the desperate inkling of time left all the mechanics of survival ran through his mind and, ironically, a recollection

36

of the great crucifix spear he had left behind. The weapon with which, standing upright, you could receive and impale a beast, the crossbar preventing the creature from reaching you.

He dropped to one knee, crouching behind the forward slanting blade, grunting with fear and concentration. The great cat came like a streak. For an instant he seemed to hang in the air above the man, then both were merged. The man grasped at the thick throat with both hands, exerting all his strength to hold off the great yellow fangs. He felt the searing pain of the clawing talons ripping at his shoulders and bunched legs, but he could not cry out. Death was upon him yet he would not give up. A shuddering tremor ran through the big spotted body bearing him down and the man struggled frantically. He tore himself free, rolling away before his senses left him.

When he opened his eyes again he was conscious only of a fierce yellow blur. He was staring into the sun and he did not immediately remember. Then he turned his head aside and started violently. He began to struggle up, urgently, then he realised that the great sprawled body nearby was completely inert, the tip of the spear blade protruding from behind the shoulder. He sank back on to his side and lay still until the shaking fit had passed. The front of his shirt and one of his thighs was soaked with the blood of the *tigré* and his own. The gashes on his chest and upper arm did not dismay him. The deeper wound on his thigh was the most formidable, and whenever he moved his leg the blood oozed freely. He tore the tattered arm from his shirt and bound his leg roughly. Then he got to his knees and for some moments he gave thanks with bowed head to the Virgin, and also to the Father.

Three times, climbing back up the slope to where he had left the bag and the *bota*, holding his leg stiff, he had to halt. In the bag he had tape and a broad roll of medicated bandage, from a box which Ramirez had given him in place of the cotton rags he had used to carry.

He poured alcohol on to the thigh wound and then bound it tightly, working as quickly as he could because of the pain. When he had douched the other gashes he lay back, the tears

37

rolling down his cheeks as he waited for the fierce burning to subside to an ache. Then he made slowly back down the slope.

Sitting on the grass, his movements hampered by his stiff leg, it took him perhaps forty minutes to skin the beast, more than twice as long at it would normally have taken him. And he had to work in the full heat of the sun, the salt sweat filling his eyes, because he lacked the strength to drag the great weight of the carcase into the trees.

But while he worked he said several more prayers of thanks, and sometimes, to keep his mind off the trial to come, he spoke out loud. Saying, *Thou are indeed the greatest tigré I have ever taken, Campeon! Bigger by two hands, I think, than the one at the river of Los Sirtes five years ago.* And another time. *How lucky that thy brains did not match the excellence of thy coat, for had thou charged without springing, it is I who would be lying here instead of you.*

When he had done he felt faint and very shaky. He was not distressed by it because after the shock of the encounter and the blood he had lost, it was natural, and to be expected. I will eat, he thought, although I am not hungry, and then I will sleep a while. He cut a large slice of the *tigré*'s liver and moved under the trees to eat the soft warm meat. There was, it occurred to him, a certain grim extra satisfaction in restoring some of his own blood with the *tigré*'s that was almost a *sarcasmo*, a bitter joke.

Despite the pain and the stiffness he slept for an hour. When he awoke the King Vulture was circling above the clearing. The bird cast no shadow now because the sun had changed position. He rolled the pelt into a tight parcel, tying both ends and adjusting the cord across his unwounded shoulder. It took him longer to climb the incline from the clearing this time, and when he got to the top he sat down and rested until the bright floating specks before his eyes had desisted. He had a considerable thirst now, and his head was aching.

By the time he reached the place of the ceiba trees, skirting the fern and sedge thickets to save his leg, the sun was almost down. He was not concerned with the light, but with the long time it had taken him, because although the bandage was still in position he could feel the steady trickle down his leg. The thought of the blood he had lost and was losing was the most worrying thing. For he knew that beyond a certain amount delirium and unconsciousness followed.

Still, he thought, it will surely be easier now, at least to the river, if I follow the *caminos* amd remember to keep the leg as stiff as I can. Even to drag it if I must. I will take a short rest here, and then try to make half the distance to the river without sitting down again, only pausing, when I must, to ease the leg pain. But, ironically, in just a few minutes, now that the sun had gone, he began to feel chilled from the drying sweat on his body and he had to forego resting longer.

He moved on again, using the spear like a crutch. It took him over two hours before he came to the *camino* that was about half the distance to the river. The periods between halts were growing shorter now, and the weight of everything had become twice as much. All the time from the ceiba trees he had been borne up by the thought of the river, using his thirst as a goad. But he was almost exhausted now, and he lay down, pillowing his head on the rolled *tigré* skin. He slept for half an hour then, turning, the knife pain awoke him. He was very cold, knowing that he should not be, and his mouth and throat were so parched that he could not summon sufficient spittle to lick his lips.

As he got to his feet he groaned from the throbbing ache deep in his thigh. While he had slept, it had taken on almost the stiffness of rigor mortis, and the pain of the other wounds had grown more acute. It was fully dark now and, in his reduced state, he could no longer ward off the thought of death and defeat. But it was the increasing feeling of dizziness and febrility, and not the darkness which forced the admission upon him. Even without moonlight, he could find his way by the stars, had done so numberless times.

He began to move slowly on again dragging his stiffened leg. Twice, scarcely realising it, he heard the alarm calls of *brockets*, bush deer. The predators would be stirring now but he did not fear them even though he knew he was leaving a

39

blood trail. He had hunted the great cats so long now that somehow, instinctively, he could almost always sense when a *tigré* was approaching. Even when he had not heard the beast's hunting cough. And then it was usually, save in the rare cases, a matter of making noise in good time. Of advertising the man presence by singing, shouting or even talking loudly to oneself. In good time, because the important thing was the distance factor. For, as he had come to realise over long experience it was when you came on them, unexpectedly, too closely . . . as in stumbling upon the den of a female with cubs, or too near to a sleeping cat . . . that they were liable to attack immediately. The critical distance was about four to five metros, and it was because within this distance the animal felt *himself* threatened. Though even then the red ones, the pumas, unlike *tigré, tlalocelotyl, peccary,* would nearly always retreat, despite the fact that there were some that ran to one hundred and eighty pounds, and could take a steer or a horse. With the red ones he had known only two cases when they had charged spearmen even when cornered.

He was stumbling now, despite the support of the spear, and his tongue protruded through his cracking lips. When he reached the end of a short tract of rising ground he had to grab at a tree to save himself from falling headlong. He leaned against it, panting. Then he slid down, got the dead weight of the pack and the hide off his back and closed his eyes.

Even more, now, than water, he wanted to sleep, to inter the pain and the exhaustion with it. But he dared not. For he knew that if he slept, the dizziness might grow into full delirium. Or that he might wake too late, for even the red ones would rip out the throat of a silent, motionless man.

The wan silver of moonlight was filtering down through the trees now and he made a great effort to concentrate. To assess how far he had come, how far, still, to the river. The thought of the river was excruciating, demanding. It was at once an end to the raging thirst and a promise of survival, the only clear thought now in his semi-crazed mind.

Holy Mother of God help me to the river.

He dragged himself up against the tree, shuddering with the

40

coursing pain, then he lurched forward again, holding the spear with both hands, leaning on it whenever he was about to fall. He was down to intervals of less than a hundred paces now, and the weight of the things on his back were four times multiplied. He was resting again, hunched on his side when he thought he heard the water. He rolled his head from side to side, striving to shut out the noises in his mind, to focus his true hearing. *Holy Mother of* ...

He rose again, staggered the twenty paces to the break in the trees and started down the slope. Then he fell, rolling and buffeting down the incline towards the water.

For several minutes he lay still, absorbing the fresh waves of pain. Fighting off unconsciousness and clinging to the flickerings of remembrance. Of the river.

Of thy mercy ... He made a terrible effort and got to his knees. He could not feel his legs and twice, crawling forward, his arms would not support him. Then, at last he was lying in the shallows.

For perhaps ten minutes he lay where he was, turning his head whenever he felt the need to drink again. He heard the soft splash of a diving capybara farther down the river and the sound reminded him. He dragged himself back up the bank to the nearest of the trees and leant his back against the bole. Ever since the fall the blood had been welling copiously from his thigh, and he was aware of the fresh warm trickles from his chest and arm, but he was too spent to re-examine himself.

He gripped his thigh with both hands, compressing the wound, and then, finally, he went to sleep, holding it, the moonlight glinting faintly on the wet sticky patch and on the blade of the spear lying a few yards higher up the slope.

When he awoke the first glimmerings of dawn were in the sky. The ache of his wounds and the stiffness of his limbs made him suck in his breath; even the smallest movement forcing a groan. But although he was still too weak to rise, his head seemed clearer, and he must have slept without moving, for the thigh wound seemed to have coagulated.

He began to attend to it, slowly and laboriously, removing the sodden cloth from the caked patch of flesh, and then re-

41

bandaging it more securely. When he had done he bent his head and prayed for two or three minutes, giving thanks for the fact of the coagulation. Then he began systematically to massage his limbs. The first time he tried to rise he could not. But he continued to rub himself until more of the numbness had passed, and at the second attempt he achieved it. He was very cold now, sometimes shivering, which was not natural, even though the sun had not yet begun to re-heat the forest. He got the spear and the *bota* and hobbled to the edge of the water.

The alcohol was like liquid fire, but after each swallow he scooped up handfuls of water to weaken it. When he felt sufficient of the warmth in his stomach he considered for a moment, then he emptied the rest of the spirit and refilled the *bota* with water.

He began to wonder, now, about the problem of the crossing. He was familiar with many miles of the river, and he knew from the landmark of the great boulder pile, two hundred yards downstream, that he had strayed a good way from the tree bridge. The thought of the bridge was overwhelming, demoralising. Time was vital now and he had no delusions about it; he knew too much of the inevitable end of any wounded creature, *tigré* included, in the *manigua*.

To get to the bridge might take hours of backtracking through jungle. To work up river, through the vine and liana tangles which frequently overhung the water itself, was utterly beyond his condition.

And he knew well enough, notwithstanding the alleviation of his thirst, and the temporary stimulation of the alcohol, that time *was* his greatest enemy. He wondered whether there was enough strength left in his old limbs to make the crossing, and, if there were not, whether the Holy Mother would regird him.

While he sat slumped and motionless he heard a rustle in the grass and turned his head. When the capybara saw him he veered and dived. He watched the huge rodent cross the river. Of course the *hass* was a swift and powerful swimmer. But nothing had challenged him from along or below the surface,

42

and the creature seemed to have had no hesitation.

If he could have stoned the water he would have had greater confidence, but that, too, was beyond him. He took a step towards the water, then halted, leaning on the spear, reconsidering the heavy, leaden encumbrance of the skin.

For a moment he hesitated, knowing that the weight and drag of it, of less than it, might be decisive. But then he thought, *No, El Campeon, thou art the greatest* tigré *I have ever fought and I will not give thee up.*

He entered the water and began to labour forward, foot by foot, thrusting with his spear and leaning against the current. The water rose from his waist to his chest. Again and again he almost went under, but somehow he kept struggling forward. He passed midstream, the water lapping his chin, and the current smoothly began to slacken. Then he saw the small bow wave moving smoothly towards him along the surface. He lifted the spear and began to beat the water, shouting as loudly as he could. He turned abruptly and fought, stumbling and threshing, towards the bank.

He dragged himself from the water as the caiman came gliding in and scrabbled his way through the reeds, pitching forward on to the grass.

After a moment or two he tried to rise, but it was too much and he lay where he had fallen for some time, shaking and gasping.

He had few allergies and his feelings towards most of the *ofensivos,* even the snakes, were of hatred or disgust, rather than fear. But ever since the boyhood incident of the Indian and the anaconda he had had a dread of having to fight in the water. Of the caimen, the *fangosos* and the *piranha.*

It had taken all his courage to try the crossing, and the narrow escape from the caiman had been very frightening. More so, in a way, than it had been with the *tigré,* for then, at least, they had fought on land. But as his mind dwelt on the horror of it it came to him that, manifestly, Our Lady had heard him, had been with him. The realisation gave him great comfort, and renewed resolve, for surely the meaning was that he could and should survive.

43

He made the effort and struggled to his feet. He gathered himself and began to plod on again, through the morning and the peak heat of midday.

In the last half mile of *camino* he had to halt and rest more than a dozen times, and when he finally came through the end of the trees on to the open ground he could not make the distance to the compound without pausing again.

The white *halcon* saw him first and, as he sank to his knees, took off from the matopolo. Then the child came from the hut. She cried out and ran to him, the old woman following her.

BOOK ONE

1. MARK RYAN

It was coming on two o'clock in the afternoon when John Ross decided to give it best. Up until then, saving times out for glassing the corries and eating a tin of pilchards each, they had been working the South ridge since eight. And the last hour or so the grumbling bouts in his belly had been getting more frequent. Right now they had reached the stage when the stabs were coming.

He wasn't unduly alarmed. Over the past year or two it had happened three or four times. Each of these times it had finally simmered down and passed after a spell. But this time it seemed to be quite a bit sharper. Maybe it was working up to the pitch when, at last, they'd cut the bloody thing out and be done with it. Anyway, it was sure enough going to be a dead-loss day. Wouldn't be missing anything.

The first feeling of pessimism, premonition of a jinx day, had started to intrude before they had begun the real climb. When they hadn't even spooked a single Roe in the timber of the lower slopes. Whereas normally, even on this south face, you put up half a dozen or more of the little fellows when you were coming up through the big trees.

He pursed his lips and went, 'Psst!', then repeated the hiss.

The bigger man a few yards ahead looked round. 'What is it, lad?'

Ross grimaced, tapping the side of his stomach. 'Bastard's playing up.'

The tall man in the oiled riding boots moved over into the lee of a big rock and leaned his back against a patch of the granite that was bare of snow. He took off the leather cap he was wearing, that was like an Afrika Korps cap, and wiped the sweat from his forehead with the back of his hand. Then he unzipped his leather windcheater to the belt and felt in his

46

shirt pocket for cigarettes. He said, 'Christ, wouldn't you know. Hard luck, boy ... Well that's about it, then.' He pressed against the boulder, hunching his back against the south-west wind that was still flurrying the snow, and cupped a match.

Ross moved up closer. He bent over the wavering flame, then straightened and let the first full swallow drift out of his mouth and nostrils and scurry away. Even despite the nagging distraction in his belly the achingly cold mountain air gave the smoke an added flavour, as if it was the first one of the day. He said, 'No, look, Mark. You carry on. I think it's a bloody write-off anyway, but you carry on, that's okay with me.'

Ryan took a pull of his cigarette. He slipped the old scuffed leather *bota* off his back and unscrewed the wooden cap. 'Here, have a good dram.'

He wondered whether to take John at his word; apart from which it did look as if it was going to be one of the jinx days. They happened sometimes, even when everything was right. And today everything was wrong, the weather, the light and the 'country'. The last two weeks had been the worst unbroken spell of out-of-the-question weather either of them had ever known. Then, a couple of days ago, it had looked to be letting up and today had seemed feasible. Say about fifty per cent normal visibility.

John, with the glasses, had called out optimistically even before he had finished parking the Brake. 'Can't see the skyline ... top of the Bens are still misted up. Be okay though!'

And it would have been too ... just so long as you could spot movement at half a mile ... if it hadn't been for the bridge.

The *Skiagh*, the north-west ridge, was always infallible after a spell of bad weather. Similarly with the four miles of peat hags along the brow of the *Meall*, the north-east ridge. But to get to these, and the other good 'countries', you had to cross the river, and the bridge had been down. Smashed by the gales, and then strewn along the Glen by the raging chin-high water. So the *Skiagh* and the *Meall* had been out. Also the

47

Little Serengeti bowl, as he had christened it the first time he had seen it and had counted a herd of four hundred in four huge 'parcels'. Which had left simply the southern 'country' of the *Vaan*. The escarpment that was the base of the three Glens running north and over which, like an isolated saw-tooth, *Kiledi*, the big patriarch Ben, presided.

The *Vaan* had always been real mean country. Sphagnum, rock and ground scrub, destitute of grazing. Stark and unrelieved, save for those ancient petrified relics of *The Great Royal Forest* that stood like gibbets along the lower slopes, gaunt reminders of the days when deer, without the Royal warrant, could be a hanging matter. It had never held more than the odd migratory 'parcel', and it was a worse prospect than ever now because for the past three or four days it had been taking the brunt of the gales.

Still, he was very reluctant to quit. Not only because he was a man self-reared to refuse defeat, even in relative unimportances like sport. Also because, as John had said, it would probably be a long time before he was here again, in the land he, an expatriate African 'Englander', loved as much as any other he had known. And, of course, you never really knew! The best Red stag he had ever had, a loner, an *Imperial*, fourteen points, had suddenly strolled into view one time when they had been almost back down to the river again after a day of frustrating wind changes.

He turned his head and looked up. They were not far below the crest of the Ben now. Perhaps an hour and a half to work the corries to the end of the ridge, well maybe two, in this knee-high stuff.

'Well, if you really mean it, John, I'll just give it a go as far as the shoulder ... if you're really okay for going down?'

' 'Course,' Ross said. 'Be fine. I'll take it easy, meet you the end of the track of the big holding pool. Shan't object to that heater and the end of the bottle either. Getting really bloody cold now.'

For a few minutes Ryan watched the other man moving downhill at a tangent across the white frozen-topped carpet. He looked steady enough, though once he slithered up to his

48

waist in one of the hidden clefts that pocked the face. Over John Ross's head, some twenty-five hundred feet below, he could see the black-green band of the tree belt in the bottom of the Glen and, here and there, the gleam of the river which wound along the twelve miles bottom past the cave of Sir Walter Scott's *Green Lady*.

He turned and began to move higher and across, bending forward against the slope and the wind. The wind really had a bite in it now. Some of the cross gusts stung like broken razor blades, and every so often he stopped to brush the tears from his eyes.

There wasn't any hurry now anyway. Taking it easily, it would take John as long to get down as it had to come up. Longer if he was careful. Then he still had a two-mile walk to the Brake, and a five-mile low-gear crawl to the salmon pool.

When he was a hundred yards short of the big ravine he bent lower, and then, when he was about twenty yards from the edge, he moved his rifle off his shoulder on to his back and made the rest on hands and knees. He fetched up at a big boulder which, for all its massiveness, looked as if one shove would send it crashing down into the trees. He turned on his side and leaned his back against it.

The ravine was one of the few places on the *Vaan* which held trees. It ran right up from the bottom of the Glen almost to the summit of the Ben in the shape of a wedge. Probably the outcome of some subterranean convulsion of centuries ago, it looked as if it had been hewn and chipped out of *Kiledi*'s side by some gargantuan axeman. Lower down it was close packed with heavy timber. But where it slashed upwards towards the top, the trees became progressively sparser, eventually petering out into a wind-whittled straggle of pine a little higher up from where he was lying.

There was nothing to be seen, nor any kind of movement.

He unzipped his jacket enough to get the binoculars resting on his chest and began to systematically scan the opposite slopes, first moving up to the misty banks on the crest and then down over the snow across the gorge, halting at intervals to quarter the ground for sign.

49

About three parts down the slope he suddenly saw tracks which ran parallel to the edge. The spoor had to be fairly new because there had been intermittent falls in the night. But at the distance he couldn't tell whether the tracks ran up or down.

The silence was deep, except that after each specially strong gust he could hear the groaning of a pine higher up the defile that was near to falling. The sound of the tree's agony was like a blunt saw champing on teak. He shifted against the rock and got a cigarette. The air was like iced Chablis now, and sometimes, during a wind lull, faint aromatic wafts carried up from the pines below.

Smoking didn't matter a damn of course if you were sure of the wind. Although a cross gust eddying from a corrie that picked up one whiff of human scent would kaput a stalk that had maybe taken painstaking hours. Which was always the most exacerbating possibility with the Reds, with their incredible scenting powers, whereas, curiously, the little fellows of the bottom lands, the Roe, mainly relied on sight and hearing. Never seemed to give a hoot for scent even when the wind carry was right at them, as he had once proved, with a cigar into the bargain.

He watched the ravine and the opposite slopes for the time of the cigarette, but nothing stirred. It was perishingly cold all right, probably more so than it would be when he finally got round to those bloody great Alaskan kodiaks two Springs hence. Just as, before that, the *jungla* of the *tigrés* would be diabolically hot. It was always the one or the other with hunting worth a damn.

Well, okay then. Pack it in, he thought. Might make more sense to go down the gorge through the trees, and maybe jump a Roe, than to slog over all that wide-open empty stuff to the end of the ridge!

He started to get up and then, as he was still on one knee, he got a kind of peripheral reaction in the corner of his eye. A flick.

After a second or two more he found the place, and then, all at once, like a film coming into focus, the parcel of hinds took

50

form, sniffing and watching before they abandoned the refuge and camouflage of the trees. He sank down again and brought the gun up.

The leading hind, always much cannier than the boss of any stag 'parcel', moved out into the open. For several minutes her keen eyes had been scanning the face of the Ben and the slopes. But she was satisfied now. She began to make across, unhurriedly, towards the edge of the ravine, gracefully pacing the snow, the five other hinds and two calves following in slow procession.

Every few yards one or more of them would pause, look around and then briefly nuzzle in the snow where it lay thinner. As with stags, the beast leading a file was not necessarily the leader of the 'parcel', the important one, if you wanted more than one. Because although they almost always milled around for a moment or two when you had fired ... baffled by the echo ... it always took them longer to decide the line of take-off if the leader was down.

But there was no doubt in his mind of the leader here. Nor of the hinds in milk, because both calves were keeping close to their mothers. The leader was the *Yeld*, the barren hind. She was the real leader all right, too. Lighter coloured than the others. A big beauty whose sterility had produced her more than average girth and plumpness. In the glasses her longer neck, a characteristic of *Yelds*, was tawny as a veldt lion's, and her quarters looked heavy.

A 'parcel' of incomers from further north, he thought. Driven south from their own ranges by the long spell of bitter weather, and then turned back from the better 'countries' by the river. Sure they were fairly good swimmers. Certainly a rutting stag, seeking hinds, would swim two miles across a loch and, later, re-cross it. But they only tackled raging white water in the last extremity, when they were in desperate case.

Inherently mistrustful of bottom lands, as always, they were retreating up the Ben now, until the *Yeld* could decide whether to try another course across the Glen, or to round the shoulder and head east.

Perhaps she was preoccupied, or tired from the climb,

51

because they were still only ambling. But then, through the glasses, he saw the first signs of developing unease, the sixth sense manifestations. The second or two of frozen concentration, the ear flicks, the raised heads turning from side to side, sniffing. It had to be their sixth sense reaction because they hadn't seen anything and the wind was unchanged, yet any minute now they would take off. Already the *Yeld* had begun to quicken her pace to a purposeful walk.

For the past minute or two his brain had been busy with the mechanics of it. The range was formidable. All of three hundred yards. He had taken a variety of game at the distance, and once a bull eland at three-fifty. But that stuff was never recommended shooting. It wasn't 'fair game', because at that kind of range you could only expect to *hit*, not to down a beast, so it was pure luck whether you might then have to trail a wounded one for miles. The light was another snag. Already the fade had set in. It would have taken the best part of half an hour to have crossed the ravine and stalked them to within surefire range, and by that time the visibility would have been too poor for precision stuff.

On the other hand he knew exactly what the Mannlicher could do. Get on with it! He thumbed over the catch and slid the bolt, then stared. There was nothing in the spout or the magazine. Idiot! His hands fled to the pouches on his chest. Nothing in the left one. He ripped open the other zipper and his ferreting fingers came away with one round. He went through his side pockets, felt his trouser pockets, but there was nothing. Then he remembered. Of all the stupid bird-brained twats!

His mind recalled the idiocy. John asking him to fix the lanyard back of his collar for him just as he had finished assembling the Mannlicher. Then the final swigs ... too many bloody swigs ... just before they started ... and then starting ... without filling the magazine.

Even so it wouldn't normally have mattered, because he habitually carried spare rounds in one or other of his chest pouches, but, of course, he had given John a handful yesterday when they had been checking the 'scope on the Mauser.

52

Jesus Christ! One bloody round. With three, even two it would have been totally different, because there was usually the chance of a second shot when they were milling. He looked at the bullet. Of course there was enough shock power generated through the tremendous velocity of that slim cylinder to kill an elephant, as he had done, providing it was truly placed. But not necessarily, even then, to drop one on the spot.

Even shot through the heart it was not unknown for a Red to run four or five hundred yards. The first time he had seen it he had been dumbfounded, because he had known the deer was well hit and yet the beast had taken off over the brow as if untouched; though subsequently it had been there, just over the crest. Hit through the stomach, or quarters, or even with a broken leg, a Red could go two miles or more.

Across the gorge a hind had climbed the broken outer steepness of the wedge now, on to the flatness of the face. One of the milk hinds and a calf were just behind her, and the others had begun to follow with the big *Yeld* having dropped back to last-but-one of the cortège.

For an instant more he hesitated, then he made a deal with his conscience. If she got away, hit, he would track and finish her with the knife no matter how far or long.

He slid the bullet in, locked the bolt, avoiding any click, and raised the 300 leaf of the foresight.

Now he squirmed down urgently into the snow, concentrating on the bead and the final calculations of destruction. Over across the defile the big hind was approaching the lip of the gorge.

Merest shade left of centre on account of the tangentical pressure of the wind. Similarly, a tiny mite lower than dead-on because of the incline. Eyes straining against the wind.

The *Yeld* scrambled up the last overhang on to the big carpet and for an instant, shaking her coat, she was three-quarter broadside, her body darker than reality against the whiteness of the snow.

Ryan sucked in a breath, summoned maximum concentration, held the bead deep in the vee, solidly, squeezed. He didn't hear the baritone boom of the Mannlicher, of course,

53

but he raised his head immediately after he felt the recoil.

The hind hadn't moved, but he knew she was hit. The other deer began to mill about, befuddled by the echoes as they almost always were, uncertain where the danger lay. He lay motionless, not giving them any hint, because with every second they wasted now the *Yeld* would be losing out. Suddenly one of the older hinds took off straight up the Ben, and at once the others broke after her.

He watched, tensed, feeling the nerve prickles of eagerness. Then he began to curse out loud as the *Yeld* began to trot after them, seemingly recovered from the first spasm of shuddering and paralysis which had confirmed that she was truly hit.

Chagrin flooded through him but then, quite suddenly, as he got to his feet, she faltered and went over on to her side, and he let go a long hiss of relief. Without the need of caution or concealment now he scrambled down the slope and crossed the ravine in fifteen minutes.

After she had gone down, poleaxed into insensibility, she would not have felt anything more, but she must only have actually died a second or two before he reached her, because there was still a faint trace of breath mist trailing from her muzzle buried deep in the snow.

He took out his knife and began to perform the urgent business of the gralloch ... the promptness of which has so much bearing on the ultimate quality of the venison ... with the sure dexterity of long practice.

Soon, the bright steaming colours of the offal, stomach bag, entrails ... crimson, cerise, blue-grey and green . . made a vivid variegated stain on the purity of the snow carpet.

When he was done he took the cord from his waist and bound the forelegs, slipknotting the hooves and making a bandolier across his chest. She was a big missy all right. By her teeth, a three-year-old ... which was surprising, for a leader, though not unprecedented ... in her barren prime, a good one hundred and seventy pounds, he reckoned. Every clear flat slope that was steep enough he let her roll and slither, swirling around, until she fetched up, breaking through the snow crust, in ground scrub or heather, each time saving a hundred yards or more of hauling.

The two burns, both winding across the face at an angle, were the toughest obstacles of the haul. Each, sunk deep in the rock strata of the Ben, involved manhandling the beast up six-foot banks of shale and boulders, and each time he had to take a rest afterwards.

It was nearly three hours later that he hauled her through the last of the trees and on to the track, and for a few moments, then, he leaned against a tree, heaving. It had been a pretty crucifying drag and he was sodden through with sweat. But he was a very strong man, who recovered quickly, and he wouldn't have missed any of it for all the cursing and the sweating.

He got a cigarette going and, after all that time and effort, it tasted fine in the keen crisp air. The Brake itself was out of sight, but he could see the glow of its lights in the hollow way down along the track which followed the river. He began to walk towards it, whistling. Not so much because of the tangible fact of the hind lying at the side of the road, as that the decision of the bullet had worked out.

When they got to the hotel there were only two locals talking with Hewie in the wee stone-flagged public bar. There was a north-easter, the same one, coming off the Loch, and they were huddled around the fire, both wall benches untenanted, because even of a summer evening it was cold as charity in the public bar.

In the lounge-bar, mind you, it was snug as a bug. There was a good log fire going in the iron cradle under the old copper canopy, and the red-gold-black tartan carpet of Hewie's clan helped to husband the heat. The cosiest corners, all newly done out in the same Hewie tartan pattern, were the inglenooks either side the fire. Real luxury. But anybody would have settled for the window seats unless they had been really stiff, because the whole wee room was snucketty.

You didn't need a ceiling light on in the Snug because the lights back of the counter were enough, and the fire threw out ambery beams on to the walls. As a matter of fact the fireplace

55

was really too large for the room, which was because the late Landlord, who had been Hewie's tenant, hadn't gone in much for class distinctions and in his time the Snug and the Public had been all one room.

Ryan threw his cap and jacket on to a corner chair and went over to the fire while John Ross slumped into a chair the other side of the hearth and began to undo the lacing of his knee-boots. They could hear the low mumble of conversation from around the end of the bar, but when it became clear that nobody had heard them come in, Ross put two fingers in his mouth and whistled.

In a minute or two Hewie came through. He was a sturdy medium-sized man in his early sixties, with the red-brown tan of the hill winds, who resembled a grizzled and somewhat shorter version of Gary Cooper.

'Well, boys, how'd it go then?'

'Later, Hewie,' John Ross said shortly. 'Let's have a fast gravy first, lad, the nearest. I'm bloody fruz.'

Ryan winked, jerking her head. 'Boy's a bit out of sorts, Hewie. Took a bad turn up the hill and missed the fun. Okay now though.'

The white-haired man smiled back. 'Och, well, we'll soon hae him richted, Marrk.'

He reached down the *De Luxe Logan* and poured out two pony glasses, then began to draw pints of 'heavy'; which is the Scottish propaganda term for weakish bitter ale that lacks the frothy head of authenticity but is reasonably tolerable.

The beer, as always, took an agonisingly long time because of the fiddling idiot wee taps that Teuton, Sassenach and others of the Ancient Order of Frothblowers always rightly regard with wonder and impatience.

Ryan moved over to the bar. He downed a whisky and took a pull of the beer. 'Leave the gravy right there and get some more of the soup going, will you, Hewie, we'll tell you when to stop. And get Morag to put a bunch of Carlsberg specials in the icebox.'

Ross came over in his red turtleneck and stockinged feet. He also put down a whisky and took a sup of beer, then felt in his

56

pocket for the old flat tin that just took four cigars. He had slept most of the waiting time in the Brake and when he had woken once again the stabbing spasms had passed. He began to rub the soles of his feet and pinch at his toes.

'A *Yeld*,' he said finally, conversationally, to Hewie. 'By Mark here. A bloody good *Yeld* though.' He turned his head. 'Come to think of it you must have worked your ass off getting that little bugger down, boy?'

'He'd been some big Daddy rising twenty odd stones he'd still be up there,' Ryan said. 'Well part of him, that is, but, yes, a good hind.'

'Uh huh!' Ross aid. 'Remember that bloody great *Royal* in the Big Horse-Moss?' He turned his head to Hewie. 'Came down in a hag. Forelegs and one antler buried in it up to the cheek. Took an hour to get him free, working up to the knees in it, before we could start the gralloch. Blown up like an elephant by then of course.'

Ryan took another swig. 'You fancy a piece of the *Yeld*, John?' he asked. 'Big venison-eating man like you?'

Ross grinned. 'Anybody mentions venison, Cathie screams, but, well, okay, I'll take a haunch for the lads.'

'Tell 'em to cook it the way Fiona invented, then,' Ryan said. ' "Venison Maryland". In square chunks like toast, fried in bacon fat. When I think of that black crap the London pubs serve up in the name of venison ... bastards should be sued.'

'Aye! Sae long as it's fairst been hung the twa weeks,' Hewie said succinctly.

Ross wrinkled his lip, scornfully. 'Aaah. Twa weeks balls! How many times do I have to tell you, Hewie. A lot of old wives crap. Like all that balls of burrying capercailzies for a fortnight.'

'Twa weeks,' the older man said with resolute obstinacy. 'And ye need twa weeks for the capers tew all the same. For to tak' oot the pine tairsty.'

'Five days for either,' Ross said heavily. 'And no burying!'

Ryan chuckled. 'I love to hear you twa primitives blethering. Beats any *Ceilidh*. You want to know how that twa weeks

57

notion got started, Hewie? Back in the coach and Highwaymen days! It took that long before they got it on to the table in the London pubs. They never tasted fresh venison and they don't now. Least of all stuff that's been gralloched on the spot.'

'Should be dark and ripe,' Hewie insisted. 'Tendered-up and tairsty.'

'Dark my ass,' Ross said scornfully. 'Dark enough now, even after a fast gralloch. *Your* dark's putrid. Will poison you yet, Hewie, I'm telling you.'

'Well, anyway, get Hamish to fix us a couple of haunches will you, Hewie?' Ryan said. 'I think I'll take a hunk for La Condesa.'

When Hewie had gone he scuffed his chin. 'How about tomorrow then . . . if the weather's okay of course? Or have you got to push-off right away regardless?'

Ross raised an eyebrow reprovingly. 'You just never remember, Mark, do you? Got a shipyard to run, man. Remember? The times the stupid buggers aren't striking over the toilet paper, or who holds the chalk, I *work*!'

Ryan grinned and flipped a hand. 'All right, all right. But I don't accept the implication. You never remember, either, I work too, mate.'

Ross laughed. 'Just kidding. I wish I could get that nice work, and I don't mean the money either.'

Ryan grimaced. 'Here we go again. Everybody who's read anything from Tarzan to Rider Haggard envies me, thinks it's a piece of cake. It's work all right, and the sweat comes in two kinds. The next piece of work I do, the physical sweat will come in at around ninety-eight to a hundred degrees humidity, on my flat feet, mate, not riding around in any Land-Rover.'

'I know, don't I? I sampled the leg-work part, didn't I?' Ross said. 'All the same the point is you love your work, mate, whereas, in case I haven't mentioned it lately, I hate, loathe and detest bloody ships!'

Ryan chuckled; he was very familiar with John Ross's periodic cursings of his lot. 'Aaah, what are you kicking about? You're a boss man with boss pay, and you don't have to

58

worry about whether you're still a good enough reporter, and you've got the most skilful hunting of the lot right here.'

'Not the same,' Ross said. 'The big variety of stuff and the danger element cancels out the skill element.' He paused. 'Like the gorilla piece you did, that was the best bit in the book, boy. Which reminds me. This next job . . . what the hell did you pick on jaguar for? Wouldn't appeal to me, stuck up a tree waiting on bloody great overgrown leopards.'

'Won't be stuck up a tree,' Ryan said. 'It has to be on foot, mostly at night.'

'No daylight hunting?'

'Not for jaguar, not for me,' Ryan said. 'According to my research there used to be a fancy outfit did it in daylight, with relays of dog packs . . . eventually put up a sleeping cat and treed him . . . but who the hell wants to shoot cats out of a tree, even nine-foot cats?'

'I do,' Ross said. 'Any time and without compunction. I'd use howitzers, grenades, poison or napalm for the whole lousy, treacherous, ignoble feline tribe without a qualm. I'm an ailurophobe and proud of it.'

Ryan grinned. 'Cheetah are okay, I'm not fond of the rest certainly. But there's a variety of other stuff there too, all new to me. Big variety of people as well. We aim to give our readers a little cultural information also, you know, not just artillery stuff.'

Ross guffawed. 'Ah, now we're getting somewhere. Big variety of two-legged cats, huh? I knew there'd have to be more to it than jaguar.'

'I am a student of the asinine human species,' Ryan said with assuming gravity.

'Not forgetting the female ass section,' Ross said. He laughed again, and pulled his lip. 'Personally, I am a devoted tit man, as you may have heard, but, boy, I'll remember those Bwangato asses till my dying day.'

'Coarse bastard,' Ryan said.

59

2. LA CONDESA

The road to the house was really only one-car width. But if you did meet the mail man or a tractor you could always drive on to the grass verge, which, in spring and early summer, was quite a sight of daffodils and crocus. From the coast road it ran back up the hillside for a mile through the farm lands, and the gradient was quite gentle though you had to take it easily at the stone bridges over the two burns that ran down to the river because they were really humpy ones. And then, again, it wound quite a bit, and you were always liable to come round a bend and find yourself right on to a hare or a covey of young pheasants or partridges who couldn't get themselves out of the lights. And sometimes, not infrequently in fact, roe would dart across. Once, a full-grown buck, taking off at a place where the roadside was banked high, had cleared the hedge and damn near landed smack on the bonnet of the car.

At the end of the last straight stretch his lights picked up the white fencing of *Greenacres*, the house they had built in midst of a ten acres enclave, in midst of the farm. He drove through the open gates and took the right-fork sweep to the garage and greenhouse building that almost concealed the small house fifty yards beyond, near the edge of the big wood. There were no lights in the cottage naturally, but Angus had raised the nearest of the three doors and he rolled in alongside the little blue car and its big buddy, the Yankee Brake.

The little blue fellow was getting on a bit now. But once in a while he took it out for an airing, and he would no more have thought of parting with it than with any of the cheerful little pictures she had painted, nor the mare, greying now, who would never see any knacker's yard.

When he had closed up and switched off the forecourt floodlight he lit a cigarette and stood for a moment looking across the grass at the house, now gradually taking on more form as his eyes acclimatised to the moonlight, the roofs pale green and the white outlines of the big picture windows sharp

60

against the dark brown of the cedar logs.

It was a pretty good house, he thought, for which he himself had come up with the basic idea of a man-sized L-shaped Afrikander bungalow, but which in all other details and respects had been her creation and delight.

Everything was very still tonight. Usually you had only to stand a moment or two to pick up the squeak of a vole, the whistle of an otter or the bass quack of a drake mallard, but now there was only the faint murmur of the burn. The burn passed under the road at the second hump-back a hundred yards back up the lane. It divided, then, to encircle 'Crusoe's island' of wild damson and weeping willows just opposite the house. In the wan light he could just make out the dark blob of a bird on the white rustic of the little bridge to the island, and then at last the silence was broken by the call of the nightjar as it flew off.

Oh God, if only there was just one light in the house. The place she had loved so much, taken such pleasure in!

Some people felt the need to dispose of things, abandon places which harboured overwhelming remembrances, but Ryan was one of the other kind. One thing I promise you, dearest, he thought, I'll never leave your house. God willing, I'll die here too. Wherever I am, wherever I go, I'll get back here to die!

He shook it off, hunched his shoulders and took the short cut across the nearest of the three lawns fronting the house, skirting the rhododendron island in the centre. He crossed the hall to the big lounge which was the western end of the house. He didn't bother with the cluster of switches which operated the concealed lighting around the walls because there was a lamp set in the Arabesque wrought-iron-work of the bar, whorled bulbs like fir cones, which gave a soft light that was quite adequate when you didn't want to read any place, or felt like a dressing-gown nightcap, or sorting out a family or business bind.

Fiona was giving him some trouble tonight all right. Even the bar gave him a twinge. The bar had three stools and all the accoutrements, but the point was that it was hidden from the

61

main area of the room in the shank of the L-shape and he could remember exactly how that had happened. Could hear her voice right now. 'After all, darling, we're not running a pub, are we? ... though I sometimes wonder ... don't want to be actually staring at rows of bottles and that blooming old beer-puller thing of yours.'

He went back of the bar and got a half-gill of Logan's in two dollops from one of the upended bottles in the rack, then drew himself a pint of bitter. He drank the whisky in two swallows with a sip of ale in between and walked over to the french windows which opened on to the *stoep*.

For a moment he stared out at the night sky and down over the green acres to the sea. But he was restless with the melancholia, familiar though it was, that seemed to be sitting specially heavily on him tonight. He took his can and went back into the hall and right along the corridor to his working room at the other end of the house. Originally it had been what the Scots call a sitting-room and the English a drawing-room, but in the end it had wound up as a sanctum-cum-gunroom.

As such it had changed its sex from indeterminate to plainly masculine, with hefty leather club chairs, sporting prints and framed African photographs. His big old batttered desk, leather-topped, solid, inherited from the Old Man, stood in the bay. Left of the bay, at right angles, french windows opened on to the other end of the *stoep*.

He went over to the french doors, unlocked one and stepped out. It was a forty by forty yards *stoep*, and not a five by two verandah, because he especially liked room to move and pace in when he was working. The air was cold and crisp, with a touch of breeze carrying just a suggestion of salt.

Three fields across to the right there was a light in one window of the turreted wing of the castle which, from this corner of the house, just protruded from the intervening mass of the Big Wood. There wasn't enough moon to make out the expanse of the bay between the twin promontories of cliffs, but he could see the pinpricked crescent of the wee 'Casino', the town's one grudging concession to the new-style investors, just off the beach. Through the twelve-by-fifties, which hung permanently beside the doors, the park and forecourt lights of the Casino resembled a miniature tiara.

He made an effort and dragged his thoughts back to the present. Which these days meant that they never got much further than about five fundamentals: young Mark, Work (which mostly, but not exclusively involved hunting-shooting plans and retrospections), Renny (which also involved young Mark), Odds and Sods (like Rugby and things-to-do around the patch) and Women (the medicinal, 'Good Joe' kind as distinct from the possibly twice but usually not more than once-in-a-lifetime-kind.

These things had also become his sleep formula though sometimes, except when he happened to be really shagged out or with a pal like John, he really had to work at it.

He had a strong notion it would be like that tonight and he had half a mind to get the car out again and go down and see Anita at the Casino.

He began to try the mental game of comparing her with Renny. The one thing they had in common was that they were both delectable, although as differingly as a pint of porter from Armagnac.

Anita was the medicinal kind, the sort you shacked-up with if you got the chance; which was the operative word because she wasn't promiscuous. With her you definitely had to rate, so that she always had a lot of libido stored up, and consequently, if you were in mutual tune, the outcome was considerably erotic. Wholesomely erotic, that was, no tedious expensive professional expertise crap (at which the Zulu maids would die 'a laffin'), because she was no tart. On the contrary, an intelligent working girl, good at her sums, who ran the Blackjack table because it left her with more money to send home to Glesca than when she had worked a comptometer in Meanthug City. About twenty-eight, medium height, natural blue-eyed Anglo-Saxon blonde with a quick wide smile and supranormally good frontage.

Renate, on the other hand, was more the kind you married if you had the chance. Not because ... saving one minor Teutonic confusion that had produced some relatives including the

63

Bavarian Aunt she had been named after ... the blueness of her blood derived from eleventh-century Celtic. But because, aside from her dark beauty and her steadfastness, she had so many other qualities you admired. Not least that she was a Countess who really looked and spoke as, you felt, a Countess should. Especially spoke. For she had the most attractive, distinguished voice of any woman he had ever heard. Though perhaps, on reflection, that was the least of her. A girl who, in the Hitler years, when the men were gone, had dug ditches, driven tractors and harvesters, humped swede and potato sacks, performed the duties of a district Vet.

A girl undaunted by a catalogue of recurring adversities which would have broken most men's spirit ... she had had to sell a hundred farms at knockdown prices when they had had her, the young lass, over a barrel for her father's death duties. Dedicated to the proposition of preserving the last enclave of her birthright, come what may. Fiona's bosom chum. With whom, it had always seemed to him, she had come as close to deep amity of the masculine kind as two women ever could.

Renate would be around thirty-five now, he reflected. And one reason why she was still unmarried ... an ironical one because it was unintentional if, indeed, realised by her ... was that almost invariably most of her suitors wound up with inferiority complexes.

All unassumingly she simply outclassed them. With horse, rod and gun. Played them piano concertos like a professional, painted them a pretty damn good landscape or came out of the trees shouldering a roebuck she had nicely gralloched herself.

Needless to say, the Piccadilly Lairds, the Mayfair commandos, the ex-chorus boy stiff-upper-lip film-actors never even got to first base. They slunk away, appalled that so fair a catch should offer so demoralising a prospect.

In the case of Anita he had progressed from nodding acquaintance quite inadvertently. There had been trouble at the Casino one evening. A fairly high-born oversexed bum of the first water, the kind given to deerstalker hats, loud tweeds and cavalry-twill trousers, had made a pass at Anita. Ryan had come to the rescue, giving the lout the back of his hand. It had

64

seemed natural, when the Casino had closed for the night, that they should go to Anita's flat.

For the time of a drink and a cigarette they had had, as he recalled, quite an intelligent chat. And then suddenly, as if they had reached a decision of mutual approval by telepathy, she had smiled and got up. And when she had returned from the bedroom there hadn't been any possibility of misunderstanding, and least of all for any tedious spoken banalities. She had simply been wearing heeled slippers and a loosely belted yellow robe, so loosely belted that when she sat down on the couch beside him it slid over her shoulders, revealing her heavy pear-shaped breasts in a gesture of offering; which, without any phoney artifice, is exactly what it had been.

She had turned out to be as demanding as she was lush, and they had mingled thrice to mutual satisfaction. If you *really* registered with her she still took a little time to make up her mind, but once she had done so she did not horse around. The first time, the appogiatura session, had been in the reddy-yellow light of the electric imitation-logs fire. It may not have been the best session. Probably the early morning one had been the best. But it had been one which he would remember. Firstly because it had marked the ending of a long passage of relative disinterestedness, and then again, paradoxically, because there had been some curiously affetuoso aspects to it, despite the fact that little had been said and nothing in the way of the usual insincerities.

He went back in from the *stoep* and got a cigarette from the desk, still thinking about it. It wasn't difficult to visualise Anita kneeling on a cushion by the fire, and he could easily make the Casino in twenty minutes, or less. All he had to do was lift the phone. Then he thought, Aaah, the hell with it. There was quite a bit of checking and preparing and tidying-up correspondence to be done tomorrow. He stretched his arms and yawned, then he went to bed.

One window of the room he used nowadays looked along the front of the house, and he heard Mrs Angus crossing the flags of the patio at eight o'clock.

65

He slipped out of bed to get the list and ballpen he had left on the dressing-table. Through the other window he could see three roe and a fawn at the edge of the wood in the high field through which the burn came down from the hill. Right now the buck was acting lookout while the others grazed the clover. He was fully mature now, six points to his sharp little antlers, and he held his head proudly, gracefully, moving his gaze in a semi-circle and occasionally tilting a little to sniff.

A hundred yards infield from the deer, five hares were playing their circus game, now and then a couple breaking off to sit up on their haunches and box each other for a few rounds before rejoining the performance.

Neither group of creatures showed awareness of the other, but had any one sensed danger all would have been alerted, much as the outrider scout of a baboon pack would draw urgent conclusions of a skulking leopard from the hate-insult calls of one of his aerial allies.

He got back into bed with a cigarette and began to check over the list while he was waiting for the tea to come along. The insect repellents, two strengths, and the rest of the medical odds and sods for bugged water, dysentery and the commoner tropical afflictions seemed to be all noted, and should be in the cupboards of the showers room. The small Winchester, the newish Mannlicher *Schonauer*, the Luger and the d.b. twelve bore, which packed easier than the s.b. repeater, were all cased and strapped. The wooden case of ammo was a bloody nuisance, but the chances of their having high velocity alloy-tipped Mannlicher stuff, or reliable shells for the Luger were remote and, often, come to that, local shotgun cartridges were an adjectival hazard.

One other thing to remember, he reflected, was to tell Angus that there were six six-foot *Abies Nobilis* saplings due on the railway wagon from up north for completion of the windbreak gap. The closure of the gap had been the final touch in the job of home-making but, for some obscure reason ... a mystery which had equally defeated the Forestry Department boys ... right after Fiona's death in the car crash four of the twenty-four trees had also died, just like that. And he had only

66

latterly got around to remembering that one thing Fiona would have wished would be to make a job of it with those beautiful blue spruce.

And this, be Christ, *would* be done, if it took fifty *Abies* to complete that handsome serrated row, because though formerly more of an agnostic than a conventionalist, there was a kind of religious little-boy notion about it. A feeling that, sometime, she just might look down and smile, and maybe say to herself, 'Well, for heaven's sake, Mark, you remembered. You really did!'

He had a good breakfast, and then he carried the spare phone through to the lounge and plugged it in.

For a second or two he thought before he dialled then, after a brief intercession, he heard the Voice. He said, 'Good morning, Voice, it's that man again. Can I come over and say Cherrio-for-a-bit, I'll be taking off tomorrow? Also, got a choice bit of venison for you, the wild stuff of course,' he smiled, 'not your tame kind.'

'That would be nice,' she said. 'Do you mean for lunch, or dinner, or what?'

'Well, lunch would be great, if it suits?'

'Well, of course it suits, dear,' she said, in that unconsciously immaculate-husky-smooth voice. 'What I meant was would you stay for real grub-up? Are you a bit pressed for time, then?'

Ryan stared out of the window. Out across the pasture 'Big Henry', the very expensive brand-new young Hereford Casanova, had a turn coming on. He had his eyes on the six selected young Aberdeen Angus maidens, now cutting him dead up the other end of the meadow, who had fussed around him, even tried to mount *him*, when he had first been introduced. (And when he, with a 'Do you mind ... when-I'm-good-and-ready-and-not-before' shrug of his massive hindquarters, had conveyed to the too-precocious, too-precipitate young heifer upstarts that, where he came from, the panting service he provided was an ultimate condescension with which he just *might* decide to favour one or all of them in his own good time.)

67

'No, not really,' he said. 'Just that I've oddments to do before taking off.'

'Well, come to lunch then, Barbara and Ian will be here. . . .'

Ryan stared through the window. Big Henry was rubbing his throat on the gate now, and the breath from his nostrils was issuing in visible portentous puffs which promised imminent and rapacious deflowering of some tarty young Aberdeen up the hill there.

Dammitall, Ryan thought, he liked them both, but not now. . . . Then she added, '. . . but they'll be going home for dinner.'

'Well, fine, then,' Ryan said. 'It will be nice to see them, but the fact is I did want to take up a bit of your private and confidential time.'

'That sounds intriguing,' Renny said. 'But I'll bet it just means you want me to look out for *Greenacres* sometimes.'

Ryan smiled. He heard Big Henry bellow his intention across the park and turned his head. The big fellow was moving up the slope towards his harem with purposeful dignified gait and already the king-size evidence issuing from his undercarriage left none in doubt that he intended to brook neither delay nor any silly-cow coynesses.

He said. 'That would be very matey of you, but I said confidential . . . confidential-personal, not confidential-impersonal.'

'Ooh, well. . . .'

'As you say, Ooh, well.' He smiled again. 'About one o'clock be okay, Voice?'

'That would be okay, N'kosi!' she said. 'Except that if you came at twelve I might show you my cacti.'

Ryan chuckled. 'Don't push your luck. Big dumbstruck country boy though I be, I'm still basically huming.'

'I know,' Renny said. 'I drew my own conclusions from your descriptions of the Bwangato ladies.'

Out over the grass Big Henry had already made his choice, firmly shouldering aside the unruminating handmaidens intent on jumping his gun, and who would bloody well have to wait their turn!

'Unfair. Us scriveners are duty bound to paint the picture.

68

Besides you forget the basic axiom that when debating any controversy it is essential to possess a knowledge of the facts.'

He heard the characteristically delightful laugh. 'For a country boy you're a bit of a glib one, N'kosi, but I think you're fairly honest.'

'Much more than that, I'm ethical,' Ryan said. 'I never told Fiona, but all my Bwangato Maintenance Orders are scrupulously remitted by Banker's Orders.'

When he put down the phone the steamy vapourings of honest mating were evident at Big Henry's abdomen and muzzle, and, stolidly contemplating the middle distance, savouring the pleasant aftermath of noble performance, he seemed quite unconscious of the randy quintet voicing their petulant objections to his selectivity and their own enforced postponements.

He got through with the packing job sooner than he had expected and it was still short of noon when he swung in through the West Lodge gates. For a half mile the drive, as well kept as *Greenacres'* road though wider, ran through thickly wooded ground dominated by immense oaks and beeches as old as sin. Then, almost suddenly, you came out into the light open parkland, and there right ahead was *Donach*. Renny's castle. Like a phantasmagoria of the long, long ago. Hugely impressive in the thin sunlight, yet not forbidding, the spaces between its grey battlements peering out like square eyes across the valley lands over which it had ruled for nearly nine hundred years. It looked, in its historic magnificence, untouched by time. Marked only by the slashes on sandstone buttresses and lower walls, where the Cromwellian cavalry had honed their swords before battering the portcullis and great doors behind which, shields and claymores in hand, the Royalist Earl and his small grim silent band had stood ready to receive them.

But when you got closer you realised that it was empty as a shell-case. That no one, any longer, slept in any of the fifty-odd spacious apartments, as disused now as the ballroom, the great hall, the dungeons, starving pit and underground passage to the smaller castle across the valley through which a Catholic

69

Queen and her entourage had once escaped their Protestant persecutors.

The rates and taxes of the soulful high priests of egalitarianism by-way-of-free-drugs-and-concrete-warrens-for-all-except Trades-Union-gaffers had fixed it so that Renny could not even afford to occupy one turreted corner. Not that, so long as its Countess drew breath, *Donach* would ever die. For she had fought off periodic propositions of Trades Union Offices, a palace of Bureaucrats and so on, and seen to it that the entail of her will was unassailable.

Ryan turned left off the main drive, along a lane that shortly divided into two take-your-pick avenues bounding the lawn before the Dower House which was called the 'Tulip'; four acres of cropped sward centered by a venerable clump of variegated rhododendron that could have concealed a squadron of tanks, and was, in bloom, a gorgeous pistillaceous blaze.

Invariably, as you negotiated the 'Tulip', from whichever direction, you were spotted from the house. Her Ladyship was already standing on the porch, and when he got out of the car she came forward, smiling, proffering her cheek in a style reserved for family and close friends that, in the courtly times, had almost become a forgotten gesture.

It was a greeting she had first instinctively accorded him more as an intimation that his great loss was shared. The dearest friend and the dearly-loved wife. A wordless message. Thereafter it had become an automatic welcome with her, but now, this time, he put his hands on her waist, kissing her on the mouth with a wee squeeze.

Just for an instant she seemed a mite taken aback, and he himself showed surprise to feel the rigid thing like a corset around her waist. He gave her another small squeeze, then stepped back. 'Hey, what's all this then, Madame? Don't tell me *you're* aiding the figure?'

She smiled, showing teeth which were not perfect, because there was one which just slightly overlapped and in so doing, curiously, gave a more attractive effect than the precisely perfect would have done. 'Well, not intentionally ... come over with a wee bit back trouble in my old age.'

70

In the drawing-room, Barbara waved hello from the couch in the bay, and Ian came across carrying his bit of pink gin. 'Well, it's about time you showed up, Mark. The place is getting overrun with Bambis I understand . . . how are you?' he smiled.

Ian Strathoun, spare and scholarly, with a clipped Van Dyck beard and horn spectacles, was something of an authority on company law. He had practised much less since inheriting the responsibilities and disadvantages of his Lairdship. A man whose natural academic manner was deceptive for he was just as conversant with the modern idiom as his teenage clutch of three. Barbara was Renny's cousin. Tall and fair, there was no physical affinity between them, but both were country girls who could not abide town-living.

'Fine,' Ryan said. 'Fine. Shade undernourished, maybe,' he grinned and patted his midriff, 'but I daresay I'll see the year out. And how are all of yours?'

'Oh, fair to messy,' Ian said. 'Touch of seasonal swine fever here and there, but nothing to worry about.' He cocked an eyebrow and nodded towards the big waist-high oak cabinet at the other end of the room. 'Beer and a dram, I presume?'

'Julian's had chicken pox,' Lady Strathoun said, taking up Ryan's enquiry. 'The others escaped though, and fortunately Ian and I had had it.' She pointed her sherry to her cousin standing smiling by the bright burning logs. 'Poor old Renny's been the unlucky one lately. Been having an awful time with her back.'

'Yes, indeed,' her husband said over his shoulder. 'You know what she's like, Mark. Stupid girl *will* lug bags of tatties, logs and things, *bound* to happen sooner or later. One of the Foresters found her spark out in one of the Rides.'

'Oh, don't fuss,' Renny said. 'I'm all right now. It just suddenly hit me at the time. It wasn't anything much really.'

'It was, too,' her cousin stridently objected. 'She's all strapped up, Mark.'

'Oh. What happened exactly?' Ryan asked.

'A disc,' Renny said. 'Went suddenly when I was lifting. Rather painful at the time, apparently I passed out.'

71

'I can imagine,' Ryan said. 'I had it happen myself once. Are you all right now?'

'Well yes, except that it's rather infuriating because there doesn't seem to be anything they can do, an operation or anything, I mean.' She grimaced. 'Consequently I have to wear this blooming belt affair, permanently, or at least for about six months, they say.'

'And, of course, you mustn't bend, or ride, or play Snap, and they don't prescribe any exercises ... that it?' Ryan asked, nodding.

'Yes. Was it the same with you, then?'

'Absolutely. Except that I couldn't trace it back to any particular incident ... had had so many odd thumps over the years, falling down the Bens, football etcetera, and with me it happened in the middle of the night, for God's sake.'

'But, obviously, you got righted?'

'Obviously,' Ryan said. 'But no thanks to the medicos. The reverse.'

'Oh? What do you mean?'

'Well, the thing they had me in was like a body belt with metal support struts up the back. Anyway, I stuck the God-awful thing for three days, then it suddenly struck me that what they said about no exercising didn't make sense. Obviously natural support is more natural than any artificial scaffolding ... apart from not letting your muscles atrophy ... So I tore the bloody thing off and literally threw it out of the window. Then I decided on a pattern of exercising and started in on it. Easy stuff at first, of course, but finally working up to the really strenuous drill. Kept it up ever since. Two dozen on the tum, two dozen touching toes and two dozen on the back with your toes tucked into two pound weights. Every morn ... or any other time if you like, but morning gets it over with.'

Strathoun covered his face with spreadeagled fingers in pretended horror. 'My God, Mark, do you mean to tell us you do that every morning? Come forward, Gunga Din!'

Ryan grinned. 'Well, or course it's a bind, especially after a heavy night. But training used to be a damned sight more of a bind, and it's a form of self-masochism that really pays off.'

72

'It sounds to me as if it could really be the answer,' Barbara said. 'And, after all, nothing ventured. . . .'

'How long ago did yours go, Mark?' Ian asked.

'Four years,' Ryan said. 'They told me I'd developed one that would come out at the drop of a hat. Load of bloody nonsense ... I've been humping beasts and God-knows-what ever since and never a twinge.' He grinned. 'Want me to do a few headover rolls, couple of back flips?'

'Well, it's the cheerfullest bit of news I've had this week,' Renny said. 'It really works hey, Bwana man?'

'Got a back like a rhino,' Ryan told her. He patted his stomach and grinned again. 'Doesn't do any hard in front either.'

A rosy-faced maid knocked and entered to confirm that lunch was ready and they went through into the dining-room. Outside, a continuing mass of heavy black cloud was riding sluggishly across the sky, obscuring the weak sunlight sufficiently to warrant lights indoors. Down the long slope and across the castle lawn a flock of the resident jackdaws noisily whirled and circled over the battlements, and all at once a roebuck followed by two does bounded across a corner of the green. Nearer at hand a rabbit, and then a second one emerged cautiously on to the open grass of the 'Tulip', only to scuttle back into the safety of the rhodies as a cruising kestrel glided easily overhead.

Inside the room the light from the clustered candelabra heightened the high gloss of the big oval table and threw transient reflections on to the portraits on the walls.

When he turned from the wide latticed windows Renny was already seated at the head, and from the picture rail behind her the fifth Earl gazed out, as if with sublime approval, over her head. He was, perhaps, the most handsome of her ancestry, Ryan had always thought, and while the fairness of the Cavalier Laird's long curls, upturned moustaches and Van Dyck beard contrasted with her darkness, she could have been his daughter; even his twin.

'I must say I'm looking forward to this, Renny dear,' the legal Laird said in his euphonic out-of-Court voice. 'Feeling

73

quite peckish, and you always feed us so surpassingly well.'

'You're always feeling peckish lately,' Barbara said, taking him up just a touch tartly in view of the possible implication. 'And it's beginning to show, I may say. *You* should think of trying Mark's daily-dozens business, dear.'

Strathoun regarded his wife with amiable disdain. 'Thank you indeed, my love. However I think I'll postpone the Ryan therapy until I'm actually obliged.'

'You have a point there, Ian,' Ryan said. 'No option with me. *Got* to keep mobile. To get the stuff, to write the piece, to pay the groceries.'

Renny snorted. 'That's a whopper if you like ... the groceries part, I mean. *You* keep mobile, Bwana Ryan, because you love every minute of it, so don't pretend.'

For a moment he kept silent, remembering some of the more than several times when he hadn't enjoyed one second of it. Like the time he had blundered on to a *rinkaals* and the two days of sweating delirium which had followed the snake's bite. The time when, hunting a baboon pack that had been raiding the shambas, *they* had suddenly turned hunter and he had *had* to drop over a dozen of them, shooting like a maniac and, this time, sweating with fear, before he had halted the wave and turned them.

He shook his head. 'Not pretending. A lot of it, sure. Maybe most of it, but far from every minute of it, I assure you.'

'Certainly, I can well believe that,' Strathoun interposed, 'which reminds me. What on earth made you choose jaguar country? Surely the climate and conditions are going to be pretty ghastly? Besides, I always thought the celebrated hunter-authors, Hemingway, Ruark, etcetera, concentrated on Africa?'

'Well, taking the last first, that's one reason,' Ryan said. 'Except that I don't count Ruark "celebrated" the way you mean ... he was a reporter, like me. A very good reporter, but he never had an original idea comparable with the Master's. Another reason is that there are some very interesting racial and political aspects where I'm going. Not just the fauna, although I never could understand why Big Ernie didn't take

74

in jaguar ... night-hunting ... or kodiak, too, for that matter.'

'Or tiger?' Renny queried. 'Correct me if I'm wrong.'

'No, you're not wrong,' Ryan said. 'But I can fully appreciate why he passed up the Indian stuff. Tiger's too damned *uninteresting*.'

'Good Lord, I always thought that tiger was a, if not *the*, pièce-de-resistance of the business?' Strathoun sounded incredulous.

'Well, not for me,' Ryan shrugged. 'Non libet.' He paused to eat, then continued. 'No man can risk wrestling those cats. So it's either the Maharajah stuff, with a squadron of elephants, which costs the earth, or stuck up a tree in a *machan* all night, bored stiff, over a tethered bait.'

'But couldn't you hunt them in daylight, African style?' Barabara asked.

Strathoun raised a patient eyebrow. 'Don't be *silly*, darling, they're wholly nocturnal beasts.'

Renny smiled and Ryan said. 'Well, that's largely right, though I've sometimes wondered whether it might be feasible with trained dog packs. Trouble is I doubt if dogs would ever bay one of the full-grown Bengali ones, so you'd never come up with him.'

'But to get back to square one,' Strathoun persisted, 'why jaguar, Mark? Apart from the fact that they haven't been so much publicised, then!'

They had reached the coffee and brandy stage now, and Ryan reached out for the silver and majolica table lighter which, once, had been a wee returning-home gift from Fiona and himself.

'Well, not *just* jaguar, Ian.' He got his cigarette lit and made the first exhalation. 'There's a pile of other stuff, and a lot of non-hunting form that interests me, as I said. But getting to the *tigrés* themselves, the point is that they're among the few beasts liable to attack without provocation. According to the oracles they have all the mean killer instinct of leopard, as you'd expect, but more aggressive confidence because they're a lot bigger and stronger than the *chuis*.' He took another draw on his cigarette. 'They're pretty few and far

75

between you know,' he continued, 'the company of unprovoked attackers. Outside of some snakes ... mamba, tommy-goff, bushmaster, anaconda ... it about comes down to most kodiak bear, some polar bear, some jaguar and some leopard.'

'And man-eating lions and tigers, Indian tigers, surely?' Renny suggested.

'No, that's different,' Ryan told her. 'With them it happens through circumstance, or accident. I'm talking about the boys who are *looking* for trouble all the time, and food only some of the time. Jaguar, leopard and puma often kill for pleasure ... every damn thing they can get a hook into, like foxes.'

'And do you mean to tell me you consider this *unprovoked* possibility an *advantage*, the aspect which attracts you?' Strathoun laughed incredulously.

Ryan smiled. 'God forbid! But let's say it's one of the things, together with night-hunting on foot, which make it a totally *different* proposition from the stuff I know ... new territory, new technique, new experience! That's what it comes to. Incidentally,' he added, 'even the anti-bloodsporters and the well-known international guild of cat-lovers can't object to self-defence shooting.'

'Oh, you'll get plenty of nonsensical letters from them, whatever you do,' Strathoun said sympathetically. 'Resign yourself. They'll all explain that you really should use a camera and, when attacked, dissuade the beast with a sternly reproving stare, or shout loudly in tones designed to intimidate.'

'Yes, I know,' Ryan grinned. 'They're a noisy cult themselves, aren't they?'

'Well, just mind *your* self-defence is adequate, N'kosi,' Renny said. 'Don't want to lose you, or have you all torn up yet. Who'd dine me out on Saturday nights?'

'Well, listen to that now!' Barbara arched her eyebrows. 'Coming from Renny, that's practically a proposal, Mark.'

'She'd never risk it,' Ryan said succinctly. 'She might get taken up on it!' He glanced at Renny, and just for an instant there seemed to be a propine intimation in her smile.

Barbara and Ian left after lunch.

'You wanted some of my private and confidential time,' she

76

said. 'You don't really want to look at my cacti, do you? What's it about, N'kosi?' She let herself settle back in the chair, crossing her legs and inadvertently unveiling a deal more of them than she realised.

She had long and beautiful legs which lost nothing from the dull sheen of the firelight. Her face was lovely, too, lightened now with the semblance of a quizzical smile, and then, also, there was that rare mellifluous voice.

All very desirable, Ryan thought. And these were only the sentient things about her. Beyond them, or should it be beneath them, he sensed, knew, was the stuff of women who had made *The Great Trek*, driven the ambulances down Bomb Alley, fired on Mau Mau thugs till the ammo ran out.... She was the kind of woman who was most eminently and elegantly feminine, yet whose repertoire did not take in hysterics, appealing helplessness and the other tedious prosaics of common feminine artifice.

And they did not grow on trees, nor issue from any standard mould! They were a pretty rare species.

For a moment more he considered her in silence. How did you tackle a woman like this without sounding like a stuffed shirt, on the one hand, or a cold fish on the other?

He said. 'Well, look, try and be very understanding and bear with me because ... well ... I'm not exactly the polished advocate type, am I?' He grinned. 'Not much in my line ... more the well-meaning-but-disastrously-undiplomatic kind, I'd say.'

She smiled, helpfully. 'I've never been terribly keen on the polished diplomatic types. You never really know where you are with them, do you? Anyway,' her lips twitched again, 'I'd say you were certainly the practical kind ... and isn't this something practical, didn't you say?'

'Yes, I did,' Ryan said. His grin was a little more rueful this time. 'And that's exactly what I mean. Probably a first-class gaffe to begin with.'

'On with you just the same,' she said lightly. 'At least I'm fully forewarned.'

Ryan leant his elbow on the chair arm and squeezed his

77

chin, compressing the cleft of it into a deeper furrow. 'Well, I think you could ... might consider adding to your staff, so-to-speak,' he said suddenly. That's a hell of an opening gambit, he thought, the real charming stuff. About as banal as hell.

She tilted her head with a little frown of enquiry. 'You mean an Estate manager? Something like that?'

'Well, yes .. cum bodyguard, cum Game Warden, cum a few other practical things, but really more than that.' Inwardly he kicked himself again. What the hell was he horsing around for? 'In fact a hell of a lot more than that!' he added, with sudden emphasis.

Her confusion lightened, and she became conscious of the little queasy anticipative feeling she had felt on the telephone, and again when he had kissed her on arrival. 'I'm not awfully sure what you mean by *more than that*, Mark? Please. Stop beating about.'

'Well, all right then,' he said. 'Here goes. Here's the pitch then. It's something I've thought about a lot, for quite a time.' He paused. 'It just seems to me that you and I, that we, might have something to offer each other that would be pretty worthwhile? Pretty kind of ... well ... a partnership that would have some starting advantages, such as quite a few common likes and interests with reasonable economics anyway ... if you follow me?'

'Truthfully I don't, wholly,' she said, just the merest shade catchily. 'You've got me a little confused.' She gave a little smile of renewed enquiry. 'I'm not really sure whether you're making a takeover bid ... or ... or what?'

He smiled back his apology, moving his head from side to side self-critically. 'Well, yes, I suppose you could call it a takeover feeler ... *feeler*, not bid ... and, yes, *of course* I'm trying to make a proposal. But, you see, it's not quite the orthodox situation, is it? There *are* these mutual complications ... that's why I'm trying to sort of push the boat out.'

The frowny look, the expression he had misinterpreted, re-lapsed into a smile that seemed to contain something other than just subjective tolerance.

'*Oh, Mark!*' It could have been a reproof. She lay back in

78

her chair and for a moment closed her eyes. 'Forgive me. I'm not being dramatic or anything, but you must admit you do have ... well ... rather an unusual approach.' For a moment she fell silent again, then she pulled herself upright, tilting her head characteristically, and now there was just a trace of mischief as well as gladness in her smile. 'Do you think you might go into any detail?' she said quietly, 'since you've just about stunned me. What are these complications?'

He shifted in his chair, considering how best to put it. 'Well you see, darling, in the first place I don't know to what extent you're already wedded . . to *Donach*.'

'You make me sound like a nun.'

'You could be just as dedicated,' he said. 'I don't know.'

'And you don't approve of that kind of dedication?'

'Don't get me wrong,' Ryan said. 'I hold *Donach* in high regard, as I hold you in the highest regard, to grossly understate the case. I'd quite likely feel the same way myself ... that's why I think I get the picture.'

'Thank you,' she said. 'I don't know about diplomacy but you have quite a quality of understanding.' She paused. 'And then? That *isn't* all, is it?'

He shook his head. 'No. Then there is the circumstance of Mark. I don't know how you would feel about him, about our father-and-son association ... whether father-and-son associations are eligible?'

She smiled. 'And not even that is wholly the question perhaps?'

Now it was his turn to frown. 'I think so ... what else?'

'The opinion of the other Mark,' she said. 'Aren't you forgetting that?'

His face relaxed again. 'No, I'm not forgetting that. We're pretty communicative, the boy and I.'

'You mean you've actually discussed it?' she asked with a note of genuine surprise.

'Oh, no. I mean I know his opinion. Of course,' he checked for an instant, 'it does raise a third problem certainly.'

'Oh?'

'He has ideas of marrying you himself,' Ryan said. 'He

79

might take a swipe at me.'

She laughed, then studied the ash on her cigarette for a moment. 'I think I can resolve one of your doubts quite quickly, darling.' She looked up suddenly. 'If I had a son like Mark I'd be very grateful, and terribly proud. Does that answer your question?' It was completely sincere.

'Conclusively,' he said. 'It also makes me very proud, and grateful. Thank you, angel, more than I can say.'

He got up and went to her, then he reached down for her wrists and pulled her upright into his arms. He kissed her, gently, and then with feeling, and then again when she put her arms around his neck. Neither of them wanted the moment to end. The barriers were down now, and it had become a very special thing.

'You're very beautiful,' Ryan said.

'So are you.'

'Undoubtedly ... except for the face. Kind of homespun. Practical, perhaps.' He smiled. 'Which reminds me, can you bear any more of the excruciatingly sensible details yet?'

She raised her face and pouted a lip. 'So soon? Is all the silly sentiment over already then?' Her voice was like the murmur of the river at night when the flow was deep and leisurely, just stroking the rocks and the reed beds, and it wasn't easy to refuse.

He laughed. 'It hasn't even begun yet. Just bear with me a while.'

'Oh well then, if we must.' She made a gesture of pretended resignation and settled herself on the couch. Her voice lowered a shade, became more earnest. 'Tell me about you and *Donach* then.'

'I think you're wedded to it, maybe that you'd never give it up for any consideration?' he said levelly. 'Isn't that right?'

For a moment she remained silent, then she nodded. 'Yes, I'm afraid it is, Mark.' There was regret, and concern in it, yet just a suggestion of defiance, too, as if she anticipated rebuke or criticism. 'And you wouldn't want any entanglement with my impractical ... impractical millstones?' This time there was a suspicion of bitterness as well as regret in her voice.

80

'I think there's,' he grinned, 'a practical answer. But first tell me this. What do *you* think of *Greenacres*?'

For an instant she seemed taken aback, then she smiled. 'It's a lovely place, delightful. I adore it.'

'Well then...' he spread his hands, shrugged.

'But I told you, darling,' she insisted quietly. 'I wouldn't, couldn't give up *Donach*.'

'Nor I *Greenacres*.... Not the same, of course, but you see the wee place has a tie for me, too.... But nobody needs to give up anything. We'd put in a good manager right here, or if you preferred we'd rebuild it, modernise it. No trouble getting the man we wanted then.'

She turned her head and stared out of the window for a moment. 'Mark. You make it all sound so,' she laughed, 'so practical.'

'It would be.' The receptive note in her voice had been unmistakable. 'More than that,' he said. 'Look, dear, I'm not rich, but I'm not stuck for a buck either. We could, well, start to build a pedigree herd say, and really stock the place again ... put down pheasant, partridge, blackcock, the lot ... and put a couple of damn good keepers in the Lodges, and really farm the arable ...'

'Mark! You're quite a character. You may not be the mad Latin type, darling, but your diplomacy is far from disastrous, I assure you. You've given me an awful lot to think about.'

He pulled her close and kissed her. 'That's what I'd hoped. Taking all in all it's a pretty fair-sized proposition, isn't it? Can we have a final Board meeting when I get back, then?'

'Of course,' she nodded. 'And, darling.'

'Yes.'

'Mind you do, then!'

He smiled and nodded. That I will, he thought. He had a feeling that was akin to elation, as if he had turned a corner into a lighter place, and he suddenly realised that there was one thing time alone would never heal for him or any man. That he had been very lonely for a very long time. Too long.

81

BOOK TWO

3. JUAN RAMIREZ

The short fat man in the crumpled white suit turned on his stool and took another look at the three men over in the corner who had come in with him. He got out his handkerchief and wiped his brow and his heavy brown jowls. His brow was rather low and narrower than his jowls. Which, save for his moustache, gave him the facial characteristics of a frog because he had a wide mouth like a monk-fish. He took the cheroot out of it and smoothed the damp halves of his moustache with his big finger, pensively.

He was a very urbane man. In fact urbanity was his strong suit. Once, even, when he had sold two upstanding Mestizo girls, twins, and the betrothed of one of the girls had used violence to burst into his office he had exercised his right of self-defence and shot the ostensible 'robber' with perfect urbanity. But now, inside the cocoon of his urbanity, he was aggravated. He had been waiting for more than an hour.

He gave a backward nod with a suspicion of his professional smile. 'Give them another drink ... a beer for the *obscuro*, too.'

'Sure,' the bartender said in English. He was a quadroon and he could handle 'teco Spanish just as well as the Honduran variety, but he liked people to know that they were not talking to some bum off the Cays because for two years he had worked in a bar in Miami. He poured two shots of rum, then added a coke and a beer and pushed the tray at the hovering youth in the starched white jacket and bare feet.

The boy padded across the big room past the door of the restaurant to the table in the corner. It was odd that they didn't provide him with shoes in this, the classiest place of its kind, the fat man thought desultorily, especially since the floor was polished hardwood for when they had the rumba band along on Wednesday and Sunday nights. But in fact he did have shoes. For his night off, on Tuesdays; had had plimsolls for two years. There was no point, he figured, for the other seven days and six nights, because he worked for tips and his keep and except for the odd drunks and the occasional Mexican whore in funds the customers were not very generous.

'He has not the virtue of punctuality, this Ramirez?' the fat man said. As an afterthought he gave it another brief token display of gold fillings to keep it urbane still.

'A lot of engagements, *Señor* Ramirez,' the barkeeper said shortly, this time in Spanish. '*Cómo siempre*, as usual.'

'*An hombré de posibilidades*, eh?' the fat man said with a touch of sarcasm.

'You said it, a man of parts,' the barman replied with counter emphasis. 'You name it, brother, he's in it.'

'But as I said, unpunctual. Annoying.'

The barkeeper shrugged. 'He said he'll be here, he'll be here. You a friend, a relative?'

'Just business.'

'Don't call him Ramirez, then. Call him Mister, or *Señor* Ramirez.'

'So. *Qué te importa?* I am a man of some importance myself, hombre.'

The bartender shrugged again. 'Suit yourself. You said business, I'm just trying to tell you.'

'All right!' the fat man said, but not too tartly because he didn't want to clam it up yet, and he added a flicker of his bonhomie smile. 'Have a drink yourself . . . have a large one.'

The bartender considered. It was early yet. Only about seven. Usually he laid off till the three *músicos* came at nine, because from then on he would be keeping up with the customers till three, maybe dawn. On the other hand he couldn't smell any other bonus from this one . . . this important-my-ass-'teco. 'Okay. *Gracias*,' he said.

He poured himself a sizeable daiquiri. While he was putting the sugar in the fat man said casually, 'I saw the boat of *Señor* Ramirez down by the bridge. What does he want with a boat like that . . . a *millionario* or something?'

'Gets fishing clients for marlin, shark, stuff like that, at

85

times,' the quadroon said. 'Then there's the collecting-up he does.'

'What's that?'

'Got men two or three points along the coast between here and Punta Quela. Skiff fishermen. Lobsters, clams, pulpos ... picks up some of his other stuff, too ... Indians bring it to the coast.'

'Other stuff?'

The barkeeper waved a hand. 'Orchids, humming birds, snakes, spiders, stuff like that. Freight plane comes once a week from Miami.' He grinned. 'Some mixed-freight, believe me.'

'So. An *exportador*, a merchant,' the fat man said. 'I thought he was a hunter?'

'Best in the country, they say,' the barman said. 'But that ain't his steady trade no more. Not many rich Sports fancy night hunting.'

'I know places where they hunt daylight with dogs,' the fat man said slowly, pedantically, to keep it going.

'And how many they get with that dude stuff?' the barkeep said heavily. He waited triumphantly. 'Juan Ramirez he gets *tigrés* every time. Ocelots, twenty-five buck caimen too.'

'As you said,' the fat man said. 'A man of *posibilidades*!'

'You name it,' the barman told him. '*Muy vivo hombré*, a real operator.'

'And with boats also?'

'That as well. Learned the boats in the war ... volunteered ... was the first man from here with the U.S. Navy ... them fast boats with the torpedoes.'

He finished off his drink in a gulp, lifted the other man's glass and mopped up a wet ring. The rum was nothing, but he felt a mite more expansive. 'You talk about *millionarios*! Twenty years ago there was a place ten miles out of town, Hacienda Los Cazadores, hunting-fishing place.' He grinned. 'Mostly indoor hunting ... of two-legged cats ... two thousand bucks a week without meals. That's where he started ... professionally I mean .. before he started taking out people on his own. They did it with dogs there, you bet, but they kept

86

running out of dogs.'

They heard the sound of car tyres on the warm sandstone dust outside and in a minute or two a man came in. He wore a white snap-brim Panama and a casual blue-and-white striped shirt cut off at the upper arms and tucked into grey slacks. His arms, brown and knotted, filled his sleeves, and he was pushing six feet, but he didn't seem that tall because of his build. The opposite of gangly. Compact. Not a heavyweight, but somewhere about a hundred and eighty-five pounds. Except for the scar down the side of his face the barkeep had always thought that he looked a dead ringer for Anthony Quinn.

He nodded to the barkeep and went out on to the terrace, the lad in the white coat following him.

'There's your customer,' the barman said. He was pretty sure who would be the propositioner. 'That's Mister Ramierez.'

The stocky man got off his stool and went slowly over to the open french doors. For a moment he stood still, using the smile that was for business in a reasonable way, then he said, 'I am Gallegos, Almagro Gallegos.'

Ramirez nodded. 'Have a drink,' he said in English. To the other man he sounded more like a Norteamericano than the bartender did.

'Thank you, but I have had three already. I've been waiting an hour,' the fat man said. There was a clear implication of complaint in his tone but he held on to the smile.

Ramirez put his hat on the chair beside him. 'Have coffee then.' He looked at the boy. 'The usual, Paco. No, wait, bring the bottle and a coke.' He glanced at the foreigner. 'Coffee also?'

'Thank you,' Gallegos said. He proffered another opportunity. 'Perhaps there was a misunderstanding of time?'

'No, I had business come up.'

'This is business,' with a touch of asperity. 'Exceptional business. I will get the others.'

'Wait,' Ramirez said. He looked at the three in the corner through the door. 'Is the business confidential?'

'Yes and no.'

'Leave them then, it will probably save more of your

87

time.'

'Very well.'

Paco was very quick with the drinks. When he had gone back for the coffee Ramirez poured himself a daiquiri and coke.

'You have a good boat,' the fat man said. 'My friends and I would like to charter it.'

'For how long?'

'How long would it take to Punta Quela?'

Ramirez regarded him dispassionately. 'Six-seven hours, not pushing it.' To himself he thought, who wants to go to Punta, by boat, for Christ's sake?

'What is the cost of a trip like that, also returning of course?' Gallegos asked.

'Two hundred a day, U.S. dollars, plus gas, plus five a day for tackle hire ... but this isn't fishing, is it?'

'What makes you think that?' the fat man said mildly.

'You didn't ask me the best places,' Ramirez said. 'The best areas are only three hours out.'

The fat man smiled his best disarming smile. 'Well, no. Not exactly just a fishing trip ... in that sense. More of a business trip perhaps, though all the fishing *aparejo* should be put aboard.'

'For appearances?'

'Don't go so hastily,' Gallegos said evenly.

'All right, you said "exceptional". What's the exceptional part?'

'The price,' the fat man said. 'The price! We would pay five hundred dollars, half in advance, plus maybe a bonus if our business was fruitful.'

'When did you want to go?'

'Next week, say the twenty-ninth day of the month. Returning the next day.'

'Or next night?'

'Corrected,' Gallegos smiled. 'Yes, perhaps next night.'

'Sorry,' Ramirez said. 'I can't help you.'

'Why not?' the fat man said, his smile receding. 'You don't like money?'

'Money's why,' Ramirez said untruthfully. 'I got a hunting client next week ... and for weeks after,' he added. The last part was true. He turned his head away. It was still hot, but the fierce daytime heat had dwindled and there was a breath of breeze working up just enough, already, to stir the fronds of the palms along the beach.

'One thousand. American dollars,' Gallegos said. He cocked his head to one side, holding out his cheroots with the confident air of a man laying down a full house. 'Is that despicable money?'

Ramirez looked at the other man's shirt. He figured the cost of the crumpled white cotton suit. But whose money? he thought. Not yours, 'teco. And the others couldn't put up twenty dollars between them.

Inside the bar the biggest of the three men had got to his feet. He came through on to the terrace leaving the other man and the Negro at the table. He was not a bad looking man, very swarthy, but whatever he had drunk had heightened his naturally surly demeanour. 'What is all the talk for?' he said bluntly. 'Is the boatman hired?'

'We are still discussing,' Gallegos said irritably. 'Take the powder, Tomás, go and wait.'

'Cojones to waiting! What has been arranged?'

'Nothing yet. I have offered Señor Ramirez a thousand but he declines.'

'All right. Name your price, boatman. Let us conclude it,' the big man said domineeringly.

'It is not price. I couldn't go anyway,' Ramirez said curtly. Even if he had not disliked the man he had begun to figure it now. Because at Punta Quela there was just the burdel for the plant workers, the bank and the Associated Fruit Company. Nothing else. Except the lighthouse on the Cay. Incidentally, he thought, I wonder if these bums realise the lighthouse has radio.

Gallegos spread his hands, recovering his smile. 'Look, Captain, name your own price, and if we can pay it we will. Is that reasonable?'

'One moment,' the big fellow said roughly. 'Is that *busi-*

ness? I will arrange the paying.' He put his big hirsute palms on the table and leant forward. 'Listen, boatman. You don't have to come even, I will handle the boat.'

Ramirez laughed incredulously. 'Go screw it, amigo.'

'What you mean? You think I can't handle boats? By God, I don't let no boatman talk like that.'

'There is no deal, and least of all for that,' Ramirez said flatly. He held up two fingers. 'And another thing. You got a forty-eight hours *saidaconducto*, right? You call me boatman again and I'll have you picked up right now, *ladino*.'

It was a word you could take either way, depending on the tone, and the other man's face darkened. He started to curse but the fat man raised his hand. 'Always you got to foul up the business talk,' he said angrily. 'Like I said, Tomás, *take the powder*!'

The big man hesitated, then turned.

Gallegos made a gesture of apology. 'Very excitable, Tomás. A bad talker.' He made an effort to get back to urbanity again and played his ace off the bottom. 'Listen, Señor Ramirez, Captain, maybe I should have told you before, but it is confidential, you understand. We have a mutual friend, it is he who sent us to you,' he said sententiously. 'El Jefe.'

'Who is El Jefe?' Ramirez asked blankly.

'Let us not make jokes,' Gallegos said. He made a small gesture of impatience. 'El Jefe Politico, Señor Cruz, Francisco Cruz ... the cousin of your wife.'

'Oh, that *hijo*,' Ramirez said. 'Well likewise with Tomás, he also can go screw.'

'What?'

'As with Tomás,' Ramirez repeated. 'My wife's relatives are a pain in the ass.'

'But I understood you were *associados*, did business ... ?' Gallegos said.

'You were misinformed then, not that it would make a difference.'

'Still,' the fat man pressed it further, 'a man of much importance. Not only Jefe, an *Ayuntamiento*, able,' he gestured in the general western direction of the border, 'to return

90

favours.' He stressed the consideration.

'The hell with Cruz, I already told you. Look, why don't you take a plane?' Ramirez said, knowing well why not. 'You could private charter from Ariatica for less money.'

'You do not understand,' Gallegos said testily.

'*You* don't! You think I'd take chances for you, or Cruz, even if I didn't have a client?'

'Chances? What chances?' the fat man said sharply.

'The chances of five to ten years, plus the boat, which is part of my business,' Ramirez said shortly. 'Who do you think you are kidding?'

'That is wild talk, unwise talk.'

'*Puta*, shit!' Ramirez said. 'Listen, amigo. I don't know you, or them. You take it out of here right now and I've never heard of you.'

When they had gone he poured himself another drink and lit a cigarette. Christ, it had stuck out a mile. They wanted to knock off the bank, or the Fruit Company payroll. Most likely the Fruit Company because they paid in U.S. dollars. Gallegos was probably one of the fringe *politicos*, the small-time leg-men on the staffs of the bigger *politicos*. Maybe one of Cruz's own. The others had looked like hard cases, but not professionals. Not smooth enough. Roughnecks. When he himself had sometimes run guns and brought back black rum and Bacardi, in the earlier days when he was still paying for the boat, it had been really organised. Like a Navy operation. He wondered whether Cruz had been the master mind, or hadn't wanted to know about it so long as he got his cut; which was usually how the Jefe operated from what he had gathered.

He finished his drink and went over to the bar. 'Well, Al, been making good time with the Facciosos!'

Alberto grimaced. 'Some big-time Facciosos! Never left a red cent for Paco here, never do.'

'Here, Paco,' Ramirez said. He scooted a half-dollar along the bar to the boy.

'I didn't mean that,' Alberto said.

91

'I know, but I feel responsible.'

'No good to you either, I guess?' the barman said. 'At least I heard you call the big ape a *ladino*.'

'No good to anybody, the 'tecos, Al,' Ramirez said. 'Even if they've got the money you've got to beat it out of them, and then they start shooting.'

'I know. Always keep a gun in the till when we get their *Navidad* parties. Some crazy *borrachons*, the 'tecos.'

In a little while a party of two men and three women came in. Upper crust locals. One of the men called a greeting to Ramirez and he nodded back, but he didn't feel social and he went out to the Jeep.

The *Wallace* bar and restaurant was the most salubrious, and probably the priciest joint in town. A Scotch and a beer cost you one dollar Honduras, say five shillings, as compared to two bucks, fifty, in a Miami bar, or half a quid in a London one. The name dated way back to a Scots buccaneer of the Teach and Morgan era, which is why you got a quarter gill for your buck and not the idiot thimbles they served in England and the States.

Either side of it, fronting on the beach, there were half a dozen or so English-style houses, with round Spanish tiles and patios, belonging to a coterie of the more affluent citizens. Other than these there were no other buildings along the dirt road till you got to the Filling Station about half way back to town. After that you entered the dirty cornea of the shanty town belt, and then, finally, the three acres of paved streets around the Plaza, Government offices and Post Office which formed the iris of the Capital.

Crossing the bridge, which was about a half-mile up from the mouth of the river, he glanced down at his boat, the apple of his eye, capacious and sturdy, yet fast. The tamarinds and spaced out cohune palms in the Plaza looked quite picturesque in the two new floodlights on the patio of the City Hall.

He drove on through the grim southern baldric of shanty town and along to his own house. It was not large. A two-storey wooden house on piles. But the white paint gleamed in the moonlight and the wood was really good stuff. When he had

92

first built it, before the scattering of modern houses out by the *Wallace*, it had been one of the best in town. A palace to the tin and crate-wood shanties. But, as he told himself nearly every time he came home, they'd have to shift. Get one set up like the *Wallace* ones. The kennels on stilts, human sties, were coming too close, now, the nearest barely a couple of hundred yards away.

He didn't mind the people as such. On the contrary. They were mostly simple friendly folk, as much a part of his life as the jungle and the sea. And every now and then they threw up real humdingers by any comparison, whether coal black or one of the various intermediate shades. But the trouble was they always brought the squalor, the stink of garbage and open sewers. You *had* to be at a distance from them because they fouled up everything.

He went up the hardwood staircase on the side of the house which gave to the front door and then up on to the balcony facing the sea. A cock *maklala* ran up the handrail ahead of him, greenish-yellow with a salmon pink underbelly, comb erected in disapproval and swishing his disproportionately large tail. When he reached the horizontal rail of the balcony the lizard turned for a second and glared, hostility in his bright basilisk eyes, then he ran along the bar on his hind legs, quick as a pheasant, and took off on to a branch of the tamarind tree which brushed the house.

Ramirez sat down beside the little bamboo table on the balcony. The homemade rocking chair plainted faintly as he settled himself. It was quite pleasant on the balcony just now. The air hung heavily, but it had begun to stir to wisps of breeze from the north-east which brought a slightly salty tang from the fish cannery down by the river mouth. When the chair creaked again his wife called out through the open door to the bedroom.

'Juan?'

'Who else? Were you expecting Zambo?' he said, maintaining the old joke between them.

El Zamo was the mail-man. A wiry little fellow, black as pitch, with a wide white smile, who was extensively rumoured

93

to possess exceptional organs. Once, in the market, a big suspicious buck had removed the small Casanova's pants by force and held him struggling for all to see that rumour was no jade. The joke, also, was because Clara could have smothered Zambo. Twenty years ago she had been tall and buxom and now, a matron of thirty-eight, she was going one hundred and seventy pounds. Not that she was unattractive or unshapely yet, or less of a performer. It was just that there was more of her, spread all over.

Mostly, she was a pretty reasonable woman too, he thought. Except when she had the gripe she made very little trouble over his other three less-official 'wives', although she was quite religious. True, they were only Indians ... about whom she had learned through Dona Maria Cruz ... and the nearest of them a hundred miles away. But many women would have endlessly complained, whereas she had largely, if not quite wholly, accepted his explanation of business considerations.

In fact, aside from the Indian women, the only regular dissension between them derived from her attitude towards Cruz, *El Jefe*, and approval of his ambitions towards their daughter, Consuela.

'*Qué passa* ... with the business I mean?' she said after a while.

'Nothing passed ... *hijos*!'

'Without money?'

'Not theirs.'

'Whose then?'

'From the payroll of the Fruit Company at Punta Quela ... bloody 'tecos!' He heard her indrawn breath and added. 'And you know who sent the crutting 'tecos? You know who sent them, eh? Cruz. Cruz, your crutting cousin.'

'Juan, he wouldn't. You are making it up.'

'He sent them, I tell you,' Ramirez said with mordant finality. 'Of course there was no mention of the purpose, that would have come at Punta.'

'Well you are guessing then?'

Ramirez swore. 'Use your brains woman. A thousand for the trip to Punta? Lucky for you, I guess well ... for Cruz, too.'

94

'Oh, Juan, I'm so glad you didn't. Don't ever.'

'Of course not. We don't need the money now, do we? And never with those *hijos* anyway.'

For a time they were silent, then she said, 'But there's still one thing.'

'What?'

'Why do you hate them all?'

'Christ, won't you ever learn? Viva la Independencia for one reason.' He flicked his stub over the rail. 'And I don't hate them *all*. I don't hate you.'

Down below, in the moonlight, a big bufo toad moved out of the shadow of the house and began to make for the mangrove patch the other side of the road.

'Well, come to bed, then?'

Ramirez laughed. 'Why not, it's better than jail.'

When he had undressed and got in she said, 'Am I really better than the Indian sluts?'

He chuckled again. 'Am I better than Zambo?'

'No, really?'

'Of course,' he lied. 'They are merely ablutions and business.'

4. 'JANE RUSSELL'

When they landed at Mexico City Ryan strolled through to the bar and studied the bottles for a moment, trying to think of something original that would be consistent with the heat and still have some kind of point to it; such as all the conventional debilitated 'long' drinks never did.

It was too hot for Logan's, even if they had ever heard of the real dew, and eventually he settled for iced beer and tequila. It was a combination that seemed to startle the taciturn barkeep out of his apathy, but in the event it wasn't too bad at all, and after he had repeated the experiment he felt a certain aperitif effect. He went through to the restaurant and

95

decided on a big Texan steak and salad, because although it was really also too hot for steak he had an idea that it might be some time before he got any good beef again.

Outside of the heat his outlook had improved from the crabbit mood he had felt on the first two legs of the trip.

For one thing it had been a good flight from Miami. The Trans-Eastern Boeing had put down right on schedule, despite having had to make a deviation on account of hurricane reports from the Gulf, there had been no porter nonsense, and this interval between planes was just long enough for drinks and a meal.

When the announcement came he finished off his coffee and went out through the Departure doors feeling more like it, and when he saw the machine it gave him a grin that had a touch of the Irish in it.

Because the once-weekly airplane to Honduras was a real old air-going tramp all right.

Among the gamut of massive gleaming jets and sleek private craft scattered over the port, the rusty old beat-up Dakota stood, straddle-legged, like a tough old crow amidst a flock of flamingoes. And the amount of stuff they were ramming into her belly, it made you wonder if they could even get her off the deck without the passengers.

He glanced around the knot of them grouped around the doors. They were a gallimaufric assembly, especially in attitudes and shades of skin ranging from a saffron-coloured supercilious-looking hidalgo type in a white suit and matching Stetson, wearing black and white shoes, down to an anxious family party of peóns.

The Captain of the aircraft leaned against the glaucous fuselage chewing mechanically, his cap tilted forward over one eye. Nearby, his aide lolled in the shade of a wing, hands in pockets and tunic on shoulder, watching the porters through smoked glasses with a similarly bored expression. They were both slim, coffee-coloured Mexicans, their faded grey-blue uniforms as old as the airplane, and the younger man looked barely old enough for an apprentice pilot.

When the porters had struggled the bays shut the Captain

96

said something to his compatriot and the second pilot called out to the passengers to come ahead.

There were two big young Negro men in front of Ryan, and when he got aboard he took the porthole seat of a double opposite to them and just back of the port wing. By now the engines were idling and most of the other seats were filled, but as the pilot began the final test-revving a woman came along the aisle and took the gangway seat beside him.

She was coloured. Off-white he supposed you would call it. Rather paler than a high-yellow. But an interesting thing about her was that although somewhere along her line there was pure Congo, technically her features were 'white'. More specifically they were Spanish white. Even more specifically, it flashed through his mind, Andalusian Spanish.

She was well above average height and, moving along the aisle, she had bent her head as if she was used to ducking doors. She wore a white calico coat which, hanging loose and open, gave a glimpse of a figure that was proportionately statuesque.

When she had settled, almost apologetically, he turned his head and momentarily they exchanged brief formal smiles. In the same instant, lowering his glance, he got a glimpse of a pale consummate bust that would have gladdened Boccaccio. But her manner was entirely circumspect, even introversive to the point of embarrassment, although there had been nothing untoward in her entry. She drew her coat together again as a normal action of modesty and smoothed the lap of her skirt.

The noise of the engines rose to a crescendo and as they accelerated to take off Ryan habitually concentrated; helping to will the old tramp into the air like a weary old matriarch swan full of eggs. When they had made a few hundred feet of laboured incline he reached up for his jacket. But before he lit a cigarette he took another surreptitious look at the woman beside him.

He would have found it difficult to explain the conclusion, but the glance confirmed his first assessment of her.

There was definitely some Negro in her, maybe to quadroon extent, probably with a preponderance of Spanish, or perhaps

97

Indian blood or, conceivably, even both. Yet the fascinating and paradoxical thing about her was the wholly European mould of her features which, especially in profile, were strikingly handsome. Not beautiful nor softly pretty, but handsome. In a way which somehow seemed scarcely reconcilable with her shyness; with an unobtrusive manner that would have been more appropriate to soft prettiness.

He dismissed further conjecturing and found the place he had got to in the book, a Ruark paperback that he had noticed on the news-stand at Miami. He had read about half of it, and had mostly found it entertaining stuff despite the fact that it was chiefly scattergunning ... which was a branch he had lost a lot of interest in over the years ... and although he himself would have begged to differ with some of the doggy pronouncements.

In fact the only acute irritation derived from the constant Pure-Gold-Simple-Rustic-Philosophies of Mr Ruark's 'Old Man' character who, it seemed to him, lagged about some fifty miles behind Big Ernie's 'Old Man' in terms of authenticity, beliefs and dramatic texture.

And except, that was, for one other embarrassment which had quite probably given Mr Ruark an equal pain, and had even more probably been contributed by a blurb writer more familiar with the wild life of Central Park. '*A classic ... no parallel in modern literature!*' the extravagant lad (or desperate hack) had written.

God Almighty, he thought. Hadn't they ever heard of Henry Williamson? Of *Tarka*, of *Salar The Salmon*, *The Lone Stag*, *The Peregrine's Saga*: of David Stephen's *String Lug The Fox*, *Six-pointer Buck*, and others which really had rated the panegyric tribute?

Not, literary Pharisee and solipsist as I'm damned sure you are, Robert, he thought, that I wouldn't have enjoyed swapping some woodland tales and theories with you. Nor have been the last, and honoured, to buy you a tot. Always supposing it didn't have to be one of those bloody fancy things taken at some fancy pub between here and the Peking Hilton, and always supposing that you'd have gone along with a jar of soup

98

and a dram or so of the real gravy!

He read two or three more pages. Good, entertaining stuff, but still, infuriatingly, for one member of the brotherhood, marred by more 'homespun' crapology about how, with a dog or his master, it was all a question of whether or not they had 'the right blood' for God's sake.

Then he made a pretence of shifting himself and half-turned his head. Her coat had worked open again and he got a further vision of the fine profile, dark, slightly slanted eyes and a superlative rising bosom that gave him a deep-down feeling in his loins. She lowered her eyes as if she immediately felt his fleeting appraisal and restored the coverage of her coat.

Across the narrow aisle on her other side one of the two bucks had given previous indication that he knew her, or presumed to, but she had brushed off his attempt at conversation with a formal nod and brief smile. For a time after that the two Negroes had conversed in lowered voices, occasionally glancing across the gangway, and sometimes sniggering.

But now the one in the aisle seat became more venturesome. He leaned across and began to importune her in semi-whispers. Mostly he kept his voice down, but Ryan heard enough to realise that he was trying to get her to go along to the toilet at the back of the plane. When finally the man put his hand on her thigh she knocked it aside and shook her head emphatically. Her face had gone a shade darker now and she stared fixedly ahead because there was nowhere else to look.

'Would you care to change seats?' Ryan said impulsively. She gave him a quick look of embarrassment and confusion, then lowered her glance.

'It's all right, thank you.' She barely murmured it but her voice had a soft mellow quality that was very attractive.

'Just thought you might find it less bothersome,' he said. 'We've got quite a time to go.'

She looked at him again, twisting the cotton gloves in her lap. 'Well . . . if you really don't mind, Sah . . .'

'Pleasure,' Ryan said.

When he stood up he gave the coloured man a studied dead-pan look of dispraisal before re-settling himself. Strictly nega-

99

tive. For a second the Negro looked as if he was going to say something, but his companion pulled his sleeve and he turned away with a laugh.

Outside the porthole the sun beat fiercely down on the rust-streaked surface of the wing, burnishing the metal with reflected glare, and inside the atmosphere grew more frowsty and oppressive. Ryan leant his head back and tried to doze, but every so often the process was interrupted by a tiny waft of perfume that had a persistent disturbing quality.

When he opened his eyes again the younger of the two Pilots was just coming out of the flight cabin. He came down the aisle, chewing lethargically, but more animate now, eyeing the passengers with his customary air of nonchalant cocksureness.

When the man drew level Ryan touched his arm. 'How about a drink, Captain?'

The brown man shrugged delicately. 'Sorry, Suh ... if we kept liquor aboard they'd all want it.' His English had a consonant Texan accent.

'You've forgotten something,' Ryan said. 'I mean *my* liquor. Remember you kindly took care of a breakable parcel for me when I came aboard?' He opened his hand, showing the bills in it.

The slim man frowned, then grinned. 'Oooh, yeh, man. That's right. That's what you did.' He put his hand on the corner of the seat and leaned over, 'Kin you remember what was in it?'

'Not rightly,' Ryan said. 'There was some Scotch, wasn't there ... ? Or it might have been Daiquiri ... plus some beer and a couple of Cokes.'

'Is that what there was, boss?' the Mexican said. He drawled it in a way which would have bristled the hairs on an R.S.M.'s neck and brought an explosion. 'Well, Sah, I'll cert'nly go lookit for you. I'll do that sure 'nough!'

The drawl and the accent would have gone along better with Hollywood chaps and high-heels, and while he spoke his eyes were ranging over the woman in the next seat. He leaned further over, grinning. 'You don' watch it, Chick, them beauts

100

are goaner bust right out, and you goaner have to ask this genelman to help you put 'em back.' He laughed insolently. 'Yehman! Finest pair of rising beauts I seen in a long time!'

There wasn't anything really malicious or offensive intended. It was just Smart Alec, funny-ha-ha stuff. Like he did all the time, with all the chiquitas. No harm to it. But she flashed him a quick look of anger and annoyance, then hunched around in her seat as if to hide her embarrassment and Ryan experienced a kindred feeling of resentment. For all the Mexican knew she could be with me, he thought! And even if the squirt knew otherwise, or even knew her personally, it made no difference.

He reached up and jerked the man's lapel, making him bend lower. 'Listen, Captain,' he said. 'Let's cut out the funny stuff, huh? Just let's get the refreshment, huh?' He said it quietly enough, with a smile, but the smile was as good as spelling it.

The younger man looked surprised. The great bulk of passengers they carried were smalltime folk. Coloureds going home, loggers, obreros, Hondurans, Guatemaltecos. Invariably obsequious, pathetically deferential to his uniform as if fearful that he might order them to jump out of the aircraft, and he was used to fooling around with them, sassying up the women when he felt like it and knowing that the men wouldn't answer back. When they had anybody of real account aboard they were usually told about it at the Departure office as a matter of policy.

He considered the appearance and demeanour of this passenger, who was prepared to make it worth his while to dig something up, and at the same time he recollected a directive that had been circulated more than once by the company. To the effect that in the airlines business you never knew whom you might be talking to!

This *gringo* could be an *importante*. Certainly he was carrying quite a roll. Aside from which he was of formidable size, and annoyed.

'Sure, boss.' He made a small conciliatory gesture and summoned a corresponding smile. 'Jus' kiddin' along. Din'

101

know the lady was a frien' of yours.' He flipped a hand and moved on down the aisle.

Ryan touched her sleeve. 'Sorry about that. Too many funny men aboard, eh?'

She turned her head and nodded. But it was plain that she didn't quite know what to say just yet. She lowered her eyes and turned again towards the porthole.

He had an intuitive feeling that her embarrassment was probably mainly due to the fact of his own presence, to his witnessing her discomfiture, because very probably ... a woman of such obvious attractions ... she was well used, if not necessarily inured to the kind of crude ploys which the bucks and the wiseguys never tried with white women. Kept for the ones who, willingly or otherwise, were wide open.

For the first time, consciously, it really struck him that for coloured women there must always be this additional disadvantage of having to put up with all this demeaning stuff from the bums, the clowns and the oglers. Both kinds.

In a little while the uniformed youth came back down the gangway with a paper sack and a concertina of plastic cups. From the Pilot's locker he had dug out a flat pint of Daiquiri from the small cache of duty-free liquor which was their little racket, and from his own, two cans of Heineken and a bottle of Coke.

He grinned expectantly. 'That your passel then, Suh?'

'That's the very one,' Ryan said. He put a folded bill into the man's slender brown hand. 'Okay?'

The other man glanced at it and nodded his satisfaction. 'Yes, Sah.'

When he had gone Ryan pulled out the folding tray from the back of the seat ahead. He set up two of the beakers, then he said: 'Well. It's a pretty limited menu I'm afraid, but can I mix you a drink?' He gave it a little smile of enquiry.

'No, thank you, Sah ... thank you just the same,' she said softly, circumspectly.

'Oh, come on. Just a wee one, not a teetotaller, are you?'

She shook her head again. 'No, Sah, but ... I'm fine ...'

'But you must be thirsty,' he drew his finger around his

102

open collar, 'in this oven.' He smiled again. 'Might help you to take a nap ... me too, for that matter ... we've still got quite a time to go.'

'You're very kind, Sah,' she said quietly.

'Well, we have a custom,' Ryan said. 'We try not to drink alone ... I'm a Limey.'

'I know that, Sah,' she said. Then, almost militantly, defiantly, 'I'm British too!'

'I'm way ahead of you,' Ryan said untruthfully. 'I guessed it. Not that it would have made any difference.' He nodded to the paper bag. 'Let's take a wee snort, and relax a while then ... compatriot.' He didn't push it. Just let it stay at being a friendly gesture.

She smiled. It was the first time she had really let go and the outcome was very fetching. 'All right then!'

'Little Daiquiri-and-beetroot-juice?'

She gave another flash of marvellous teeth in a smile, still semi-diffident, but which made him feel as if he had just given her a bunch of roses. 'Well, thank you.'

He poured a fifty-fifty rum and coke, then got a half glass of Daiquiri and a can for himself. 'God save our Queen,' he said lightly. 'Her tax men and all.'

The last bit seemed to have her foxed at first and she wrinkled her nose, but then she said. 'Yes, Sah, God save her!'

It was said so respectfully that it caught him off balance, and he glanced up to confirm that it was sincere. Not sarcasm. Certainly he'd experienced this extraordinary allegiance before. In Nepal, in some parts of Kenya, Hong Kong, the Falkland Isles and other unlikely seeming places. But it was still a bit unexpected. Paradoxical.

She didn't smoke, but eventually she took a repeat drink. In the ordinary way, what with the socialising effect of the drinks and all, you would have taken it from there. But there didn't seem to be much point to setting up an involvement, even should she be receptive, just as he was coming up to the business end of the trip, for all that he was beginning to get quite an inclination.

103

Moreover, he had now a notion to convey that not every John in the book was necessarily on the make, well at least not like blundering carthorses anyway.

He laid back his head again, and shortly, with the heavy stuffiness and the soporific aid of the liquor, he lapsed into a doze.

When he came to fully again they were flying lower, just coming up to the approaches. He got up and went back down the aisle, and for a few minutes, he watched the pattern spreading out below from a rear window that offered a much better view than the portholes.

The approaches reminded him of the swamp areas of the Bwangato country. A great expanse of matt-brown mud flats and green mangrove swamps, intricately laced with weaving blue channels, that were also strongly reminiscent of the Everglades.

Off the coast the Cays stretched north and south in a wavering irregular necklace that roughly followed the shoreline. They were like haphazard blobs of green ink from the pen of a drunken cartographer, and while some were no bigger than rafts, the size of a carrier's flight deck or less, others of the islands looked to run to some acres.

They were steeped in history, too, of course. The first tentative havens of the original buccaneers. Of Teach, Morgan and the others who had scourged the Main, and, ultimately bequeathed much hard-won mainland territory, as well as their British names, to descendants now agglomerated into a fantastic present-day population whose complexions covered half the spectrum.

The thought reminded him again of the woman back along the gangway. Her original forebears could well have been a Spanish or British seaman and a Negress, mulatto or mestizo girl.

When he returned to his seat she was sitting upright, checking her papers and ticket in a small caiman-hide handbag. She looked up and smiled, and he wondered if her more relieved air was because she was nearly home, or because she would soon have more manoeuvring space for the wiseguys and the Big

104

Dealers.

'Just about coming in, then?' he said.

'Yes, just about.' She nodded and then looked down at the bag in her lap. 'I'd like to thank you again, Sah ...' she said quietly.

'Lord, forget it,' Ryan said. 'My pleasure!' Oddly he felt a touch of embarrassment himself.

When they had finally crunched and ground to a quivering halt, he stood up and got her suitcase from the rack. The label on it said *Miss Ida Morgan*. In a way it seemed like a let-down. Too un-exotic. Carmelita Del Rio, or Dolores dos Something would have been more like it, more belonging. But then he had another thought, harking back to his earlier musings, and which gave him an inner smile.

Morgan, begod! How about that?

The name which had paralysed the Spanish rulers of long ago, had conjured the repeated embarrassments ... and covert approvals ... of successive British Ambassadors to Madrid, as well as British emissaries throughout the emergent Caribbean countries.

Ludicrous, of course, yet quite a thought. That from some-where way back, maybe through some wayward interlude, the name of the great Captain-Buccaneer-Governor, the man who had led that fantastic British handful on that fantastic over-land march to Panama, had persisted and sub-divided down the years to this coloured beauty.

Certainly he had been a man for interludes, had Morgan. By all the legends more mindful of a lady's talents than her colour, and this had been his favourite coast. His real home.

Maybe not quite so wildly fanciful at that, he speculated! For in his prime the old pirate had bestowed his favours pretty widely, and those inheritors of his virility were not likely to have eschewed his name. The name would not be unknown, he fancied, between the Cays and Maracaibo!

He stood aside and they exchanged nods as she followed the two Negro men and the family party past the younger Pilot standing at the door. Then, unhurriedly, he put on his jacket, loosely knotted his tie and reached down his mac.

In the packed adobe oven of the semi-dilapidated Customs and Immigration hut everybody was talking and nobody listening. There was a door in the corner marked *Restaurant*, in faded white paint. Right now he was neither hungry nor thirsty, just bored and boiled, but there would be some baggage-unloading time yet. And then likely a basic English, or basic Spanish session about the guns and the ammo and stuff.

He walked along through the scattering of cane tables and chairs to the far end of the bar and was about to get a beer from the Chinaman in the soiled white tunic, when he felt a touch on his arm.

'Mistah Ryan, Sah?'

'That's right.'

'Señor Ramirez,' the coloured man corrected himself, '*Mistah* Ramirez, send me fetch yo. No come himself, he caught up in business. Come along to yo dinnah time.'

He was a sturdily built mulatto in a chewed-up straw hat, faded khaki shirt and blue jeans rolled above his chocolate calves. There was an effort of concentration in his speech, his eyes half closing like he had memorised it, and afterwards he grinned widely as if in self-congratulation.

It was a simple enough message, yet not so easy to pick up as you might think because of the curious Creole accent, which always takes a little time to assimilate. Technically English, at least basically, the pronunciation often makes it as abstruse as broad Glaswegian to a Cockney. And, of course, as he was to discover, that was only the half of it, because this kind of Creole English took in inverted word sequences, and vernacular phrases which derived equally from Spanish, French and Christ-knew-what. Though, curiously, their Spanish was said to be largely unperverted.

'Qué va!' He tried it in Spanish. 'You go along and look for my stuff then!' When the mulatto's face showed understanding he continued in Spanish, '*Dos sacos*, two bags,' he held up two fingers, 'then three ... three gun cases and one case of munición, all with my name ... Ryan. See.' He got the ballpen from his jacket and printed RYAN on one of the small card-

106

board doily mats on the bar counter.

'Si, Señor,' the brown man said. But then he relapsed back into Creole again as if he was on his mettle over it and didn't realise that, right now, it would probably be a sight easier for both of them in Spanish. 'Yassah, ah go lookit, then wait fo yo outside by car.'

As he padded out, the woman in the white coat came through the door from the Customs hut carrying her case, immediately followed by the two Negroes off the plane. Without looking around she walked rapidly across to a small table against the wall which had only one chair to it. It was clear that she was trying to ignore them, but the two men persisted, laughing and fooling around, and then drawing up chairs to hem her in. They were obviously pestering, trying to hustle her.

Again? Ryan thought. Does she get this stuff all the time for God's sake? Not that it made any difference to the annoyance he felt, because these bums had already been warned off the course.

He ground out the butt of his cigarette. Ida saw him coming first, then the less obstreperous of the bucks, the one who had been in the window seat in the plane. The more fanciful one had his back to him.

'I've been looking for you, Jane,' Ryan said emphatically. 'Come on over here.'

She looked up expectantly, then started to rise but the more ambitious man swung around. His shiny black face showed surprise at first, then rancour and a resentment that went much further than he would have felt towards another coloured man.

'Who' hell yo think you are, Whitney. Who ast yo come bustin' in?'

'Shut your face, boy,' Ryan said curtly. There was a White Boss ring to it, so the black man thought, though the truth was that up until then, no question of skin had entered Ryan's mind. He would have felt, reacted similarly towards any member of his own Hall, club, fraternity ... whether white, black, brown or sky-blue-pink.

107

'Shut your face and blow, *boy*!' he said again.

He tapped the third man's chair with the side of his foot and the Honduran drew aside.

Intrinsically, the third man was an unassuming, even introvert man who was always getting inveigled into situations by Alberto and he knew damn well that Alberto was way out of line now, as he so often was. Even among their own crowd down at the fish factory Alberto was always stirring it up with somebody's woman. And this woman was no dime-a-dozen chick. And this Whitey wasn't going to take any of Alberto's lip either, you didn't have to be a genius to figure that.

He pulled at his companion's sleeve but the glowering man ignored him as he had known he would.

Alberto rose and balanced on his feet. He smelt frustration again and his face was working with resentment. Given two more shots of rum he would probably have taken a swing at this Whitey, but he had now an untypical presentiment that if he did he might this time wind up on the losing end.

The prospect of further disparagement, personal devaluation, added to his resentment and involuntarily his hand went to his hip.

Inevitably, the implication of the knife made Ryan grin with anger. He thrust the crumpled corner of his mac into the Negro's stomach, jabbed him with the hard muzzle of the empty Luger. It was an instinctive action, a bluff, except that there was no bluff in the expression on his face, and when Alberto got the message he felt a further prickling of apprehension. And the feeling grew in him that this one might not be the same as the little fracases he was used to, that this time he could wind up with holes in his belly.

He moved back from the table staring uncertainly, letting his hands fall to his sides.

'Come on, Jane,' Ryan said again. The quieter Negro shifted some more and she came out past him. Ryan took her case and they moved down the room till he gestured to a table near the bar. He let his expression relax and smiled. 'Just won't leave you alone, eh?'

She was still tensed up. 'I'm really *very* sorry,' she said

108

quietly, distractedly.

He waved a hand. 'Hell, it wasn't your fault. Are you waiting for someone then?'

'Just for the bus to town,' she said. 'It'll be along soon now I hope.'

'Well, that's all right then, I've got a driver somewhere. Soon as my stuff's ready let me drop you off.'

'Oh, no, really ... caused you 'nough bother already.'

'No bother, a pleasure.' He leant forward a little, smiling. 'Come on, now, forget about them. We'll just have one for the road and get going?'

Some of the stress left her expression. 'Well can I pay for it then, please?'

'Not this time. Maybe next time I run into you.'

He had just fetched the drinks from the bar when the mulatto came through from the door of the Customs hut and he signalled him over. 'Got the stuff then, hombre?'

The Honduran grinned equivocally. 'Got de bags yo name on, Sah. They ready fo Customs.'

'All right,' Ryan said. 'I'll go get my papers stamped. But when this lady has finished her drink you take her through to the car, then come back and find me.'

The mulatto figured it in English for a moment. Then he grinned, proud of his perceptive ability. 'Yessah.'

'Right, then,' Ryan said. He smiled at Ida. 'I'll be as quick as I can.'

In the Customs hut there were only two passengers still to be cleared now. The Immigration Officer wore an air of wearied authority. He was a man of lowly beginnings who had never quite got over the incredible authority vested in himself. But he was not officious, and his bulk gave him a reassuringly friendly air.

He thumped the passport, glanced perfunctorily at the other papers and pushed them back with the brief professional smile that, he always hoped, conveyed the broad understanding of one man-of-the-world for another.

'Have yosel' a good visit, Sah. *Ah* recommend de *Palace*.' He waved a hand. 'Fact ah use it masel'!' The commenda-

109

tion was obviously unchallengeable.

Ryan nodded. He picked up the wad of papers and moved across the hut. The Customs man sat in his shirt sleeves at a deal table which was piled with yellowing forms, stencilled sheets, a miscellany of rubber stamps and other dusty trivia. He was as coal black as his colleague, but, contrastingly, a thin niggly man. With a soured expression that basically derived from the fact of no peaked cap and jurisdiction only over goods ... mostly dime store jewellery or half-drunk bottles of cheap bourbon, at that ... instead of human subjects.

Unlike the fat man with the cap he began to study the documents laboriously, his lips moving slowly as he silently spelled out the words to himself.

Outside on the strip one of the Dakota's engines coughed and then caught.

Ryan hoisted his bags on to the bench next the table. 'These here are mine.' He indicated the boxes on the floor. 'And these are the guns and ammunition.'

'*Guns!*' The business suddenly took on an unusual import-ance, and the thin man jerked upright, all his latent authorita-tive instincts aroused.

'*Hunting guns,*' Ryan said heavily, impatiently. 'You're not being invaded yet.'

The scraggy man stared, then he sighed and reached re-signedly for the inevitable forms he hated so much. Later, down at the *Kwikservice*, he would brood over the incident that had nearly amounted to something at last.

At the front of the building a big old Buick sedan stood on the loose red gravel. The front fender was twisted and the tyres were thickly coated with heavy red soil powdered with grey dust as if it had been alternately ploughing through wet earth and then dry stretches of alkali-flat.

The girl was already in back of the car, and there was a stranger sitting on the passenger side of the front benchseat who was more pretentiously dressed than the mulatto. In a short-sleeved yellow aertex shirt, with blue cotton pants and an old soft hat. His ebony forearm lay along the top of the seat

110

and as Ryan approached he raised two fingers to his forehead and grinned indolently, showing his platinum-edged teeth.

Ryan stared cursorily back. He was sticky-hot, getting crab-bit again, and there was the further nark that this character, Ramirez, the professional, had not been here to meet him and take care of the formalities as, by any professional standards, he should have been.

And he wasn't in the mood for sharing cabs or Creole conversation just yet.

'Who's he, and who invited him anyway?' He jerked his head to the mulatto.

'Oh, he jus' come along case yo needed extry help, boss,' the driver said vaguely. 'He de cab owner . . . ah his driver.'

'Is that so,' Ryan said testily. 'Well next time you tell *Mister* Ramirez to be here himself, boy. You just tell him that from me.'

He opened a rear door and got a glimpse of long shapely legs and rounded knees, abbreviated by a skirt that tautly suggested abundantly swelling thighs and hips. It was maybe irrational, but the brief vision and the look on her face, as if she thought there might still be more upset pending, dispersed some of his irritation. He smiled reassuringly. 'Sorry for all the delay, Jane . . . the Generalissimo back there . . .'

When they were moving he began to feel more relaxed, and at this first sight the scenery was engrossing. On both sides of the road the thick lush vegetation was occasionally splashed by blotches of vivid colour.

Verdant mangrove swamp backed by a secondary growth of clotted marsh shrubbery, officiated over by monkey-tail palms and cabbage palmhearts that, in turn, were commanded by great towering *nargustas*, their lower branches hung with lichens.

The prevailing greenness was regularly relieved by the red, yellow and bright-orange floral patches, and soon they began to get fleeting madrigal glimpses of the wide green river that escorted the road to the Capital.

Despite the late afternoon heat, saving for a few stretches more exposed to the full force of the sun, the red dirt of the

111

road looked soft and moist from the last of the erratic ten-minute rain squalls which had exploded at midday; lashing the foliage and peppering the ground with the force of hail.

Some of the bigger potholes were near hub-deep now, but the mulatto made no attempt at avoidance, and after the third violent shake-up Ryan leaned forward. 'Look man, cut it down ... slack off for God's sake. We're not in that much of a hurry,' he suggested.

'*Siento*, sorry, Sah.' The driver half turned his head and nodded, but the man beside him snickered and leaned across. 'I think the Inglés in another kind of hurry, eh?' he grinned. 'He pick up the girl on the plane, now he in big hurry to take off her pants, so you got to go slow.' It was said in a patois of Spanish, out before the driver could stop him, and Ryan had got the gist of it. He looked at the girl. She was staring out of the open window as if she had not heard, but she probably had.

God almighty!

If these characters and the two on the plane were typical of local attitudes there were going to be some incidents before this trip was over all right!

He tapped the one with the hat on the shoulder. 'Listen, *hijo*,' he said in Spanish. 'I don't know if Mister Ramirez or I are paying for this cab ... either way it's me ... but if you *hijo*s say another word, you *hijos* are going to walk! Comprender?'

'Yes Sah, mister,' the mulatto said promptly. He had never heard of psychoneuroses or compulsive urges himself, but he had learned to recognise sincerity from the end of his father's belt and he took his foot away from the clutch to nudge the other man's shin.

The unsuspected understanding of the Inglés seemed to have confused the cabowner, but in the instant of awkward silence which followed it came to him that if, additionally, his little impropriety got back to Señor Ramirez there would be further repercussions.

He groped for the conciliatory words. 'Mah 'pologies, Sah. Jes' jokin', Sah. No 'fence taken, ah hope?' he added urgently.

112

For a moment Ryan let him stew, then he said. 'All *right*. Just look out for the bomb craters from now on, huh?'

He glanced at the girl. She was watching the two Hondurans, sitting rigidly upright now, both staring fixedly ahead. There seemed to be just the suggestion of a smile on her face and he felt his own lips relax into a grin despite his anger.

Suddenly, a mile or so farther on, the mulatto began to slow right down. He gave a sudden exclamatory curse and they craned forward.

For maybe a hundred yards or more the road was alive. The red dirt covered with a living, moving, undulating carpet.

Once, as a boy, and one other time since, Ryan had come across a migration of frogs; countless millions of tiny bright-green fellows making their hazardous annual trek from the shallows of an adjacent Loch to subsequently disperse themselves over the fields, dykes and hedges. The phenomenon right ahead had come similarity. But the little frogs had not been repulsive! Rather, in their small Olympian leapings, to the contrary. Amusing.

The car had stopped now, but then the mulatto changed his mind and began to move forward again.

'Wait. Hold it,' Ryan said. He got out of the car and walked towards the hustling loathsome armies obliterating all sign of the road.

Unlike the frogs the land crabs had no uniformity of size. Mostly the creatures were about the dimensions of a man's fist. But there were small ones, the size of a golf ball, and a prolificacy of Colonels and Generals which, he guessed, must have run to eight and ten pounds apiece.

About twenty yards in from the fringe of the mass a pile-up had occurred. Evidently the big green ground lizard had blundered, or perhaps been circumnavigated by the decopods' flanking patrols and now he was in process of being eaten alive almost without any slackening of the general advance.

The whole disgusting animated pattern was shot with colour because although the majority of the crabs were crimson or yellow-backed specimens, others were purple or blue, as if invested with some kind of inter-tribal conjugations.

113

He moved forward a few paces and, prospectively, or aggressively, a big pop-eyed yellow-black outrider, perhaps activated by an instinctive consciousness of unlimited support, came side-skittling towards him. Ryan kicked the creature back into the writhing mass and walked back to the car.

With the frogs he would have waited a while, but he had no similar sympathy for these nightmare scavengers. And they were still swarming out of the mangrove roots in such undiminished numbers that it might have taken another hour yet.

Sometimes, in Africa, he had watched armies of *Siafu* ants and, even playing a blowtorch on the head of their columns, failed to deviate them. But somehow these crabs were even more repugnant than the big ants. And God help the man or animal prostrated or incapacitated in the path of their myriads of tearing pincers, he thought.

He nodded to the mulatto and the car moved crunchingly forward leaving a bloody mashed and squirming double trail that was redder than the road, the ones picked up in the mud of the wheels producing an irregular thudding of hard shells against the undersides of the wings.

If he had been on more affable terms with the Hondurans he would have asked if the crabs were edible, as they almost certainly were, and, in such case, why the people didn't harvest these periodic effluxes?

For instance, as British country folk seasonally harvested the elvers coming up the rivers, by the boatload, with nets and buckets.

He knew something about the crabs from mugging-up on general fauna aspects of the country, and clearly what they had run into was one of the 'egg-washing' migrations to the sea which, about this time of year, were probably going on en masse in most of the coastal areas.

Practically every coastline in the world is the habitat of various types of crabs, but in some tropical lands the distinction was that they were not just marine creatures. They got all over.

In fact some genera were primarily land animals, even to be

found at high altitudes, though even these Sierra types made these incredible pilgrimages of species-perpetuation to the original source of their evolution, the sea.

A while after the crabs they passed a log cabin on a spit of higher ground in midst of a quarter acre hacked from the lush yellow-green wilderness. There were three turkey-vultures on the roof. Two were gimlet-eyed adults intent on anything that went, but the third was a sleepy adolescent who had chanced on a dying iguana and was full of the lizard's meat. Other single-room cabins now began to occur at intervals, the wide gaps between them gradually lessening as they came nearer to the perimeter of the town.

He was familiar with the squalor belts of East African towns, Nairobi, Mombassa and the rest; which in fact clung to the outskirts of nearly all White-founded African places. They were defilements of the African scène ... for which White and Black shared equal responsibility ... more hideous than any Western slums, if no more so than many Islamic, Hindu and Oriental variations. But in terms of sheer pathos, the pathos of hopelessly foredoomed human endeavour, the shanty town they were now passing through was more pathetic than anything he had ever seen before. Came nearer to an ordered hell.

The rows of sun-bleached bare wood huts were less like oversize packing cases than crates. The untrimmed boards left gaps between the layers that in places let in, or exuded, according to the hour, thin slats of sunlight or lamplight. No, that's too loose, he thought! Big kipper-boxes on stilts came nearer to it because, when you considered the teeming picanninies, they would obviously *have* to have some kipper-box system for sleeping; some kind of dormitory order.

God knew how the cratewood ghetto survived, because the obvious hazard that hit you was fire. Just one careless cigarette-end, one persistent spark from a garbage bonfire, one upturned fish-oil lamp and the whole flimsy tinder-dry warren would go like a forest fire. Go faster than a forest fire, because all the houses were shored-up on piles, some leaning awry. Poised for it.

115

Overall hung the sagging smell cloud. A heavy conglomerate odour of open sewers, stewing iguana, decomposing garbage, soured water butts, rotting fish-heads, merged and intensified by the heat and the still, limp air. Maybe it had no more God-awful stench than the unplumbed kasbahs and suks of 'modernised' Egypt and Tunisia he thought. It was hard to fully recollect. But it was sufficient.

As the shanty belt gave out the stink grew less, devolving to an aroma, and then a taint, and then finally to a constrastingly pleasant alfresco atmosphere of quenelle and slowly cooling macadam and masonry.

They were crossing the bridge and he was leaning out, engrossed with the variety of small and medium craft, when she touched his arm.

'If I could stop off anywhere here then, please?' she asked.

'Of course.' He snapped his fingers and called out to the mulatto to pull in. 'Are you sure this is far enough, suit you all right?' He smiled. 'Nobody's in any hurry, remember.'

She nodded, smiling back. 'Right here will be fine, thank you.'

He took her case and got out of the car. 'Well, adios for now then, Jane, and glad to be of service. I hope I'll see you around the town, sometime.'

She smiled and nodded again, then, just as she was about to go, she yielded to the temptation and turned. 'Why do you call me Jane?'

Just for a second he was taken aback, then he grinned. 'Don't you get the pictures, the movies, here, Jane?'

'Yes.' She frowned.

'And you've never seen Jane Russell?'

'Oh!' He watched the understanding grow, then the hesitatory smile and the conjecturing whether he was really paying a big compliment, or laughing at her.

He put some convincing emphasis into it, 'You've got everything she's got, Jane.' He winked. 'Maybe more, look out for yourself, now.'

When the car had made around three sides of the Plaza and

116

he saw the *Palace* just off the square he almost winced. Some Palace!

He himself hadn't given the hotel aspects much prominence in the somewhat pragmatic correspondence with Ramirez. But he had taken it for granted that there would be a civilised pitch at the beginning and end of his stay.

The mulatto drew in and hooted a couple of times before he got out and went in through the glass door of the place.

In a minute or two he returned with two boys. They both looked about fourteen, and except that one was taller than the other they could have been twins, brothers anyway. Slim, softly-spoken, good-looking lads with café-au-lait complexions and black crinkly hair, in washed-out cotton jeans and alpargatas handed down from someone who had bigger feet. The taller one was fully compos, but the other lad still had a face full of sleep because he had just been roused out of an extended siesta. The extended siesta was because this week it was his shift to sit it out till dawn, against the thin possibility of some late bum with the price of a rum, or some logger in town for a ball who wanted a bonito steak, or who was booked-in and had got to be ass-heaved and keelhauled up the stairs. Part of the service, though few remembered or appreciated the worth of it next day.

The driver carried in two of the guncases and the boys got the rest.

'Is this with me or Mister Ramirez?' Ryan said.

'With you, Sah?'

'All right, how much?'

The mulatto figured. He was torn between wanting to make a buck, and what his employer had said about going real easy on account of Señor Ramirez. He conquered his instinct. 'Five dollars, Sah.'

'Dollars Honduras?'

'Yessah.'

It was a cheap ride. 'Okay,' Ryan said. 'Ten dollars, American.'

He peeled off the bill and the mulatto beamed his appreciation because the difference was around fifty per cent per buck.

117

And, if this patron didn't chisel him out of it, it was the kind of transaction that rarely came his way.

The boys started up the stairs off the hall carrying his stuff, but when they started across the landing to the second floor he jibbed. 'Hey, wait a minute, muchachos!'

There wasn't much sign of other guests and there didn't seem much point in extra stair-climbing just for the exercise. He made a gesture covering the adjacent doors. 'How about one of these ... easier?'

The taller boy shook his head uncertainly, as if not fully comprehending. 'No, pliz, Señor ... Mister. You follow me, pliz.'

Ryan said it again, this time in Spanish, explaining that the idea was more convenience.

'Si, si, Señor,' the other lad said. 'But above,' he pointed upward, 'for the *importantes*, for the friends of Señor Ramirez ... *with the air conditioning.*' There was pride in both his voice and expression at the announcement.

On the second landing a door opened on to an outside balcony which ran the length of the place, and hence the three apartments off it were each twice the size of the six first-floor rooms below.

Looking out from the balcony towards the south beaches, maybe five or six hundred yards distant, there was a depressing vista of shanty tops. But immediately below there was a courtyard, part hidden by the luxuriant blooms of a cultivated *cherimoya* tree. The flowery foliage also half-concealed a metal stair which ran down the wall like a fire escape.

A humming bird hung, whirring, over a sprig of the blossom, and as he followed the boys along the balcony a small yellow iguanid lizard, mottled brown gular fins apprehensively raised like the dorsal of a shark, ran up the trunk into the deeper concealment of the more closely knit higher branches.

The taller muchacho unlocked the centre door, and as soon as he had put down his share of the baggage he went across to the air-conditioning unit in the corner and switched it on. As soon as it started to whirr he turned with a smile of renewed pride and vindication.

118

'Really works, eh?' Ryan grinned. He threw his mac and jacket on to the bed. 'Got any Bacardi or Daiquiri in the place, hombrés ... Señors?'

'Si, Señor,' the taller one said.

'*And* cold beer?'

The smaller one smiled his added satisfaction. 'Si!'

'Even ice?'

'Of course, Señor.' Again with a suggestion of pride if not deprecation.

'*Well*,' Ryan said, 'that's not bad. That's not bad at all, muchachos.' He ferreted around in his pocket and found two half dollars. 'Bring up a bottle of Daiquiri, and a couple of cold beers and a carafe of ice water, Señors. But pronto, muchachos ... *al instante*, eh, hombrés?'

Both boys started for the door but Ryan called out. '... Momento! How are you called, Señors?'

For an instant they looked at each other. 'I am Ricardo ... Reechard ...' the taller one said.

'And your chum here, El Soñoliento?' Ryan smiled, 'the sleepyhead?'

Both boys grinned, the smaller one sheepishly. 'Also Ricardo, Señor.'

Ryan crinkled his brows. 'Aren't you two brothers, then?'

'Si, Señor,' the taller one said. 'But our mothers ...'

The other boy interrupted him. He was the serious, the introvert one, and it was the first time he had spoken. 'We have the same father; this is our father's hotel.' There was no disapproval of his half-brother in it, but there seemed to be a note of resignation as if it was an outworn joke.

'Well, in that case let's make it easier for all of us,' Ryan said lightly. 'From now on,' pointing to the more sedate boy, 'you're Wee Dick, and you're Big Dick.'

This time the smaller lad chuckled, too, and after they had closed the door he heard them laughing on the balcony. '*Beeg Dick y Wee Dick!*'

After the near-derelict impressions of the place gained from the street, the interior, and the room itself was a tolerably pleasant surprise. The linoleum was clean and the wardrobe

119

closet and dressing table also smelled of polish. The bed looked pretty new, as did the tiny bathroom, which had a handbasin and shower.

Obviously the 'cold' water wasn't going to be really cool till about midnight, but while he was taking a luke-warm shower he heard one of the boys knock and come in with the drinks.

He had a couple of drinks in the nude and then lay down on the bed with a cigarette. It was cloyingly, oppressively hot. Even with the small conditioning unit on full it felt like about ninety. The dry African heat of plains and desert had never bothered him. But this heavy humid stuff, heavier, it seemed to him, than some of the West African fever-trap areas he had hunted, was going to take some getting used to. He dozed off, wondering whether it would be less ennervating in the jungle itself, as it was in the gorilla country of N'gi.

When he came out of his nap it was turned nine o'clock and a bit cooler. Downstairs in the small hall Big Dick had taken over the chair of vigil by the door, and now there was a woman back of the little reception counter in the corner. She could have been pure Mexican or Spanish, and save that when she smiled widely she showed part of her upper gum, she had Latin good looks. Maybe in her late twenties and hence, by racial tendency, very mature, though not really portly yet.

He returned her smile and went through into the bar. It was empty except for the man behind the counter and a big brown-skinned genial looking woman in a bandana headdress who was desultorily polishing a glass.

The proprietor moved along the counter enquiringly. He was a biggish, cheerful looking man, and even though his features were beginning to blur now with middle-aged self-indulgence there was no doubt that he was the father of the two boys, or that the buxom woman with the head-scarf was the mother of one of them.

'Mister Ryan, 'ennit?' Surprisingly, he spoke exactly like a working man of the English Black Country. 'Welcome toe the *Palace*. Everything all right . . . anything yo want?' He held out his hand.

'Well, I'm beginning to feel a bit peckish,' Ryan said,

120

'What's on the bill?'

'Well, nah,' the Patron said. He jerked his head to his wife and she moved around to them, smiling. 'Come here, luv, and tek Mr Ryan's order.' He wrinkled his nose. 'We can do yo fried chicken, or roast iguana ... I'm having that meself ... or mutting chops, or fish a'course.' He specified one or two local varieties.

'Too hot for meat,' Ryan said, 'hot meat, anyway. I'll take the *bonito*, cold and soused. Say a couple of middle-cut steaks and a bit of salad or such?'

'Every time,' Jorge said. 'Norra bad pick either, yo could doe a lot werse.' He spoke to the plump smiling woman in Spanish. 'Two cuts of bonito, *saturamento*. Good cuts. For a big hombré, like me,' grinning, 'with two eggs, hard, and pimentoes, and a bottle of *manzila* ... the *manzila* will be a present!'

'A present ... *por nada*?' Her eyebrows lifted questioningly. 'Now we are *millionarios* all at once?'

He shot her a glance of sufferance. 'We have Inglés, *de encima Inglés*, all the time? Por favor!' He made it sound patiently sarcastic but he ended on a note of authority. '*A present* ... Querida.'

'Qué va,' she said, also with sarcasm. 'Of what importance? The rich Inglés cannot afford the wine, so ...' She shrugged, but it was all quite good-humoured, as if she was well inured to his irrational grandiose gestures.

Ryan grinned his understanding. He summoned up his best Madrileno accent. 'This of the *manzila*, Señora. El Proprietario is very kind, but I agree with you ... it is too much. Please charge it.' He watched her face change. 'And perhaps you will join me in a glass when you serve it?'

She put a hand to her mouth and exchanged a look of embarrassment with her husband. 'Gracias, Señor.' She turned and went towards the far door leading to the kitchen, then looked back at Jorge and laughed. '*Tonto!*'

'*Tonto* yourself,' he called back. 'You're the one put yer foot in it as usual. Wot'll it be, Guvnor?'

'Just a beer for now,' Ryan said. 'And where did you get the

121

Brummagem accent then?'

'Ay, that's not bad,' Jorge said appreciatively. 'Yo have the Spanish, and yo got me spotted too?' He poured half the beer and pushed across the misted bottle. 'Well, that's where I got it ... Bermingham! Mekkin' tanks all through the war. Med some money I did. Then I come 'um and bowt the pub.'

'But this is your country?' Ryan asked. 'You're local?'

'Ow, yes. Fower generations ... but I'm British, mind.'

Ryan smiled. Commercially Jorge was clearly an opsimath who had made it fairly late on, but he *had* made it, and would undoubtedly be counted a plutocrat by the country's general standards. And his basic political outlook seemed to closely correspond with Ida's. 'Well, in that case we better have another,' Ryan said.

The five small tables in the little dining-room across the hall were dimly lit, either because the two ceiling lights were low-powered, or because the current was lacking. Somebody had broken one of the shades and from the fluff on the bulb the accident must have occurred some time ago, though otherwise the room looked very clean.

The broad languidly turning blades of the big old fan suspended between the lights cast intermittent shadows on to a battered mahogany sideboard that was covered with a miscellany of sauce bottles, cigarette cartons and upturned glasses.

Facing the door, like a defiant declaration of political integrity, there was a large framed print of *The Monarch of the Glen*. It seemed absurdly out of context, and yet somehow as unequivocably declarative as if it had been the Union Jack itself. Yellowed somewhat, with time, yet still forcefully conveying pride, nobility, rugged grandeur.

There was no one else in the room and as he sat down at a corner table Big Dick came in with a bottle. He nodded and the boy drew the cork and poured out half a glass. In the light the wine looked pale yellow. It was pretty good, chilled and dry, not unlike chablis. He took a sip then raised his thumb and winked. '*Buena!*' The boy smiled his satisfaction and set down the bottle.

122

In a few minutes he was back with a tray. The *bonito* was excellently tasty, and the salad was crisp from the ice-box. Even so, although the food was cold, by the time he had finished he was making extra sweat. Oddly, the coffee was not so good. He pushed the cup away and was pouring more wine when Jorge came in. Now he walked with a limp, which hadn't been apparent in the bar, and Ryan suddenly realised that he had some kind of artificial leg.

'Message for yo, Mr Ryan, one of Juan's, Mr Ramirez's boys, just brought it.' He held out an envelope.

'Thanks,' Ryan said. 'Sit down and have some of the house speciality. Good stuff.'

'Don't mind if I doe,' the stout man said. He turned a chair so that he could stretch his stiff leg out beside the table.

There had only been three exchanges of letters with Ramirez, and it had been clear that the hunter was not much for correspondence, nor given to supplying overmuch detail. His initial reply had been typewritten; in the stilted phraseology of a Second-former who was having a hard time with a tough subject. It had contained some inventive phonetical spelling, and just sufficient information to take the business further.

At the time of receiving it Ryan had visualised the hunter performing the irritating chore, and then, perhaps, getting it typed out by a friend at the Post Office or the Police Station. One salient let's-get-this-quite-straight point made with simple clarity in the letter had given him a particular smile.

'*I see that you have hunted African cats,*' it had run, '*so you will no that it is no good to run when the cat comes and the reason I tell you this first is because I had one man (he was a good shot and had also hunted African cats BUT NOT AT NITE) and when the cat came he took off and we had a bad axxerdent.*'

But right now he was in no mood to be amused at any of Ramirez's vagaries for the hunter's failure to meet the plane still rankled. The note was written in longhand, in the bold legible style of a pupil raised to the old copybooks formula. '*Dear Mr Ryan, I sent a car to pick you up the airport and I*

123

hope they got you to the Palace OK. I no it looks like a hell of a dump but you will find the room and the chow are not bad. Tell Jorge anything spechal you want and he will fix it sure. The reason I coud not come in I run into some trouble with my boat which is part of my bisiness and has to pick up the langostas just the same when I am up country. Also I will need it for you anyway after the tigres because you said you also want to fish marlin. Right now the boat is nearly fixed and I will meet you up at the Palace eight tomorro nite.' There was also an afterthought footnote which said: *'You have not lost out any time anyway because were we will go it has been blowing real hard and sometimes these huracáns take two-three weeks to let up.'*

Well, that was some explanation, he supposed, though it was still pretty casual considering he, Ryan, was doing the paying. He put the envelope in his pocket. 'Some casual character Mr Ramirez, eh? Pretty cool, eh? He doesn't show up to meet me, and now all he's worrying about is bloody lobsters.'

The chubby man chuckled. 'Yes, the boy told me.'

'You know him well?' Ryan asked. 'For long?'

'Since before the war, since before he began to really make the dough.'

'Know's the score, eh?'

'Don't give it a thought,' the shorter man said. 'Yo got the best there is.' He brought out a serrated metal case from his breast pocket and held it out, raising his eyebrows in recommendation. 'Mild. Yo can inhale 'em.' After Ryan had taken a cheroot he continued. 'Fishing, toe, you can't go wrong with him.' He glanced down at his leg. 'I'd a been fishing with him this would never have happened.'

'How did it happen?' Ryan asked.

'Well, I used toe fish with Juan, every once in a while,' Jorge said, 'fun fishing for the big stuff yo understand. Then this one time, 'bout five years ago, he couldn't make it,' Jorge said, 'and I was narked so I went anyway.' He shrugged. 'With a bum, a *ladino*, a dumb bum. After a while I hooked a good 'un, a *tiburón*. Yo know ... a blue 'un. Nothing special mind

124

... had plenty better blues with Juan ... one about three hunderd pound but a bastard!' He blew a derogatory puff of aromatic blue which dawdled in the heavy air. 'Well, yo know how it is. With a good 'un it has toe be a two-man heave with the gaffs and the bum loused it up, fell on his back as the fish come aboard. I got the fish right on top of me, acrost my legs ... and he bit clean through my shin.'

'Nasty!' Ryan said. He shook his head. 'That was really the hard cheese.'

'Yo said it,' Jorge agreed. 'I ain't been to Cherch since, I don't mind tellin' yer, I don't reckon I desairved that.' He was silent for a moment then he grinned. 'I tell 'em I'll gu to Mass again when I've growed a new leg and not befower.'

Ryan took a draw and inhaled it. Right enough they were pleasantly mild. 'I can imagine how you feel. Still there's another way of looking at it. You might not have made it at all, you could have lost too much blood.'

'Ar, I suppose.' He rubbed the back of his neck and grinned again. 'Meks a good excuse, though. They don't get nowt out of me no more.'

For a short while after Jorge had stiff-legged out, Ryan sat on, finishing the wine. It was on his mind to take a stroll as far as Main Street and the Plaza, but he felt relaxed, lazy from the food, and there were a couple of duty chores he could take care of. He went back up through the hall and halted on the balcony to finish Jorge's cigar.

There was a good moon risen now, but just as he got leaning comfortably it was overcast by cloud. When it emerged again and his eyes became fully accustomed he could dimly make out the reflective glint of the sea beyond the end of the town.

The soughing of the surf was just audible, punctuated by the chirruping chorus of the crickets from the intervening shanty area, and down below, in the courtyard, he could hear the faint enigmatical scurryings of the rats and the fainter, wispier sound of roaches. The foliage of the cherimoya tree drooped flaccidly, its silence occasionally disturbed by the small rustlings of a tree lizard at the buds.

125

He flicked the cigar butt in the direction of the raider, raising a few sparks and a tiny scurrying, then went inside and stripped off. From one of his bags he got a pad and two envelopes, one for Mark and one for Renny. The letter to Renny involved no complications and only took about ten minutes, but Mark's took a lot longer because it had to be a professional job. Sufficiently professionally descriptive of things and places to make up a little, he hoped, for the big divide between them, and always implying that this was only a temporary circumstance.

When he had done he lay down on the bed in his pyjama pants and took up the Ruark book. But he had come to a part now where the gay blade was explaining *ad nauseam* how he addressed Miss Olivia de Havilland as 'Livvy'; along with the breath-taking pet names and known-only-to-intimates inanities of sundry politicians and various theatrical exotica.

The name-dropping stuff scarcely rose above the standard of *Vital Confessions* and was so jarringly arch that it almost audibly tittered. He dropped the book and transferred his thoughts to the more practical considerations of fishing *tiburón*, and 'nite' hunting.

5. AGARRADA

It was very early when he woke and when he went across by the mirror he got a shock that jerked him out of the semicomatose in a hurry. His upper arms and back were a solid pincushion mass of tiny red bites.

The pricks were smaller than ordinary mosquito bites, and the extraordinary thing was that he hadn't felt a thing during the night. Nor, for that matter, beyond a minor itchiness, did he yet feel anything akin to what the effects would have been with common mosquitoes.

Not that that necessarily meant anything. This might be some kind of local pest which could have a more delayed-action outcome for all he knew. Certainly, by mosquito standards, he had collected twice the number of bites capable of setting up a heavy fever.

He cursed volubly out loud. So much for their bloody skeeter grilles. Why were these tropical peoples always, basically, so bloody inefficient? Then he noticed the open bathroom door. The skylight of course! He had slept in his pyjama pants, on top of the bed, and he must have turned on to his stomach when he was dropping off.

Still cursing he got the drawstring medicine bag from his case and fished among the tins, tubes and repellents for the quinine tablets and the alcohol. Bolting the stable of course, but there wasn't anything else to do except maybe get stuck into a bottle of the more refined stuff if he got the well-known pulse and muscular messages, as he had done more than once in successful disregard of skilled opinion.

With the departure of the crickets and the rest of the audible noctivagants it was still completely quiet outside save only for the sporadic chidings of a distant rooster. But as he was taking the quinine he caught the soft sloppety sound of a footfall and went out on to the balcony.

Down below the woman who had been at the desk in the hall was in the act of unlocking the street door of the courtyard. He whistled and waved her to come nearer.

He was still only wearing pants and slippers and when he saw the nonplussed look on her face he realised she might think he had suddenly developed romantic ideas, was making a play.

Despite the preoccupation of the bites he grinned. Even by laissez-aller tropical standards the idea of crumpet at this unshaven hour of the morning was a bit far out.

'Nada ... negado, Señora!' He put his hand behind his back and turned to demonstrate, holding up the square bottle of alcohol. '*Catástrofe!* Come up here and help me out.'

For a moment she continued to hesitate, still a shade disconcerted and not yet wholly clear, but then she crossed the flags under the tree to the stair.

She had a floral-patterned yellow bandeau on her head this

127

morning and it suited her well, bringing out the well-fed almost boyish softness of her face. Except for the sultry quality of her eyes her manner was quite circumspect. But the tired elastic of her old cotton blouse had worked down over one of her bare shoulders, revealing the upper swell of a breast that was just perceptibly lighter coloured than the pale fawn of her arms and shoulders.

She seemed unconscious or unconcerned with the display of bosom she was offering, but her languid earthy appeal lost nothing by it.

'I've run into a little trouble,' Ryan said. 'Got really bitten over in the night. Could you give me a rub around?'

'Rub around?'

He changed it into Spanish. '*Masage*, with the *esperitu*.' He held out the bottle and turned, showing her his back close up.

'Ah!' She put a hand to her mouth, then giggled. '*Los pequeños*, the tiny ones!'

'They're not bad?'

She shook her head, smiling. 'No, Señor. Not like the *ofensivos*, the swamp ones. From them ... *enfermedad*, the illness.'

'Well, just the same, if you'll oblige,' he said. He took her wrist and led her into the room, then handed her the bottle and lay down on the bed. The alcohol was pleasantly cool on his back.

'You are the bookkeeper of the hotel?' he asked after a minute or two.

'That and other things.'

Her fingers had none of the roughness of a domestic worker. I'll bet, he thought. And very nice for Uncle Jorge, too. He half-turned his head. 'Of the boys? Which one is yours ... *El Pequeño*?' For an instant he thought he sensed withdrawal. 'Both are handsome,' he added, tempering it.

She smiled, then, at the implication. 'Si ... him!'

'And how do they call you?'

'Paquita.'

'*Muchas gracias*, Señora Paquita then,' he said, knowing

128

well that it was not Señora.

'Senorita,' she said, easily enough and without brazenness, but equally without implication of apology.

They've got it organised all right, Ryan thought. Practical acceptance. I'll bet the priests have themselves a broadminded time too. 'Well thanks again, Paquita,' he said, bypassing the correction, 'I hope I can do the same for you sometime.' He turned on to his back and grinned. 'It would give me very muchas pleasure.'

She didn't seem all that anxious to go, and she put a hand on her hip, tilting her head and regarding him quizzically. 'You want me to be eaten by the *pequeños* also?'

'Just a little . . . just enough.'

She laughed and started towards the door.

'About some breakfast?' Ryan said.

She turned and leaned against the jamb. The fringe of her blouse barely covered the tantalising point of her breast now and he had a job not to be too precipitate. 'Some fruit and eggs?' She wrinkled her nose. ' 'Amburger? *Cuarto hora*, feef-teen minutes.'

He glanced at his watch. Incredibly it still wasn't nearly six yet. 'Fruit and eggs will be fine,' he said. 'But make it later, say eight o'clock?'

'Si, eight o'clock.'

He heard the low whistle just as he was getting another cigarette and went out on to the balcony again. Paquita called up softly from the foot of the stair. 'Sometimes . . . usually . . . I have much trouble with the *claraboya*, the skylight in my room. It takes much strength. . . .'

Ryan smiled. 'No trouble at all. A pleasure. I'll see to it tonight.'

Already the mounting yellow scourge had begun the process of burning through the ice-cream blanket of the cumulus, the big massed cloud banks out over the horizon that were awaiting the arrival of the Trade winds. Soon you would be able to fry an egg on the flagstones of the Plaza.

But for the moment, on the balcony, it was, and would be for another hour, the pleasantest time of the day. The air still

129

hung heavily, somnolently, but occasionally it bore torpid wafts of breeze from the sea which, though barely strong enough to disturb the upper leaves of the *cherimoya*, were like gentle invigorant douches.

Before he went back inside he watched a skein of black geese, daguerrotyped against the sky, passing right overhead before planing down towards a distant group of Cays. The birds reminded him of similar echelons coming in at intervals from frosted fields, in the dawn light, to settle on the ice-free patches of the Loch, and then to rise again, wheeling in panic as the guns roared.

Outside in the street he turned left on an impulse, away from the Plaza towards the ghetto area he had seen from the balcony. The street itself appeared to head straight for the coast, petering out a couple of hundred yards along, but just a stone's throw from the hotel a narrow dirt road came in at right angles. He turned up it and was right away into the shanties.

A white-haired mestizo sat hunched on the rickety steps of one of the first huts, gutting fish in a pail.

Ryan lit a cigarette and began to stroll. There was nothing much in his clothes to denote the alien. The bush shirt and trousers he wore, both khaki, had seen plenty of service and even his Safari cap was very similar to the cotton baseball caps which a number of the men were beginning to prefer to straws and sombreros. But the veteran had him figured all right. Probably the as yet much lighter tan of his face and forearms, he thought, plus his foreign walk; upright and long-striding.

He nodded as he passed. But the old man merely stared back impassively, suspiciously. Maybe they really paid rents for these rat-traps, had rent collectors, he thought, or maybe he was just a naturally ornery old bugger with a touch of the gripes.

Conversely, farther along, a massive young coal-black Mammy, tattered green *shantung* exposing her vast polished ebony thighs as she bent over a fishbox pram, turned her head

130

to flash a huge smile that implied goodwill and even, he felt, content.

Well it beats hell, he thought, how these womenkind ... the jet blacks down to the palest Asian yellows .. all cursed with probably the worst living standards of any land where English was officially spoken, yet seemed to exude a general attitude of beneficence. In fact taking the women as an example, they had a kind of natural shyness that had a lot more charm to it than the moronic sophistication of bingo, pot and juvenile punks created by the 'permissive' Evangelists of 'The Flatulent Society'.

At a corner of the street he turned up left again along an even narrower bisection of the warren. In the time of the continuous rains, if the river burst its banks, he had been told, the ghettoes were transformed into areas like paddy fields of red mud, or again, after the periodic calamity of a tidal wave, into courts of white-crusted salt like saline-marshes. But right now the baked dusty ground around the piles of the shanties was pitted with the holes of minute crabs.

A lot of the huts had water storage butts, old ironbound casks, but the water was green, alive with minute aquaria. God knew how they used it and survived, even despite the staggering hazards which, over time, human guts could become inured to.

At the end of the alley he came out into Main Street and turned down east towards the Plaza. The sun was already beginning the climb from temperate to irksome now, but one or two of the *borrachóns*, the outright bums, were still slumped against the walls along the wide front portico of the Government building.

There were two chief reasons why the portico was a favoured pad; providing you had a sack to insulate yourself against the ultimate chill of the flags. Firstly, because the long stone canopy over the columns gave protection whenever there was a heavy dew. Then, also, it was raised a foot above the level of the Plaza and the street, and of no really rewarding interest to the rats. Any time now the few far-goners remaining would get rousted out of their twitching fantasies, because

131

despite the nocturnal tolerance of authority the unwritten law required their dispersal at sun-up.

Most of the defeated ones had long since shuffled off down to the market by the river, because early-bird foraging was the essence of the desperate daily business of survival. Get down there real early, while they were still busy unloading the ice wagons, toting the open fishboxes, you always had a chance in the bustle and confusion of kicking a spilled fish under a fold of the tarpaulin walls. Or even, sidling through the aisles of benches, of knocking off a *tataroga* egg, or a couple of the smaller *caracasha* ones!

Just a couple of *tataroga* turtle eggs would see you through till tomorrow's market in a pinch. But you needed four *caracashas*, because they were only about half the size of hen eggs. The scaly *dobar* fish were a pain in the ass, because they were so much big mouth and teeth, that, like lousy *piranha*, there wasn't enough flesh to take the ache out of your belly except with the ones too big to get under your shirt.

But if you could slip a freshwater *lukanani* perch into your pants, which you'd already tied around the bottoms, you were making out. (Half, raw, behind the market ... or cooked if your stomach could wait long enough for a fire on the waste lot back of the school ... and half before you shucked down for the night on the Town Hall patio, or under one of the derelict trucks back of the *Kwikservice Garage And Eats*.) And if you could palm a small *bonito* you were really set.

In the corner of the Plaza there was an *Excusados*. The convenience was shaded, and even decorously overhung by a screen of lopped tamarind trees. The cerise bean pods contrasted colourfully with the delicately feathery pale bluish foliage, and it would have been an unusually picturesque urinal save for one less decorous feature. There was a large white-cast Cupid over the door, and somebody had carefully painted the genitals of the fat cherub a bright crimson.

Ryan grinned to himself. You had to hand it to 'em. The international brotherhood of craphouse artists. Or maybe this one was intended as a calculated affront to Catholic modesties, because the religions were reckoned to be about equally di-

132

vided, with the Catholics much the more militantly puritanical.

He moved on down the street to the bridge. A gathering throng of people was beginning to pass both ways now. Pretty soon you would have to step off the narrow sidewalk to make way. Most of the folk seemed to be women. The mammys with a little money who, accordingly, got the pick of the market, and the still poorer ones concerned more with bulk value for outsize families than quality when the uppity customers had all been taken care of.

The river, green and sluggish here, as it neared the sea, lapped the landing quay which adjoined the market. Opposite, a quartet of vultures peered superciliously down from the roof of a warehouse at the more energetic scattering of gulls gliding and calling over the market and the water.

At the seaward end of the quay men were unloading crates of bottles and stencilled cases from a coastal steamer, and nearby a variety of lesser craft, from skiffs to fishing boats that resembled 'Fifie' Seine-Netters, were moored side by side.

One boat just below the bridge, a cabin cruiser about forty feet that looked as if it could move, stood out from the rest like a snipe among widgeon.

There was a girl in the stern, pushing a long-handled mop, who seemed to be out of context with her job, yet in keeping with the class of the boat despite her bare legs and feet. She was a local, in the near-white category, he guessed. But there was a look of caste about her that proclaimed upper crust. Maybe only local upper crust, but manifestly not of the ordinary rank and file.

For a second she looked up as if she had suddenly become aware of being under scrutiny. She was very good-looking in a kind of saintly claustral way, and her oval face reminded him of some celebrated painting ... it could have been one of the Renaissance Italians, or maybe one of Goya's Spanish noblewomen ... that, right then, he just couldn't recall the title of. They took a good long look at each other before she turned away and he moved on.

In the tarpaulin cavern of the market, overlaid by a compounded smell that, perhaps through some cancelling process

133

of the more repellent odours, was not outrightly offensive for all its richness, the first stall was run by a sad-faced man with deepset eager eyes who could have been a Malay.

There were glass jars of striped candy and various other highly coloured boiled sweets on his bench, but his specialities were frijole beans, and tortillas, cooked while you waited over cohune charcoal, and which, disregarding the audibly flatulent effects, you washed down with tepid *gaseosa*.

The vegetable stalls were well stacked with artichokes, red and green peppers, sweet potatoes and fruits. But only a few offered any variety of the more exotic stuff. Mountain Cabbage and the delectable 'Palm Celery' which is cut from a particular group of the endogen species.

The fish pedlars were of much more biological interest. As well as the commoner species, most had wickerwork tubs of live crustaceans ... crabs, lobsters, crayfish ... all indiscriminately piled on top of one another in slowly heaving mightmare heaps of eyes, claws and pincers. One or two of the fancier enterprisers, too, had *calamar*, small cuttlefish and octopi, and the eyes of the creatures looked equally alive.

But this unanimous predilection for liveness ... the proof of freshness in a climate where putrescence and lienteric consequences developed fast ... was even more evident on the counters of the fleshers.

Here, apart from some ready butchered meats of indeterminate freshness, most of the more substantial stuff was also offered in the live condition.

River tortoises and small turtles lay on their backs feebly treadmilling, trussed chickens hung upside down in bunches, while here and there gyved aguti 'rabbits' or wriggling armadilloes also waited on a buyer and the knife. The edible lizards, chiefly grey-green iguanas, laid belly up in attitudes of prayer, were secured, ironically, by the meshing of their claws through the skin pads of their own 'hands' and feet.

He watched one grinning stripped-to-the-waist purveyor behead, gut and skin an *aguti* in a few seconds, while at the next stall, another butcher uncurled and peremptorily carved up a squeaking balled-up armadillo for the pot. (An edentate

134

creature, which needs to be roasted in its jacket of bony armour as soon as possible after gutting, the armadillo was cleaned with despatch. But almost as soon as its wet excrescence of blood and viscera squelched on to the bench, the *cobarra* flies, savagely voracious kindred of the common house fly, were swarming about the Negro's hands and he swung the creature around to disperse the cloud before packaging the twitching carcase.)

The majority of women took their meat in the live, or semi-live condition. Unceremoniously ramming the fowl, reptile or marine creature into their coloured strawbags. But some, for the extra dime, had their selections cleaned and butchered on the spot, and the cobblestones were sheened and slippery with the fish and lizard heads, with the varicoloured slime of entrails and the dung pellets of the living food still unsold.

He ate a late solitary lunch of cold iguana, served up by Wee Dick, that was as good as jackal and nearer to turkey than chicken, and afterwards he went upstairs to join the national siesta.

For a time he read some more of Mr Ruark's libretto. He had come to a sequence which was quite enjoyable stuff, notwithstanding the grizzled profundities of the author's grizzled veteran, but eventually it induced a long drowse.

When he went downstairs again, some time after four o'clock, the place was still deserted and by the precepts of the sickeningly blithe spirit who had coined the idiot phrase, it was still too hot for other than 'mad dogs and Englishmen'.

But outside in the street some people were moving freely around, and he had one little business matter that needed taking care of before Ramirez came.

He found the letter in his case and then went along the street, making right across the Plaza. The building he was looking for was at the back of the Town Hall. One flight up the bare wooden stairs there was a landing with two or three doors. One was marked *Enquiries*, in English, and, alternatively, *Informacion*.

From the narrow counter inside you could see about one half

135

of a large general office. Two white-shirted clerks sat at littered tables, one sucking *gaseosa* through a straw. A third, younger than the others, was leaning against an open window. He came across to the barrier, his plimsolls hardly audible on the bare boards, as if the interruption was a relief.

'Mr McVee in?' Ryan said. He got a card from his wallet and held it out.

'Yes, Sah.' The boy nodded and crossed to a door in the corner.

Save that he was a Civil Engineer, and the head of some Government department primarily concerned with forestry and mining, Ryan was not wholly clear what McVee's position was because the official had replied to his letter on plain private stationery. But he was a contact, finally suggested by the Press Association, when he had first been organising the Safari, who had been very helpful and on points of information not supplied by Ramirez.

In just a minute or two the boy returned and raised the hinged lid of the counter for him to follow.

McVee was short and thick set. Mahogany faced with a clipped brown moustache and hair that was greying at the sides and thinning on top. His shirt sleeves were rolled up, showing the golden hairs on the smoked leather of his forearms, and his tie was pulled down below the vee of his open shirtcollar. He gave an impression of efficiency and energy that seemed out of context with the climate and tempo of the country, and Ryan could visualise that at times the clerks in the outer office would be required to perform on the double. He held out a brown hand that had quite a grip to it.

'I called to thank you for all your trouble and help,' Ryan said. 'In London they didn't hardly seem to know the latitude.'

McVee made a grimace. 'I ken that well enough ... I hope they discover it before Castro does.' He indicated a chair. 'You all fixed up noo, organised?' His voice had the pleasing undulation of a Fifer, a lilting intonation that is as beguiling as the soft brogue of the Southern Irish.

'Well, I think so,' Ryan said. 'I'm meeting Mr Ramirez tonight.'

'Och, well, your troubles are over ... or beginning,' the older man said. 'But I believe you're well used tae the hunting?'

Ryan shrugged. 'Well not this kind. I'm familiar with the basics, African style, and,' he grinned, 'the essential tight ass qualification known to all, you might say.'

McVee chuckled spontaneously. 'I went with him myself ... Ramirez ... once, soon after I first came out here. The deer part was all right, but, mon, I'm telling ye, I didn'a like the other stuff, the all-night business.'

'I prefer the broad light of day myself,' Ryan smiled, 'but your cats aren't very co-operative. Did you have any luck?'

McVee shook his head. 'Not me. After the first try I stuck tae the daylight. But Juan got a couple, one of 'em *was* in daylight, tae. Verra unusual.'

He shook his head reminiscently. 'Mon, I won't forget that one ... put the fear of God into me I don't mind telling ye! It happened just after dawn one morning. We were just bird hunting for the pot, and we came around this corner of the *camino* and here's this hulking cat, a real big bastard, eating an armadillo. Well, all we had was shotguns ye ken, with just No. 6 birdshot, but the crazy bugger lets go at him without hesitating.

'The Laird only knows why it didn't charge ... whether it was the suddenness or the noise ... but the brute just roared and dived into the bush.'

He paused for a moment and then went on again. ' "Come on, we'll get him now all right," he says. "He won't go far now, not with all that lead up his ass. He'll lay up and wait for us now."

' "By Christ he'll wait in vain for me," I told him, "are you out of your mind, mon? Follow that great bastard ... *in all that dense stuff ... with birdshot?*"

' "Hell, we got four barrels," he says, "that'll be *enough.* Give him yours in the face ... blind the bastard."

' "Not in a million years," I said. "Not wi' a Tommy gun! Forget it, forget the whole thing." But, ye know, he wouldn'a have it.'

137

' "Well, all right, get under that tree," he says. "I guarantee he won't come for *you*, if you stay still, even if he gets past me."

'Well, I didn't have much alternative if he was going in anyway did I? And he was right enough about the cat not going far. He couldn't have got ten yards when the bastard came. Man, ye never saw anything like it! At the last minute he dropped down and gied him both barrels in the belly, simultaneously, just as the bugger sprang. Blew the guts oot of him!'

Ryan wreathed his lips critically. 'Not good. Not good at all. That acrobatic stuff is for the birds.' Clearly Ramirez was a man of impetuosity. Any African Pro would have gone for the rifles and then returned to follow up.

McVee opened a drawer and then pushed across a box of Senior Service. When Ryan had taken one he took the stubby, curved pipe in the hardwood bowl and tapped out the ash. 'Yes, well, that's the way he daes things. Still, there's nae doot he gets the results all richt.' He blew out a puff. 'As a matter of interest, why did ye pick on *tigrés*, anyway . . . aren't they the nastiest proposition then?'

Ryan smiled. 'Well I suppose the short and silly answer is . . . that's why! They may not be the super heavyweights but they seem to be the nastiest, as you say, and I have a theory about it. I think it's because they don't have any opposition . . . except man . . . all their own way, all the time.'

'And this is what interests you?'

'Well, it's one thing,' Ryan said. 'There are tom leopards who will argue out a kill with a lion, *and* come out of it with the grub, especially if their girlfriend is around. And, I've seen a task force of daddy baboons dissuade a leopard off one of the troop, and a mother *kudu* rout a pack of hyenas. But the *tigrés* have got it made.' He pinched his nose and grinned. 'Besides, I get paid for it.'

'That's the best reason,' McVee said. 'Providing it's enough.'

Ryan returned the smile. 'Can't complain. I could get more for doing Bengal cats, because a lot of non-hunters have a

138

glamour thing about them, but personally I'd sooner go fishing.'

McVee smiled. 'Well, I agree about the fishing.' He made a circle with his second finger and thumb. 'Man, we've got the fishing here. Tarpon,' he waved a hand towards the window, 'marlin, barracuda, shark, they're all oot there.'

'Yes, I know,' Ryan said. 'I intend to get round to that end too, you bet.'

For a moment McVee was silent. He moved his pipe and regarded it reflectively, then he looked up. 'But ye know,' for a fleeting instant he was all Scot and there was a wry note in his voice, 'I'd still tak' the salmon.'

He was just the smallest bit carried away now and Ryan nodded sympathetically. 'I'm a Hielander myself,' the stubby man continued after a minute. 'But I sairved ma forestry time in Ayreshire ... I fished the Doon ... there wis a place nae sa far frae *The Cottage* ... hoachin' wi em.'

'It will be Rabbie's ye're takkin aboot, will it no?' Ryan said prosaically. 'Up watter or doon?' He made it his best imitation of the lilt and the tongue. 'Frae the Auld Brig, I mean.' He grinned.

McVee stared at him, a smile of incredulity slowly spreading on his face. 'Mon ye canna mean ... ye dinna mean....'

'Sure I do,' Ryan said grinning. 'It's got tae be the howkin' holes at the Weir, or, the ither way, it's got tae be the deep 'un around the second bend frae the mill?'

McVee slapped his knee. 'I go tae hell ... it *is* a small world, eh?'

'They're just as good as they ever were, according to what they tell me,' Ryan said. 'Wi' wurrms, spinners, flees or the cleekit,' he smiled.

The other man gave a shake of his head, smiling, widely, incredulously. Just for a moment, in his fancy, he was *hâme*. Reliving the thrill of a twenty pounder streaking away with the line, hearing the calls of coot and curlew.

'How *about* this man, Juan Ramirez?' Ryan said after the pause.

Reluctantly McVee came out of his little reverie. 'The best,

139

nae better ... but ye'll need to watch him, mind. I don't mean he isn'a a hundred percent. What I mean is he's a man who goes for results ye ken ... the one way or the other. He takes chances ootside of the beasts.'

'What kind of chances?'

'Well, we're not supposed to ken him, but we do and he knows I ken him. If he's not getting the results he wants ... *tigré*, ocelot or whatever ... he isn't over-concerned about going into other people's territory. Deep into it.'

'Risky?'

'Verra risky,' McVee said. 'Sometimes they shoot first.'

Ryan frowned. 'Pretty drastic stuff ... just for poaching?'

'You don't know them, especially the *politicos*,' McVee said. 'They've been trying tae tak' over this enclave for a century.'

'I wonder they don't get away with it,' Ryan said. 'The living standards you're stuck with. I was looking at some of the rummies and bums this morning ... incidentally where do they get the money for it.'

McVee shrugged. 'That's one of the universal mysteries, but I ken where Juan Ramirez gets his frae. All over!' He chuckled. 'A mon of many parts, is Juan, and he doesn'a like oor neighbours over the Border even a little bitty.'

'A rugged individualist?'

McVee grinned. 'Anything from orchids tae gun-running, and we still don't know whether he was for or against Castro ... though I gi' him the benefit of that doot. He's nae Quisling, like some.'

Ryan got to his feet and put out his hand. 'Well, thanks again, and for the filling-in. It would be nice if we could have a bite together when I get back ... bit of fishing too, maybe?'

'I'd enjoy that,' the Scotsman said. 'But just a minute noo.'

For a second he considered. The big, saturnine Englishman ... he reminded him somewhat of that one-time superlative slugger, Max Baer ... had given him a smile or two, and, after all a mon wha knowed the Bonny Doon ... 'Of course I dinna knaw exactly where he'll be takkin ye,' he said. 'But we've Resthouses in some parts; north and south. Might be useful tae

140

ye noo and then. Tell Juan to let me know where you're going and I'll radio the boss boys for ye.'

'Very good of you,' Ryan said. 'Radio phones eh?'

'That's nothing, we've even the horseless carriages,' McVee smiled.

'Here's tae us,' Ryan grinned. 'Wha's like us?'

He got back to the *Palace* some time after seven and took a couple of drinks and a shower. Promptly at eight Wee Dick came through to the bar to tell him that a car had arrived from Señor Ramirez. He was a bit annoyed that, again, the hunter had not come personally, and, irrationally when he saw that the driver was the same mulatto who had met the plane, the feeling increased.

The outer air was just as heavy and oppressive, but in the pale bluish light of the single floodlight hung from a palm the white front of the *Wallace* bar and the sound of the surf lent to an illusion of coolness.

There were three or four people in the hall but he knew instinctively which was the hunter even before he came forward.

'I would have met you if I could,' Ramirez said. 'But we had to get the boat fixed. You understand. Important.'

'So I gathered,' Ryan said flatly. He did not return the other man's smile and Ramirez made a further gesture.

'Just one of those things. Took longer than we'd thought, I only got through an hour ago,' he said with a brief gesture.

'Okay,' Ryan said shortly. 'Just so long as we take off tomorrow then.'

'Sure thing, we're all set now, be around first thing in the morning,' the swarthier man nodded. 'You impatient to get at the cats then?'

'Not specially the cats,' Ryan said. 'I just don't like hanging around. Besides, I've seen the market, and some of the two-legged cats ... that's all there is, isn't there?'

Ramirez grinned. 'I meant the four-legged kind.'

'I know you did,' Ryan answered. 'Of course some of the other sort might be all right, for afterwards ... but after-

141

wards!'

Ramirez grinned again. 'Check. I'll bear it in mind.'

It was plain enough that the Inglés was somewhat aggrieved, but he had the feeling that there was nothing much to it, that they would get along. And he had a pretty good hunch that there would be no complications of loose bowels with this one, which was always quite a consideration.

'I guess there's something else I should apologise for,' he said. 'I always buy dinner for the family, the wife and my daughter, before I leave town for a while . . . kind of habit . . . and I wasn't here yesterday.'

'Listen, *Cazador*,' Ryan said deliberately, 'I'm the client, remember! You don't show at the airport or the hotel, now you want to run off again. . . .'

'No, no, it's just I got them with me now, but they'll leave right after we've eaten,' Ramirez said.

There were only two other couples in the Restaurant, and the two women were seated at a table near the door on to the terrace. The elder one, in a black gown, had the air of a duena. Both wore lace mantillas over high combs, but the younger one was attractively dressed in white.

Crossing the floor Ryan realised that she was the girl he had seen from the bridge, and aside from the clothes she now wore, she looked even more appealing close to. So much so that he was suddenly glad he had put on a fresh shirt and slacks, and involuntarily he wiped the palm of his hand on his hip.

'You are already a hunter, like Juan . . . in Africa . . . I believe, Mr Ryan?' the elder woman said almost before he was seated.

She was a plumply attractive woman, who was probably a lot of fun in her own element, he thought. But right now she gave an impression of being on best behaviour, projecting an effect of naivete and self-consciousness.

'Well, yes, you might say I was in the business for a time,' he nodded.

'But more importantly, a writer?' the younger woman said with interest. She had a voice that was more modulated than her mother's, and her accent was more American than Creole.

142

'Well, that, too,' Ryan smiled. 'But with me the hunting has to come before the writing so I guess *it's* the more important.'

'Not for my money,' Ramirez grinned. He spread his hand. 'I give you some real good hunting ... you write about it ... so more clients.'

Ryan smiled again. 'Well, you just do that, Cazador, and I'll see about my end of it.'

The menu, laboriously handwritten, took some deciphering. But when you had it figured the choice offered was not bad at all. In addition to the no nonsense food you took-and-liked at the *Palace* and the *Kwickservice Eats* there were some higher falutin' dishes like Clam Chowder, Chili-con-carne, Shrimp Creole. And the fruits included pineapple, huckleberries, cranberries, melon and checkerberries.

'I saw your boat this morning,' Ryan said when they had given their orders. 'Your daughter was cleaning it up. Looked very elegant ... in fact they both did.' He glanced across at the girl and she returned his smile.

Ramirez watched the exchange before replying. 'Yes, pretty *rapido*. A hundred-and-fifty horse. Consuela likes it, the fishing also.'

'I hope she'll come along when we get round to it, then,' Ryan said.

Consuela smiled back, and again Ramirez looked at each of them reflectively. He cut a chunk from the steak on his plate and chewed, then he said suddenly. 'You married, Mr Ryan?'

It was quite casually said, inconsequential, and yet there was something in his expression which plainly conveyed—'lay-off, man, don't get any ideas.'

Ryan felt a faint prickling of resentment. 'I have a boy, but I'm not married,' he said brusquely. He felt a certain pique at the hunter's tacit rebuff and, he deliberately withheld any further amplification. In fact he was considering whether to deliberately solicit the girl's interest when a man came through the door from the bar and, raising a hand, called a greeting to the elder woman.

He came over to them at once. A heavy-set man, with large

143

identical gold rings on the third finger of each hand, whose bulk was beginning to show above and below the constriction of his belt.

'Ah, Francisco!' At once Clara Ramirez was all cordiality and fluster. 'What a surprise ... a business visit?'

The stout man smiled demonstratively. 'That it should happen more often, Clara. Such a pleasure to see you, *prima* ... and my lovely Consuela too!'

He was well enough barbered, but the blue of his beard still showed through his olive complexion and his flat moustache was too long, Ryan thought, extending further than the corners of his mouth. Also his head was almost round, close set on his shoulders, though the predominant characteristic about him was his eyes, which were yellowish, like a feline's, but flat, like some snakes'.

For a moment his glance ranged lingeringly over the girl's face and bust, then he reached down for her hand and pressed her reluctant fingers to his lips.

Other than a single expressionless glance Ramirez had offered no acknowledgement of the newcomer's presence at all, but now his wife shot him a look of embarrassment and entreaty. 'Juan, please. A chair for Francisco, *please*!' Still Ramirez continued to eat, ignoring her request as if he had not heard it.

For a second or two longer she waited, impotently, the colour rising in her cheeks, but he merely continued to chew and she looked away seeking to carry it off.

'Señor, er, Mister Ryan...' she made a gesture of introduction. 'Señor Cruz, mi primo, a kinsman! Señor Cruz is a *Jefe* and an *Ayuntamiento* of my country.'

Ramirez smiled and gave a short laugh. The rebuke for himself in her voice was nothing, but her ludicrous pride of relationship was an obscenity beyond stomaching.

'*This* is your country, my paloma, and for ever be grateful for it,' he said mordantly, still without taking his eyes from the drumstick he held.

'Ah, always the jocoso, the droll one, eh, Juan,' the fleshy man said with a pretence of geniality. He extended a pudgy

144

hand. 'I am pleased to meet you, Señor Ryan, but ... I am interrupting your meal ... I will wait for Juan on the terrace, Clara ...'

'Do not bother,' Ramirez said shortly. 'As you seem to have overlooked, I am occupied.'

'I am leaving tomorrow and my business is with you,' the *Ayuntamiento* said heavily. 'I am sure the Señor and the ladies will excuse you for a few minutes.'

Ramirez pushed away his plate. 'If the business concerns the *hijo*, Gallegos, and the other *ladinos*, it is already finished,' he said curtly. 'It never began.'

The stocky man got a cigar case from his breast pocket and then a gold lighter. 'Per'aps, per'aps not, Juan. But there is also a personal matter ... you might say a family matter. Of much mutual importance I think.' He smiled at each of the women in turn as if he had their understanding.

'What family can that be?' Ramirez said scathingly. 'Nothing of this family will ever concern you ... *Jeficito*.' He used the diminutive in the secondary, insulting sense of meaning a two-bit politician, a small-time piker.

The other man's face had turned darker now and a vein became apparent in his short neck. He seemed on the point of an explosive reply, but he swallowed it. 'All the same I will wait, Juan,' he said gutturally. Nodding to the two women he made for the door on to the terrace, jerking his head peremptorily to Paco for the boy to follow.

When the sloe-eyed mestizo girl had brought the fruit and nuts Ramirez got out his cigarettes. The annoyance still showed in his face but when he was lit he blew the first inhalation to one side in a stream, and grinned across. 'I apologise for the *hijo*, compradre? Seems like I'm apologising to you all the time. Now I got to do it again for this *teco*.' He shot a resipiscent glance at his wife, 'But don't worry, *he* ain't going to hold us up.'

'That's all right,' Ryan said lightly. 'Happens all over. Just a bit of family disagreement, I gather ... an *agarrada*?'

Ramirez chuckled outrightly. 'Hey, that's pretty good. Come to think of it they told me you had the *idioma*. How about that, Mama? I have the *agarrada* with Cruz all right, don't I?'

'Juan.' There was reproof in her expression, but she changed it to a pleading look. 'Don't provoke Francisco no more. He is of much influence and importance and ... *cómo siempre* ... he only wishes to make the business with you. He *said* that.'

Ramirez regarded her with a look of exasperation. 'You know what I think of his kind of business,' he snorted. 'Whereas with Mr Ryan here I have real business. The business of *tigrés*. And whereas Cruz is a punk, as are his friends ... *hijos de puta*, all of them.'

'But at the least speak with him,' she persisted. 'You don't *have* to make no business with him. You can ...' she waved a hand vaguely, 'give the excuses. ...'

He shrugged his disgust at her obtuseness, then something occurred to him and he grinned. 'You know, Mama, maybe you are right at that.' He got to his feet. 'Order me coffee also, and more wine, too, because I shall be right back.' He patted her head as if humouring a child, and winked at Ryan. 'Five minutes for Cruz then, or maybe less I think ... to make the *permanent* excuses this time!'

She started to speak, but he was already moving towards the terrace door and Consuela put a hand on her arm. '*Nada, pues nada*, Mamma, let it be,' she said softly. 'He does not mean what you think.'

Ryan signalled to the mestizo girl to bring another bottle of the *manzila*.

From where he sat facing the two women he could see past them on to the lighted terrace. Ramirez was leaning on the rail, and Cruz was at his side, speaking emphatically and occasionally gesturing. He was not as tall as the hunter, by a couple of inches, but he had the bulky aggression of a boar. Ramirez looked around and for a second or two he obviously spoke with vehemence, then he turned his head and spat as if in emphasis.

The tableau of the two men was like a film without a sound track but Ryan could sense the rising acrimony between them.

146

The waitress came with the new bottle and he went through the motions of sampling it and refilling their glasses.

The next time he looked he saw Ramirez turn from the rail, and Cruz make a gesture of anger. Then, suddenly, the hunter put his hand on the other man's chest shoving him violently away, and repeating it. The shorter man staggered back, then he lunged forward and struck Ramirez in the mouth, moving with surprising speed. The taller man ignored the blow then, for a few seconds, he waded into the *Ayuntamiento* like a dynamo, both arms going like pistons, really dealing out the punishment.

The bulky man gave ground, then his head jerked back and he disappeared from view, leaving a fragment of white suiting on the broken rail as he went down on to the sand.

Ryan felt the grin spreading on his face. The final thump which Ramirez had handed out had looked like quite a haymaker, but save for the faint noise of splintering wood the other sounds had been drowned in the noise of the surf.

Neither of the women seemed to have heard anything, and the few other diners were unsighted, with their backs to the windows.

He switched his attention to Consuela. It was not difficult to understand why she was manifestly the apple of her father's eye. Nor even why his paternal instincts seemed to be abnormally developed, for the two were opposite in almost all respects. Her elegant style and manner were in marked contrast to the hunter's personality, and yet were complementary to it.

In other circumstances he might have been tempted to improve his acquaintance with her. But it would not have been very bright to offend Ramirez's sensitivities at this stage of their business.

'Well, I hope you will be able to join us for the fishing,' he said casually. 'I understand your father has quite a nose for locating the big ones?'

She smiled, acknowledging the invitation and the tribute. 'Yes, he is very good,' she said, with obvious pride. 'For three years he has killled the greatest of the *espadas* taken here, the

147

king marlins.'

Ramirez came in from the terrace. There was a suggestion of redness at the corner of his mouth, but he seemed to be pleased with himself. 'You were right enough, Mama,' he said, nodding. 'I should've made things more clear to him a long time ago.'

'It was all right, Juan?' she said quickly, doubtfully. 'There was no trouble?'

'Trouble?' He gave a little shrug. 'Well, of course, a little of the *agarrada*, you understand, a little of the business wrangling ... but no trouble.'

'But where is Francisco, then?' she asked, still dubiously, uncertainly.

'As you told us,' he answered easily. 'The Jefecito ... El Jefe ... is of much importance. His next important business was also urgente. I don't think he'll be back.'

'Well, you were certainly very quick,' Ryan smiled derisively. 'It is obviously a nonsense that business is done more quickly in the colder countries.'

Ramirez grinned. He lifted his refilled glass and took a drink of the wine. 'Listen. A piece of news over McVee's radio ... he told me you'd been to see him and I was there later ... I think you're going to be lucky. It looks like we may have got ourselves a special cat. Near Parmeque, village in the Punta Quela country, a girl killed. We were going there anyway.'

Ryan raised his eyebrows. 'You mean *tigré*? A man-eater?'

'Not yet, just a girl-eater yet. But he'll get to it now, if somebody don't get to him first.'

'That's something for the book,' Ryan said. 'Have you ever had any before? I mean you yourself?'

'Only two in my time. One took four kids and two men, over a period, before we got to him. There's an old hunter up north, though, seen several over his time.' He finished his wine. 'How about you? You ever run into any of these kind of killers?'

'Also twice,' Ryan said, 'lioness and a leopard. An African blundered on to the lioness when she had cubs, after that she had the taste for it. The other was an old slowed-down *chui*

148

... maybe starving ... who found out the women in the shambas were a pushover.'

'That's always the size of it,' Ramirez said. 'Well, ninety-nine times ... what you said about old cats. I bet you ten bucks this is a big old cat when we find him.'

'You seem pretty sure about finding him.'

Ramirez grinned. 'Damn right I am. More than ever now he'll stick to his patch. Besides we'll call him, or it may be a her, but I bet you ten bucks more it's a him.'

'No complaints with that,' Ryan said. 'I'll take it. What time can we get started in the morning?'

'Eight o'clock be okay? I got to check on the gas and things?'

'All right,' Ryan nodded. He glanced at his watch. Surprisingly it was ten-thirty already. 'Well, I think I'll take an early night.' He looked around for the mestizo girl but Ramirez raised his hand. 'Let me get you a cab.'

'No, leave it,' Ryan said. 'On second thoughts I think I'll walk, get some air.' When he had taken his leave of the women he lit a cigarette and nodded to Ramirez. 'Well, Cazador, buenventura, then, for twenty bucks!'

Ramirez showed his teeth. 'You bet. Buena caza ... *Bwana*, ain't it?'

Consuela watched the Englishman go. Very big, flat backed and wide across the shoulders. Much older than herself, though younger than *El Jefe*, she thought, and still taut around the middle. He had come to hunt the *gatos*, as her father sometimes called the great spotted ones, and, appropriately, he moved somewhat as they did, flowingly, without seeming effort. She would look forward to the fishing.

'This of Francisco ...' the older woman started urgently, but Ramirez cut her short.

'Aaah, the hell with Cruz, Clara, *forget* Cruz.' He finished his coffee. 'I think we will each have a glass of cognac, no?' He signalled to Paco and got his tin of cheroots from his pocket. 'You know something, Clara, I think I will get along with this Inglés.' He grinned. 'And afterwards you may get a fine present, *paloma* ... you, too, *gatita*.'

149

The street to the *Palace*, which was lit only by a couple of bulbs fifty yards apart and a small auriole of yellow light from the hall of the hotel, was deserted.

Approaching the place he hesitated for a moment. He wouldn't have minded another drink before bed. But he didn't fancy being roped into a session with Jorge tonight. Then he remembered that in any case he still had a shot or two of Daiquiri and some beer standing in the handbasin. He passed the front door and tried the wicket-gate in the wall. Typically, it was still unfastened.

In the moonlight the cherimoya looked stately, ethereal. After all the tawdriness of the shanties and the shebeens the courtyard was like a temple with a domed ceiling of stars. He took a step forward, then he noticed the small square of curtained amber light that had been hidden by the tree. He halted and leaned his shoulder against the bole, fishing in his pocket for a cigarette, considering.

It may have been the grace and tranquillity of the place, but, paradoxically, a medley of recondite thoughts which were irrelevant to the symbol of the light began to run through his mind. He had never had much time for organised religion. (Least of all at those times when you were suddenly plunged into crucifying personal tragedy. Its fanciful crap was for the purblind and the wishful thinkers more than ever then!) And in its fatuous illogicalities, arrogations, postulations, above all in the sickening sycophancy of all the dog-collar species, the dogma had always given him a big pain in the neck.

For where *was* the Love and Kindness, still less the justice, in Nature, in Humanity? Any hunter, observing all the hate and the cruelty and the injustice, knew a sight better than that.

Not that he had ever had any time for atheism, because that dogma was equally unconvincing. Though with the shattering blow of Fiona, that had seemed to so conclusively testify to the nonsense of Belief, to the tenet that the empiric reality was hell and not heaven, he had come very close to it.

But then, as the jagged pain had dulled, it had come to him increasingly that he still had the lad, a part of her at least. And

150

that save through Belief there just was no other hope of ultimate reunion. Just nothing else to hang on to.

Renate was a different thing altogether. A happy circumstance, involving deep affection that might well increase, blossom, though it could never supplant what he had had with Fiona.

And even Renate was ten thousand miles away. And meantime here he was, a pretty standard guy named Ryan, and who still had to eat and sleep and work and live it out like all the rest, the serene and the unhappy, the bereaved and the unbereaved. A man who, ipso facto, could thereby use such superficial distractions as offered, and thank you for that, anyway.

He hawked, spat out some of the dry chaff taste in his throat, wiped the sweat beads off his face and crossed the flags.

Intriguingly, the door opened even before he could tap on it and a puddle of soft yellow light lapped his feet. *Esplendoroso!* This time she was really laying it on the line. She leaned back against the door jamb, arching her back, pouting her breasts, smiling. Now she had high Spanish heels, which supplied an extra touch of élan and height. Her blouse hung much lower over one bare rounded shoulder than it had the first time, barely containing the nub of her breast, and she had fixed a small red bloom in the hair beside her ear.

'About *los pequeños* and the skylight,' he said, deadpan. 'Not too late to fix it is it?'

'Nada.' She shook her head and smiled again, extending her hand in a gesture of invitation. On the threshold he took her face in his hands, tilting it while he kissed her.

Except for the smaller windows the room was more or less a duplication of his own. There was a low table with a bottle of Daiquiri and one of *manzila*, with two glasses. The liquor, too, then! All in all it was quite a compliment.

'You wish a drink, Señor?'

He nodded. 'By all means, chica. You think of everything.'

She poured a glass of the white rum, and some of the wine for herself.

'*Paquita es muy querida.*' He grinned and raised the glass to

151

her, then took it in a swallow and seated himself on the end of the bed. In profile her breasts were not large, but she had wide inviting buttocks.

She put down her glass and went over to him, slowly, with some pretended hesitancy, moving in a calculated way that advertised the rounded spread of her hips. He took her by the throat again and began to kiss her seriously.

Her lips, succulent as a peach, with a faint wet taste of wine, stimulated the urge in him that had begun at the sight of her framed in the doorway.

'Well, and how do you find yourself, Paquita?' he said softly, in the *idioma*, 'because I find you *mucho hermoso*.' He moved his hands along and down over her shoulders, kissing her hard in the soft corner of her neck and feeling the quiver of pleasure.

'I find you also *mucho hermoso, Señor*,' she said huskily. The anticipation in her voice was unmistakable, as if she had been waiting a long time and was way past stalling around. '*Muy hombré* . . .'

Even so she was no professional, he thought. Nor yet the rustic unsophisticate either. Apparently it had just happened that the cut of his jib appealed to her, released the chemical reaction, and, like himself, she believed in making your own opportunities.

'*Mucho sentimiento*, Paquita,' he said. 'You are delicious.'

'Señor . . . Querido . . .' For answer she grasped the sides of his head and kissed him ardently.

He slid her blouse down over her elbows and kissed the dark upturned nipples of her breasts, already stiffened with eagerness. Impulsively she pulled the blouse over her head and dropped it on the bed, then put her arms around his neck, pressing her breasts against him, and kissed him lastingly.

He kept up the teasing and caressing for several minutes. Kissing behind her ears, lifting her breasts and brushing her nipples, and when she turned, so that her head lay back on his shoulder, he continued the fondling; kissing the soft widths of her shoulders and cosseting her breasts, still prolonging the outcome.

When he felt for the catch at her hip she brushed his hand away and unzipped the fastening herself impetuously. She kicked the skirt aside and turned again, lips parted in anticipation, breathing deeply, tigerish in her intensity.

Now, except for her shoes and stockings, she was fully revealed. Relatively small-breasted but voluptuously hipped.

'Querido!' She pressed against him, her hips writhing gently back and forth in a spontaneous importuning movement. Ryan kissed her again, then he swept her up, pressing his face into the satin substance of her stomach until she squirmed with pleasure. He laid her on the bed and she lay face down, expectantly, while he stripped off.

Her back and hips were like velvet and for a while more he caressed her until she suddenly turned and flung her thigh across him, dragging at his shoulder and holding up her mouth. He moved deliberately at first, prolonging sensation until he sensed that there would be complete and mutual fulfilment. Then, finally, he drove into her with mounting vigour until she ended the silence with a long drawn-out sigh of satisfaction.

Later in his room, he considered the teeth marks in his shoulder. She hadn't quite broken the skin, but she had done a better job on the lobe of his ear than the *pequenos* would have. He grinned at his reflection in the mirror. *Muy viveza* all right. Some *suculento*, Paquita!

6. BUENA CAZA

He heard the truck arrive as he was finishing his coffee. It was an open Dodge that looked about three tons load, with sensible kingsize tyres, and there were three men squatted on the tarpaulins in back.

The heavyweight one, Tom ... Tomãsco ... seemed to be the muscle man. Ebony. Pure African origin. A big man, almost Ryan's height, in a raggety straw sombrero and white

153

singlet. Taciturn demeanour, except that sometimes he was startled into a grin as wide as a *demoiselle*; which is Creole for tiger shark. His bare feet were like half-size turbots top side up, and he looked as if he could have held up the truck while they changed a wheel.

The two others had European strains from somewhere back along the line. Almagro, the apprentice hunter, was a *café-au-lait* coloured man about twenty-seven or eight, also of obvious durability, but in a wirier, lither way than the big fellow.

Manuel, cookboy, 'washerwoman' and general handyman of the party, had about him an air of extrovert geniality that pleasantly contrasted with both the moroseness of the big buck and the thoughtful manner of the novitiate hunter. He was not short, of medium height, but without the implication of formidableness that was implicit in the other two.

By the time they had left the shanty belt, on the road south, the sun was beginning to bear down, making little dazzle patches on the metal of the hood and sucking up the humidity that was secreted in the increasingly abundant vegetation.

Ryan reached for the rag in the cubby and wiped his hands. He got the cigarettes from his shirt pocket, shook one loose and offered it.

'By the way I hope you picked up the whisky I ordered, the *Scotch* I mean? That's one little indulgence shouldn't be forgotten,' he said.

Ramirez sniggered. 'You quite a drinking man, eh, Bwana? Got you worried huh?'

Ryan was conscious of a prickle of annoyance. 'That's my business, Cazador,' he said curtly. 'And if you did forget you can turn around right now.'

A spot of colour appeared in the other man's cheek and his expression changed. 'Well I didn't forget, *Mister*,' he said slowly, deliberately. 'Took some trouble over it ... it's not plentiful ... like the other stuff you asked for. But any time you want to turn around,' he waved a hand, 'we'll turn around all right. Like right now?'

'That would cost you something wouldn't it,' Ryan said flatly, 'say about two Grand, plus the lawyer's fee? Because

154

this isn't for free, is it? I'm paying for it, aren't I, and for the whisky, and everything else. So don't give me any temperament, friend, because you made a deal with me that will stand up and I've come a long way.'

For a moment they looked at each other with something like hostility, then Ramirez turned his head and spat out of the window. Ryan took out the alligator pear which Paquita had given him when they were leaving and began to chew the fruit, staring ahead expressionlessly.

They were coming on to the real rough stuff of the beat-up dirt road now, and a few miles farther on they began to leave the marsh and water-scrub area for more varied country.

On the seaward side there were still tracts of mangrove, habited now by egrets and pale-cerise coloured herons hunting the brown-backed red-billed *uca* crabs and other small fry which scuttled between the reed tufts and the twisted roots. But now the semi-marine bush was gradually giving way to the beginning of rain forest. To the great entwined profusion of a *Caliente* 'country'. Terrain which, scorched by the sun but nourished by the spasmodic torrential downpours, produced fantastically colourful medleys of flora, notwithstanding the relatively infertile soil.

Vast towering nargustas and great hardwoods, immense dignified seigneurs of the forest, presided over a multi-tinted consortium of less spectacular species, ranging from mahoganies, ceibas, breadfruit and coconut palms, many of them blazoned with common parasitical orchids and harassed by suffocating creepers, down to the plebeian stratum of palmettoes, tree ferns, graceful lilies and, ultimately, armadillo grass.

In itself it was all worth seeing, and maybe Ramirez hadn't really intended anything snide, Ryan began to think. And, of course, by the professional's tradition it was *his* show! He *had* to be the skipper of the outfit. Certainly he himself had never taken any African party of strangers on any other basis.

He thought about it some more and swallowed some of his bile. 'Sorry if I blew a gasket, man,' he said at length. 'Maybe your kind of heat works on the liver. Not all me though ...

155

you also get out of line, mate.'

Ramirez gave him a short glance. Then he grinned. 'Like with Cruz, for instance?'

'No,' Ryan said. 'I was in favour of that. Like not meeting your customers and like what-the-hell's-it-to-you-how-much-I-drink.'

'Okay, let's forget it. We just got fouled up again eh, Bwana?'

'Call it morning-itis,' Ryan said. 'Let's begin again. With the formalities. My first name's Mark.'

'As you know, Juan, or John ... what you prefer?'

'I don't prefer anything,' Ryan said. 'Anyway, I thought up one of my own that suits you better.'

'Como?'

'Marciano!'

Ramirez smiled. 'Some battler. I wish I was half that good.'

'You looked useful,' Ryan said easily. 'And then, of course, we seem to have Mister Liston back in there.'

'Tomãsco?' Ramirez chuckled. 'Well, that makes you Max Baer, seeing you're bigger than the both of us.'

'They better look out for us then,' Ryan smiled. 'We seem to have assembled an All-Stars outfit.'

Ramirez skirted a hub-deep crater the width of an elephant pit, then changed down for a juddering stretch of iron-hard murram parallel striations that stretched across the way like inverted gutter pipes.

When they had jolted over the stretch he turned his head. 'I guess I ought to explain about that *hijo*, Cruz. I dare say you wondered about him?'

'Not much,' Ryan said. 'Seemed pretty obvious anyway ... little personal *agarrada*!'

'Well, that's right enough.' Ramirez smiled at the recollection. 'But there's more to it than that.'

'Politics you mean?'

'Well, yes, in a way.'

'Go ahead,' Ryan said, 'though it's not my department I should say.

156

'But you know about the 'tecos?' Ramirez insisted. 'You know how it is with us and them?'

'I can guess,' Ryan said. 'I expect they follow the well-known pattern ... always running out of *lebensraum*. And your grass is greener?'

'That's them, that's the *facciosos*,' Ramirez said. He spat over the side. 'Ragged-assed Batistas in fancy uniforms!'

Ryan nodded. 'Who want to take you over, strictly for your benefit of course. Isn't that it?'

Ramirez returned the nod. 'And how!' He shook his head from side to side. 'Your politicians never seem to catch on with *facciosos*. Look what they fed Batista, look what they still take from Franco, Salazar ...'

'I'll make a confession,' Ryan said. 'Or maybe it should be an apology. We don't have many politicians now. Just Brothers and Comrades. The Comrades are very good at organising the Brothers ... of course they're much brighter than the Brothers ... and, incidentally, the Comrades would be happy for you to be taken over.' He grinned. 'I know it sounds crazy, but it's a hell of a crazy set-up these days.'

Ramirez frowned incredulously. 'But if you mean the Commies ... the Reds ... would want the *facciosos* here that's crazy, man. Don't make sense.'

'Yes it does,' Ryan told him. 'But we'll get to that. First off, do I gather you think they're different then ... the Comrades and the *facciosos*?'

Ramirez considered. The way it was now with Castro the Cubans didn't seem to have won much, except slogans. Still, the Batistas, unspeakable obscenities ... 'Yes. Yes I guess so,' he said finally. Irresolutely.

'Not for my money,' Ryan said. 'Not any more. The only real difference between them is that the *facciosos*, all nationalities of them, support Religion. And different labels, of course, Gauleiters, Commissars, Ayuntamientos, what-have-you. But the set-ups and the methods are the same. The knout, the concentration camp, liquidation, no genuine trials, Secret Police, one Party, the same bloody formulae as ever!'

'Well, maybe,' Ramirez rubbed his chin. 'But they were the

157

ones stood up to Franco weren't they?'

'I know something about that,' Ryan said. 'My father fought on the Jarama river.' He finished eating. 'Do you know *who* it was who sold the pass to Franco, betrayed the Spanish Democracy? The Comrades ... just as soon as they realised the people weren't going to stand for a Commie Government even if Franco was beaten!'

'But that still don't make sense,' Ramirez objected. 'They fought all through.'

'Not the organised Commies,' Ryan said. 'They quit the moment the word came from Moscow. And it makes sense all right, ice cold long-term Commie sense. Their strategy's always been to take over the takers-over ... damn sight more popular than taking over a working democracy. Never made any secret about it either. It's all right there in their manifestos, for all the Brothers to read, but they're too busy playing Bingo and nationalising the fish-shops.'

'Well,' Ramirez shrugged. 'Facciosos or Commies, we know the score with the *puercos*. Pure poison.'

'Amen to that,' Ryan said. 'But what I'm trying to tell you is, don't look for any help from the bunch of Wet-Dreams *we've* evolved. And if your neighbours ever do get away with it, in no time at all you'll be Sieg heiling the hammer-and-sickle, not the 'tecos' flag.'

'*Libertad o Muerte!*' Ramirez said with emphasis. 'Why don't you write about it?'

'Sorry,' Ryan shrugged. 'As I said before, I apologise, but it's just not my line of business, Cazador. The Brothers wouldn't want to know anyway. They're all cluttered up with the really weighty stuff like nationalising the fish-shops and ending the Inhuman Slavery of the forty-hour week.' He paused for a moment. 'With Cruz, though, it goes further than politics doesn't it?'

'Consuela,' Ramirez said shortly. 'The punk wants Consuela! Imagine, a *hijo* like *that*, even if he wasn't a 'teco,' he added vehemently.

'Where's the problem? You're the head of the house.'

'No problem, kind of complications, though.' For a moment

158

he considered how to explain it. 'I got a good wife, Mark, but about some things she is very dumb. She thinks like a 'teco ... the old Spanish ways. For her things like marriage should be *arranged*, and what counts is if the man is important. And she worries. The way she figures it Cruz is a bigshot, an Excellency, also a chief of Police and all that stuff ... would be good for Consuela and good for me.'

'How good for you?'

Ramirez reached for the Coke in a wire cage on the dash and offered it, but Ryan shook his head. He took a swig himself. 'There's times when I got orders for particular orchids, or skins, and we've been unlucky. I'm not interested in, what you call it ... the goose chases. I get orders for stuff, I fill the orders. Over the border there's sure-fire "countries"; also I got friends there, trappers ... I give 'em the *trampas* in the first place ... and they get fair prices from me.'

'You're talking about Cruz "countries"?'

'Sure.'

'For which El Jefe could give you the *salvoconducto*, turn the blind eye, if you played ball with him. Or again he could throw you in the can, or you could have an accident? That the risk?'

Ramirez curled his lip. 'Aaah! There's no risk ... a cinch.'

'McVee disagrees,' Ryan said. 'He thinks it could even be a fatal risk. He thinks you're the only one ever gotten away with it.'

'He was sounding off about it, eh?' Ramirez grinned.

'The subject came up,' Ryan said, 'and I don't think McVee is a fool either.'

'Well, it would be a risk, say for *him*. But, man, I know those "countries", I've hunted 'em ten years.' He made another gesture. 'I can lose those punks any time at all.'

'Well,' Ryan shrugged. 'I'd still say your wife has a point.'

'Aaah, as I said, *estúpido*, dumb. She believes what Cruz tells her, she even thinks that *hijo* would be good for Consuela. Like I said, good in bed, with the cooking ... but the dumbest of my wives.'

Ryan cocked an eyebrow. 'Wives, plural? You run a harem

or something?'

'I got three others,' Ramirez said prosaically. 'I have to move around this country, don't I?'

Ryan laughed. 'Well, I'm familiar with the *lobolo* system, cheaper-by-the-dozen, but I didn't know you boys went in for it.'

'Matter of being practical,' Ramirez said casually. 'In this business you got to be practical, Bwana.'

'Fill me in,' Ryan smiled. 'I'm here to learn.'

'Well, it ain't really what you might think.' He put the tip of a forefinger in his ear and wiggled it, pulling at the lobe. 'Clara's the only legal one, like that the others don't count. Indian marriages!'

'But why *marry* 'em? Where's the percentage?'

'Right where they live,' Ramirez said. 'And I could un-marry any of 'em if I wanted.' He reached into the cubby of the dash. 'You want some real fruit?'

'No thanks,' Ryan said.

Ramirez got a nectarine from the locker in the dash. When he had taken a bite he made a gesture with it. 'First, I am bubbies with the Indians. Get their co-operation, get the best of their stuff. Good business. Second, it keeps the women faithful, gives them a rating, no horsing around with the *vale-rosos*, no fornicating. The Headman take care of that ... they're all Bossmen's daughters. Third,' he grinned, 'well, they're all pretty good, you bet ... younger than Clara!'

'Well if you put it like that,' Ryan chuckled. 'I suppose it makes sense?'

'I'm here to tell you,' Ramirez said.

For a while they were silent then Ryan said. 'This Cruz. After the business last night won't he be really looking for you from now on? And does he *know* the "countries" you work ... his "countries" I mean?'

'Likely! They got their ways of getting Indian information, but,' he grinned, 'I got mine too. And what he never knows is *when* I might take the notion, or which "country", because I don't even know myself.'

'Well,' Ryan shrugged, 'most men have the poacher instinct,

160

most hunters anyway ... I'm following a wounded one myself. I don't think much about whose territory it is ... but, where I come from, you don't get shot for it.'

Ramirez smiled. 'I don't get shot either, Bwana. Who's going to get shot?'

'Well, not me, Cazador,' Ryan said. 'I'll tell you that for nothing.'

In the fierce heat of noon, abruptly, surprisingly, they came to a cabin that was set back off the track in a small compound of hard-baked murram and old knee-high tree stumps. The store was quite isolated, and better made, more solidly constructed than the town shanties. Low slung, with walls of palm logs and a thatching of plaited pandanu, which makes more durable roofing than coconut or straw, it looked as if it could stand up to hurricane onslaughts and probably had.

At the front there was a portale of woven reeds, stretched over a framework of bamboo, that was like a car port. Beneath the awning there were two benches and some stools with dished tops, made from sections of big mahogany logs.

There were five Mayans outside the cabin, all swathed in their blankets despite the heat. Two were men, small and wiry-looking, in shapeless straw hats, who sat at one of the benches in the shade of the portale. But, typically, the three women, hatless, waited patiently outside in the full electric glare of the sun. They were stockier than the men and one had a child on her hip, but the other two were younger.

Ramirez slowed right down, reducing his dust cloud to the minimum. He cut the engine and let the truck coast on to the burnt trodden soil in front of the cabin. When they got out of the cab the two Indians got up and moved out from under the awning as if it was automatically required of them as a matter of deference. One carried his unfinished bottle of gaseosa. Their faces were impassive, showing neither curiosity, resentment nor any kind of positive feeling.

There was an open hatch under the awning which ran the length of one side of the hut and the man behind it looked pure Cantonese. He was an old man who had lived out two wives. His first, more or less of his own race, had come with him from

161

the town forty years ago. The second had been a strapping young black woman whom he had also brought from the town after due bargaining with her parents.

He had acquired her for the comfort and pleasure of her wide buttocks, and for free labour, but one day she had strayed into the fringe of the jungle and trodden on a *gecko*. It may have been that in feeding her to fatness, obliging her to consume vast meals of pork fat, manioc and other starch roots traded-in by the Indians, the diet had sapped her natural resistance, but whereas no more than a day or two of sickness should have resulted from the poisonous bite of the lizard, she had developed a fever and died.

That had been when he had still been capable of enjoying his plump and obedient black goose to the full. Now he had been old for a long time, with fragile hands like November foliage and deep wrinkles in the skin of his neck, although his eyes were still clear, unvanquished.

He watched them come in out of the sun, sipping his grey maize-coffee and smiling a welcome for Juan Ramirez. Behind him, in the dimness of the store, you could just make out a miscellany of trading merchandise, pots, pans, knives, implement, machetes.

On the wall at the end of the counter there was a coloured picture of the Virgin and Child, and beneath it a metal crucifix. They seemed incongruous emblems for a Chinese, but maybe they were intended as signs of respect, and testimonies to his right of endenizement, Ryan thought.

The second, less pacific, yet complementary symbol of Chinese resolve hung from a centre post behind his head. A .45 Colt that was as old as himself, but still in good working condition. It was a long time since he had fired it. But in his earlier days there had been occasions when the warning roar of the gun, supplementary to his quiet resolution, had offset his own apparent frailness; proclaimed that none could expect to rob him with impunity. The warning demonstrations had always been sufficient. Except once. When a half-breed Carib full of mescal had tried to take his first wife, and then he had shot the *ladrón* dead without hesitation.

162

'Heinekens, Wu, all round?' Ramirez made a gesture to the boys. He looked across at Ryan. 'How about you, Bwana, some mescal or tequila with it? Stiffen it up?'

'No, I'll take a pukka dram with it,' Ryan said.

'Fetch Señor Ryan a bottle from the truck,' the hunter called to Manny. 'One with the White Horse on it.' He turned back to the old man. 'Well, Wu. How are the sons? Still putting the bite on you?'

The trader put five beer cans on the counter and began to open them. He shook his head slowly from side to side but his smile was gentle, belying his pretended disapproval. 'Not knowing!' He nodded towards the direction from which they had come. 'Still with third uncle. Only come here when they are broke.'

Ryan took a pull of the beer. It was not quite luke, just about drinkable. The old man handed him two paper mugs and he filled them, pushing one along to Ramirez ... He jerked his head. 'Strictly no liquor for the boys, eh, Cazador ... Right?'

Ramirez nodded, 'Damn right. Only Tom takes it anyway ... when he gets the chance ... Manny never tasted it in his life.' He took the beer out to the others and Ryan carried the whisky and the beakers.

When they had seated themselves at the other bench, Ryan inclined his head. 'How does he make out for customers ... here in the middle of nowhere?'

'Better than you'd think,' Ramirez told him. 'Get's a truck load of loggers every once in a while, but his steady trade's with the Indians. They come in from forty miles around.'

'I think he had some guts,' Ryan said ruminatively. 'Little old fellow like him setting up here on his own. What does he do for burglars, send a pigeon to the gendarmes?'

Ramirez laughed. '*Es muy yesca*, Wu, of much spunk! That, and his cannon, and because he had a real firm notion to make a buck.'

'How about the sons?'

'They were okay at first,' Ramirez said. 'Grew up here. But finally they go to hankering after boots and shirts and damn

163

fool luxuries like that, and now,' he grinned, 'they're city slickers. They work for their uncle at the *Kwikservice Eats.*'

Ryan smiled. He nodded to the bottle. 'Have a dram of the good stuff.'

Ramirez pursed his lips indecisively. 'You're getting me into habits, Bwana. I don't normally hit that stuff till later.'

'I know,' Ryan said. 'But we're not operating yet. Go ahead.'

'This time, then, but after this we stick to the rules. Right?'

'Right,' Ryan said. He smiled to himself, remembering a joke with an N'derobo tracker he had once had quite a time ago. 'Except for Manny.'

'Manny?'

Ryan sunk his drink and mopped the sweat beads from his brow and neck. 'Just a wee kid-on, a bit of fooling ... with your okay?'

'Like what?'

'Just give him a dram,' Ryan said. 'See how it takes him.'

'I told you ... he's never tasted hard stuff.'

'That's what I mean.'

'Wait a minute, Bwana,' Ramirez frowned. 'Don't go spoiling the boys with liquor, or money, or anything like that.'

Ryan crossed his heart. 'Not a chance, don't worry. Chances are he'll swear off for life anyway, first taste of whisky is pure poison for anybody, if you remember.'

'Okay then,' Ramirez said doubtfully. 'Try him if you want to.'

Ryan winked. 'Hey, Manny.' He jerked his head. 'Over here, *montero.*'

The other two boys smiled at the 'hunter' tribute, and their smaller partner beamed widely.

Ryan poured out a half cupful. 'Understand you've never tasted the wine of my country, *muchacho*?' He held out the cup. '*Caballo blanco* ... strictly for *Importantes*!'

The brown man looked at the cup, then at the smiling Inglés and his patrón. Ramirez nodded and he took it. 'You have to drink it in one swig,' Ryan said. 'Essential. Not like the beer.'

164

The Honduran nodded. He put the cup to his nose and smelt it. The odour was not encouraging but he took the drink on a gulp.

For an instant his expression remained questioning, uncertain, then his face took on a look of utter disgust. Ugh! He half-retched, then he began to swear in a mixture of Creole, Spanish and English, until, gradually, the obscenity of taste began to dissipate. He grabbed the can he had put down and swilled the remains of the beer around in his mouth before swallowing it.

'What! You don't like it?' Ryan said with feigned astonishment. He shook his head, continuing the pretence of seriousness. 'Well, that case, *muchacho*, you never will.' He got a note from his pocket. 'Better get us all some more beer . . . take your taste away, put your fire out.'

'Si, put the fire out.' The brown man put a hand on his stomach and grinned ingenuously. Save in extreme circumstances his natural amicability was never disturbed for more than a few minutes, and now that the vile taste was fading he felt after all a certain compensating warmth in his stomach.

While he was getting more beer some kind of an altercation seemed to have broken out among the group of Indians outside in the compound. One of the two men seemed to be arguing with the two younger women, making gestures which suggested that he was forbidding something. The older man took no part in it, staring detachedly in front of him as if unconscious of any disturbance.

Suddenly, one of the women broke it off with a shrug of defiance. She turned abruptly from the protesting man and moved into the shade of the portale, the other following her more diffidently.

Hesitantly she approached Ramirez and muttered a few words in dialect. Ryan watched with interest. It was obvious that she was importuning him in some kind of way but her manner was so completely opposed to the Western, or, come to think of it, African or Oriental way of it. There was no grimace of invitation on her expressionless face, no spurious smile. She could just have been proffering a basket of black

165

beans at the roadside. It looked like some sort of a purely unemotional we-have-to-eat-and-I-got-this-to-hawk proposition.

Ramirez listened in silence for a few moments without looking at her. Then he spoke shortly and made a negative gesture of indifference and dismissal.

'An invitation into the bushes, but Uncle there isn't in favour of it?' Ryan said. 'That it?'

Ramirez smiled. 'That's not bad guessing for a guy who don't speak the dialects. But even if we'd got a packet of salvarsan for the clap they ain't like Carmen Mirandas are they? I said we'd settle for the floor show.'

The bolder of the two women beckoned the other to come closer. She said something in a low voice, and then they both dropped their blankets. Underneath, each wore a kind of coarsely woven billowy skirt, but from the waist up they were naked.

They began a kind of foot-shuffling dance, rotating slowly in opposite circles, but there was nothing very erotic about it, the movement barely shuggling their brown breasts, which were firm enough but boyishly unattractive. Emphatically, they were in no danger at all of further defloration, still less of assault. Even Tomásco, who was not given to undue aesthetic requirements, felt only a mild interest in a performance that he had seen more effectively executed a good many times before.

Yet, ironically, the Mayan glowering in the background, who could, feasibly, have been the husband or the father of either of the women, was now provoked to action. Suddenly, impulsively, he started forward angrily.

Ramirez rose. He gripped the Indian's arms, pinning him. While he held the man he spoke rapidly in the dialect, but not threateningly, reassuring him. The Mayan ceased struggling and the old man called to him from outside. He muttered an imprecation and Ramirez released him.

Momentarily the women had halted their shuffling. Now, unconcernedly, they made to resume, but Ramirez tossed a coin to each and waved them away.

'Another guess,' Ryan said grinning. 'You told Montezuma,

166

there, there was nothing to worry about? No takers?'

Ramirez put down his drink and felt for his cheroots. 'You're quite a mind reader, Bwana.'

Ryan looked across at the caked dirt on the women's feet and shins and wrinkled his nose. Even if they had been hosed down first you could have smelled the body odour at six feet. 'Not difficult,' he said. 'You can smell lion stink down wind at twenty yards, especially lioness, but those ones would spook the lions.'

Ramirez laughed. 'Some local broads, eh, but the ripest I ever smelt were the New Orleans chippies. Some of them *really* hummed.'

'You'd wonder how some of the Cockneys ever do business,' Ryan said. 'But I never saw any white ones could outpace, outsassy the Masai ladies ... they practically put 'em in your mouth ... except the Bwangato—they were something again.'

'Real hustlers?'

'Ischium artists, assologists,' Ryan said. He smiled at the other man's puzzled look. 'The Masai worship their genital organs, the Bwangato their asses ... at least their women's asses ... even decorate 'em.'

'I'll be Goddammed.'

'I'm not kidding you. *Nekbwes!* Thing like a small plate which hangs over their backsides from a waist string ... focuses the attention like a ... a ...'

'Target?' Ramirez suggested.

'Very apt,' Ryan laughed, 'Right on the button. The ones less than forty-five round the buttocks don't have a chance. They're broads all right. According to science their backsides first developed as a store of body fat against times of starvation.'

The recollection reminded him of an old story. 'Did you ever hear the one about the inquisitive lady Zebra in the Open Zoo?'

Ramirez shook his head.

'Well, she jumped the hedge into the next field. Then she went up to one of the sheep and introduced herself. After the formalities she said, "Oh, by the way, what do *you* do for a

167

living exactly?" "Oh, I just eat and eat," the sheep told her, "and then they come and take the wool off me!"

'The next hedge she jumped there was a herd of cows, and she repeats the enquiry. "Oh, well, I just eat and eat and then they come and take the milk from me," the sow says. The third fence there was just a big old bull in the field. The Zebra minces up to him and starts in again, same line, same question. The old bull just bends one eye over her plump quarters, then he stops chewing for a moment and says, "Look, Honey, you just shed those striped pyjamas and I'll show you what I do for a living!"'

They lunched on cold iguana and turtle eggs, and when they were ready to leave the old man came out of the store. 'Adios, then, Wu,' Ramirez said. 'Send me word when you have a good *collection* of ocelot, the price is good.'

The Chinese raised his old fustic hand in affirmation and goodbye. 'Buena caza, good hunting, Juan!' His quiet, gentle manner seemed somehow out of context with the resolute spirit of the man of the wilderness he was, Ryan thought.

'I am in favour of Wu,' he said later as they got into high gear. 'Quite a character. We could do with a lot more Chinks like him.'

Ramirez nodded. 'Uh huh. Mrs Wu was a humdinger, even in my time.' He grinned. 'I'd been a lot younger I might even have risked the cannon with her.'

They came to the ferry in the late rays of afternoon. The craft was a real homespun job that resembled a water-borne pagoda on a platform of balsa logs, and the superstructure looked as old as hell, but Ramirez seemed to have no qualms about it.

It was strictly a self-service transport, fitted with double-handed windlasses by which you manhandled your own vehicle across, and if the last user had left it on the wrong side you had to take a *dory* across and fetch her back. But now it was ready at hand and Almagro and Tomásco held the sides firm against the ramp of the bank while Ramirez edged the truck on to the platform, the deck of the boat bucking and partially submerging with the weight of the vehicle.

When they were in motion, Ryan lit a cigarette and leaned back against the truck. From across the river, tangentically, the sun-rays cast a dazzling sheen of reflection on to the water and he pulled down the peak of his cap against the glare.

A hundred yards downstream a fish, a big one, arced out of the greeny-brown glass like a salmon relieving its waiting monotony. Perhaps one of these big *lukanani* perch, he thought, or, more interestingly, tarpon, even.

When he shifted his gaze he saw the snake at once, slithering down an incline of the bank. It was not very large, about three feet, but its red and yellow markings glinted brightly in the sun before it took to the water.

Almagro and Tom had struck a rhythm on the windlasses now and the raft had made twenty yards or so, moving on an elliptical course against the sluggish thrust of the current.

He turned and reached into the truck for the canvas holster belt of the Luger. The snake was nearly parallel with the back of the craft now, swimming with its head held stiffly out of the water like an umbrella handle. There was already a clip in the butt of the pistol and he was about to begin the fun practice when he felt a hand on his arm.

'Just a minute, Mark,' Ramirez said, 'and don't try for the *minit*, the little dog, leave him.' He pointed. Near to the place where the first snake had appeared, two others, nut brown and thicker, were now slithering down the baked mud of the bank. Hard behind them their pursuer, silvery grey, with the shape and webs of an otter, hit the water with a soft splash. Oddly, the swimming action of both reptiles, snaking near the surface of the water, was quite different from the periscope style of the first one.

The otter gained rapidly on them. As soon as he overtook the nearer reptile his head drew back, neck contracted, and then flashed forward in a lightning strike. For a moment or two both creatures disappeared in a flurry of water, then, some yards from the swirl, the *guina marten* surfaced, his lashing victim gripped firmly in his small dagger teeth.

Ryan smiled, 'Bedamned. Like a cross between a mongoose

169

and an otter, the little fellow. Didn't give a damn for the boat either.'

'No, they never quit,' Ramirez said. 'Real cussed. Good skins, but I'd never hunt 'em because they mostly live on the *ofensivos*.' He glanced at the Luger. 'You like the little guns, eh?'

'Insurance,' Ryan said. 'Saved my bacon with a *chui*, a leopard, one time, ever since then I've made a habit of it. Besides, I haven't hunted nights before, except croc, I might louse it up with one of your cats.'

Ramirez smiled. 'Well, maybe you got something. But you won't need any insurance here ... I'll be there too.'

'What's so different about here?' Ryan said. 'You need it all the time, especially the if-only-I'd-had-a-gun times, especially the snake times, especially *you* do!'

'Oh!' The hunter cocked an eyebrow. 'How do you figure that?'

'From the scrape you've got there,' Ryan said laconically. 'That's a cat rake isn't it?'

It was a calculated guess, but the hunter's expression confirmed it. Involuntarily, his fingers went to his face, moved down over his cheek.

'As I said, killed a good tom leopard with this little Kraut gun once,' Ryan said. He threw his cigarette butt into the green water. 'I'm bloody glad I had it, boy, it's the reason I didn't end up in strips.'

Ramirez laughed. 'All right. Maybe a point. Maybe I'll get me one some time.'

'You should,' Ryan said. 'Specially now you've got this *Jefe* business an' all. Another thing. You never had a busted firing pin with a wounded one lying up for you just ahead? Don't knock the little guns, boy!'

Across the river the road became even more of a track. Serpentining ahead through heavy jungle towards a distant mountain range dominated by one particular peak that sometimes showed above the tops of the big timber. But to the east, flanking the course of the river, there was an elongated tract of

170

semi-open ground like rough meadow land.

In some ways it was similar to the occasional cirques of razed ground ripped and gouged out of the jungle by hurricanes, save that it lacked the typical residues of tornado action, sundered stumps and trees transformed into gaunt witches' shapes. Instead, it was relieved here and there by clumps of polewood mangrove, small groves of cabbage palm, and curiously beleagured islands of tall razor grass.

It was terrain which, once, before some subterranean tremor had caused the river to recede, had been wholly marsh and bog. *Akalche*, which is the Mayan word for low-lying areas of mainly secondary growth with few big trees, and currently it was largely overgrown with coarse armadillo grass.

Ramirez edged the truck off the track and began to drive slowly over the tufty ground towards an isolated group of mammee trees. As they came nearer, the blanketing foliage of the mammees became suddenly animated, disgorging a variety of creatures that had been feeding on the big pink apples, and the silence was shattered by a medley of alarm cries.

A screeching mishmash of crimson, green and yellow-green parrots and macaws took off in a cloud of vivid colour, and a troop of black howler monkeys fled chattering and screaming for the greater safety of the jungle fringe.

'I think we'll stop off here, tonight,' Ramirez said. 'Farther on isn't so good.' He glanced at the angle of the sun above the treetops. 'But the light will last for a while yet if you want to fish or take a look around while the boys fix camp?'

'What had you got in mind,' Ryan asked. 'With the gun?'

'Oh, caiman ... alligator, more likely caiman ... maybe a capybara.'

'Sounds okay,' Ryan said. 'But first we'll just break the rules.' He grinned. 'At least I will. Sweat and all.' He went over to the truck and got the remains of the midday whisky and two beers. When he came back, he said: 'Just for my benefit, what's the difference between your crocs and other bastards?'

Ramirez took the beer. 'Not much till you get to recognise 'em. Size mostly. With the caimen the big teeth don't show

171

like with the 'gators, and they got heavier armour. They come in two colours, mostly black but there's some, kind of yellowy. The other thing is you can wrestle a 'gator, but not a big caiman.'

'How big's big?'

'Most blacks run ten–twelve feet, full grown, some make fifteen-eighteen. That big enough?'

'I hate them all,' Ryan said. 'Nastiest bastards of the bloody lot, the saurians. The African ones are bloody canny too. If you want a real load of croc hides you've got to do it at night.'

'That goes for here, with bait and a light,' Ramirez said. 'But sometimes, usually, I can call them close in.'

'I'll bet,' Ryan said sardonically. 'You ought to tell the *Reader's Digest* about that one.'

Ramirez experienced a quirk of resentment. 'You don't know it all yet, Bwana,' he said. 'You want to try it?'

For answer, Ryan went over to the truck. He uncased the Mannlicher and got a box of the new-style alloy-tipped soft nose that were replacing the old lead-nosed kind. When he returned to where the boys were pitching the tents, Ramirez was waiting. He was carrying a big bore single barrelled shotgun now, and around his waist he had a coil of the slim *cordel* which some skiff fishermen use for big marlin and tiger shark.

There was a big treble attached to the rope, bigger than a shark hook, more like a small grapnel, the points being set in cork stoppers to avoid ripping into his clothes when he was moving.

'What's the cannon for?' Ryan said enquiringly. The point of the heavy tackle was obvious.

'We just might see a *hass*, a capybara; they're worth taking,' the hunter said shortly. 'This ain't a bad place for them either. I'll leave the big stuff to you,' he added drily, 'since you know all about it.'

Ryan returned the grin. Maybe he had that one coming. For a moment he cogitated, thinking back to what he had read up. Then he remembered. The capybara were big rodents. Very big rodents. Full grown they were said to be as big as pigs. Amphibious, with heads shaped like those of giant water voles.

172

'Useful, huh? Good eating?'

'Good as pork,' Ramirez said. 'Likewise the leather, better than buckskin. We get a good *hass* we'll have ourselves some pork fillets that thick.' He made a circle with his finger and thumb.

'How big do they come?' Ryan checked.

'Good boar will run to a hundred-and-thirty, hundred-and-fifty pounds. I got seven *hass* in a bunch once, a family, caught 'em on the open savannah.' He grinned at the recollection. 'They can't run far, no stamina on land.'

Ryan grimaced. 'Hell did you do that for? Who'd want the lot for God's sake?'

'The Indians, that's who,' Ramirez said. 'My buddies, remember. I don't waste good meat or good leather, Bwana. They fetched 'em all in you bet.'

Ryan put five rounds in the magazine of the Mannlicher and one up the spout. 'Well, Okay, let's get started then.'

On the far side the jungle wall groped greedily towards the water, overhanging it in some places, as if trying to recapture the highway it had grudgingly conceded.

But on their side the going was not so formidable. Sometimes, relatively open stretches of *akalche*, intersticed with furrows of razor and kunai grass, made it easy as moorland. And at first they were able to skirt the places where the creeping avalanche had issued its probing elements of stunted cohune palm, pigeon plum and ginats that, in turn, had been halted by the overburdened soil and then defeated by the parasite rattans and the creepers.

But increasingly, as they followed the course of the river, the *akalche* tracts became sparser, and the protruding jungle barriers thicker, so that at times, now, Ramirez had to draw the machete on his hip and cut down outriders of thorn brush and matted lianas.

They moved on through the diffused shadows of ginat groves and came out on to another narrow strip of hard brassy light between the river and the forest. Here the ground was hot and dry, and curiously, the dead *akalche* had made way for an

173

advancing embranglement of 'dumb-cane'; scabrous young pine that looked as if it might successfully defy the slower advance of the big timber.

The unusual chest-high afforestation had a tangy ambrosian smell, and a kind of fairy glen aspect, as if it might have been the habitat of forest sprites.

Just a couple of hundred yards farther on a promontory of mahoganies and great hardwoods marched almost to the water's edge, and now they heard the soft noise of inrushing water. The stream was quite shallow, but over the years it had gouged deeply into the forest floor.

They let themselves down to the edge, sprang across and scrambled up the six-foot dyke the other side, grasping the broken lianas which still clung to a fallen giant straddling the mouth.

A hundred yards ahead they could see the fall which stretched diagonally across the river between the two outcrops of spume-lapped boulders like a mill race.

The cascade itself, no more than five or six feet deep, would have been child's play to salmon or even brown trout, but below it the level fell again to a stretch of white water that would have taxed a good fish.

Above the fall, where the river maintained its relatively leisurely pace, there were darker surface patches, here and there, indicating deep pools.

'All right, we'll try it here,' Ramirez said shortly. 'And listen, Bwana, if I bring one in, let him come in real close, four or five yards, before you thump him.' He waited. 'You got that all right, Mark? He's got to be close.'

Ryan nodded. He grinned. But there was still scepticism in his expression.

He had known a Hieland poacher who could call buck rabbits to the other side of a stone wall. And a keeper who could simulate the squeal of trapped rabbit well enough to fool fox and stoat. The same man, too, could call dog foxes at night, with the wail of a vixen, which was even more difficult. And according to his enquiries, since underwritten by McVee, there seemed to be no doubt that this man, Ramirez, really could

174

'call' jaguar.

But calling crocs, caimen ... they were all the same silent bloody villains ... took some swallowing. Was something he would believe when he saw it!

He worked down on to his stomach and watched Ramirez slither down the bank and get down on his haunches, resting on his elbows behind a fringe of reeds. When the hunter had settled himself, he stretched forward. He covered his nose and mouth with his palm and began to make a deep humming noise that was something like the droning of bees, only deeper and more resonant.

The hunter kept up the humming call for two or three minutes, then he stopped abruptly and both men stayed still, watching.

After a similar interval the hunter began again.

Now that the light was fading even the later bird calls seemed to be petering out, and there was only the soft slushing sound of the water as it passed over the fall farther along.

The silence grew deeper and then, suddenly, was rent by the single harsh abbreviated squawk of a macaw from across the river.

For all his doubt Ryan felt an irrational twinge of anticipation. Even in strange country you could somehow always tell an alarm note, and the bird's cry was very reminiscent of the scolding screech of an African parrot, glimpsing a prowling leopard, or some other hated killer. Irrelevant but jarring.

Just for a moment he thought of jaguar, but then he dismissed the idea. Few leopards moved before sundown, and the *tigrés* were much later hunters. More likely the bird had been startled by a kinkajou, or a tree lizard.

He rested his chin on his forearm, smelling the musty odour of rotting vegetation which came from the jungle behind him, borne on the almost imperceptible wafts of the evening breezes.

For the fourth or fifth time Ramirez called, and the sound seemed to roll across the surface of the water. Nothing stirred. There was no sound or sign of response but then, just as he was beginning again, he broke off sharply.

175

For a second or two more he remained listening and peering through the gap he had made in the reeds, then he looked back over his shoulder, grinning and jabbing a finger towards the water. He made a gesture signing Ryan to listen hard, cupping a hand round his ear.

Still nothing seemed to have disturbed the stillness. Then, suddenly, just for a few seconds, Ryan heard it, the susurrant drone of a swarm that was not a swarm.

Just briefly, Ramirez called once more, then he lay still, staring through the parted reeds and unwinding the cord about his waist. Ryan took a practice sighting. The light had dimmed appreciably since they had set out but it was still fair enough, he could see the foresight all right.

It was impossible to judge the direction from which the message had come, but some ten seconds or so later the problem was resolved. He saw the bow wave, about fifty yards out, approaching diagonally from the direction of the fall. It was not very pronounced, barely cutting the surface of the water, but it was unmistakable, and he nodded down to Ramirez to confirm his awareness.

He pressed the catch over to *fire* and wiped the sweat drops from his eyes and forehead with the back of his hand. With any kind of crocs it had to be a precision brain shot to kill instantly. Heart and lung shots were no good, unless you were in a boat and had a Gaffer with you, because death was never immediate, and invariably the stricken creature either sank, or was taken by others of its kind once it was really bleeding. And it had to be precise because the armour was incredibly tough, capable of deflecting even softnose if the shot wasn't bang on.

In the opacous murk of the water the submerged body of the reptile was invisible, but from the distance between the snout tip and the eye knobs it was no half-grown snapper.

When the smooth arrow wave had neared to twenty yards he began to concentrate fully, laying the bead on the spot back of the eye knobs and holding it there, following the glide. At fifteen yards he sucked in the final breath, brow furrowed, and began the squeeze. Ten yards ... eight ... then the baritone

176

boom of the Mannlicher split the silence and Ramirez, below him, heard the tearing slap.

The big saurian reared half out of the water and fell back again in a lashing, swirling crescent. He knew, instinctively that he had nailed him, but as the creature straightened, broadside, he gave him another one in the neck.

Ramirez sprang to his feet. For a moment he swung the looped cordel like a lariat, then he cast out over the caiman. He let the leaded grapnel sink, then began to draw in across the carcass. When the big treble-hook lay against the reptile's side he jerked powerfully, sinking the barbs into him. He called out over his shoulder. 'All right, let's get the bastard out then.'

Ryan slid down the bank, grinning. Save that they did it with a rod, the hunter's performance reminded him strongly of what the really expert salmon poachers called *howking*, casting over lying salmon and then foulhooking the fish with a snatch at the instant of contact. 'Boy, you *howked* that swine like a real Scotsman! Here, let's give you a hand.'

Ramirez was dragging on the rope now, bringing the heavy log-like body into the shallows in a ponderous glide. For a second or two he studied the carcase, but this was a dead *ofensivo* all right, not a stunned one. Each man took a foreleg and they dragged the creature up through the mud of the reed bed.

When they had the caiman properly beached the hunter took a handful of mud and slapped it over the pulpy patch ... big as an orange ... where Ryan's high velocity softnose had exploded the brain area. The mud would discourage the *cobarra* flies and, more pertinently, reduce the blood smell likely to be picked up by scavengers. He did the same with the neck wound though it, having missed the vertebrae or other bony resistance, had produced only a tomato-sized laceration.

The black caiman was a well-nourished bull, about twelve feet long.

Ramirez rinsed his hands in the water and wiped them on the sides of his pants. 'Well,' he sidekicked the caiman's tight yellowy belly with his boot, 'the way I always look at it with

177

these, that's a lot more fish in the river anyway. Not a bad hide, at that. We'll send the boys out in the morning.'

'Not likely to get ripped up in the night?' Ryan asked. This was one country where they didn't have to allow for the omni-present *fisi*, the hyenas, and the jackals, but there would be other carrion eaters.

'The only chance is a pack of wild dogs,' Ramirez said, 'and that ain't very likely. But we'll settle him on his belly. That way any of the cats will figure he's just sleeping and they'll make a detour, believe me.'

'While we were bringing him in I was wondering about *piranha*,' Ryan said. 'I know we were only five minutes or so, but they tell me they're pretty quick once there's blood in the water?'

'Too bloody right,' Ramirez said. 'Bastards can strip a deer to the bones in less than that, but they don't get up this far. They don't like the rough water, and they wouldn't climb the fall except in a big spate.'

The beginnings of dusk were not far off now and when they came to the place of the figs the shadow patches had visibly deepened. The gaps in the parasol of high foliage were edged in soft red-glow now, instead of the hard glare, and the kinka-jous had gone. Ramirez halted abruptly and Ryan, following, almost collided with him.

'*Hass* . . . look!' He whispered it.

Ryan stared over the hunter's shoulder, following his gaze. He scrutinised the bank and the immediate *akalche*, then suddenly he saw the trio of heads in line, half way across the river and about seventy yards ahead.

He followed Ramirez, bent double, and both men dropped down at the edge of the bank. The distance was much beyond the effective range of the shotgun. Ramirez rolled aside and gestured him to move up. 'Try it, soon as they land.'

Ryan elbowed forward to the brink. By the time the leader was twenty yards offshore he was ready, his brain automatic-ally busy with the mechanics of it.

The caiman had really been barndoor stuff, and, normally, so would this be. Here, in this limp flaccidity, windage, gaug-

178

ing a cross current, the other considerations, just didn't arise, and elevation or the reverse didn't come into it because the Manny was smack-on, flat, up to four hundred yards.

But there were two things. It would have to be fast, because the capybaras weren't going to hang around once they landed. And it wouldn't be any good to thunk one just anywhere, because likely the *hass* would instinctively fling himself back into the water, his second element, and make out far enough on muscular reaction to preclude a repetition of Juan's *howking* technique.

The other thing was the light. Because the pig-rodents were going to land right smack between himself and the blood-orange rays illumining the horizon of the treetops.

The capybara came out of the water at an angle of forty degrees. He looked about two feet at the shoulder, and his coat glinted iridescently as he turned his head sharply to verify the presence of the two females. Simultaneously with the movement, Ryan's straining, screwed-up eyes got the foresight over the four finger area just back of the shoulder. He grunted softly with the effort of seeing the bead and squeezed off just as the cape's head came back preparatory to the swift rush up the bank.

The capy went over on to his side with a squeal that rose and then faded like the dying wail of a reed-pipe. Smitten with a shock power that had pulverised his heart. The two sows whirled in the shallows, their alarm honks contrasting with the mortal cry of the male rodent, and made for the deep water, diving as soon as they were able to.

The capybara lay just clear of the water's edge. As they came up to him a foreleg lifted fractionally and fell back, presaging the final shudder before complete immobility. He was a young boar come lately to maturity. His light brown hide was tautly drawn over his sleek corpulence and the heavy roundness of his tailless hams bespoke succulent meat.

'That wasn't bad, Bwana,' Ramirez said. 'Not bad at all. You thump the cats like that and we'll do all right.'

'He was a co-operative piggy,' Ryan said. 'Stood just right, just long enough!'

179

When they came in sight of the truck and the two tents across the final lengthy strip of *akalche*, Ramirez halted, put two fingers in his mouth and whistled. At the far end of the *akalche* strip one of the boys looked up and stared, then Tom and Manny began to trot towards them.

Both boys grinned widely when they saw the capybara, and the smaller man helped Tomãsco get the carcase on to his shoulders. As they approached the tents, appetising odours of cooking wafted towards them from the barbecue grid which Manny had set over a glowing heap of cohune charcoal.

'You already cooked the *largartos*?' Ramirez asked.

'Si, Jefe, they are ready.'

'Well, it won't matter.' The hunter shrugged. 'Wrap 'em in fig leaves and gauze, they'll be okay cold tomorrow. Right now we're going to have rib-roast *hass*.'

The mulatto nodded his approval, grinning. '*Mucho excelente*.'

'Yeh, well listen,' the hunter said, 'don't skin him yet, just cut out plenty for all of us, then sack him up. We'll be taking him in for Yano tomorrow.'

It was really coming on to dusk now. The daytime pests, the bottle flies and the *cobarras* had disappeared as the sun went down. But now was the time the *pequenos* and the mosquitoes took over. Stabbing the heavy air, searching for blood, especially thin-skinned, easily gotten blood.

The smoke gusts from Almagro's separate fire, a piled heap of greenery with a charcoal base, offered some deterrent though. And if you supplemented it with periodically renewed smearings of repellent, plus a dram of the real dew, and a decent untipped cigarette with a taste to it, this was the second-best time of the day.

While they waited Manny set out five coconut mats around the barbecue, and a steaming pot of potatoes. The *hass* meat, with Tomãsco's help, was already sizzling on the red hot grill. Ryan watched the cookboy's procedure with interest. Tin plates and everything! It was a lot more sophisticated than everybody taking a thumb and finger into stewing-pots of jackal stew. Real dude stuff. And even so completely fresh,

180

rare and unhung as it was, the *hass* meat was as good as roast pork at the Savoy. White, tender and really succulent. It might have been how the beasts fed, or the climate ... maybe something of both ... but one thing for sure was that even 'hung' impala was never in the same street as this fresh roasted *hass*!

He finished chewing the length of a piece, holding the chopped-off hunk of rib like a slice of melon, tearing the white meat off with his teeth.

'Pretty good, Juan. Pretty bloody good. Better than tapir?'

'Depends if you're a beef or a pork man, I guess,' Ramirez told him. 'That's about the difference. Me, I'd sooner take the pig meat.' He tossed a stripped bone on to the charcoal and reached over for a turtle egg. 'But there's one little fella beats 'em all for my dough ... river tortoise. That's real swank eating.' He spread his hands a yard apart. 'Come a fair size, too, but they're not so common ... too many other critturs go for 'em, caiman, piranha, even the cats if they spot one in the shallows.'

'Tortoise? Don't you mean turtle?' Ryan asked.

'No, tortoise. *Hikiti*. Strictly freshwater.'

Down by the river the bullfrogs had started to sound, and out across the *akalche* the cicadas were beginning to add their chirrupings from a dozen different directions. They ate in silence for a while, only subconsciously aware of the low chorusing of the small noctivagants and the occasional sizzling of damper stuff from the slowfire.

Ramirez stretched on his side and took a sip of coffee. He yawned and jerked his head in the downstream direction. 'Not a bad *hijo* you got back there, Mark. Make a pretty good hide.'

Ryan nodded. 'Yes, but I don't want it. Had my fill of crocs. You take it?' He drew on his cigarette and blew a tight stream towards the darkness beyond the firelight. 'You know something. Juan. In Africa the most hunters get killed by elephant, but it's the bloody crocs who kill the most *people* by ten times. The biggest vilest bloody menaces God ever debased the waters with!'

181

Ramirez smiled. 'Not here, they ain't, Mister. We got one here the caimen will get the hell out from.'

'Huh?'

'The really big bastard,' the hunter said. '*El Fangoso*. Anaconda!'

'Christ, yes. I'd forgotten them.'

Ramirez jabbed a finger. 'Well don't, ever, if you're crossing water. They're not common, but they're bloody curtains. You don't see *them* coming.'

He spat a lick of nicotine over his shoulder. 'I've seen *fangosos* with half a caiman sticking out their gullets. You carve one up you wouldn't believe the stuff in his belly. Take any goddam thing in the water ... tapir, swimming *tigré*, buffalo, you name it.'

Ryan squeezed his chin. 'You ever had any accidents with them personally?'

'One kaput accident,' Ramirez said succinctly. He flipped a hand. 'Wading this same goddam river, further west. We lost an Indian. Poor bastard gave one yell and disappeared under.' He paused to finish his coffee. 'There was one other time after that ... wading again, just a shallow crossing. You don't expect them in anything that shallow. Anyway Almagro saw this one coming, then we both did, thank Christ! Mostly you can't see 'em. They lie on the bottom and they look black, but out of the water they're kind of brown-yellow with banana yellow underbellies.'

'You beat him to the bank?' Ryan asked.

The hunter shook his head. 'No. We could never have made it, we were half way across, but we both had guns. We each gave him two barrels of buck-shot before he could hit us. I doubt we killed him, but,' he grinned, 'it gave the bastard something else to think about while we run for it.'

'Have a dram,' Ryan said. He poured three fingers into their coffee mugs and called across for Manny to bring a couple more beers.

There was a half-moon rising now, beginning to throw faintly glinting streaks on the black glass surface of the river. He watched the thin grey smoke column rise from his cigarette

182

and mushroom out on to the still heavy air, then he gestured with the cigarette. 'Well, you've certainly got the *ofensivos* all right, Juan,' he said languidly. 'Caimen, anaconda, the snakes ... not forgetting those God-awful spiders.'

'Aaah. Don't worry about the *arañas*, that's a lot of story-book crap,' Ramirez said deprecatingly. 'I've never been bitten by a Widow, the little black-and-red bulbous bastards, but the big tarantulas, the bird-eating ones, are twice as poisonous as the Widows and I've been twice bitten by them, getting orchids. The first time I threw up a few times for a couple of days, the second time, nothing ... maybe the first time acted like a vaccine jag ... But they never killed anybody, except maybe children.'

'I'm not *worried* about them,' Ryan said, 'I just naturally hate the sight of crocs and crawlies. I don't *like* the bastards!'

'Christ, who does?' Ramirez grimaced. 'But you get used to 'em, and you could go a month without seeing any.' He picked at a fragment of meat in his teeth with a matchstick. 'I'll tell you one mean little bastard to look out for though, Bwana. Green hairy caterpillar. Some bloody *ofensivos* those, about as long as your big finger. You've only got to touch the bastards and it burns enough to make you yell. Worse than a scorpion.'

Ryan gave a rueful grin. He shook his head from side to side in self-rebuke. 'Christ! I must have been bloody crackers picking on this chamber of horrors you've got.'

Ramirez raised a questioning eyebrow. 'You don't have the snakes ... the *ofensivos* ... in Africa? I thought they had their lot, too.'

'Sure! But everything about it's different. Beginning with the climate,' Ryan said emphatically. 'Africa's quite an island, so they've got a lot of "countries" and a lot of variety. Some, in the West, are as god-awful steaming as yours. But the "countries" I know best, East and Central, it's hot all right, but it's dry. Kind of hard to explain but it doesn't take it out of you like here. You can march all day but you're not *buggered*, just tired!'

He paused and took another draw. 'The other thing is that it's *daylight* hunting ... outside of sitting up for some stock

183

raiding *chui* ... You can *see* 'em boy.' He paused for a moment. 'I'll tell you something else for nothing, Juan. I'm just as shit-scared as the next guy, but it makes a big difference when you can see what's coming. That way you're breaking even at the worst!'

The swarthier man smiled. Right now he felt friendlier towards this client, no, this *compradre*, than he had towards any man for a long time. Than he had since he had first met, and come to understand the old man, El Viejo. 'Forget it, Bwana. I've killed a lot of cats and I still get the prickles when I hear him coming. But you'll see 'em all right, don't worry about that, and night hunting is like with the *ofensivos* ... you get used to it.'

'Well,' Ryan shook his head again in mock dismay. 'When it comes to them I don't know what God was thinking about ... all these bastarding horrors to plague us. Maybe they're all the two-legged bastards down the ages reincarnated, re-born and quadruple re-born?'

The hunter chuckled. 'Hey, that's pretty good. I like that. Sure they are. Right down to Hitler and Batista and Huerta and the 'tecos and Cruz ... only he ain't dead yet, and anyway he's only a sawn-off *hijo*.'

The stuff with the White Stallion on the label was mellowing them up some now and Ryan laughed. He finished off his drink and topped up both mugs before lighting another cigarette. 'Well, you might as well give me the full nightmare, Juan. How *about* the snakes-of-the-country? I know you've got two real malignant bastards, jumping "Tommygoff" and Bushmaster. Right?'

'Well,' the hunter grinned, 'we got quite a selection, but those are the real *bad* bastards right enough. Either one will hit you ... and I mean hit you ... just because you're there to be hit. With the "Tommygoffs" you got to get yourself into the habit of looking out for him, because you know where he's going to be anyway.'

'Where's that?'

'Ninety-nine times curled around the top of a tree fern or a palmetto, like a bird's nest.'

184

'That's about the level of a man's head,' Ryan said. 'Cosy. What's the range of his jump? Somebody told me they could make ten feet?'

'Baloney,' the hunter said. 'Five or six at the most.'

'Well, that's different,' Ryan said heavily. 'That makes a hell of a bloody great difference ... considering you could be inside a couple of feet.'

'Relax, Bwana,' Ramirez smiled, then laughed outright. 'Don't worry about the Tommys. In the first place me or Almagro will be in front, and in the second place we know where to look ... the fern and palmetto patches ... it's kind of second nature with us.'

'Christ. A man ought to have a suit of armour to hunt this country,' Ryan said wryly. He threw his butt into the glow. 'Well, let's get to the other bastard, *El Demonio*, the kaput bastard.'

'A *real* fugging bastard, that one,' Ramirez said soberly. 'Makes me think of what you said about God and the *ofensivos*.' He put a more reassuring face on it, smiled and shrugged. 'What I mean is, you really got a point with those ones ... but ... no worry ... we know 'em and they send you the message first.'

'All the same ... ?' Ryan asked.

'Come up to around twelve feet, Bushmaster,' the hunter said. 'Light brown with dark brown triangles down his back, edged around with white. Very thick. Rises up about chest high and strikes like a ganger's hammer. Man he *strikes*!'

He took a pull of his cheroot and watched the glow fade off the end, considering. But this guy wasn't a playboy hunter, he was a brother professional, and as he had already decided, a *compradre*, so no bull.

'Don't bother about the Tommys, Mark,' he said. 'But bother about looking out for this one. Like you said, he's the kaput bastard ... about two minutes flat! On the other hand you might never see one ... you could go two-three months and not see one, or see two in a day ... and, like I said, he gives you the message before he comes, hisses loud and clear for maybe half a minute or more.'

185

'Oh, well, that's a cinch,' Ryan said, with heavy sarcasm. 'All that time, you could take a cup of tea first.'

Ramirez grinned. 'Well, you *could* almost take a quick swig ... so long as you're carrying a cannon. He's one reason why the front man, me or Almagro, always carried a d.b. cannon.'

'Obviously *you* haven't had any accidents with them?'

'No,' the hunter shook his head. 'Seen two guys dead of *demonios* in my time mind. With one they cut the bastard to pieces with machetes, but he still had his fangs right through the guy's forearm. That's what I mean about hitting hard.'

Ryan sat up and reached for the bottle. 'Very impressive, very encouraging. Maybe I should start checking my return tickets.'

'Not if you want value for your money,' Ramirez said. 'I wouldn't give you no discount.' They looked at each other then, simultaneously, both men laughed.

'You've got snakebite kit of course?' Ryan asked.

'Sure,' Ramirez said. He tapped the leather-cased sheath knife on his hip. 'Right here.'

'You mean you don't carry any serums,' Ryan said sharply, incredulously.

'Listen, Mark,' the hunter said easily. 'I been hunting this country near twenty years. I'm still here, ain't I? Also, I'm a bush doctor.'

'What's that mean? That if somebody gets a Tommygoff in the neck you'll take a knife to it?'

'I might, or I might do it the Indian way.'

'What's that?'

'You won't believe me if I tell you.'

'Try me.'

'They eat dirt,' Ramirez said. 'Handfuls of it.'

'You're damn right I won't believe you,' Ryan frowned. 'What bloody good would that do?'

Ramirez shrugged. 'I don't know what it does. But I know it works ... not with Bushmaster of course, but with the others. I've seen three Indians hit by Tommygoffs at different times, and they're still around. No surgery, just dirt.'

For a moment Ryan thought about it in silence. Conceiv-

186

ably, perhaps, soil, or rather *some* soil, possessed antidotal or absorptive properties. There could be an element of chemical truth in it, for all he knew, or possibly it had to do with the old faith-healing, mind-over-matter stuff.

'Well, just the same, Juan,' he said finally, 'if I run into any snake trouble you can forget the dirt prescription, just stick to the old knife-and-suck treatment, I wouldn't want to arrive at the pearly gates in a state of vomit.'

'Don't give it a thought,' Ramirez grinned. 'I nearly always bring my customers back alive!'

From somewhere across the river, beyond the synedrous wall of the jungle came a thin death squeal. Ryan nodded in the direction of the sound. '*Tigré* on the move?'

'*Acuri*, jungle rabbit. More likely a *ninit*, or ocelot or bush dog got him. They come on one close up he's easily caught, runs in a circle when he's really scared stiff.'

The deep silence descended again, mantling the forest and the river. It was quite different from the African night, Ryan thought. Certainly there were some similarities. The common backcloth pattern of the insectivora, the occasional, barely audible rustlings in the grass, the cicadas and the other chirrupers. But it was subtler. Lacking the sudden nerve-jangling gibber of hyena, the growling grunt of an old lion hunting carrion ... or the angry frustrated roar of a younger one ... the malevolent abrasive cough of a stalking leopard, the weak alarm cry of a dikdik.

And outside of the *acuri* there had been no sudden strident noise of fear, or killing. Everything was softer, stealthier. Even the river bank creatures entered and left their element with ghostly insinuating plops that scarcely disturbed the water. There was, however, the same thought you had to sleep with. In the African context, of skulking, darting hyena removing half your face or foot. Here, of snake.

'Your night is different somehow,' Ryan said. 'Lies heavier.' He yawned and stretched his arms. 'Almost ready for the sack this early and I haven't done a damn thing.'

Ramirez nodded. 'You done much night hunting before?'

187

'Not really. Sat up for leopards a few times. Village raiders!'

'There's just a couple of other things about it,' Ramirez said. 'Just so we're organised.'

'Okay, go ahead.'

Ramirez stroked his cheek. 'Well, the way we're going to do it there's two things you got to remember all the time. First is, even if you don't nail him to the floor first-off it'll be okay because I'll be there with the stopper, the cannon. You got to remember that, Mark. The other thing is that however it goes you got to stay *put* . . . that's the must one.'

Ryan's face relapsed into a smile. 'Okay, Cazador. You don't have to spell it out, goes for all cats doesn't it?' He poured himself a final short one. 'Tell me something. No bull. Can a man wrestle these cats of yours?'

Ramirez considered the other's man substance. The breadth of his shoulders, the heavy thews which filled his shirt-sleeves. 'It's been known,' he said. 'I only ever tried it but once myself.' He touched the scar on his cheek. 'And after the first round I got help from a couple of Caribs . . . it wasn't a real big cat!'

'What do you call a real big cat, anyway?'

'Two hundred, two fifty pounds! Around eight-nine feet nose to tip! They been taken up to four hundred pounds but that happens about as often as Carneras with fighters.'

'That's what I thought,' Ryan said. 'They've got a lot more chest and less waist than the *chuis*.'

'So they tell me,' the hunter said. 'From what I've heard they're just as mean, but a lot stronger. Take a big bush cow, tapir, or a steer, no trouble. *That* ain't easy, considering the thickness of a bush cow's hide, but the thing I've never been able to really figure is how they got the strength to drag a crittur twice as heavy as theirselves.'

He shook his head reflectively. 'But, I'll tell you one thing, Bwana. We're going to get ourselves a good cat here, and he's going to be the only one there because he's going to be a big old bastard that's got too slowed down for *hass* and *peccaries*, hogs.'

188

'Still seems a hell of a tall order to me,' Ryan said doubtfully. He waved a hand towards the black mass of the jungle. 'Finding one particular cat ... in that I mean.'

'No, you got it wrong. I'm telling you, there won't be another cat on *this* boy's manor, you bet. They all got their own little patches, and they don't range much ... except when they're tomcatting. Lazy bastards. He hears us call he'll come fast enough.'

'Lulu's back in town?'

'Nada,' Ramirez said. 'Nothing like that. Of course a lady in season would have him scouring the patch, sure. But the reason he'll come is because he's got strong ideas about some young punk working his territory.'

As he went over to the tent some tiny creature scurried away between the tufts, and the soft rustling reminded him of more lethal noctamulants. Like the ones who lie browsing by day but descend the palmettoes by night to hunt dinner.

The boys were already settled in the larger tent now, and he fixed the folding wire frame of the net which draped down to his waist. He unfastened his belt, but he kept the Luger by his side.

He remembered thinking, when he had first been planning the trip, that it would probably fall a lot short of African standards. Would not be in the same big league. Now he was not so sure.

These cats were not so hefty as lion, but they were a lot more formidable than the *chuis*, their African cousins, who, in turn were in many ways more formidable than lion. Again, while Africa was big and savage it was also noisy and overt. Whereas this country was not so much savage as lethal, silent, covert. A brooding corner of the earth.

He glanced over at the half-curled form of the man occupying the other half of the tent. It must have taken plenty of guts, knowledge and imagination to hack a real living out of this forgotten, basically hostile enclave. Clearly, as McVee had said, a man of parts, of *muy yesca*, much spunk.

He rolled on to his side and slept.

189

7. PARMEQUE

When he awoke, dawn had already broken and Juan had folded back the flaps of the tent. He turned on his side and for a moment he had half a mind to sleep some more, because despite the hardness of the ground beneath the kapok, he felt lazily relaxed. But finally he pushed aside the netting and sat up.

He reached for the cigarettes and moved over to the open end of the tent. Before he lit one he spat out a lick of liquor-and-tobacco taste, the perennial daily reminder of the trivial pleasures, and at the sound, Manny, squatting by his cooking fire, turned his head and smiled good morning.

Right overhead a big white cloud drifted slowly across the backcloth of the cirrus. Perhaps appropriately it had the shape of a big capybara, even to the profile of an open, panting mouth. And, amusingly, the *hass* was being chased by a smaller cloud that looked like a dassy, an African rabbit, that was nuzzling the backside of its much heftier relative.

Over across the river, above the undulating line of the tree-tops, a white eagle hung like a small puffball of smoke etched on to the blue canvas of the gold-streaked lower sky. Straggles of woolly white mist, like thin streaks of tobacco smoke, were suspended low and wavering over the dark gloss of the water, but already the first luke rays were taxing their vapoury substance.

A pleasant mingled smell of maize coffee and meat and eggs already frying over the refurbished charcoal filled the air.

Manny straightened up from his kneeling position and came over with a mug. It wasn't quite like real coffee, or even the canned stuff, but it was hot and wet and not unpalatable. Cleansing to the palate.

Ramirez was over by the truck, but there was no sign of the other two. Then he remembered the caiman. No doubt they had gone for it.

When he had finished the mug he stripped off his shirt and

190

went down to the river. Even now, before the sun had raised its temperature to any extent, the water was not cold, and very inviting.

A swim would have been damn good, and he would have taken a chance of *piranha*, which normally only came in on a blood taint anyway. But that still always left the possibility of anaconda and caiman and, much likelier than either, bearing in mind the sluggishness of the current here, bilharzia. The hellish minute worm that went straight for your anus and bored on through you until it was into your liver.

In Africa you could almost always judge the kind of water that would be free of the parasite fluke ... *spruits* with a fair flow of current and cress ... just as you passed up the reverse kind, like here.

He slipped off his trunks, just retaining the plimsolls he wore at night, and waded into the shallows to his thighs. When he had given himself a good splattering and towelling he came back out a little farther along, through a fringe of reeds and up the slope of the bank on to the armadillo grass and *akalche*, and picked up his trousers.

Ramirez had already begun eating, and there was a second plate of meat and eggs ready on the grill over the fire.

'Buenos días!' He had just settled himself and started to eat when he felt the hot itching sensation around his calf. He put the platter aside and pulled up the leg of his pants.

There was a patch on his leg the size of a bath plug, and even as he stared it seemed to be dilating and spreading like an increasing stain.

Ramirez swore. 'Hold it, *leave it*!' He ran across to the truck and came back carrying a bottle. He splashed a dose of the raw alcohol over the living amoebiform mass, waited a moment and repeated it.

'*Warri-ticks!*' He took the rag that was wrapped around the bottle, soaked it some more and began to rub over the patch. In a moment or two he sponged it clean. He rolled the rag to a ball and threw it on to the fire, the flames spurting up from the effect of the spirit. Then, finally, he looked up at Ryan with a grin, shaking his head with mock resignation. 'Man, you can

191

find 'em all right . . . and those ones ain't common.'

He took up his plate and began to eat again. 'You must of walked through 'em bare-legged. They hang on reeds and stuff, in bunches, like little swarms, waiting for something they can feed on to brush against 'em.'

'As I said before you've really got the lot here, boy,' Ryan said vehemently. 'Really the bloody lot!'

'Quite some anyway,' the hunter grinned. 'Real little bastards those ones.' He held an egg poised on the point of his knife. 'You never run into ticks before.'

'All the time,' Ryan said. 'But the ones I know are much bigger, and they don't come in those kind of swarms. You feel 'em quicker and you put a fag end on their asses before they can burrow.'

'No good with these. Not once they've hooked on. They bust off with their heads under your skin, sets up an infection. Only thing I know that'll shift 'em is real hard liquor.' He nodded to the watching man by the fire. 'Manny collected a bunch once. *Demostrar* for Señor Ryan!'

The cookboy rolled up a leg of his tattery jeans. Just below the back of his brown knee there was a lighter-coloured scar patch about three inches square, which looked dished.

'I hope you had some kind of anaesthetic,' Ryan said. 'Or did you just slug him, because that looks like real bush surgery?'

'Well, I guess it was at that,' Ramirez smiled. 'We were all out of alcohol at the time, so Tom and Almagro held him down, because we still had to cut the piece out.'

'So help me I should have brought one-forty proof Kruschev vodka, not whisky,' Ryan said, 'for application as well as consumption, and in case you run out.'

Ramirez laughed. 'Well, there's one painless way with the *warri-ticks*, only the catch is you have to be near a *billum* pool at the time.'

'What the hell's *billum*?'

'Little fish.' He held up finger and thumb making a small gap. '*Enanos*, midgets. You strip off and lie in the pool, not moving. The *billum* take every goddam *warri-tick* off you,

192

don't matter how firm they're hooked in. They suck 'em out!'

'Bully for the *billum*,' Ryan grimaced. 'Except that while they're doing their stuff you're probably collecting a backside full of flukes and a bunch of leeches on your *cojones*. No, I think I'd stick to the hooch!'

The track beyond the river had first been hacked and hewn out of the jungle many generations ago as the logging gangs had moved methodically and laboriously on through the areas of lesser timber ... wake-chewstick, prickly-yellow, pigeon plum ... to the zones of the great mahoganies and the giant hardwoods.

Down the years, from that beginning, it had been worn into the red murram earth by the great ox and bullock wagon teams, and the rains had laved it and the sun had cemented it.

Presently, in the hollows, it sometimes bore marks of heavy-duty tyres deriving from the supply truck that went through at regular intervals. Also, less frequently, from the lorries of road gangs, periodically sent from the Capital to burn and machete back the permanent encroachment threat of the jungle from either side.

As it advanced towards its end it became even less of a track and more like a widened *camino*, a deer trail, that, in places where the trees overhung and reached out entwining arms, was like a living tunnel.

The air, in the first hour or so since they had struck camp, had been pleasantly fragrant, still retaining something of the relative coolness of the night. Balmy and somnolent, yet lightened by small wisps of breeze that carried the merged scents of lilies, balisiers, fern, the bright yellow heliconias and other jungle flowers and plants that edged or carpeted the small glades and borders of the forest.

Maybe the dawns, as Ryan conjectured, lacked something of the pellucid glory and expanse of African sunrises. Yet, in the brief interlude before the tyranny and travail of an even more punitive sun than he had known, before the big day-long sweat that snuffed out the perfumes and transformed the taste of

193

cigarettes to mouldered straw, they were impressive. Exhilarating.

But the unbridled heat was never long delayed and soon, in places where the big trees stood back, the waves had begun to shimmer across the track again.

Near midday they came to a bridge over a stream, and when they had crossed Ramirez halted the truck in a patch of dappled shade beneath the fleur-de-lis foliage of a group of oil palms. The heavy timbers of the bridge looked as old as time, their sides overlaid and crenulated with pads of moss, yet still, seemingly as solid and substantial as when they had first been laid.

In the clear shaded water beneath the bridge a dozen or more fish, the size of pound trout, were bunched in a group, their tail fins fanning lazily back and forth as they maintained position against the gentle current.

Ramirez flipped a hand. 'You want to take a dip, go ahead. That's good water, Mark, you can drink it.'

'Not a bad idea,' Ryan said. 'Maybe not much point before bedtime though ... be steaming again in ten minutes!' All the same he began to make his way down the steep bank beside the bridge.

A few yards along there was a sand and gravelly stretch at the edge of the water, and a little farther still the stream twisted out of sight. Right on the bend a bed of chest-high fern rode down the slope of the bank almost to the water's edge, like a toe of the jungle.

He was about to skirt the feathery green when he froze.

The tail of the snake was wound around a mangrove root for purchase, but the rest of its four-foot body was stretched along the strand in an animated ripple.

The hindquarters and feebly sinuating tail of a lizard protruded from its jaws, and the forepart of the victim made an elongated bulge behind the reptile's head. Every few seconds the snake tensed and then made another constricting effort in the laborious process of swallowing the smaller reptile whole. Involuntarily, Ryans hand went to his hip, but then he remembered that he had left the pistol in the truck.

194

In the strong light the snake had a ferine, extravagant beauty of colouring. Vividly banded, in black, red and yellow, every time it contracted itself its brilliant wide stripes glinted in the sunlight. In its complete preoccupation it was still unaware of his presence, and in any event it was obviously in no case to offer any extraneous threat.

For a second or two the struggle engrossed him. From what he could remember the snake was probably one of the *coral* species, of which some, seemingly, were non-poisonous.

Juan was probably still there on the bridge around the bend, but going back for a gun would be bloody ridiculous in the circumstances. He began to look around for a sizeable rock, then he remembered a little tangle of branches, storm residue, just along back.

He retreated from the fern and picked out a strong branch, breaking it down into a stave of five feet or so. Then he went back through the fern. The coral was still fully committed, but now, as he came through on to the strand, it heard the crunch of his boot and writhed around, hissing, for all its dilated jaws.

Instinctively, despite the burden of the lizard the coral coiled, rearing itself to its natural posture of stabbing attack. But it could not possibly disgorge the creature from its jaws.

Ryan moved closer and lashed at the feinting splotch of colour. The first blow was too high, but it shifted the creature to the edge of the water, spread-eagling the coils. Now it seemed to fully realise its situation, and began to move across the strand, still carrying the encumbrance in its gullet. His second heavy double-handed blow caught the snake squarely across the back, lifting it in a shower of pebbly sand into the middle of the stream.

'Drown you bastard!' He grinned with satisfaction.

Even without the deadweight in its throat it was a virtual certainty. For he felt sure that he must have broken the creature's vertebrae.

For a minute or two longer he remained watching the bank edge lest the coral should manage to beach itself. Overby there was a momentary turbulence. But there was no further sign of the creature and the far bank was almost sheer.

195

He lit a cigarette and began to move further along, keeping to the edge of the water. The incident wryly reminded him that here, in this country, it was maybe even more to the point to practice the very precept he had lectured Ramirez about ... to keep a gun permanently on the hip ... and he smiled to himself with self-reproach.

Fifty yards farther upstream there was a little fall, between the rock walls, where the water came down over a flat shelf into a pool before resuming its normal leisurely pace again. The base of the gorge was strewn with boulders which, on this side, straggled out on to the bank, and there was a miscellany of lumber and flotsam piled against the rocks like a beaver dam.

He climbed over and up the boulders to the six or seven feet higher level of the shelf.

All along the opposite side the wall of the jungle was almost flush to the water's edge continuing uninterruptedly. But on this side, curiously, there was a hemispheric open patch of bare ground for about twenty yards, which, from above, must have looked like a bald streak on the scalp of the forest.

The red earth was devoid of growth. As if it had been blasted over with napalm or sodium. And in midst of it there was a shape like a low cupola, rising to a pyramid of perhaps six feet. It was a strange, oddly malignant-looking phenomenon, which baffled him for a moment. But then he realised that it was a version of the same thing which had various African forms.

He fended around for a sizeable stone and flung it into the dome of the heap with some force. The rock broke through the crust of baked earth, bedding right into it, but no eruption of racing minutiae occurred.

He was still carrying the branch and he plunged it deep into the heap several times, but it still remained inanimate.

When he returned Ramirez was still sitting on the bridge where he had left him. He didn't mention the snake; but he jerked his head back the way he had come. 'You've got some of the damnedest things all right, Cazador ... back there ... I've seen some ant castles, but not that big. That's what it was,

196

wasn't it?' He made an illustrative gesture. 'Bare as a baboon's backside!'

The hunter flipped away the butt of his cheroot. 'You must've run across one of the big old nests. Old as hell,' he said.

'You mean abandoned?' Ryan asked. 'The bugs taken off for likelier parts?'

'Could be. But not always. Parasol ants! Sometimes their heaps look dead when they ain't. When under the outer crust every tunnel, every drainage pit is solid stiff with 'em.'

Ryan got up on to the bridge and they started towards where the boys were waiting at the truck nearby.

'I took out a bunch of Yankee scientists one time,' Ramirez said while they walked. 'We hunted around till we found a big heap, then they excavated it and I watched. Seen plenty heaps of course, but never seen one really dug out before.'

'Interesting?'

The hunter nodded. 'Beat hell! Man, they're better organised than us! Those heaps run ten-twelve feet deep. They got rooms, corridors, clean air shafts, highways, even garbage and mortician squads.'

'Yes, I know about that part,' Ryan said. 'It was the size of the thing got me. If colonies that size took a notion to move in on a house, a village, they'd take some stopping? Easier to move the village?'

'Doesn't seem to happen,' Ramirez pondered. 'Anyway you'd stop 'em with fire or something.'

'Not if they're like *Siafus*, you wouldn't,' Ryan dissented. 'Those are the African big ones. They'll suddenly turn up sometimes, just out of nowhere, a bloody great column stretching for God knows how far. Fire doesn't work. Bastards just keep coming ahead, climbing the heap.'

'That so? Well, these boys I took out fixed 'em all right,' the hunter told him. 'They worked on the heap for a week, digging around, photographing and all that. Then, when they finally got through, they sprayed the heap with some stuff. Must have been something special. The Goddamnest thing you ever saw. The stuff didn't kill 'em ... sent the bastards

197

crazy ... they killed each other. The whole bloody nation wiped itself out!'

There were three vultures in the dead Mammee that was the herald of Parmeque. The tree stood like a petrified sentry, its whitened branches reaching up like a High Priest importuning the heavens, supporting the trio of *buitres* presiding over the lower order of several crows in the well of the court.

The street, beginning a few score yards beyond the tree, contained about a hundred yards of habited places, then, a similar distance farther on, petered out into the bounding jungle.

In the heavy rains it rapidly devolved into a shin-deep channel of churned red mud. But right now it was as hard as stone. With a top dressing of red-grey dust.

The straggle of buildings either side made you wonder. The nucleus of the interspaced one-storey adobe houses with the piebald effect, cracked, replastered and replastered again, were very old. The precursors of the place. Perhaps in the beginning well set apart. But, over time, they had been joined to and debased by the crude intervening shacks. Shoddy latter-day intruders which desecrated and demeaned the crumbling dignity of the old cottages.

Diagonally opposed, across the street, there were two frame buildings that were in better shape than the rest. Bigger and more pretentious.

The first looked to be some kind of a general store. Hardware, pots and pans, meal sacks, machetes in leather sheaths and yellow shirts with black edging bands around the cuffs and collars. (The latter for the adornment of the occasional fancy dresser, such as maybe a road ganger on location, who wished to make time with the local girls. Or a local buck who had hit a week-end winning streak in the permanent nightly crap game for pennies and centavos that had worn an oblong pan in the dirt back of the store, and even preserved its form through the rains.)

The other place was patently the most important structure of the settlement. It resembled two box cars piled one on top of the other. Nevertheless, it was a two-storey building, not dissimilar to a Western saloon of the period of Mr William Hicock, and its railed boardwalk portico, providing a frontal area of shade, added further credence to the Western American impression.

For all his ennui Ryan almost laughed outright when he saw the sign above the door. *Tropicos Hotel.*

When it came to dramatic, if unintentional, comedy you had to hand it to 'em. No doubt the branch of Harrods back there, with the shirts and hardware, would be the *Emporio Magnifico,* or something similar.

Inside the saloon the heat was in some ways even more insufferable. Despite the open door and shutters it reared to meet you like a bake house fug agglutinated with tobacco smoke.

Three white men were sitting at a table which comprised the only furniture beside the wall-benches either side of the door. But, contrastingly, the man behind the bar had a skin as jetly piceous as Tomásco's.

As soon as he saw who they were he grinned widely and called out a greeting. Ramirez nodded back, and when the Negro had lowered the sound of a small radio that was giving out guitar music from one of the shelves behind him he turned and went through a door at the back.

Out back he had a small Heineken icebox for special customers, and just recently he had received another cylinder of gas by the Government truck.

In a minute or two he returned with an armful of bottles which were the same as the ones on the shelves but, miraculously, misted over with cold.

One of the men at the table, a red-faced blond crew-cut type, watched the performance of the special treatment with an expression that changed from surprise to annoyance.

The cold beer was a real treat. Ryan finished a bottle off and put it down with an appreciative exhalation. He picked up another of the bottles and took it out on to the porch.

'Sam.' Ramirez hooked his finger, and the Negro moved closer. 'Where's Quetyl?'

199

'*Sta dormido*, boss, I wake her.' He went out again through the door which bisected the shelves and shouted something in Creole or Spanish, or both.

While he waited Ryan came back in again. He had a new bottle of the White Horse *Logan-de-Luxe*, but excellently smooth as it was, in this climate you still needed a beer with it. He said, 'I gather from Almagro that this is one of your enterprises?'

The hunter nodded. 'Three years ago. Sam runs it for me ... Sam and Quetyl.'

'That's the lady you mentioned ... goes with the place?'

Ramirez nodded again.

Ryan smiled. 'Got to hand it to you, Juan. You're a hundred per cent organised all right.'

There was a sudden noise of raised voices and commotion from outside and both men turned. The two Indians who entered had the slim brown bodies of youths, and they were grunting with the effort of lugging a young caiman because, although the legs and jaws of the reptile were bound, every now and then it lashed and struggled powerfully.

The caiman was about five feet long and its back was as black as the faces of Sam and Tomãsco, though less shiny.

The Mayans got the creature on his back against the side of the bar and one of them began to speak to Ramirez in dialect.

The hunter listened in silence, but it was obvious that he was not really interested in the Indians' pitch, and after a minute or two he said something in their own tongue and waved them away.

'You plenty mean Cazador, Juan. No buy fine little snapper from these boys, isn't that it?' Ryan smiled.

Ramirez grunted. 'Yeh. Every now and then I get an order for one and send word through Sam, but they try it every time they hear I'm coming. Keep 'em penned for a month sometimes, feeding 'em piranha and dobar.'

The Indians had now begun to importune the trio of construction men, lifting the caiman on to the bar for their closer inspection, but it was obvious that the white men had no knowledge of the tongue. The blond one called out to Ramirez in a

200

strong German-American accent. 'Hey, Mister, what's with these conches then? They trying to *sell* us this croc or something?'

The hunter nodded. 'You can have him for two bucks, give 'em three if you feel generous.'

The blond man guffawed. 'Stoopid bastards. They think we *eat* croc or something?'

'Why not?' Ramirez said. 'You could eat that one all right.'

'You mean you can really eat *those*?' one of the other men said incredulously.

Ramirez reached a nectarine from a bowl on the counter and took a bite. 'How long you people been up country?'

The second man wiped his neck with a red bandana but, oddly, he left the beads on his nose. 'Six months!'

'And you never et iguana yet?' the hunter asked.

'Sure, two or three times, it's like chicken.'

'Well, *he'd* be like chicken . . . that had been fed on fish.' He took another bite of the smooth-skinned peach. 'Or you could carve him up, make your wife a fancy case. Or you could tame him . . . they're not trying to con you, Jack!'

The reptile on the bar top began to struggle violently, slapping the wood with heavy blows of his tail, and it took both the boys to hold him.

'Some fugging pet that,' the crew-cut said derisively. 'Tame *him*! Fugger'd have your foot off.'

'Not if you kept him fed,' Ramirez said. 'Or you could ring his snout . . . he'd tame down all right, *and* sleep as long as you wanted.'

'Sleep?'

'Sure.' He moved along the bar and said something to the Indians and they struggled the caiman over on to its back. Ramirez dealt the creature a sudden heavy slap across its belly with the back of his hand. Then he bent down until his head was almost against the caiman's snout and began to make a deep humming noise that was different from the sound with which he had called the big caiman for Ryan.

Almost at once the reptile's struggles disisted and in a moment or two it lay completely inert, as if anaesthetised.

201

'I'll be buggered,' the second construction man said. 'What you do to him, man?'

'Acts like hypnotism,' the hunter said. 'As long as you don't touch his belly you can do what you want with him, he won't wake.' He unfastened the cord around the saurian's snout and opened the long jaws, then he put his hand in the creature's mouth and let the jaws close on to it, easily, until only his wrist was showing.

'Jesus. That's one up yours, Herman,' the second man laughed. 'That fugging croc's asleep all right.' He chuckled again. 'How d'you wake the bastard?'

Ramirez re-tied the cord. He posed both hands over the reptile then dug all his finger tips into its belly. Immediately it began to squirm and lash again. For a few seconds he let the beast struggle, then he repeated the 'hypnotising' procedure, leaving it stretched motionless again, like a dead log.

While he was getting himself another beer the door behind the bar opened and a woman came in. Her skin was paler than those of the Indian boys, more café-au-lait, but she was manifestly Mayan and good-looking, as some of them are, by any standard. She wore a low-cut white blouse which was in the Mexican style, except that it had wide ornamental bands following the neckline and around the abbreviated sleeves. The bands were decorated with a red-and-black Indian design of alternating squares, diamonds and crosses, and she had another one sewn midway around her cotton skirt.

The jet blackness of her eyes and hair . . . centre-parted and drawn tightly down over her temples on either side . . . lent intensity to the whiteness of her teeth. In one ear she wore a gold ring, but it was her only personal adornment.

'This is Quetyl,' Ramirez said. For a second or two he spoke to her in the dialect and, hearing his own name, Ryan realised that he was being introduced. He smiled and nodded and the girl smiled back. She was softly spoken and he liked her at once.

'What do you think of her?' Ramirez asked dispassionately. 'Give her a year or two and she'll probably be as fat as a bush cow, like most of 'em get, but, right now . . .' he smiled at her appraisingly, 'reckon you've seen worse, eh, Bwana?' He saw the look on Ryan's face and chuckled. 'Oh, it's all right. No English. Just a little Spanish, if you give it her nice and easy. And don't get me wrong, I do right by her.'

'I'll bet you do,' Ryan said dryly, 'and I don't blame you, only I hope it won't take more than one night. I can think of cooler places than here.'

Ramirez laughed again. 'Don't worry, we'll be in McVee's Resthouse by tonight. Quetyl's going to send a message ahead to the village right now, the one where the kid came from that the cat took.' He lifted the flap of the bar to let the girl through. 'Have yourself a couple more beers. I'll be right back before you know it.'

The blond crew-cut got up from his chair and moved along to the bar. He was not drunk but they had been working at it pretty well all morning and his voice had got progressively thicker.

He screwed up his eyes in a look of accusation and resentment. 'Well now, *Sambo*, we'll just take some of that *cold* beer, this time, *Sambo* . . . like you got for these guys,' he said pointedly.

The 'Sambos' had been insulting and denigratory, but the Negro gave no sign. 'That beer come from Mr Ramirez's pussonal icebox, Suh,' he said evenly. 'This his place and that his beer. Ah knew he'd be here at noon, you see.'

'No I don't fuggin see,' the blond man said with slow offensiveness. 'But *you* better fuggin see, black boy. *You* better see we get the right beer from now on.' He was a biggish man, about two hundred and twenty pounds, with heavy muscles turning to fat. Somewhere between Ryan and Ramirez in size, about Tomásco's height.

'Go ahead, Sam,' Ryan said. 'You can blame it on me if the boss squawks, and you can always start another stack afterwards.' He gave the blond man a little nudge with his shoulder. 'Cool off, Krauty, it's too bloody hot for arguing.' He pushed along the whisky bottle. 'Have a dram.'

The crew-cut stared back confusedly, his expression a mixture of recalcitrance and anger. 'Don't call me Kraut, English,

203

don't do that.'

'No offence, Krauty,' Ryan said equably. 'I said have a dram.' He still kept it nice and friendly, but for an instant he turned and stood fully upright before putting his elbows back on the bar again.

For a second the blond man thought about it. There had only been one time, with a Swede who had turned out to be an ex pro, when his bull strength hadn't been enough. But he wasn't getting any younger and this bloody English had got shoulders like a gorilla. He had a maddening feeling of frustration and his enmity instinctively reverted to the Negro.

He leant across the counter as the black man came back in with three more cold beers.

He said. 'Listen, nig. The yeller doll with the ring in her ear. That's your baby, ain't it?'

'No, Suh, not my baby.'

'We heard different.'

'Ah don't know what you heard, Suh,' the Negro said shortly, 'but it ain't so.'

'You're shacked up here with her, ain't you, and she ain't here for ornament, is she?' the florid man said, with harsh exasperation.

'Don't talk like that, Mister,' the black man said. There was a touch of agitation in his voice. 'Ah told you ... she ain't my baby.'

The blond man turned and called out to the two at the table, derisively, mimicking the Negro's voice. 'You want to know something, boys? She don't belong to the nig, she ain't his baby, and he don't know nothing about it.'

He turned again and stretched forward across the bar top. 'Listen, black boy, ten bucks ... then these guys, that's thirty bucks ... real American bucks, Sambo ... only I got to be first, see. You fix it!'

'Don't talk like that, man.' There was a tinge of deeper emotion in his voice now. 'You don't understand. She belong to Mr Ramirez, this whole place belong to Mr Ramirez. You talk like that any more you got to leave, Mister, Suh.'

The crew-cut's face grew redder. He leaned forward again,

tapping the bar. 'Listen, *nigger*, you fix it with that yeller piece, see, or I'll twist your balls off.' His anger was getting out of hand now, but then, for the second time in his life he made the discovery that friends, like bastards, come in all colours.

'Shut your face, Krauty,' Ryan said irritably.

Ever since the crew-cut had begun to sound off he had felt his hackles rising. 'You make too much bloody noise for a little fella. Shut it, or it'll be shut for you.'

'What! You mean by the croc expert?' the blond man's voice rose stridently. 'That nigger-loving whop? I could take that bum apart,' he said wildly.

'That nigger-loving wop could paralyse you, fat boy,' Ryan said offensively, 'but I mean *me*.' He paused. 'Of course you can wait till the "Wop" comes back if you want.'

'No, Suh, boss,' the Negro said suddenly. 'He can't wait that long, this man's leaving right now, his friends are leaving too.' He brought the shotgun up from under the counter and stood back with it. 'Ah 'sure you they're leaving!' He still had control, but he had the cataclismic look in his eyes now, the penultimate thing. He wasn't fooling.

The other two men had already got to their feet. One was spare and round-shouldered, with hollow cheeks and sun-faded brown hair. He understood the look on the face of the Negro because he had been around longer than the others, and it reminded him of one time when a bunch of Carib labourers had run like crazy, with machetes.

'Come on, Al.' He shoved the other man. At the door he turned. 'Don't push it, Herman ... you always got to louse it up ... I'm telling you, don't push it.'

'He's right, Herman,' Ryan said. 'You don't want your guts all over the floor, do you? Take it out of here, boy.'

The blond man hesitated. He started to curse, then it tailed off. His cheek muscles were working, but his face had gone paler. He turned around and went out after the others into the yellow glare of the street.

205

8. NIGHT HUNT

The big stately nargusta tree, which had been spared for the purpose, threw a pool of early evening shade over the stoep of the Resthouse that gave an illusion of coolness. It was only an illusion, of course, because the sweat was still coming out all over. But, stretched out in the old full-length cane chair, with a couple of tepid ales and a pint of gravy alongside, it was not to be despised. Luxurious even, Ryan thought, if you counted Turkish baths with a counteracting liquid intake as luxurious.

And it created an atmosphere in which to think properly ... belatedly, apart from odd moments ... of things which a man should dwell on sometimes. Contemplate and enjoy; not brush over and dismiss. Such as one's ain folk. One's lad, and, to use an old-fashioned expression that nevertheless best fitted, one's 'intended'.

From Parmeque it had been a laborious business of following what had originally been a deer *camino* ... widened by hand and kept open first by the passage of mule and buffalo wagons and then, eventually, by jeep and truck ... the sides of which often dragged along the truck or prodded at the screen with protuberating growths.

The Resthouse, a teak bungalow set in a compound that had been hacked out of virgin bush and kept clear by order of a succession of forestry and mining bosses, was a small enclave surrounded by jungle. And whoever had picked the site and organised its building had known his onions.

The river was three or four hundred yards distant, through the first wall of jungle, but the boundary of the compound on one side was a stream. And the stream water, Ramirez said, was good. Furthermore, there was a bath-house shed beside it with a shower that, though somewhat primitively constructed, worked well enough.

For most of its length the stream was shaded by the fringe of jungle giants. Accordingly, from late afternoon onwards, the water began to cool slowly so that the added luxury of a midnight shower was always available. Pretty bloody good in midst of nowhere!

Ramirez came out on to the verandah and flopped down in the loop of his hammock. 'Well, how're you making out, Bwana?'

Ryan flipped a hand. 'Good stuff, Cazador. A good place. Once that stream really cools all we'll need is a couple of your wife's friends.'

Ramirez smiled back. 'That wouldn't be any problem, the village ain't far. But we got other things to do, ain't we?'

'Tonight?'

'Well, sure. Anyway, I thought you were rarin' to go?'

Ryan pulled himself upright. 'Well, fair enough. Let's go then.'

'Oh, not yet.' The hunter raised a hand. 'Around eight o'clock will be soon enough.'

'All right. Hadn't thought we'd be organised till tomorrow,' Ryan said. 'The guides and so on.'

'They're already here ... were here ahead of us. It'll take about half an hour to the place they found the clothes and stuff, they say. We'll be back at sun-up and you can get a bath with your breakfast, the best time anyway.'

'Uh huh. How do they fancy the chances incidentally?' Ryan asked inconsequentially. 'The Indians, I mean.'

'They ain't keen to go,' the hunter said. 'From his pugs that's a big old cat out there, they say, like I figured, and he's got the taste now. But once they've led us to the place we won't need them any more. After that I'll always be able to find it.'

'Well, I hope you're right,' Ryan yawned. 'Might as well sweat for a big 'un.'

The hunter grinned. 'You'll sweat all right, Mark. Me too.'

'You mean when we see him?'

'No. I mean when you hear him coming and you can't see him, that's the sweat part.'

'The calling you do,' Ryan said, after they had smoked in silence for a while. 'I suppose it'll be about the same as a hunting leopard?'

207

'Maybe. I wouldn't know,' Ramirez said, 'I never heard an African leopard. Wait a minute though, you can judge for yourself.'

He got up and went inside. In a minute or two he returned. He tossed the big round gourd into Ryan's lap. 'That's the little grape makes the music, calls *tigrés* like you won't know the difference.'

The gourd was a little larger than a football. It was hollowed out to the outer rind, which was about three eighths of an inch thick and as hard as the heel of your boot. Around the circumference there were four rows of holes, parallel but differently spaced, through which ran woven strings like thick thread. The strings passed alternately in and out the holes, like the lacing of a boot, and the ends, inside the gourd, were looped. The neck was just large enough to admit a man's hand.

Ryan examined it with interest then handed it back. 'Go ahead then, let's hear some cat music.'

Ramirez put his hand in the gourd and began to work the strings with his fingers. The sound was like a deep-throated sawing growl. He continued it for a minute or two then ceased, grinning enquiringly.

'I'll be damned,' Ryan said. He grinned back. 'That's it, boy, that's exactly it. A hunting leopard. A bloody great big hunting *chui*!'

'Well, they sing the same, then, but ours must be real outsize *chuis* then, because that's a hunting *tigré*, Mister, male or female.'

'Let's have another look,' Ryan asked. He took the gourd again and turned it around in his hands. 'What is it, anyway? Some kind of musk-melon?'

'No. It's the fruit of a particular kind of jungle vine. Not common, but you can always find 'em if you look long enough.'

'Inedible, I suppose?'

'Yeh. Taste like hell, but they play all right, eh ... when you finally get the hang of it, that is. The strings are mulehair, don't ask me why, but nothing else works as well.'

'That figures,' Ryan said. 'After all the bow of a violin is horsehair. These strings are the bow and the gourd is the resonator, the amplifier.'

'Is that so?' the darker man said. He laughed. 'I'm a goddam *músico* and I never knew it.'

'I doubt you'll make Carnegie Hall,' Ryan said. 'But there'd be quite a market for those things in three African States, plus India and Indo-China. You could make an instructional lecture tour of it when you retire. Professor Ramirez and his infallible grape!'

'Not a bad idea,' the hunter said. 'I'll have Yano start raising a crop of these buffaloes' balls.'

They crossed the stream and entered the heavy jungle with the two Mayans leading. Either Indian could have led them singly but for the return to their village, if the white men were unsuccessful, the raised voices of two men were more inspiriting, and two stabbing spears, and two casting spears, more adequate than those of one man.

The stars winked furtively through gaps and rents in the ceiling of the forest, and the moon was not yet of great assistance. Even so, the slim brown men moved easily enough ahead, avoiding the heavier vine-choked tangles of palmetto and secondary growth, and finding passages through dense cover where an inexperienced man might have taken half an hour.

There was no special need of stealth as yet but, instinctively, they made almost no noise, walking on the heels of their small feet and feeling with their toes for dead twigs and brittle debris.

Every once in a while, momentarily, they halted to check their course, peering up at the stars through the topmost tracery of the great giants rearing three hundred feet or more overhead. Later, too, they began to pause more frequently to listen for a moment.

They had no misgivings of direction ... what they were listening for was the further confirmation of the stream ... and they had no need to attempt haste, for presently they had full confidence in the white men's guns. Moreover even a *tigré* who had discovered how easily humans could be killed, would

209

almost certainly never attack a party of men.

But they knew, also, that when El Cazador was making the *tigré* sound ... this Cazador who had killed more *tigrés* than any other their old men said ... none knew, until the last, the direction from which the great cat would emerge. And they could not stay with the white men because El Cazador would never permit more than one other man to hunt with him in this way.

Hence, when they had found the place, it was their intention to avoid the hazard of running on to the *tigré* themselves, and to settle until dawn in the crotch of a tree. For although the *tigrés* were good climbers of the lesser trees, even the lowest limbs of some of the great hardwoods, which a man could reach easily enough through the trailing lianas, were almost a spear's throw from the ground and afforded complete security.

In the deeper vaults of the *mattoral* it was like entering a vacuum, Ryan thought. There was no remote stirring of air, and all the foliage was covered with a clammy film, as if warm invisible mist had risen from the forest floor.

Still, the moon was risen higher now and the wan silvery ponds of the small clearings provided brief sensations of relief from the overall pattern of darkness and brooding silence.

Strictly speaking the silence was not entire. For if you stood still and listened intently you could pick up small rustlings at times, and once, from a good way off, the anguished squeal of a jungle rat echoed faintly through the twisting black-green avenues. But beneath the tiny, barely audible sounds, there was a profound quiet that was almost tangible. Resentful. Like the atmosphere of a great tomb, the sanctity of which has been violated by alien intruders.

About fifteen minutes farther on the two Indians halted again, and this time, concentrating, Ryan himself heard the faint rilling of the stream they had been seeking.

It was not much more than a brook, about five or six yards wide, shallow and pebbly, a wandering aisle through the cathedrals of the forest.

Here and there a shaft of moonlight, filtering down through the overhead of foliage webbing, cast a fretwork of reflections

210

on its surface that fluttered correspondingly with the movement of the leaves.

They crossed the stream, hauled themselves up the opposite bank and for a few moments lay where they were, resting, smelling the moist fusty odour of the forest floor at close proximity. The terrain was beginning to change now and a little farther on they began to file through a grove of tamarinds, and then, abruptly, they came out on to a *camino* of unusual translucence.

The trail wound ahead through the jungle like a watercourse overgrown with moss and armadillo grass. In parts it was overhung, but in the straighter stretches, between the patches of black shadow, you could distinguish it for as much as fifty yards even in the pallid light.

There are many forest creatures, large and small, who, when seeking water or escape, rarely deviate from particular trails or 'runs' that have served them and their kind for long generations. (Nor is this tendency as advantageous to their enemies as might be supposed, for it allows the more innocuous creatures full use of the only advantage they possess—speed. Thus, the rabbit following his run, and never deviating from it, the roe deer fleeing along trails he has used since first he wobbled forth, clearing familiar obstacles unhesitatingly, outpacing the swiftest dogs.) And the trails of the larger beasts are adopted and perpetuated by many lesser forest creatures.

The *camino* they were following now had probably been created by generations of bush deer, and widened by the regular lumbering passage of tapirs. By a variety of fauna which had moved, or flitted, listening, along its way. Ant-bears and capybara, families of rooting peccaries, tiny fifteen-inch *mazama* deer who so closely resembled the little African dikdiks, all using it at different times of day and night, seeking the safer drinking places of the stream.

In the hollows where, during the rains, the overlay of grass and moss root-rotted and grew thinly, the spoor of the forest creatures was very varied. Cloven imprints of the deer species, and the hogs, were superimposed on the spatular, knuckle-shaped pads of other beasts and their enemies.

211

A dank smell of rot and ordure drifted sluggishly over their faces, borne on a torpid breath of breeze. In parts the trail narrowed, but often all four men could have walked abreast.

Ryan closed up beside Ramirez now, and as they moved through a bend where the jungle walls impinged more closely, he felt the wispy brush of foliage across his face. The sensation at once reminded him of the snakes who struck from the fronds of fern and palmetto . . . *at about the level of a man's head* . . . and he dropped back, feeling the hair prickle on his neck.

Just a short spell farther on the Mayans, moving slowly now, halted and turned. One of them pointed to the great tree which stood back a yard or two from the edge of the *camino* and, coming closer, they saw the spear driven horizontally into the bole. The Indian gestured to the weapon and spoke briefly in a low voice until Ramirez nodded.

'This is where they found the remains of the girl. The first place was at the edge of the forest, near the village. That's where he took a quick feed; then he brought the rest of her up here, hid her up and finished her off the next night.'

'Quite a haul,' Ryan said.

'Not for a grown cat . . . nothing . . . grown cat would haul a big *brocket* buck, a bush deer, twice as far. But after he's et he's got to drink, right here suits him fine. This here's the middle of his patch all right, and I bet he uses this trail all the time.'

'Maybe. But if the kill was two-three days ago he could be twenty miles away,' Ryan said sceptically.

'No.' Ramirez shook his head. 'He could be but he ain't. I'll give you a hundred he's within a half-mile of us right now. This is *his* patch, and they've kept this place baited for us since. Tied out a fowl at sundown to keep him extra interested. Believe me, he won't leave his patch so long as it holds easy meat.' He shifted the sling of the shotgun to his left shoulder and took the gourd from the Indian.

Ryan took the flask from his hip pocket and held it out. When the other man shook his head he shrugged and took a good swig. He checked the magazine of the Luger and recocked it, then he unslung the Mannlicher and adjusted the

212

lamp on his forehead. The lamps which both men wore were like surgeons', only more powerful, and they threw a beam of wider diameter than a gun torch.

'All right, let's get started.'

The hunter nodded and moved off along the *camino*. Almost at once he began to work the gourd, and in the heavy silence the sound, guttural and jagged, purposely larger than life, had a nerve-jangling effect when you were waiting for it.

As he followed, Ryan saw one of the Mayans begin to swarm up a liana into the higher darkness of a big matopolo, the other waiting to join him.

Ramirez moved slowly along the trail. Every several minutes he broke the silence with the throaty rasping call, then halted to listen for a moment or two.

After a while, from some distance ahead, away off the trail, they heard the chittering alarm call of a deer. It could have been a tribute to the hunter's performance, or something which it had seen rather than heard.

Ryan stiffened. His finger curled around the trigger. But there was no other sound or manifestation and Ramirez began to move slowly forward again. Two or three minutes later the jittering call of a *brocket* sounded again, this time from no more than a hundred yards ahead.

It could have been another animal, but it was probably the same one. You would suppose, he thought subconsciously, that when they heard the cat sound they would get the hell out of it, and keep going. But for some unaccountable reason, unless it was that they were fearful of running on to another cat, they rarely moved far away before stopping again to listen.

When the deer sounded Ramirez halted again. He listened then gave the gourd call and listened again. Ryan moved up close and nudged his arm.

The hunter gave no sign for a moment, then he shook his head and began to move forward again, maintaining the same slow gait and keeping within the deeper shadow of the *camino* wall, periodically punctuating the silence with the gourd for fifteen-twenty minutes more before he stopped again.

'Well,' he took his hand from the gourd and brushed the

sweat from his face with his forearm. 'I think he's gone visiting tonight, I don't think he's going to show.' He shrugged. 'Either that or he figures two against one is chancy.' An hour passed, and another, keeping to the same pattern of regular pauses to call and listen.

Now and then wisps of breeze, remnants from the savannah far beyond, sent gentle undulating ripples through the heads of the grass. Ramirez yawned and spat. 'Well, let's go, getting chilled already.'

As he got to his feet a *brocket* called from somewhere way back in the direction they had come from. It was the first incisive sound that had broken the silence for some time. He jabbed his finger. 'Well, he could still be there, it was only a hunch. Bastard could have been sizing us up all the time, or figuring a place to try it.'

'Trying to make up his mind you mean?' Ryan said. 'There being two of us?'

'Yeh, that.' For a moment he kept silent. The thought which had occurred to him was plainly a stupidity, above all it was an unprofessional stupidity for which, later, he would probably call himself a lot of names. But there was an aspect of it which appealed to him, and it would be interesting to discover this African hunter's reactions. 'Of course there's one way to find out,' he said easily.

'Like imitating the buck back there?'

'No. Like us splitting up. Me going ahead, that ought to bring him out if he's there, that ought to solve his problem.'

'How far ahead?' Ryan said.

Ramirez thought. The dumbness of it came home to him now, the second thoughts. But he had committed himself, and if he backed down now it would have backfired. He would seem like the yellowbelly. 'Say a couple of hundred yards!'

Ryan sat where he was. He got his flask and took a drink, then lit a fresh cigarette. He said, 'Bear with me a minute, Cazador, I've got the cramps.'

While he massaged his calf he considered. This was a lot of silly, irresponsible crap. Kindergarten *'Cowardy, cowardly custard'* stuff, from way back when some other kid 'dared' you. It

214

wasn't how you hunted a *chui* who had taken to human flesh. It was how a bloody fool would try it. Gunga Din bravado stuff. And what he should have said was: 'Grow up, boy, we're supposed to be here for fun.'

But the nonsense needled him, touched a responsive chord of equally incondite recklessness. 'All right, go ahead! If either of us gets jumped I take it the other comes fast.'

'Faster than that,' Ramirez said. 'Start coming when I give you an owl hoot, that'll be when I'm far enough ahead.'

Ryan watched his form grow dimmer, and then disappear in the farther darkness of the *camino*. He laid the Mannlicher across his thighs, curled his finger round the triggger and waited.

When he heard the owl call he rose and clicked the catch of the rifle over to hair-trigger. From here on anything coming was going to get two h.v. softnose, the fast, shoot-first snapshot treatment.

He began to retrace the trail, straining his eyes, memorising the pace they had made before so as to keep the distance which Ramirez had said.

He had only gone a few paces when the cat sound broke the silence. It would be Juan, of course, and at the distance it was much less jarring but remarkably authentic. The perfect facsimile sound of a big hunting leopard. Too bloody perfect, it suddenly occurred to him. How, at this distance, *did* you tell it from the genuine article?

Another hour dragged silently by without incident. The *brocket* had not called again, and between the intervals of Ramirez's calling only the faint brushing sound of his own slow footfalls had been audible to him.

The gourd calls seemed to be getting more distant and, for some reason, coming at increasingly longer intervals, Even, it seemed to him, as much as fifteen minutes between, though it might have been less.

He quickened his pace a little for the next two hundred yards or so, then slackened down as he approached an elbow turn of the trail.

Around the bend he could see dimly for perhaps forty yards,

215

then for a similar distance before the semi-visible stretch ended in an overhung tunnel of black shadow.

He began to move through the heavy darkness of the passage, carrying the Luger again now, and conscious of the beating of his heart and the tightening of his sphincteral muscles.

Then, suddenly, he heard a sound and swung, but even as he wheeled he felt the grip on his arm and the hand over his mouth. Ramirez whispered urgently, *'Just beyond the curve ... edge of the track ... take him.'* He whispered again. *'About thirty yards, switch on when I tell you.'*

Ryan began to steal forward on the balls of his feet. As they came out of the thicker gloom he saw the bend and edged forward until he reached it, then halted.

For a minute, two minutes, both men stood quite still, listening, and there was nothing. Then he heard it, a sound he recognised, the crunching of bone. He inched forward until he knew he had cleared the bend and froze.

The feeding sound ceased, then began again. He concentrated, focusing on the intermissive crackling noise until he could dimly make out a vague form like a log on the track. He felt the squeeze on his arm but he didn't need a signal now. It was different, but the anticipative feeling was one he knew.

He sucked in a breath, pressed the button on his belt and swung the gun up. Red diamonds, glinting in the edge of the light, then, as he felt the wood against his cheek, he moved slightly and got the whole tableau in the beam.

For a fraction of an instant he felt surprise at the relative smallness of the quarry, no bigger than a hyena. Then, as the cat rose, ears stiffly pricked, jaws dripping, staring back into the light, he got the foresight on his chest and squeezed.

The stab of orange flame transpierced the white light and the staccato boom tore through the heavy silence of the forest.

The smitten creature sprang awrily, its death and pain scream almost impinging on the echoes of the gun. It fell on to its back in a half-somersault, then on to its side.

Instinctively, Ryan held the white prism on the scrabbling body, but he knew where the shell had gone and that no creature of this size, well hit, could take a softnose carrying the immense shockpower of the Mannlicher and come again. He let the gun droop in his hands while they waited for the convulsions of the yellowy form to slacken.

'Okay, Bwana,' Ramirez said shortly. 'You pinned him.'

In the light of their headlamps the sleek twitching feline body looked ambery coloured, almost as orange as the rump of an *acuri*, and the rosettes not so dark and defined as they would be in daylight.

Alongside the beast, the brown-skinned remains of a *laaba*, similar to an *acuri* but proportionately far larger than a hare is to a rabbit, lay spreadeagled in a mess of dark blood and blue-green entrails. Maybe forty pounds of solid meat, the *laaba*. An innocent of the forest. Torn, lacerated, part-eaten while still alive, it had won a measure of posthumous justice through the incidence of a relatively small, high velocity projectile.

Ryan moved the cat on to its back with his foot. Distastefully. 'Some bloody *tigré* that,' he said disparagingly. 'A bloody kitten, a *gatita*, what's the idea, Cazador?'

Ramirez looked up with a requiting expression. He was already squatted beside the ocelot now, preparing to slit away the suety semi-transparent membranous layer which divides the hide from the body.

'Where's the beef, Bwana? You thumped him good, and you got yourself a real good ocelot. About fifty bucks worth. You get some more like him and you've got a coat will have the women fighting to oblige you.'

Ryan watched him moving the knife carefully and deftly along the belly edges, easing out the guts and stomach bag intact, making a good job of it. He had a feeling of let-down and anticlimax, but after a moment or two he grinned and shrugged ruefully. 'Well, that takes care of the real business for tonight, anyway.'

'Don't worry about it,' Ramirez said. 'We'll get to him all right. Right now we got a *micho* here that's better than a poke in the eye.'

'A *microbio*, you mean,' Ryan said, but not too disgustedly because there was some satisfaction in the evidence that he was settling in, getting the hang of the light bogey.

217

When he had finished the skinning and rolled up the pelt the hunter stared up at the gaps in the treetops. 'Be coming up dawn soon.' The night was beginning to dissolve now and the heavy velvet overhead was gradually taking on the lighter shade of late twilight.

A while before they came to the place where they had left the Mayans Ryan smelled smoke, and when they crested a short incline of the *camino* he was surprised to see a fire going beneath the tree which the Indians had first blazed with the spear. Also, that three other young Mayans, and Almagro, had joined the two who had first led them out.

As yet there was still a dark content in the air, but the light eddying through the trees gaining strength perceptibly now. In an hour or two the dulled foliage would begin to sheen and eventually to shimmer in the heat again.

Coming nearer to the fire, the savoury smell of wood smoke and coffee, transcending the jungle odours of damp earth and fern, reminded both men that they had not eaten for long enough.

When Ramirez had spoken briefly with the Indians, they settled down to the food. It was more than welcome and they were on to their second mugs of coffee before the hunter spoke. He nodded to the Mayans squatting nearby. 'One of the boys will take you back to the house when you're ready, Mark. Do you want to go now, or do you fancy a doze first? No hurry, of course.'

'What do you mean, take *me* back?' Ryan said. 'Aren't you coming?'

'Not yet,' Ramirez put his palms on the grass and stretched out his legs. 'Got a job to do first, but you can go ahead and get some sleep, we'll be working again tonight, remember.'

'What's the job?' Ryan asked.

'Oh, just for our friends here. Meat! That's why they're here now. They're not all that steamed up about the cat or the killing yet . . . just another *accidente*, and they figure we'll get him sooner or later anyway . . . Meat's what they get really worked up about.'

'Any particular kind?'

218

Ramirez shook his head. 'No. Damn near any that comes. Of course what they really go mad for is bush cow, tapir. But they'll settle for *hass* or *peccary*, you bet ... what comes. ...'

'Well, tapir is on my list, mate,' Ryan said.

'Yes, but don't worry about that yet. We'll get *anta* all right, even if we have to use Indian dogs, this is just for what you might call the political handout stuff. The bonus.'

'I see,' Ryan said. 'Well how long were you thinking of?'

'Say till midday. Not after that, I'll tell you. No hogs or bush cows by then, they're going to have to eat corn and Mammee apples!'

'Okay then,' Ryan said, 'count me in too. Two guns better than one. Should speed it up.'

'We got two guns already now Almagro's here.' Ramirez nodded to where the younger hunter had leant a 30.06 Winchester against the bole of the tree. 'But you're welcome if you want to come along, only,' he grinned, 'there'll be a lot of walking to it. The Savannah ... end of this *camino* ... farther than we went last night.'

'Don't worry,' Ryan said. 'Not too old yet.'

He stretched out on his back and made an O with his lips, watching the wee puff of smoke make a ring before it slowly distintegrated on the turgid air. Above him a small maklala lizard was stalking yellow 'doctor' flies on one of the lower branches of a nearby nargusta. The tiny basilisk moved almost imperceptibly, just an inch or so at a time, towards the knot of flies feeding on a minute excresence of sap where a macaw had honed his bill. Then, suddenly, the lizard made a lightning dart, its tongue flicking.

That's how a *chui* comes, he thought. Slowly at first, bit by bit. Bunched. Then all at once like a yellow streak. Very fast indeed. But not fast enough, mate! Not fast enough to beat the tonnage of a seven millimetre moving a bloody sight faster, or the pulverising close range blast of a dose of buckshot in your evil yellow face, as the case may be.

Probably the greatest satisfaction of all, more than stopping a charging buff or elephant ... both of whom were noble beasts who only attacked in self-defence or desperation ... was

219

to hand out the big poetic surprise to the *chuis*, or any of their murdering villainous kin.

Come and get it you ignoble yellow-bellied bastards. See what it feels like! That's how he had always felt with all cats.

He wondered whether these overgrown *chuis*, the *tigrés*, would operate and react similarly. Come as soon as you overstepped the margin which, in their brains, precluded flight. And whether they telegraphed the last minute charge signal with their tails. Most probably they did. But, of course, the difference would be that with these, in the dark, you could forget about precision shooting. It had got to be snapshooting, the fast stuff. Get one into him pretty damned quick. Maybe it wouldn't kill, but with the power of the Manny behind it, anywhere in the neck, chest or shoulder it would stop him long enough for another, or two.

'I think I will take a nap, Juan,' he said. 'Let's give it an hour to settle the grub before we take off?'

'Sure thing, Mark,' Ramirez said. 'Suits me.' He stretched out himself and watched the red and yellow glint of the true dawn gradually lighting the gaps in the ceiling of the forest.

'What's for tonight, then?' Ryan said. 'We coming back here again, give it another try?' It was still early morning and they had been walking for about two hours, were nearing the end of the *camino* now.

'No, I don't think so,' the hunter said slowly. 'I been thinking about that. What we'll do is this. Almagro brought along a couple of fowl. We'll tie 'em out here tonight, but I'd like for you to try another beat. Then, tomorrow night, we'll be back here. The way I figure it if he takes the fowl ... no bother ... then it's a leadpipe cinch he'll be back the next night.'

'Intrigue him, you mean? Associate the place with easy pickings?'

'Yeh, it'll bring him on,' Ramirez nodded. 'Specially if he's a cautious old daddy like I'm damn sure he is. Specially if he heard some of the calling last night, but maybe missed us after I quit.'

220

It was still pleasant walking yet. Still fresh enough to enjoy a couple of cigarettes before the yellow heat reduced the taste of the tobacco to contaminated straw once more.

'All right, where's this new beat then?'

'The river,' Ramirez said. 'They tell me they keep hearing *tigré* along the river. It mightn't be our boy, of course, but what the hell, you wouldn't object if it was just a relative?'

'No. But there isn't a trail along the river, is there? Be bloody awkward going at night, wouldn't it?'

'The opposite,' Ramirez said. 'It's dude stuff, by dory. Canoe. Almagro is very good with the dory. With the gourd too.'

'Almagro?'

'The dorys only carry two men.'

'Wait a minute, let me get this straight,' Ryan frowned. 'Just where will you be then?'

Ramirez looked away. 'Well ... Parmeque, I got business there. But I'll be back by morning, don't worry.'

Ryan laughed sarcastically. 'So that's it, eh? I know your business, friend. I wouldn't blame you either, except you've got prior business right here.'

'Okay.' Ramirez shrugged. 'I'll stay if you want. But you'd be doing me a favour, Almagro too. And it won't make no difference, it's still the river either way.'

For a time they marched in silence, then Ryan turned his head. 'How good is Almagro? and no bull.'

'A hundred percent,' Ramirez said, 'and I don't mean fifty. You think I'd send him with you if he wasn't?'

'All right then,' Ryan said finally. 'But after this we stick to business?'

'Nothing else but,' Ramirez grinned. 'You got my word for that, and maybe I'll give you a discount on the bill.'

'Never mind the discount,' Ryan said. 'Just so we gather some of these wee *gatitas* of yours.'

Almagro and the others had left half an hour before them. They had gone ahead, fanning out, two to either side of the trail, against the chance of picking up fresh tapir sign. They saw them waiting now as they approached the end of the

221

camino.

After the semi-tone visibility of the jungle the hard bright light of the Savannah, undiminished by any pantheon of collective foliage, had all the contrast of high noon and twilight. Save that, perhaps half a mile out on their left, a dark promontory of jungle pushed out like a serpent's tongue, the plain looked wide open to the horizon. But it was quite different to veldt or prairie. Less uniform and much more varied by differing stabs of colour.

Predominantly, the brownish waist-high grass stretched out like an endless saffron seascape, but it was piebalded with meadows of armadillo grass and inset tracts of *akalche* and bogland. And further relieved by sporadic thickets of low brush which blazed like yellow gorse, and aloof islands of tall albescent pampas grass with silvery panicles that wavered in each breath of breeze like assegai blades.

'This is your big country, eh?' Ryan said. 'A pity your cats don't use it more, Juan, I like the light.'

'They do use it sometimes,' the hunter said. 'Remember I told you you get the odd one lying up. Mostly a real hungry one that's missed out on his hunting for a day or two, or one that's ranged out too far at night and is resting up ... they're lazy bastards. But it ain't really their kind of "country". They don't like the open light or the heat. Sometimes, too, there's the odd old slowing-up one figuring on jumping a hog or a fawn.'

'Or a tapir?'

Ramirez shook his head. 'Not often. They try it sometimes if they're real famished, but it takes a real big powerful cat, and at that there'd better not be any trees around.'

'You mean the little old "hippos" have a comeback?'

'Sure, if there's trees or water around. If there is, it's three to one the *anta* will make out. It works like this. The cat's got jaws like a vice and big incisors. He goes for the back of the neck, behind the ears, but he *has* to get through to the spinal chord. Well, the old *anta*'s hide is hell of a thickness, and tough as the sole of your boot, and even under that his spine is set deep in thick fat. And if it's not a big distance the *anta* can

222

carry the cat till he gets to a tree, because he's helluva strong in the legs.'

'Thumps the cat against the tree you mean?' Ryan asked.

'Damn right he does,' Ramirez said. 'Or if there's no tree he'll charge right into a thorn thicket ... the thorns don't bother *him* ... and the cat gets a face full, maybe gets blinded. Those bumb old bush cows ain't so dumb believe me.'

He shaded his eyes and looked out after Almagro and the Indians, beginning, now, to spread out ahead of them through the tall grass.

'I come up at the end of a contest once,' he continued. 'Collected a free *tigré* skin. The cat was upwards of two hundred pounds, but the *anta* was easy twice that, or more. He'd really flattened that *gatita*, must've bust every bone in his body.'

Ryan chuckled. 'Blessed are the meek vegetarians, and good for the little old "hippos".'

'Well, that's right enough,' Ramirez said. 'Bush cows will run from practically any damn thing ... peccaries, wild dogs. And the crazy thing is none of them could make any impression on his hide. They got teeth like razors, too. One gets surrounded and bayed he'll kill a dog with one bite.'

'I had 'em wrong I guess,' Ryan said thoughtfully. 'I thought of scaled down rhino at first, but it's hippo they take after. Hippo graze the edge of the bush, but they always stay in range of water, very good swimmers.'

'Yeh, well, that's like the *antas* all right. They can swim under water so long you'd think they'd drowned,' Ramirez agreed.

He nodded towards the area where a black-green tongue of the jungle jutted out into the *lavrado*, the Savannah. 'See that tree-line up there, sticking out like a long jetty? Well, back of that there's quite a lake. Never hunted it much but the boys claim it's good tapir "country". Probably is, it's got the feeding and the water they want.'

As they began to approach the tree belt an increasing number and variety of birds began to take off from the fringe trees and head back into the heavy timber of the jungle, the mingled cries of the sundry parrot and toucan species raising a squawking chorus.

Near the tip of the promontory it was no more than a hundred yards deep, and, threading through the trees, they seemed hardly to have entered the cavern of shadow before emerging again into the bright light.

The sudden panorama of the lake was almost startling. Even in a land where bright hues were commonplace, its concentration of primitive colours struck the sensibilities like a lurid canvas. Thick beds of brilliant purple, yellow and crimson heliconias, balisiers and wahas crowded almost to the water's edge. Between them, and dividing the colour belt from the big timber following the periphery of the lake, were green plots and aisles of short grass and *selaginella* moss that looked as if they had been mown or cropped.

Even the great trees, ceibas, mahoganies and hardwoods, draped with bright, green vines, surpassed their forest contemporaries and were dotted with a variety of orchids that stood out like freshly minted coins.

The lake itself, supporting tracts of water lilies like cream and yellow dinner plates, contained a host of water birds, rafts of common duck, muscovies, their black, white-faced *wasisi* relatives and various other kinds. According to bent, the place was a duck hunter's, or an ornithologist's paradise.

For a few minutes Ryan stood still, absorbing the vividness of it. He was a man who instinctively first thought in terms of likely game content, extent of cover, kind of going, when studying any new wild terrain. But he was not insensitive to the aesthetic aspects of scenery and grandeur, and the spectacle of the lake impressed him greatly.

He overtook Ramirez and nudged his arm. 'Phew! Some botanical garden eh? I wish I had a colour camera so they'd believe it.'

'Huh.' The hunter looked surprised until he followed the other man's sweeping gesture. 'Oh, yeh. It's a pretty place, I guess.'

He began to move along the bank, here and there pointing out spoor in the moss with the toe of his boot, cloven imprints, some as large as the span of a man's hand, and pugmarks.

'They were right enough, there's tapir here all right, plenty of other stuff too.'

He whistled to Almagro, farther long the bank, and gestured him to bring the others. When they came up he exchanged the shotgun for the Winchester which the younger hunter had brought from the Resthouse, and for a moment or two he spoke to the Indians in dialect.

As soon as he had finished, the five Mayans and Almagro started back the way they had come and then, when they were through the narrow tree belt, began to move out across the open plain, in diverging lines until the two groups of three were five or six hundred yards apart.

'They're going to make a drive, beat the plain towards us here at the lake, is that the plan?' Ryan said.

The hunter nodded. 'Yeh. We'd probably put up an *anta* working round the lake, but this near to the banks we'd have to be fast and lucky. He'd be into the water before you could really get a bead on him. Besides, at this time there ought to be some out grazing the *lavrado*, there's a herb in the grass they're always hunting for. Almagro will take them out a mile or so, then they'll make a bow and head back here. Try to head anything in the grass or the thickets this way.'

'I'm beginning to feel at home,' Ryan grinned. 'I like the sound of that, boy. But we're not in any hurry for a while this end, then?'

'No. But we'll move along nearer the end of the trees before we settle though, because anything making a beeline for water in more likely to come in that end.'

They began to move along the bank, taking it easily, every so often slashing with their caps at the small dancing fly clouds that rose from the grass.

In some places there were no reeds and you could look directly down into the water, which had a greenish tinge but was relatively clear in the strong light.

Ryan squatted on his heels for a moment at an edge of the bank that jutted out like an abutment. Thumb-sized beetles were crisscrossing each other's surface tracks in and out of a fringe of duckweed, and a water scorpion, front legs shaped

225

like the pincers of a crab, scurried across the surface for cover.

He was about to rise and move on when his eye caught a sinuous dark shape on the bottom. It was only a few feet out from the bank, resembling a five-foot length of ship's hawser in the form of an S, and there was no movement. He snapped his fingers to Ramirez, just ahead, and pointed to it. 'Hell's that, Juan? Pretty sizeable for a water snake, isn't it ... baby anaconda?'

Ramirez stooped and peered, then he looked around for a stone. 'Eel. Electric eel! Not much to the *fangosos* or *piranha*, not lethal, but you bump one when you're fording a river and you get a hell of a shock. Knocks some guys cold.' He tossed the rock in a lob and at once the snake-fish came to life, squirming away in a swirl of disturbed mud.

Ryan spat into the water after the creature. He pushed the peak of his cap up off his forehead and grimaced. 'Great bathing you've got in this country, boy, I can't wait for a swim!'

The other man laughed. 'Keep thinking about the shower back at the house.'

'What I'm thinking about just now,' Ryan said, 'is that when we get back to town we'll make a deal with the Army ... for a case of grenades! *Then* we'll stone the pools and the fords how it should be done.'

Ramirez chuckled again. 'You'd need depth charges for the *fangosos* at that!' He swabbed the back of his neck with a bandana the size of a napkin and jerked his head. 'Come on, let's get set up. Almagro will be a while yet, but we might get a crack at something meanwhile ... deer, peccaries.'

'Wait a minute. We do that we're going to spook any tapir?'

The hunter shrugged. 'Maybe. Depends. But it's your party, Bwana. You see something good you go ahead, it'll be some kind of meat for 'em, and we'll get *anta* for ourselves later this trip anyway.'

Towards the end of the narrow tree belt there was a stretch of bank that was wider than the rest and cut back into the trees in the shape of an ellipse for thirty yards or so. At the far end of it a fallen Mammee straddled the strand. Its topmost branches lay in the water, but its lower limbs and bole were

226

overgrown with a magenta creeper, making a natural barrier that you had to either climb or skirt around.

'Real cosy,' Ramirez said. 'You got a ready-made blind right there, Mark. Go get yourself set up, and I'll get dug in somewhere along this back end. That way we'll have crossfire for anything coming through the trees, and two chances for anything coming along the bank either way as well.'

'Okay,' Ryan said. 'But give me a sign when you're set, I don't want to thump you, or get one of those cigars you're using.'

For a moment or two he watched the hunter go. Quite a character, Juan, he thought idly. Probably a sight more accomplished than me, even if he couldn't write a thesis. (Although come to think of it if he ever wrote one on *la manigua*, the jungle, his practical knowledge ought to be more than compensate for any literary defects.)

Yet even his innate academic qualifications were not peanuts either. How many men knew the score in English, Spanish, Mayan and Carib? And, in a land of great poverty and less than little opportunity he had made it the really hard way. In fields that called for more than average guts and physical stamina as well as organising ability.

And above all he was the kind of man in whom, indefinably, you felt reliance. Which was quite a point. There were some celebrated professional African hunters he knew, with whom he had always had the feeling that in a tough situation you would be strictly on your own, notwithstanding the code!

He turned and walked over to the fallen Mammee. Before the wayward tailend whirlwind of a hurricane had uprooted it from an advance position in the jungle fringe it had been a tree in mid-growth. And he had no difficulty in finding a place, in the crook of a vast sundered branch, where, ducking under the creeper tangle, he could rest his rifle and elbows on the bole quite comfortably.

He took his knife and cleared a space in the vine foliage which gave him a pillbox view of the stretch of bank, then settled himself to wait.

He had a small sachet of dried fungus powder in his pocket

227

which Ramirez had given him and he cast a pinch of it into the air. He was not quite sure of the scenting powers of tapir ... though with those snouts they were likely acute ... but such air current as there was was coming across the lake.

After the strong light of the Savannah and the bank the dappled shade of the hide was quite pleasant, like sitting in the dimness of a theatre watching a wide stage that was bright with colour.

The air hung heavily, and the sounds of droning insects, the distant quack of a foraging drake and the occasional strident where-are-you call of a wayward parrot wanting return to his flock were the only noises etched on the general pattern of silence.

It would be quite a spell yet before Almagro and his beaters were likely to send anything this way, and for a second he toyed with the idea of a quick cigarette. But then he dismissed the thought and bent forward to lean his chin on his folded forearms.

He half-closed his eyes and let his mind ramble, lazily, over disconnected mental jottings and things a long way off ... Mark, Renate, *Green Acres*.... Then, suddenly, he realised that his torpid wandering gaze had registered something, passed over some movement down along the skirting of the jungle.

Or had it? It could have been a momentary interruption by a bird or lizard, or a light-pencil percolating through foliage disturbed by a breath of breeze.

But he had long since learned that often the only clue to a winged partridge in the grass, a wounded buffalo in ambush, was the merest flick of wing or ear. Like the single uncontrollable ear twitch of one deer when your glasses would otherwise have passed over a whole tawny 'parcel' of them, standing frozen still and perfectly camouflaged against the tawny background of the hillside, cannily waiting for the danger to pass.

He returned his gaze to the spot, screwing up his eyes in concentration, scanning the place bit by bit. And then suddenly he got it. A yellowy tail tip, etched against the matted green of vegetation, which sometimes gently twitched.

228

He brought the rifle along the trunk until the stock was under his chin. Very slowly, because the creature was in the same circumstance as himself, surveying the open ground, and fortuitously, must have arrived there a few minutes after himself.

Five minutes dragged by without incident. Probably Almagro's party had disturbed him on their way back through the trees, Ryan thought. Now he would be very much on the alert, aware of the proximity of men, and likely on his way around the lake to the far shore before lying up again.

Suddenly the tail tip disappeared and the cat padded stealthily out just a few steps into the open.

In the bright sunlight he was very handsome, as almost all the murdering felines are, Ryan thought, but he felt a throe of disappointment that it was not a *tigré*.

For a second, wondering whether a shot now might louse up the main chance of tapir, he hesitated. Just to speak or disclose himself would almost surely send the creature bounding back into the trees. But, of course, there was nothing certain about the prospect of bush cow, and the beast was still a cat.

He lowered his chin and squinted along the faint bluey gleam of the barrel. The cat had turned threequarters away from him now, but at this range of forty yards almost any-where would do for his size. Even straight up the anus which, considering the tearing excruciating pain the bastards meted out to fawns, mother creatures in the act of birth and a legion of other defenceless ones, he sometimes thought was the poetic way, appropriate retribution.

If you gave it them that way, as you sometimes did when there was no choice, they knew about it all right. Because usually, then, with a high velocity, the bullet travelled right up as far as the chest cavity. But, instinctively, even with these, he automatically inclined to the professional disposition. To the preference for a single precision shot.

He gave a low whistle and began to squeeze as the cat turned, stiff-necked and ears pricked to listen, as he had known it would. The timing was right and he came on to the place back of the shoulder just as he fired. The ocelot half sprang

229

into the air and fell on to its side with only the sound of a deep hissing of breath like air escaping from a punctured tyre as its forelegs pawed at the ground.

The fact that it had not screamed did not wholly surprise him because the reaction, though unusual, sometimes inexplicably occurred with various creatures, as if the vocal chords had been suddenly severed, though hitherto he had experienced it only with shots that broke the neck, whereas this one, he knew, had pulverised the heart.

There wasn't any point in moving, and he wasn't very interested in the dead cat stretched out there in the sun like a yellow labrador lying idling in front of his master's porch.

He ejected the spent shell and pushed another into the magazine to keep the gun fully charged, then he laid it horizontally between the bole of the tree and the hole he had made in the creeper foliage. The faint, pleasantly-acrid smell of cordite still hung around the proximity of his screen, taking time to melt into the laden atmosphere.

It could be, of course, that they would be cussing his guts. That the sound of the shot might have turned an *anta* they had put up. Depended on how the echo had disseminated through the trees and over the water.

It was a fact ... which perhaps might not have been mysterious to acoustic experts ... that if you, the shooter, were still unobserved, five times of ten, no, more often than that, an animal, or a group of animals—especially a group of animals —would completely misread the echoes, take-off right at you.

And hearing had nothing to do with it, because usually those with the keenest sense of hearing, like most of the deer species, always seemed most at sea.

Maybe it was why, hunting at night, all the big cats sounded off. Jaguar and leopard their throaty, sawing growl, lion their deep resounding grunts. Maybe the instinctive idea was to confuse the victims, make them unsure whether they were running away from disaster, or into it.

Certainly it *did* confuse them, because, at night, they only ever seemed to run a short way before halting and giving themselves away, or lapsing into fatal hesitation.

He was about to settle down with his chin on his forearm again, when he heard a crashing rushing sound which, ironically, he could not properly place himself, beyond that it was coming through the trees. There was no pretence of stealth about this oncomer, but in the seconds of his realising the location of the sounds the beast had already burst through the fringe scrub of the trees and out into the open back of him.

He tore at the mat of creeper behind him, but before he could get a rifle sight on the creature the tapir had crossed the strand and plunged into the water. A young one, maybe half-grown, or less, still marked with the white spots and flank stripes of a calf.

So luckily it hadn't mattered, because he wouldn't have fired anyway. In fact it was probably a good thing that the calf had seemingly been well ahead of Almagro's party, because three of the Mayans had bows. And if the youngster had broken cover near to them it was a cinch they would have tried it. Wounded him. Because their big arrows, the ones with which they tried for tapir, usually vainly, could have pierced the calf's immature hide, and they were tipped with poison, curare.

He lowered his rifle and watched the calf swimming across the lake. Only the ears and snout of the youngster showed above the water, just like a baby hippo. Then, suddenly, his smile faded and he stiffened.

A turmoil of water had risen at the *anta*'s side, and for an instant a glistening shape the thickness of a palm trunk cut the surface and seemed to ride over the calf's back. For a minute or so the green sheen of the water was lashed to foam. Then, just as abruptly, the heaving tableau sank from view, leaving a residue of spume and turbulence to resettle and dissolve as the anaconda dragged down its frantic, drowning prey.

Ryan swore vehemently beneath his breath.

Another disturbance came to his ears, abruptly dispersing his angry revulsive thoughts.

At first it seemed more distant than the swishing rending sounds of the calf's progress had been. But as it came nearer he got the same impression of some cumbersome creature blundering and bursting through the tangles of secondary growth between the dark columns of the trees.

Well, there wasn't going to be any slip-up this time.

He leant on the bole, listening. Tensed, but fully organised now. Professionally orientated. Catch set to hair-trigger, thumb stroking the wood in the personal mannerism which was his own habitual prelude to fast action.

He waited, becoming increasingly surer now of the approximate point at which the *anta* ... there was no doubt in his mind that it was another *anta* ... would burst through into the open any minute now. Then, just before he got the full picture of her sepia-grey bulk, the whipcrack of a rifle fractionally transcended the ripping sound of sundered brush and the heavy padding of thrashing ponderous feet.

He realised that Juan had got a view of her a second or so earlier, fired and hit ... there was no mistaking the familiar slapping thunk ... but he hadn't downed her. Nothing like it.

The big female tapir come on across the grassy open stretch in a trundling rush, and it raced through his mind that it was not, now, just a matter of collecting four hundred pounds or so of Indian food.

Even allowing that the *fangoso* was fully occupied with the calf, the bush cow wouldn't have a chance once the piranha and the caimen got the taint of her blood.

The old girl deserved a cleaner end than the shocking agony of piranha, or the slashing attacks of reptiles who would have given her passage had she not been hard smitten.

He had the foresight on her now, and then she made it easier for him, suddenly swerving as she neared the brink and raising her snout, as if, all at once, she realised that in her wounded state the water no longer offered traditional sanctuary but more danger.

Momentarily she halted.

About four feet at the shoulder, her trunk-like proboscis gave her an almost elephantine profile, but her deep rotund body and widely spatulated feet were nearer the shape of hippo.

232

Her thick heavy legs and her sides were coated with grey mud, as if she had been wallowing, but her back and neck looked almost nutty-brown in the sunlight. She half-wheeled, raised ears seeking the sounds of pursuit which had still not yet reached the man's ears, and he saw the crimson patch just forward of her shoulder from which the red rivulets ran.

She began to turn again towards the water, as if she still clung to the natural decision of her instinct, and at that instant of her hesitation Ryan fired.

The high velocity 7 z 57 took her in back of the shoulder joint just as she was about to plough forward into the water. She froze, and then began to rock, snorting, semi-anaesthetised by shock more than pain. She was not yet dead, nor down. In another moment she would have hit the water, carrying Ramirez's bullet, and swum until the devil fish or the reptiles had smelt her blood. But he had read the trembling sign of gathering paralysis too many times before not to know that, now, she would not take another step. Even so he moved the foresight, made it very precise, and gave her instant deliverance through the centre of the neck. The *anta* crumpled and went down, her forelegs collapsing first.

He laid the rifle against the tree and mopped his eyes and forehead clear of the sweat drops, then felt for a cigarette. Funny that, like the cat laying forty yards in the other direction, she had made comparatively little noise, he thought. Even hit with exact accuracy, in the ear place, *N'dofu*, whose trunk was as long as these tubby ones stood high, invariably let loose *his* final chilling scream. A buff's dying bellow, the clarion epitome of spent valour, carried out over a great area of veldt, and even a smitten *chui* habitually voiced his guttural scream of hate and defeat.

As he bent down, forcing out through the tangle of *pareira*, he heard the first echoing sounds of Almagro and the others, calling and beating towards the lake. He started towards the body of the tapir, then saw Ramirez emerge from the edge of the trees at the far end of the strip. He waited for him. As he came nearer, the hunter grinned, giving the thumbs up sign.

'Buena caza, Bwana! A good cat, too. You're really going to get that coat, eh?'

When they reached the stream ... they had left Almagro with the Indians, of whom one had gone ahead to fetch enough men from the village ... their shirts were sodden through and white-streaked with salt. It was something after three o'clock now and they had walked non-stop from the lake. But they would make the Resthouse in another hour or so and that would allow, Ryan told himself, a sleep of five hours.

By silent mutual consent they flopped down near the stream for a brief respite before the last stage of the denser jungle.

Ramirez settled his back against a tree. He felt in his pocket and brought out two globular fruits that looked like small nectarines. 'Wild melocotón.' He held one out.

Ryan smiled incredulously. 'Christ. Do you pull 'em out of the air or something?'

The hunter took a bite. 'Almagro. He knows I like 'em. Doesn't miss much, Almagro.'

The fruit was not fully ripe, but quite pleasant, with a peachy flavour. When he had eaten it, Ryan fished for his cigarettes, but he had finished them.

He caught the cheroot Ramirez threw, lit it and stretched out full length, pillowing his head on his clasped hands and peering down over the damp mat of his chest.

Your jungle is more complex than anything I've known before, Juan, he mused to himself. Including the Ituri. A greater variety of flora. Here, with yours, you kept hitting whole areas which were as different from each other in the general riot of growth as the segments of a kaleidoscope. It would be a hell of a place to lose your compass all right. A man could cut trail for a week, a month ... in circles!

Earlier, when they had first set out in the morning he had remembered how the Indians had checked direction, and, where there had been gaps, he himself had sometimes taken note of the topmost foliage of the big timber. By and large it showed a westerly consistency, like orchard trees inclining from a prevailing wind. That was one way you could take a

234

basic bearing, assuming that there really was a prevailing wind up top at several times of year. But there didn't seem to be another damned thing you could set your sights by if you were good and lost.

While he rested and smoked he cogitated about it. But it continued to defeat him, and when they got up to go he came out with it. 'By the way, there was time once when I got myself lost for a couple of days ... a place called the Bwangato "country" ... I was just thinking, you ever get lost in this? It wouldn't be difficult.'

'Well it happens, certainly,' Ramirez said. 'Twice with me, in the beginning. The second time I calmed down and used my head.'

'What happened the first time?'

'I was lost all right, for two days. It was when I was a kid, about twelve, hunting turkey. In the end the Indians found me ... trailed me ... Quetyl's tribe.'

'Scarifying?'

'Plenty. After that I leaned the business, you bet.'

'Carried a compass?'

Ramirez shook his head. 'No, you don't need a compass.' He made a short sweeping gesture. 'The *mattoral* isn't like the sea, more like a jigsaw puzzle. You get to understand the pieces and, then, there are half a dozen ways.'

'Like what?' Ryan asked.

'Well, one way is when you find a river or a stream,' the hunter said. He jerked his head back. 'Say like that one, but it doesn't matter if it's only a trickle, or which way it's running. From that you know the shortest direct line to the sea.'

'But that wouldn't be conclusive,' Ryan objected.

'It is when you fit it in, add it to some of the other things.'

He halted and stared up and around for a minute or two. They were passing through a kind of dell now, a semi-open place created by the downfall of a big mahogany. The clumps of tree fern which had benefited from the extra light and space occasioned by the fallen giant looked much the same. But, following the hunter's gaze, looking more closely, Ryan saw that they were not. Not quite.

235

Ramirez moved over to a particular cluster that was thicker and more robust looking than the majority, the rhizomed stems bearing fronds that reached maybe seven or eight feet in height. He took his knife and chose a central stem that was perhaps three inches in diameter near the base. The blade went through the plant easily enough, and then he cut through the stem again a bit lower. He held up the section . . . a piece some four or five inches long . . . and grinned. 'Jungle dead reckoning!'

Inside the green outer rind the substance was like pale yellow cheese, but following the periphery . . . marking the thickness of the rind . . . there was a distinct contortionate line like a marginal ring, as if you had drawn it with a pen and compass. The line almost completed the inner circumference, but not quite. At the penultimate point each end turned at right angles to the outer rind, so that the whole outline was like a frying pan with a handle about the thickness of a pencil.

Ramirez pointed to it. 'There. You cut through a stem and that neck, that handle, always points due north!' He held out the knife. 'Here, cut off two or three more and you'll see they're all the same, all pointing the same way.'

Ryan cut two more of the stems and verified it. He pushed back the peak of his cap and shook his head from side to side. 'Well, that's one for the book all right. Bloody odd.'

Ramirez shrugged. 'I don't know . . . plenty things more bloody odd. More bloody odder I think that the seals eat *medusas*, Portuguese men-of-war, the matopolo, the strangling fig, growing on top of another tree. . . .'

'Well, that's right, now that I come to think of it,' Ryan said. 'There are odder things. Best stew in the world is jackal, best *screw* in the world is a coal-brown Zulu . . . there's a couple of bloody oddities right enough . . . But the fern is more interesting.'

Ramirez laughed. 'Bring a couple of them Zulus with you next time. Now you got *me* interested.'

When they came, finally, through the last of the trees, there were several other Indians, older people, gathered around a

236

cooking fire in the compound.

Both men were tired now, hungrier than termites. As hungry as hunters. And the smell from the Indians' gourds of *pinole* porridge of maize and mesquit beans, and Manny's simmering posnet of cured *hass*, plus fresh fish, roasted, was really fine smelling.

Most of the Indians rose and two of them, older men, came forward to meet them. Typically, their faces were uncommunicative, gravely set, but their manner implied anticipation.

In a few brief sentences Ramirez told them that there was meat coming, for the whole village. Then he dismissed them to their porridge.

Manny had already despatched Tomãsco and now the big fellow came trotting back from the stream, with a fresh bottle of *Logans* and an armful of Carlsbergs. When he had put down the bottles, grinning, he went back to the bath-house and waited.

The beer was only just off tepid yet, but it was manna. Ryan stripped off his shirt and made for the bath-hut, carrying a bottle. Four times Tomãsco filled the *Heath Robinson* contraption for him, and by the third time of filling, even though the stream water was not much cooler than the beer, he was whistling.

When at last he came out he called to Ramirez, eating on the stoep. 'All yours, Cazador! You not going to swill the bugs off then?'

The hunter grinned back. 'Not here, Bwana. No time. I got a real tub and a bathmaid to fix my back in Parmeque, remember?'

'Fix you on your back you mean,' Ryan said. He laughed. 'Well, it's as good a way as any I suppose, depending on the lady's enthusiasm.'

Inside the house he took a little time looking out fresh pants, socks and a shirt, bundling up the dirty stuff for Manny to wash, drinking another properly adequate Scotch-and-chaser, and by the time he got to the food on the stoep Ramirez had disappeared.

But in a minute or two he heard the truck start up and the

237

hunter drove around the corner of the house.

He halted in front of the verandah and put his head out of the window. 'Well, buena caza for tonight, Bwana! ... and get yourself some sleep, it'll be a long night. I told Manny to call you at nine.'

Ryan stretched his legs luxuriously. 'Might alter that. Might just make it ten.'

'Well, suit yourself, but nine would be better. Like to see a good cat, or a couple more of the little 'uns when I get back.'

'We'll see,' Ryan said. He held up an egg on his fork. 'By the way, see if you can dig up a couple of hundred those cheroots of yours.'

After he had finished eating he settled himself in the battered reclining chair as Manny brought out a billycan of fresh coffee. It was the time, now, when the hard intractable heat was beginning to lose its edge, and before the frogs and the cicadas had started up. The exhaust note of the truck had faded away and, save for the occasional faint sounds of Manny moving inside the house, everything was very still and tranquil.

The first ocelot hide was tacked out on the wall along the end of the stoep. They had salted and powdered it, he saw, and it looked a pretty good skin. Larger, too, than he had supposed it would be now that it was spread out. It still didn't interest him greatly, but the cat had obviously been in prime condition, well nourished, and maybe it would be a bit of fun to collect enough of them for a coat at that.

For Renny ... or Consuela Ramirez if father really came through with the cats and the fishing! Or even 'Jane Russell'? No, for Renny of course. Be your age, Ryan!

Not that Consuela was not very interesting, and intriguing. Nor that 'Jane' was not something the Parisians wouldn't have raved about. They'd have raved all right! Jane Russell with just a touch of the old Josephine Baker-in-her-heyday! Consuela, too. Goya type, Consuela. In her case with a touch of that Italian wench, what was her name ... Cardinale or Martinelli ... or one of those.

But, come to think of it even if Renny hadn't taken priority,

238

an ocelot coat would hardly be a very appropriate gift for either of the others. In this climate. And especially not for Consuela, because she was likely to be bored stiff with the sight of spotted fur. Coals to Newcastle.

It would be nice to buy Consuela a dinner though.

He stopped wool-gathering and glanced at his watch. Then, reluctantly, he hauled himself upright and went inside for the more apposite relaxation of the camp bed.

9. COODOI

It was just after nine when Manny brought fresh coffee. He got off his cot and took his mug out on to the stoep, rubbing the sleep mucus from the corners of his eyes.

The Indians had gone, and in the pale light you could just make out the last lingering wisps of their fire across the compound. Almagro sat at the foot of the steps smoking a cigarette, the headlamps, the big gourd and a long single-barrelled shot-gun beside him.

'All set then, Almagro?' Ryan stretched and yawned.

'Si, Señor,' the slim man said. 'Whenever you are ready.' The night air was still heavy and torpid but he wore a cotton hip jacket over his singlet and it occurred to Ryan that later, down the river, he might need more than a shirt. He went back inside and found his spare bush jacket and the canvas shoulder holster for the Luger that had been an intelligent afterthought for the trip because, sitting in the dory, the pistol would otherwise have been awkward. He carried the stuff out on to the stoep with the Mannlicher and a box of ammo.

'Right then, Almagro.' He started for the steps, then checked and snapped his fingers. How thoughtless could you get? He moved to the door and called out. 'Nearly forgot the *importante*, Manny. *El vino del Scotland*. Don't ever let me forget that, compradre.'

When the sturdy man brought the whisky he filled his hip

flask, then took a good swig from the bottle. The cookboy watched him as if in mild remonstrance, and when he put down the bottle Ryan laughed and wagged a finger. 'Don't you worry about it, Manny.' He changed his tone to imitate Ramirez's voice and gesture. 'I'm telling you, man, we're gonna have *tigré* steak for breakfast. Couple of *jovencitos* like us, we don't need no boss hunter, eh, Almagro?'

Almagro smiled and the shorter man laughed. *Los Inglés!* And the *Americanos* also! Peculiar men. Some were poor hunters, or no hunters at all, but the good ones were pretty Goddam all right. *Sólido*, like El Cazador himself.

Ryan watched Almagro from the corner of his eye as they walked. He had good shoulders, and he moved well, lithely. And his permanent air of alertness, even about the camp, was intrinsic and unobtrusive. His nose was just a shade hooked maybe, but he was a good-looking fellow, in the Mexican style, and if his features were a bit thinly chiselled, his chin had a set to it. Not a rough-house fighting man, Ryan thought, but probably with the superior qualities of tenacity and lasting endurance.

It just remained to be seen whether Almagro had the quality which was indispensable to his business. The self-belief through which you controlled the fear. The trick of self-persuasion that, as distinct from the rule in most other professions, did *not* become easier through experience. The mental chore which you had to cope with every bloody time. Because the simple fact of it was that you could just as easily balls-it-up with your fiftieth bloody feline villain as your first, for all your superior primatial intelligence. Wind up with a stinking, scabrous, berserk, flea-ridden, bone-lazy, ignoble *ofensivo* on top of you ... and against whose tearing septic hooks you had only the defence of honest fighting ... not because your eyesight had defected, but the resolve part of your mechanism.

But, aside from his own instincts, one thing for sure was that Juan Ramirez was not a man to suffer bums or chancers. It was most unlikely that Almagro didn't have what it took.

When he saw the Indian *periagua*, the dory, he had some misgivings. It hardly looked adequate to take their human

240

weight of maybe four hundred pounds, aside from the clutter of equipment.

'Christ. Some battleship this, Almagro. You sure this little basket will stay afloat?'

'Si, si, Señor,' the younger man said seriously, nodding. He was not quite sure whether the *Inglés* was joking.

'Hm! You hunted much by dory before, Almagro?' Ryan asked.

For a second the olive-complexioned man considered. Ramirez had always impressed upon him the importance of being accurate in matters of description and detail. He held up both hands. 'Veinte. Veinte times!'

'Okay,' Ryan said. He jerked his head towards the intermittent beds of reed along the bank, some protruding twenty yards into the main flow. 'Just I don't fancy trying to outswim the caimen, particularly in that kind of stuff.' The younger hunter smiled his serene, guarded smile.

The place where the dory was beached was one of the many constrictions of the river. Here it was only about a hundred yards wide, but in just a short way downstream it had spread to a span of two hundred. Or perhaps more, because in the wan light of the half-moon the sheen on the water did not reach as far as the paludal fringe of reeds and mangroves which fronted the high black jungle walls on either side.

Almagro, in the stern, began to head them diagonally towards the left bank.

Ryan jerked his head. He spoke softly over his shoulder. 'That the side the cat took the child along?'

'Si,' Almagro said. 'The village is not far ahead, though one cannot see it from the water.'

'When are you going to call?'

'As soon as we are past the turbulence ... around the next bend. It is not formidable,' he added. 'But it would be better to hold with both hands.'

'The bank has become a regular beat with him, the cat we want, I mean?' Ryan asked.

'Yes. Since the child, his spoor is frequent, they say, but the river is always a good place for them. El Cazador does not

241

believe that this cat's "country" will extend far beyond the village, hence there may be the chance of others.'

They were through the bend and into the rapids almost before Ryan realised it, steering for one of the gaps between the straggle of big flat-topped rocks irregularly strewn across the river. The water was not really violent, but beyond the rocks there was a stretch of twenty yards which was sufficiently agitated to make spume . . . or to capsize a careless paddler.

He laid the gun in the prow and Almagro took them through the sluice between two of the great slabs and into the calm with a minimum of buffeting.

They seemed now to be coming into an area of marsh where small streams, some only a few yards wide, debouched from the mangroves into the river. Then, unexpectedly, Almagro turned the dory towards a larger tributary. It was about thirty yards wide and its mouth was completely draped with a screen of vines and lianas that trailed from the high archway of the big leaning trees to within a few feet of the water.

After the dull gleam and grey shadows of the open river, the tributary was pitch dark, like entering a cave. Just for a moment Almagro's lamp diffused the blackness, revealing the dense farrago of twisting, gesticulating mangrove roots which hedged the water on both sides, and they heard a muted sound of scurrying, followed by a succession of soft plops.

Sitting in the prow, Ryan got a fleeting glimpse of one of the creatures as it dived. It looked like an *acuri*, but it was twice the size of a jungle rabbit, more. Perhaps twenty pounds, with a white throat and white stripes along its flank.

'*Wapishana!*' Almagro said very softly. '*Tropa* of *wapishana*. This is a place for them . . . hence for the small cats and the *tigrés*.'

Now he laid his paddle down between his knees and reached behind him for the gourd.

The current was much slower than the river. Negligible. A few quiet paddle-thrusts kept you moving like a drifting log.

Ryan felt a touch on his shoulder. 'I call now, Señor,' Almagro said. 'If a cat comes I will tell you where I see him, like this.' He gripped Ryan's shoulder more firmly. 'Then use

242

the light.'

'You mean you can see, in *this* tunnel?'

'Not at first,' Almagro breathed. 'But if one answers we will hear, and when he comes we will find his eyes.'

In the confined area of the cavern only faint sporadic glimmers of moonlight from the scattered rents in the overhead mass of vegetation relieved the density of the gloom, and the sound from the gourd, amplified and echoed by the acoustics of the tunnel, seemed more penetrating than it had along the *caminos* of the forest. But Almagro had been well schooled and the cat sound was impressively authentic.

An hour passed in slow movement. Drifting, until the momentum from each brief thrust of careful insonant paddling had been expended, occasionally ducking festooning lianas and boughs that rode against the boat and rubbed their clothes. And in the intervals when the gourd was silent the quiet, save once in a while for the faint sound of an errant rodent seeking the sanctuary of the water, was contrastingly deep and pregnant with inner secrecy. Everywhere, the musty smell of rotting debris was so accentuated by the confinement that you could almost taste the stuff itself.

Manifestly, the tributary was primarily a preserve of the smaller amphibians and noctivagants. And except for the felines who hunted them, the larger game stuck to the less claustrophobic areas of the forest, for there were no sudden alarm calls of deer or peccary.

Another hour passed. Gently paddling, drifting, ducking, peering into a murk sometimes faintly illumined by a dull sheen of sieved moonlight.

Then, almost stealthily it seemed, the heavy blackness began gradually to lighten. They were nearing the end of the creek, for that is what it was, coming back out on to the river.

About ten minutes later they reached the lower mouth of the channel and Ryan felt the relief of coming out of one of those long railway tunnels when you were always waiting for the collision with an oncoming train that never happened.

A short distance ahead, he could just make out the dark bulk of a fallen tree which lay in the water at a tangent from the

243

mouth, like a flying buttress bridging the gap between the bank and an outcrop of big rocks.

'Get her over there,' Ryan said. 'Lay up for a while.'

When they were lying gently against the rocks he lit a cigarette without consulting Almagro, and then felt for his flask. He was not critical, or dispirited, but right now he didn't much care what Almagro thought, or didn't, or about the rules. Even the treated tobacco seemed tolerable . . . out in the open, after that Godawful foetid tunnel, which had produced bloody nothing!

He took another good swig and held the flask over his shoulder, but Almagro declined, and a moment or two later he caught a tiny squelch and a wisp of coffee odour from Ramirez's battered thermos.

In the tunnel they had repeatedly run into clouds of mosquitoes and *cobarras* at times, and even the copious smearings of repellent he had given himself had not been a hundred percent effective. But here, near midstream, it was pleasantly free.

When he was part way through the cigarette he half-turned around. 'We going back up river now? Try the main banks?'

'If you wish it, Señor, but I think we should return the way we have come.'

It was on the tip of his tongue to tell Almagro to forget it. That hereafter they would try for cats the less obnoxious ways. Then he remembered that they were both so-to-speak on their mettle to come up with some results that had not been set-up by Juan. And, too, that some success was probably more earnestly desired, more important to Almagro, the novitiate professional, than to himself.

He scratched an irritant spot on his neck. 'What about the paddling? Going back is going to take more, and if we do spring a cat it's going to have to be very quick stuff, no option.' He tried not to sound too malcontented.

'Of course, Señor,' the slim man said earnestly. 'There will be no difficulty. I will make the paddling and the calling as before.'

'All right,' Ryan said. 'All right. We'll do it the bloody hard

244

way again . . . this time, anyway.'

As far as the channel entrance he shared the paddling, then he took up the Mannlicher and left it to Almagro to keep them moving.

About every ten minutes or so, once they were well into the tunnel again, Almagro shipped his paddle and called with the gourd. But less stridently than formerly. Just enough, now, to be picked up by tufted ears which might have heard the earlier calling and were now more closely situated. Then, suddenly, just as he was about to call again, he stiffened and leaned forward.

'*Tigré!*' He mouthed it. Very quietly, though his instinct was to shout it in self-justification.

Ryan sat motionless, moving his thumb against the wood. He was conscious of the massive silence of the jungle around and over him, but he heard nothing. After a minute or two more he leaned backwards, twisting his neck and shaking his head, but Almagro nodded insistently. He waited another two minutes. Then he caught a faint rustling, somewhere out on the right bank.

Almagro inched the boat towards the other side. He let it move gradually back, feeling the mangroves from root to root, until the stern edged into the soft sucking embrace of a reed bed. He took up the gourd again and barely drew the thongs, emitting a sound that was little more than a throaty murmur this time. Like the vocal evidence offered by a cat who was young and unsure of himself.

Nothing. Then both men heard it. A rustling that was much nearer and more definitive.

Ryan peered towards it, straining his eyes against the blackness of the jungle wall, conscious of the hair pricklings and the constriction in his chest. Still there was nothing above the almost inaudible squelching of the boat against the mud.

Then, suddenly, he felt Almagro's hand on his shoulder. 'There!' He followed the direction of the other man's arm, switched on his lamp and brought up the gun. Still there was nothing, then, moving the beam along the bank edge he passed through a red phosphorescent gleam of eyes and brought it

245

back.

The big cat's head and shoulders protruded through the mangroves, looking down into the water as if he were about to dive. He straightened up and stared into the light, but even as his lips drew back to voice his snarl of warning and uncertainty Ryan found the white foresight and his finger closed on the hairtrigger.

The cat reared high, his scream cutting through the booming echo of the gun, then he came down again on his forepaws and turned. Ryan tore back the bolt and rammed it home again in a movement. Get him! It went through his mind that sometimes *these* cats, wounded, would attack a boat. *Get him!*

He flung up the gun again, firing on the instant of overlap and this time Almagro heard the heavy thunk of smitten flesh merged with the crash and flame of the rifle.

Both headlamps were focused now, and for a second or two they sat motionless, watching the threshing, heaving shape half-hidden in the mangroves, until the movements began to slacken.

Ryan released a breath. He wiped the sweat drops from his mouth and brow with the back of his hand, feeling the grin coming. 'Well, for Christ's sake, we got him, boy ... without the boss hunter.' He chuckled. 'Looked like a pretty good cat from here, too?'

'Yes, a good one, Señor,' Almagro said quickly. 'But is not *tigré ... leon ...* puma!'

He pushed the dory free and began to paddle towards the place. When they were near enough he grabbed some roots and hauled himself out, then roped the stern stanchion while Ryan clawed his way on to the bank.

In the light of the torches it was hard to decide the creature's real colour. But certainly it was no *tigré*. Longer legged, red-tawny, more slender, not the wide squat breadth of chest. The differences were much the same as between a cheetah and a leopard, except that this one had no rosettes, no markings to speak of.

On the other hand it was no kitten, or else it was a hell of a big kitten. Say one-seventy-one-eighty pounds and about eight

246

feet nose to bulbous tip.

'Goddamitall,' Ryan said. 'Wouldn't you know? What our Montana friends also call a "lion". Some bloody lion! Overgrown weasel'd be more like it!'

Almagro looked up from his knees in some perplexity. 'But, Señor ... look at his size. Vasto, truly an *ejamplar*! The best *leon* I have seen.'

Ryan took a hold of the puma's ear. He pulled up the head and pushed back the lips to see the long yellowy fangs, then he bent down and pulled the body out straight, trampling back the crackling mangroves and the shrubs. He was a good puma, all right. But who the bloody hell was interested in pumas, 'mountain lions', bullshit like that? The most cowardly of all the cowardly felines. Sheep killers, for Christ's sake, who couldn't face up to a half-decent dog never mind a man-ape.

'You think he's worth skinning, then?' he said doubtfully.

'But of course, Señor,' Almagro said emphatically. 'We get a fine skin from him. *Excelente*.'

Ryan rubbed his shin. He *was* a big one all right. Certainly bigger than most African leopards, even the odd exceptional tom. He began to feel somewhat mollified. It was a different kind of pelt, anyway. Most probably Mark would like to have it.

Almagro returned and with the machete began to clear a small area of bank to work in. When he had done, Ryan holding the lamp, he started in with the knife, making the long belly slit and easing out the stomach bag, heart, entrails, buff and liver. He slid the pile of offal into the water and turned the carcase upright to drain out the blood, then began to free the pelt.

For a few moments Ryan watched the young hunter work, then he remembered that there should still be a drink in the flask he had left under his clobber and he threaded back to the boat. He got the flask and started back through the mangroves. Almagro had worked three parts along the carcase now and one of his feet was puddling the mud of the bank edge.

Ryan took a good swallow and pocketed the flask. He was just about to feel for a cigarette when his lamp picked up the

247

small ripple on the black surface of the water. It looked like a drifting twig, vee-shaped, but then it suddenly occurred to him that it was moving laterally across the channel, not along it. The phenomenon was within two yards of the bank when the realisation hit him and in the same instant he whipped the pistol from his armpit and shouted. '*Move.*'

He fired as the thick stubby forelegs lifted the long black lunging snout out of the water and Almagro flung himself forward across the body of the cat. Then again as the great jaws whipcracked together, and twice more, from his hands and knees, aiming more deliberately, as the caiman slid back into the water and began to lash about.

'*Bastard, you bastard!*' He found himself almost yelling it as he turned towards where Almagro sprawled, watching.

'Hail Maria!' the young man said, as if to himself. He was quite self-possessed still, but his mouth was tightly drawn.

'Yes, a close one.'

'It was the blood and entrails, of course,' Almagro said. 'I should have remembered it would bring them.'

'Happens all the time with the bastards,' Ryan said. 'The African ones snatch washerwomen and children all the time.' He held out the flask. 'Here, take a swig of vino Inglés, boy.'

'No, Gracias, Señor. I will finish off the skin and we will go home.'

Ryan shook the flask. 'Aaah. Come on, drink it.' It was practically an order. 'And take your time. We're in no hurry now. There'll be some more along, I daresay ... get some more practice soon.' He grinned and thrust the flask into Almagro's hand.

He turned his lamp on to the water. It looked as if he had hit every time, because the big shot-up saurian was on his side now, and even as he watched the reptile began to turn on to its back, the lighter colour of its belly shining wetly in the head-lamp. He fetched the rifle from the dory, replaced the two rounds he had used on the puma, and settled himself in a comfortable position. Without realising it, he grinned, venge-fully. *Come ahead you bastards, the food is all free!*

He had half-finished a cigarette when the first interruption came. One moment there was nothing, then, suddenly, some-where about where the caiman had sunk from view, the water was boiling with turbulent ripples. *Piranha*.

For about five minutes it continued, while the school re-duced the reptile to a shell of hide and jawbones. Then the violent agitation began to slacken and the water gradually re-verted to calm.

Almagro stood upright. He had the pelt scraped down and bundled now. 'Ready now, Señor?'

'No, not yet,' Ryan said. 'Give it a while for the big thugs now the fish have cleared.'

Just a short spell afterwards they saw the kind of gentle bow wave they were waiting for. He took all the time he needed, beaded the eye nobs and mashed the caiman's brains. In the next fifteen minutes he got two more before the hell fish caught the fresh blood scentings and the turmoil of churned water began again.

When he woke and went out on to the stoep in his plimsolls and pyjama pants it was going ten o'clock, but although the heat was well risen, it had been raining just previously and despite some sluggish puffs of warm breeze from the jungle it was a little more tolerable than usual.

Directly overhead a group of dark thunderclouds rode slowly across the blue backcloth, undoubtedly a presage of hurricane or at least fierce rains to come, but from its direction it looked as if the ultimate tempest was destined for farther inland.

Manny came out on to the verandah with tea and a can of water and when he was through shaving Ryan went over to the 'sentry box' shower by the stream. There still seemed to be nobody else about, but by the time he had started in on the eggs and fried liver of tapir, Almagro came around the side of the house.

He smiled and nodded, but at the same time he had a cer-tain air of awkwardness about him that was uncharacteristic.

Ryan grinned back. 'Well, Cazador de *leon*,' he stressed the *leon*. 'Qué para, what goes, as they say?'

249

The slim man smiled again and murmured something inaudibly. He looked away for a moment then back again, seeming to brace himself. When it came he spoke quickly. 'Señor, I would be pleased if you would accept this small gift!' He held it out, a hunting knife complete with sheath, pretty new.

Ryan stared back in surprise. He took the knife and turned it over in his hands. It was an excellent Sheffield make, hardly used. Probably the best, or one of the best of the young hunter's personal chattels, he thought. 'What's all this about, compradre?' he said with a look of surprise.

Almagro clenched his hands at his sides. It was not only that he had little experience of such a situation. There was also the thought that a rich man, as this *patrono* surely was, might laugh at the triviality of it, and he had considered the matter with some misgivings before making up his mind.

'Señor, you saved my career,' he said finally.

Ryan crinkled his brows. Then he understood, and for an instant he almost laughed, but the expression on the younger man's face made him check, avoid any appearance of flippancy. Instead he gave a little shrug of implied disagreement. 'If you mean what I think you do, Almagro, it was nothing at all. Anybody would have thumped that bastard. What else? *Qué te importa!*'

The brown man shook his head. 'No, Señor. To me of the greatest importance. Had the beast taken my leg, even my foot, then I would have been finished.' He spread his hands in a small emphatic gesture.

Ryan frowned. 'Hm!' He held up the knife to the light and made a show of inspecting it again, reading aloud the maker's name. 'Well...' He put it down beside his plate. 'That's a *bloody* fine knife, boy!' He looked up, smiling. 'In fact that's my knife from here on ... compradre!'

Almagro smiled and turned to go, but Ryan said: 'Hey, wait a minute. More to it than that isn't there? Sit down and have some coffee.'

'Señor?'

'Sit down, I tell you,' Ryan insisted. He turned his head and shouted to Manny in the house to bring some more coffee. He

250

said. 'All right, let's say I did you a favour, then ... but you did me one, too.' He forked a chunk of liver and chewed for a moment. 'Pretty good *leon*, eh?'

'Yes, sir, Señor,' Almagro said seriously. 'I think so.'

'I think so also,' Ryan said. He finished another mouthful, kidney and egg this time. 'But I want to tell you something, Almagro. I shall keep this knife, with remembrance, providing you also accept a small gift from me, to commemorate the *leon*.'

He got up and went into the house. When he returned he held out a folded twenty-five dollar bill. 'I know it's not the same, boy, but, you understand, I've only the guns right now.'

Almagro rose. His face showed perplexity and he shifted his stance. 'Señor. It is too much!'

'Nonsense,' Ryan said. 'For a puma like that? For an *ejemplar*?' He waved it aside. 'Besides, a custom ... Inglés ... called fair-do's.'

They heard a whistle and saw Ramirez coming across the compound from where the truck had drawn up. He had a carton under his arm and when he came up on to the stoep he put the package of cheroots on the table. 'Well, Cazador, no sign of our special friend?' Then he saw the puma skin. 'Well, that's quite a *leon* you got yourselves anyway.'

'Naturally,' Ryan said. 'Almagro and I, we're only interested in *ejemplars*, we don't bother with the ordinary stuff, that's for the bums ... the bar-hunters!'

Ramirez bent down, grinning. 'Well, he's a sure enough *ejemplar* all right. Say eight feet, maybe around one-seventy, one-eighty pounds?' He glanced enquiringly at Almagro and the younger man nodded. He turned and shouted, 'Tomãsco. Come here and spread this cat skin.'

The big boy was nowhere in sight but in a minute or two he came out from somewhere around back of the house. He came up the steps and bent over the freshly treated pelt on the boards.

In the hard daylight the colour was very tawny. Redder than a real lion, though similar, in a way, Ryan thought. Which could be the reason for the gross misnomer, *leon*. In the sense

251

that, if you disregarded the distinctive black line down the tail to the tip of the bulb there was the same dirty-yellow under-belly, dirty-yellow inner-sides of all four quarters, throat and under lip. Not to mention his recollection of the cat in death.

Chop some inches off his legs and he would have come nearer to the shape of a maneless *simba* than *chui* did!

An Indian came loping across the compound from the direction of the stream. He looked like one of the two Mayans who had first led them, but it was impossible to tell from his blank expression whether he brought good or bad tidings.

He halted at the foot of the steps and began to address Ramirez. When he had finished, the hunter nodded shortly and replied briefly in the dialect. He turned and began to pour himself some coffee. 'Well, Bwana, keep your fingers crossed, we might hit it tonight. The cat took the fowl again. They're going to tie out two more tonight.'

'Let's not count our chickens yet,' Ryan said cautiously. 'Could be any damn thing. Could be one of those, couldn't it?' he nodded towards the puma skin. 'Or ocelot, or dogs? Or any damn thing?'

'It could be, but it ain't,' Ramirez said conclusively. 'It was our boy all right. By now they know his prints better than their own.'

They entered the jungle soon after dark, roughly following the same line as before, and except that he sometimes stopped briefly to check the ceiling, Ramirez's unhesitating progress was uncanny. At the same time they went more slowly than when the two Indians had led them, moving at half-pace through the pools of heavier darkness and carefully skirting the drooping finery of the palmetto and tree fern groves.

When they came finally to the place where the cat had finished with the Mayan maid it was still only shortly after eight o'clock. As they had approached the tree the pair of fowl had set up a squawking flapping chorus, but soon after they had settled down to occasional barely audible cluckings of enquiry.

Ryan moved back into the shadow of the big tree which still held the Mayan spear, and watched Ramirez unsling the gourd

252

and adjust the sling of his big single-barrel.

'We going to stick around here this time?' he said quietly.

'For a while anyway.'

'Well, no bullshitting around ... wandering off...' He tapped the pistol on his hip. 'You don't know how close you came to it last time.'

The hunter's teeth showed dimly in the gloom. 'Don't worry, I'll be right here. He'll come to us this time.'

'Are you going to call from here then?'

'In a minute.'

'The fowl will sound off, of course,' Ryan said.

'Sure. All the better.' Ramirez grinned again. 'He'll come all the quicker if he figures some other cat has found his little ... er...'

'Sinecure?' Ryan offered.

'Yeh, that.'

He moved out past the tied fowls to the edge of the *camino* and peered both ways for a moment before returning to the tree. 'This is a good place all right,' he said softly. 'It runs straight both ways for forty-five yards. When I figure he's close enough, we move out to the fringe ... I don't want him too close all at once.' He gave a little nudge with his elbow, and again his teeth showed in the darkness. 'We're going to hit it, Bwana,' he whispered. 'I got the feeling.'

As soon as he began with the gourd the birds set up a raucous burthen of alarm clucking, flapping their wings in ineffectual attempts to free themselves from the bough. But after a time, accustomd as they were to two-legged primates, it seemed to enter their birdbrains that the gutteral threat sound was coming from the man and they became semi-assured, reverting to sporadic throaty chucklings.

Three or four times more in the next hour Ramirez called, and after each sounding they concentrated but there was no answering sound. Ryan watched the tethered fowl on their compulsory perch. Lucky birds, you pair, he thought. Well, maybe you will be.

A slight fitful breeze had sprung up overhead. It came and went at short intervals, producing a faint soughing in the tree

253

tops which was like the far distant murmuring of surf.

Ramirez moved forward again and called from the edge of the track. As the low, harsh resonance tailed away, the wan glimmering light in the camino began to fade. The cloudbank pared, then obliterated the thin rays of the moon crescent, and in the moment of complete darkness both men heard the sound.

Ramirez stiffened abruptly. For a moment more he remained still, listening, then he moved quietly back against the tree.

'You heard him?' Ryan nodded.

'Not far. Maybe five-ten minutes,' the hunter whispered.

He moved the short distance to the birds. The lighter shade of their plumage was just discernible in the gloom. He grasped the staked branch and shook it lightly until both fowls had set up their alarm chorus.

Ryan felt a little tug on his arm and they began to edge forward, moving on the balls of their feet. At the fringe of the heavy shadow they paused, waiting for it.

The sound came again. It was not vociferous, but laden with arrogance and menace, a proclamation of omnipotence, and this time he would have put it at no more than a hundred yards along the track.

Ramirez pointed to the ground and breathed in his ear. 'Take him from here, I shall be opposite.' He bent low and crossed the track.

Ryan edged farther outwards until he was standing in the shadow of the camino wall, but clear of foliage. He was conscious of the coldness of the barrel held across his chest, the chilled sweat on his face and neck. With his free hand he felt for the switch of the headlamp, straining his eyes along the deer-path. It was desperately vague, but, increasingly, he picked up the impression of a blurred something that was darker than the grey-black of the camino, moving towards him.

For another half-second he waited and the blur became more positive, more picturised. He moved the stock higher against his chest and switched on the light. The beam

254

ploughed short, then lifted and picked up the full reflection of red diamonds but, incredibly, fractionally, there seemed to be no outlined form against the blackness of the background.

A feeling almost of bewilderment raced through him, then he heard the drawn snarl and the light gathered the gleam of fangs conjoined with eyes. He got the white bead under the suspended triangle of red circles and white teeth, held, and squeezed off.

Strangely, he was fully conscious of the crash, and even the flame tongue over and above the yellowly light. The blurred shape along the track seemed to lurch backwards, its maddened roar following the echo of the gun, but even as he worked the bolt it bunched and came, revealed.

In the fraction of time left, he fired again, a snapshot flyer at the bulk streaking towards him. He barely noticed the tearing rip across his braced, lowered shoulders but he staggered from the impact. He wheeled, tearing the Luger from his belt, shouting: '*Shoot. GIVE IT THE BASTARD!*'

Dimly he heard Ramirez's shout, but his gaze still held the threshing form a few yards farther along the track and he levelled the pistol as the other man grabbed his wrist. 'No. Leave him ... *leave him* ... you got him, man, *you got him*!'

He shook off the hand and rounded on him, his face livid with rage. 'Fug you, Ramirez!' He almost shouted it. 'You did fugging nothing, worse than nothing. Why didn't you give it him when he came? *That was your job!*'

'I would have,' Ramirez said urgently. 'But it wasn't necessary. If he'd come again, I would have, but I knew you'd *got him*, man. I heard it, both times.' The animation in his voice grew less, changed to a note of gratification. 'And you know what you got, man? A *coodoi*. A *coodoi din*, for Christ's sake! Man, you got the luck all right.'

He made to approach the prone, spasmodically jerking body on the grass, but Ryan swung him round.

'*Luck!*' The seeming utter irresponsibility of it almost made him choke. He hit the swarthier man a heavy slap across the face with the back of his hand. '*Luck* ... you bloody birdbrain! Where I come from *you'd* be bloody shot for that kind

255

of luck. Your job was to throw the nails into him when he came. You call yourself a professional, you're a fugging amateur, Ramirez, a fugging amateur! I ought to slap you down.'

Ramirez stood still, hands hanging at his sides. His expression slowly changed and he let the gun fall. 'Any time. You can try it any time ... Professional!' he said curtly.

'Don't push *your* luck,' Ryan said mordantly. 'Just don't push it another inch. Just go do your job for a change,' he groped for the right insult word, '*aficionada!*' He turned his back, breathing heavily, and felt for his flask.

Ramirez did not reply. But as he went towards the tree for the knives, the feelings of anger and mortification in him made him turn. He said, 'Christ, you're a professional. You ought to know then. These things happen, don't they? We ain't playing softball, are we? I lost him. I got the lamp off him and I couldn't pick him up quick enough again. All right! Maybe for that I had the slap coming. But we're still here, ain't we? And we'd still be here if he'd come again.'

'No thanks to you, *tonto*,' Ryan said. 'No bloody thanks to you!' He lit a cheroot and took a good drag, waving the other man away. He was still breathing deeply, but gradually, after another drink, he began to feel calmer.

He watched the hunter working, on his knees. The rage was still simmering in him, but what Ramirez had said had some substance in it. In this business you had to accept that the beasts had a say in it, that once in a while the technique got fouled-up through no lack of proper application. And by now he had begun to develop more interest in this *coodoi*, so called.

He moved slowly over to where Ramirez was gralloching the beast.

The big *tigré* had bitten through one of his own paws in his final bewildered frenzy, a phenomenon which he had seen before with leopard and lion. He had two tomato holes in the chest, one off centre ... and he was entirely black!

Ramirez glanced up shortly. 'Some *coodoi*, eh? Some *coodoi din*! Look at that skin, black as night.'

There was no animation or concession in his voice, but it

256

was obviously an approach, an attempt towards restoration of the relationship.

'I'm looking,' Ryan said shortly, sardonically. 'And the hell with *his* bloody skin anyway, get to mine . . . *bush doctor*!' He pulled off his shirt and turned his back.

Ramirez glanced up in surprise. For a moment he stared, then he stuck his knife in the ground and went over to the tree. In a minute he was back with the bottle.

The main scrape was about ten inches long, running from the hump of his shoulder across the blade of it. There were two more superficial scratches either side of it, but all were relatively surface gashes.

The alcohol burned and needled deeply. Ryan flexed his shoulders against the stinging. 'It doesn't feel like much?' he said shortly. 'But give it plenty anyway, all these bastarding cats are walking septicaemia. . . .'

'Don't tell me,' Ramirez said. 'I thought he went right over you but he must've got you with a hind hook.' When he had done copiously swabbing the scratches he cut strips of medicated plaster. 'I'm real sorry about that, Bwana,' he said awkwardly. 'I didn't know . . . it's all right, though.'

'Aaah. Forget it,' Ryan said. 'As you said, it happens; just it really gets you het up.' He felt for his flask and held it out. 'Take a dram. Go on!' He picked up his shirt. It was still better than nothing and he buttoned it on, then went for his bush jacket from the stuff beside the tree. He got a fresh cheroot lit and returned to where Ramirez was finishing with the big cat.

Up until now, in his angry agitation, he had virtually ignored the creature. Ramirez pulled open the wide, heavy jaws for him to see. One of the big incisors was blunted, broken off at the tip, and some of the back teeth, the bone-crushers, were ground to stumps. But, by Christ, he was a hell of a big cat, and his fur shone like black velvet!

In strong light you would be able to see the shadows of the rosettes beneath the coat, similar to a leopard's, except for the central black spot. But right now he was glossy black as anthracite.

257

'Well, that's one bastard won't bother your friends any more,' Ryan said.

Ramirez nodded. 'Yeh. This *ilegítimo*'s an old bastard all right! Funny thing though, he ain't all that old. I'd say between middle and old, and he'd et well enough. Maybe too well, lost the speed for deer, slowing down to hogs and humans.'

'He came fast enough for me,' Ryan said, with a remaining suggestion of acrimony. 'He covered the ground all right!'

'Yeh, but it was him being a *din*, back as tar, a *coodoi din*. He'd been an ordinary one you'd have seen him plain, got him the first time. Anyway,' he lifted one of the powerful bowed forelegs, strong enough to twist and break a bullock's neck, then let it fall, 'you sure got yourself a *tigré*.' He cocked his head to one side. 'Say nine feet end to end, say rising two-fifty pounds. That's not a bad *tigré*.'

BOOK THREE

10. S.S. *BONITO*

They had hunted the country within radious of the Rest-house for two-three weeks now. Ten nights along the caminos, alternating with days on the open savannah, and others of just idling and fishing for lukanani and tarpon. (One time 'howk-ing' lousy piranha, six or a dozen at a time, because you didn't need hooks or tackle for them. Just a hunk of bloody meat and yank them when they took.)

The nights had produced two *tigrés* and four ocelots. The days a wide variety of game. Tapir, peccary, brocket, savan-nah deer. . . .

In the village they had a lot of smoked meat cached now, and not even the oldest women, who were older than the oldest men, had ever had so much protein before.

The toothless ones stewed the meat till it was tender as pap, but they also supped all the blood they wanted. The blood seemed to be what their glands most craved, and responded to, Ryan thought; whether the medical pedants applauded or otherwise.

The days on the savannah had been interesting. But the sun had been bloody punitive. His tan matched Ramirez's now. Slumped there in the old cane chair on the stoep, he could have been a Mexican. Or a Honduran. Despite the automatic-ally augmented daily intake of liquid, lime juice more than hard stuff, he must have shed the best part of a stone now, he thought, and when he was moving he felt faster and more poised.

High overhead a bank of thundercloud rode across the sun, temporarily dimming the brazen noon glare, taking the sheen off the puddles remaining from the morning downpour. Directly above the house a heavy clap shattered the somnolent calm and was almost immediately followed by a more distant rumble. The rain came soon after. Suddenly, as it always did,

260

in a furious downpour of drops the size of tit's eggs.

He shifted in his chair, squinting through the wet haze which already almost obscured the rainbow forming over the jungle roof.

'Christ, they don't know anything about rain in Manchester, or Greenock, this is the real monsoon stuff,' he said.

Ramirez smiled. 'Yeh, it looks like the beginning of the big Wet all right, but don't worry, it won't bother us for a week or two, takes time to move north. That's why we come south first.'

Ryan listened to the rustling sound of the beaten foliage from the periphery of the jungle and the dull machine-gunning on the roof of the house. He reached for the whisky and raised an eyebrow. When the other man nodded he poured out a couple of half mugs again, and got two more beers.

'Up north, the Corozoale country, it'll still be dry for quite a while yet,' Ramirez offered.

'Tell me about that country again?' Ryan said.

'Same as here, only better, and without the rain. Plus a couple of other things.'

'Like what?'

'Like more cats, plus buffalo, plus *marudis*, turkey. . . .'

'You're just thinking about your belly,' Ryan said.

'I bet you ten bucks you'll eat the *marudis*,' Ramirez said. 'They're real bonus eating, but like I said cats and buffalo, too. 'Teco buffalo at that . . . which makes 'em all the better.'

'Being strictly illegal?'

'That's right. But don't worry, we'll find you plenty of action this side of the borner. Almagro knows it well, and there's the old man, El Viejo, knows every cat patch, every damned camino in the territory.'

'You hunting the other side is grudge stuff, or, put it another way, some kind of point of honour?' Ryan posed.

'Well kind of, sometimes,' the swarthier man said. He twitched his shoulders. 'Anyway I never been up there yet without I took a couple of cats and a bunch of *marudis* off the 'tecos . . . specially when I didn't need 'em.'

'It sounds like the good old free enterprise principle of

261

taking out ivory and rhino horn regardless,' Ryan said. 'They still do it, of course ... but they really throw the book at them.'

'Yeh.' Ramirez seemed reluctant to talk about it.

'Yeh, what?'

'Yeh, they'd throw me the book.'

'Listen,' Ryan said. 'The way I picked it up, your friends over there might really enjoy that, might throw you a sight more than the book, like a few rounds of hardnose?'

Ramirez smiled. 'You got it right there.'

'Well, why d'you do it, then? Where's the percentage?'

'In handing it back,' Ramirez said. 'In kicking their fat asses.' He drew in a mouthful and blew out a puff. 'Look! The 'tecos were skinning the Corozoale for thirty-forty years, maybe longer. Specially the Cruz bunch, this Cruz and the one before him. They got *everything*. Everything Viejo, the old man, got, everything the Indians got ... for *nothing*! The bastards didn't pay them a twentieth, didn't pay them peanuts. ...'

Ryan shrugged. 'Even between the Wars the African *smouses* were getting ivory and horn for a handful of salt, leopard pelts for a foot of bright wire. ... What they call trading in a buyer's market, bloody murder, but it's legal.'

'Okay, okay,' Ramirez said. 'The old man and the Indians didn't know any better, but that wasn't the half of it.' He took a short swig and studied his mug. 'They'd been getting all that stuff, all that time, nobody interfering. Then the old man got torn up by a cat. Pretty bad. Couldn't operate any more, at least not the only way he knew. The 'tecos brushed him off, wouldn't even stake him a bag of meal. They still got the Indians' stuff, but the old man nearly went, of starvation.'

'Square-shooters,' Ryan said. 'The really altruist kind. But you said *got*, they don't get the merchandise any more?'

It gave the Honduran a grin of pleasure. 'Better than that. I've had my own *perreira*, Mayans and Caribs, in *their* "countries" for long enough. And El Viejo's doing better than before.'

'He recovered?'

262

'Yes. Rest and some real food ... tough as *cordel*, the old one.' The recollection seemed to give him more pleasure. 'I reckon I saved his bacon, then,' he grinned, 'and I cooked theirs. The first thing, I taught the old man the *trampas*, the big gins, so that it didn't matter so much about his bad arm, his shooting arm. Then, over time, making trips with some of Quetyl's people, I got a grupo of their Indians organised. The old man is still the best, but the 'teco Indians bring a fair cache across ... everybody does better, except the 'tecos.'

'It sounds like fair-enough business,' Ryan said. 'Except that sooner or later they're going to take a couple of shots at you, I'd say.'

Ramirez smiled. 'They have. Twice.'

'Obviously they missed?'

'Not the first time. The first time they got one of us, one of Quetyl's people. We got him out and across but he didn't make it.'

'What happened the second time?'

'The second time they didn't get us by surprise,' the hunter said laconically. 'We had scouts overlooking the valley. The *ladinos* got all the surprise.'

'How did you make out?'

'They don't like being on the other end,' Ramirez said. 'They made a strategic withdrawal ... that's what you call it, ain't it? ... Later I heard there'd been a funeral in El Pazo.' He flicked the butt of his cheroot over the rail. 'A couple of Cruz's *vaqueros* got hit by Bushmasters, something like that.'

'Serious stuff,' Ryan said, 'and more to it than merchandise, I think? Viva Independencia! Isn't that really what it's all about?'

Ramirez looked up without replying; he gave an affirmative nod. 'Sure.' After a moment or two he said. 'Well, do we pull out in the morning then? Suit you?'

'Suits me,' Ryan said. 'Yes, let's get. I suppose we have to go back to town first?' he added.

Ramirez nodded. 'Only one road north, we don't run to helicopters yet. But if you'd like a change we could dory down river to Punta Quela?'

263

'What's at Punta Quela?'

'The *Bonito*, the fruit boat. Runs twice a week down the coast, it'll be there Sunday, day after tomorrow.'

'Well, that sounds okay,' Ryan said. 'You mean just the two of us?'

'Yes. The boys can take the truck back to town ... all the heavy stuff ... We can make the coast about Saturday night-Sunday morning.'

That night the wind came through the compound in gusts of gale force, reaching a crescendo about midnight, and the beating of the rain on the roof was like hail, more sustained than formerly.

In the morning the area around the house was littered with fronds and foliage. But the air was fresher than it had ever been before, as if the storm had revitalised it, and down by the river the intricate vegetational web along the banks had been transformed into a glistening wash of browns, greens and yellows.

The going was easy, and in the lead canoe the two white men maintained a comfortable pace that, without pushing it, steadily ate up the miles. Twenty yards back the two Mayans trailed the baggage dory behind their own.

Even when the yellow tyrant had fully risen, permanently maintaining a dancing haze band across the surface of the water a hundred or so yards ahead, it was still relatively pleasant. For by now Ryan had become accustomed to the set of the dory, which somehow seemed easier to handle in daylight. And, by contrast with the confinement and obscurity of the dense jungle, on the river there was a great deal to be seen.

The variety of bird life, particularly, was impressively diverse. Quail and snipe hunted the bank edges, duck of varying sizes ... including a species of muscovy as large as the domestic breed ... abounded in the reed beds and inlets. From time to time, rounding a bend, they would put up rafts of *wasisi* fowl. Black duck about the size of pintails, with white throats and cheeks, and chestnut breasts, that took off in flocks so packed as to momentarily diffuse the glare of the sun.

264

It was about six o'clock of the following morning when they began to near the end of the jungle, and when, rounding the last bend before the river mouth, they saw the lighthouse out across the Bay, Ramirez steered for the bank. They left the Indians then, and took a short-cut across a tract of sand and scrub towards the harbour.

As they got nearer the ground rose steadily and, cresting the rise, they saw the *Bonito* alongside the wooden jetty that ran out from the white sand.

She was a fairly shallow draught one-funnel coastal boat which had obviously taken a good beating over her time and was in some need of repainting, but she still looked solid. Clyde-built.

The jetty was right at this near end of the harbour front, and there must have been some reason for its seemingly eccentric positioning because the long white warehouse of the fruit company was two-three hundred yards down along the other end.

Back of the warehouse façade there was a juxtapositioned sequence of parallel corrugated-iron roofs that looked like elongated Nissen huts. And between the fruit company and the jetty there were maybe a dozen one-storey small-time enterprises. Little one-man tobacco warehouses, chandlers, junk stores, a pawnshop. Shacks. In varying stages of bleached disrepair. Two of the proprietors were slumped against their doorjambs like cud-chewing oxen leaning their weights against a tree.

At varying intervals along the wharf, fronting the row of mercantile ordnances, irregularly spaced palms and flamboyan trees made isolated puddles of beckoning refuge and, sometimes, a prop for a citizen who was either sleeping it off, or just browsing over humanity's idiocies.

Behind the harbour's maritime boundary the squat tin pyramid of a church reached above the low roofs like a stubby renegueing finger. Like an admonition against Christ knew what. Or against everything.

Aside from the straggle of trees and the stark whiteness of the big warehouse only two other splashes of colour lent any

265

variety to the ashen-grey aspect of the harbour's face.

Along about half way one place, painted pastel blue, stood out like a budgerigar in a row of sparrows.

There was a bench seat in front of it and a parasol umbrella-table with two or three chairs, and just opposite half a dozen skiffs and two or three piraguas gently rode the water. The boats' sails, emblems of lasting poverty, were faded and patched, except for one whose bright crimson canvas looked brand new and, thereby, disproportionately resplendent.

Hardly anybody moved about the wharf itself, but, contrastingly, the fore and aft decks of the *Bonito* were already peopled with patient, expectant passengers.

Their complexions ranged from coal black to cinnamon, and, inevitably, there were many examples of features ... captivating outcome of their polygenetic origins ... which were, so-to-speak, fundamentally out of character. Stalwart negroids of both sexes with the faces of Mediterranean whites, fragile saffron men of originally Asian descent with negroid casts of features....

Some of them had impressively beautiful eyes for all their passivity and expressionlessness, and the same look of enduring bovine resignation. They were all perfectly aware that the boat would not leave till noon, but there was always the disturbing thought in their minds that, just this one time, it might sail ahead of schedule. (In which remote contingency few would have expected any explanation, and fewer still presumed to seek one.)

Outside of such 'risk', too, there was also the consideration of winning yourself a place where you could rest your back and maybe later, when night fell, even stretch out full-length.

It was coming ten o'clock now, into the period when even walking called for conscious effort. In the humid heat, the sweat patches on shirts and blouses spread surreptitiously, and some sought vainly to revivify themselves with woven fans like fly-swatters.

'I want to make a call on the fruit company manager,' Ramirez said as they approached the wharf. 'Just a bit of business.' He flipped a hand. 'Ten minutes ... you're welcome to

266

come along if you want?'

'No, that's all right, you go ahead,' Ryan nodded. 'I'll just take a look around.'

'Have a drink at the *Quita Penas*,' Ramirez suggested. 'Or you could try a plate of the rissoles. Pretty good.'

'That the blue place?'

'Yes.'

'I might do that,' Ryan said, 'otherwise I'll see you back here.' For a moment he watched the hunter go, then he turned and squinted out over the bay. Except for the white fringe of whispering surf along the beaches either side of the wharf the sea was smooth as a pond, matching the colour of the bistro.

He began to stroll along the extent of the wharf. Across from the fruit warehouses there were three iron bollards, strong enough to take the hawsers of a steamer. But they were all encrusted and rusted-up as if they hadn't been used in a long time, and the awry remains of the jetty jutted from the water.

It was near to high tide now, but the water lapping around the derelict jetty looked only deep enough for skiffs and light craft. Evidently the bottom sand piled up hereabouts and probably it hadn't been worth the cost and labour of periodic dredging.

You could have fried eggs or tortillas on the board front, and even walking took some effort, but the mushroom tops of the bollards were too hot to sit on.

The other side of the street, next to the blue, 'Sorrows Away' bistro, an old man sat on a low stool mending a net.

He wore a tattered straw hat and rolled-up jeans, and his bare torso and shanks were the colour of malt vinegar. In the open-fronted shed behind him there were aluminium floats on piles of netting and coils of *cordel*.

Farther along from the chandlers there was a hardware store, a shop offering bright coloured Lancashire shoddy cloth and cheap Birmingham jewellery, and then a funeral parlour. The funeral parlour had plain deal coffins at eight Honduras dollars, which you could paint yourself, or de luxe caskets, ready stained and with brass ornaments, at twelve-fifty. The

267

doors of the fancy shop and the hardware store were open, but all the other places seemed to be locked up.

The wharf ended at the Bank, a square two-storey concrete building with latticed windows above the small general office where the manager had his quarters. It stood on the corner of a street at right angles to the front, which looked as if it eventually petered out in the jungle hinterland of scrub and sand dunes, and didn't seem worth investigating.

He went back along the front and halted at the parasol table. Some Punta Quela boulevard café! But the table and chairs were clean polished, and there was the sound of a fan from the dark interior.

After the glare outside he had to take off his Polaroids and stand for a moment, but when his eyes were readjusted he saw that everything was just as clean and spick inside.

There was only one other customer. An old man, smoking a stubby pipe, who sat on a bench under the open shutters, a small glass of some colourless drink in his dry brown hand. He could have been the twin brother of the chandler next door, and he doffed his head slightly in a way which probably derived, way back, from Spanish or Portuguese courtesy.

Ryan unslung his rifle and stacked it carefully like he always did. He was always careful with his guns. Some fellows slung 'em about anyhow . . . and then wondered why, with a 'scope or a foresight that had been thumped on a rock or fallen on the floor, they were firing a mile out. You looked after a good gun and it looked after you.

From back of the bar counter the *proprietario* watched him with interest and, when he turned and straightened up, flashed him a friendly smile.

He was a very pleasant looking man, who could have passed for Spanish or Cuban, in a brown snap-brim straw fedora and a white singlet, and he looked as clean as anything in the place.

'Is not a stick-up, Señor?'

It was just a bit of bonhomie, not wiseguy stuff, in keeping with his air of good humour.

Ryan smiled back. 'Not unless you've got *vino Inglés* hid-

268

den up?' he said in English.

On the shelves there were tequila and mescal, dark and clear rum and cola and orange.

The patron smiled again. He slid a hatch in the wall behind him and called out in Spanish. 'Lirio, Liriosita ... a special customer. That you bring the cognac *Inglés*, the three-sided bottle.'

In a minute or two a woman's face appeared at the trap. She had about the same colouring as the man and her expression was animated with curiosity.

The brown man put the bottle on the counter with an air of pride.

'Señor, the whisky!' It was a quart of *Standfast*, half full.

'Well done,' Ryan said. 'And some beer?'

'Of course.'

'Have a shot yourself, landlord,' Ryan said. 'And my friend the net maker here, or whatever it is he takes, since he is also a fine-looking man.'

'*Gracias, Señor, gracias*. Though he is not the net maker, the net maker his brother. He is the ... ah ... mortician.'

'Ah, so.' Ryan said. 'Well that's a hell of a trade all right, but he's still a fine looking man.'

The bartender grinned and called across to the old man in the indigenous Spanish.

'The Cazador here has it in his head to buy you liquor, Francisco. Do not ask me why, except that he says you have a good face, and that he is clearly an *Inglés* or *Americano*. You can have the best, he will not mind.'

'He is *Inglés*, then,' the old man said. 'For they are more perceptive, and he has a good face himself.' The depth of his voice belied his age and his delivery was like a peasant of the Algarve. He made a gesture with his pipe. 'Say that I will accept, Arturo ... and do not cheat on the price.'

'That is not of your business,' Arturo said grinning. 'What price did *you* charge for the *ladróns*? Double for foreigners, you said.'

'For foreign *robbers*, I said,' the old man sharply corrected. 'Besides, an *Inglés* is not a foreigner, in that sense. An ally.'

269

Arturo shrugged. 'We do not know that he *is Inglés*, but, all right, I will add merely ten cents.'

'I wish I could speak good Spanish,' Ryan said in good Spanish, making it deadpan. 'But the *Inglés* are very bad at languages.'

For a second there was silence. Then the old man chuckled. '*Qué tal*, Arturo?'

The younger man drew his hand down his face, covering his grin. 'Your pardon, Señor.'

Ryan waved it aside. 'Aaah. *Qué te importa?* Let us have another drink, *muchachas*, and a dish of the *rissoles*, eh?' They grinned at each other, mutually enjoying the foolery of the language joke.

The drinks were pretty tepid, of course, but what the hell. They took the straw taste out of your mouth, and when the rissoles came they were really good, much better than tortillas. Made you realise you hadn't really eaten since dawn.

He finished off a third of the meatballs and wiped his mouth. 'That of the *ladróns*,' he asked casually. 'You had blackwater in the jail here or something?'

'No, Señor,' Arturo said. 'Not like that. A hold-up, a week ago! Four men try to hold up the pay office. There was one in the boat got away, they got one in the jail still and,' he nodded towards the old man, 'Francisco, he get the two stiffs. Foreigners, 'tecos.' He looked over his glass. 'You know about 'tecos, Señor?'

'Sure,' Ryan said. 'Viva Independencia!'

'Yes, sir, like that.'

Ryan looked at his watch. He finished his beer and put a red bill on the bar. 'That your flag shall always fly, amigos,' he said with a smile.

'*Eterno*,' Arthuro said soberly.

The old man got to his feet. He held out his palm. '*Permiso*, Señor. Another drink before you leave, a grace?'

For a moment Ryan hesitated. But only a louse could have refused the old man's gesture. He dipped his head. 'Ah, well, *Gracias* . . . a beer then, if you please.'

'Indeed.' Arturo was not to be outdone. 'With the house,

270

Señor.'

'Cojones to the house,' the old man said sharply. 'The Cazador is my guest. *I* pay!'

Arturo raised his hand in denial, but then, as if resignedly, he let it fall and winked at Ryan. 'Ah, well, why not ... Capitalist. All that extra money of the *ladróns*.' He grinned at Ryan. 'They had enough money for their own caskets anyway. Amusing, eh?'

'What you might call unintended tourist trade,' Ryan smiled. He downed the fresh beer in a swig and nodded to each as he went out.

He saw Ramirez coming towards him when he was half way back along the wharf. 'Business go off all right?'

The hunter grinned. 'You might say I won a couple of hundred. Might even stake you to a ball when we get back.'

'It must have been a pretty fast game?'

'Yeh. Crisp.'

'Like cops-and-robbers?' he said intuitively.

For a moment Ramirez frowned, then he grinned. 'You tell fortunes, too, Bwana?'

Ryan chuckled disavowingly. 'Not even with tea leaves, must be pure telepathy, plus maybe the association of ideas, as they call it.' He jerked his head. 'The boys in the bistro have just been telling me about the hold-up fracas they had here recently. Seems some of your friends from across the border really walked into it.'

Ramirez smiled mordantly. 'Yeh, well it had to be the Company or the Bank. They had an extra guard in each ... guys who could handle a sub ... waiting ... and they don't get but two strange launches in here in a year.' He spat the butt of his cheroot on to the sandy dirt.

'But *you* knew when it was going to happen?' Ryan said. 'I have that feeling.'

The hunter smiled. 'Give or take a week! Let's say I kind of forecasted it.' He turned his head abruptly, the satisfaction and the amusement gone for a moment. 'You think I should've let those *facciosos* heist *us*, maybe knock off some of our people too?'

271

'Christ, don't get me wrong,' Ryan said. 'I'm only sorry they didn't get the boat as well.'

Ramirez's expression slowly relaxed and he grinned with real amusement. 'You want to know something—they did! When he could see they'd fouled it up the one in the boat took off, ditched 'em ... beached the boat about forty miles up the coast.'

'Good stuff,' Ryan said, then added: 'How about the one in the boat though. Do you reckon he could make it across country?'

Ramirez considered. 'Hell, he'd have a gun, maybe some money ... a down-payment for handling the boat ... he could've. I could've.' He grinned. 'I dare say you could've.'

At the jetty there was still a straggle of passengers going aboard, and on the decks it was getting so that people had to weave and sidle to move around.

'It looks like Saturday night at the Palais now all right,' Ryan said. 'There wouldn't be any cabins, of course?'

'Four, with double bunks.'

'But all booked a month ago, of course?'

'Don't worry about that. Every time I get down here it turns out they had me booked two months back.'

Ryan grinned. 'Don't tell me, just let me guess. The Captain's father-in-law of yours?'

'It'd make it cheaper, right enough,' Ramirez said. 'Got no daughters, though.'

When they saw the two men coming along the jetty, carrying rifles, an increasing murmur arose among the passengers, and more of them began to crowd over to the gangplank side. The taller hunter in the peaked Safari cap and dark glasses had them puzzled, looked alien. But as they came nearer there were some shouts of recognition for the more indigenous-looking man beside him.

Nodding here and there, Ramirez pushed his way through the curious grinning throng towards the bridge. Above him, at the head of the stairs, the Captain stared down at the passengers with an expression that seemed to combine tolerance and resignation. When he lifted his cap to scratch his head and wave Ramirez ahead, the combination of his shining brown pate and grizzled ear tufts invested his broad black face with a kind of serene Pickwickian aspect.

As they came up the ladder he accompanied his smile of welcome with a spanking prolonged fart that was not so much in contempt of general etiquette as because ... save in the presence of his Owners and the fruit company manager ... he had long since given up trying to control a weakness that took him frequently, and always when he laughed. Primarily the affliction derived from a daily diet of vast quantities of tortillas, split-peas and beans that his ageing sphincteral muscles could no longer reliably contain. And he had elected to retain his diet, without hesitation.

In the wheelhouse, after some mutual clapping of shoulders and a further brace of tearing explosions from the Captain, Ramirez made the introductions. Meanwhile the Skipper's wife, a hefty duenna of similar ebony complexion, sat smoking a cigar on the padded seat bisected by the wheel and compass box. She was obviously inured to, if any longer mindful of her husband's punctuative lapses for she gave no sign of embarrassment.

By the time they had taken a round of bacardi-and-limes the temperature in the wheelhouse was fully a hundred degrees, despite the fact that all three windows of the forward side were wound down.

The air, more than usually oppressively cloying, was laden with the threat of storm, and twice there had been heavy rumbles overhead. They were almost at the scheduled time of departure now, and already the penultimate siren blast had been given.

From the bench along the starboard side of the wheelhouse Ryan stretched his legs luxuriously and, now and then, took a sip of maize coffee with his rum. After the drinks and the introductions he had left it to Ramirez to make the social chitchat with the Captain and his wife.

As he gazed out over the jetty there was another rumble, followed by a sudden waft of torpid breeze which stirred the fronds of the palms and flamboyans, producing a sound like the whispering swish of maraccas that was audible above the voices of the passengers.

Now the first random taps began to patter on the wheelhouse roof. Minutes later a cloud shivered and burst, and then the big rain pellets began to hammer down in furiously rising tempo.

As many of the passengers as could pushed and jostled into the small Saloon-cum-Eats-Bar amidships. Others sought any kind of cover they could find. Only three, Mayans, two men and a woman, passively seated against a bulwark, made no effort to seek shelter, merely pulling their blankets over their heads.

The Captain put down his drink and crossed to the wheel. He peered out at the gathering rain curtains, then at the clock above his head, and reached for the siren cord. As if conjured by the final blast, three latecomers, two men and a woman, appeared suddenly from the misting background at the far end of the jetty. The men sprinted ahead, shoulders hunched against the driving rain, the woman following twenty yards behind them.

She had a straw suitcase in one hand and a bundled coat was gathered under her other arm as if she had just left a car and had had no time to put it on. As she hurried forward her breasts moved effusively with the effort, and once, catching her heel against a loose-ended board she almost fell. The rain was streaming down her face and neck, over the redness of her mouth and on to the sodden skin of her dress, which was the same pale yellow colour of her headscarf. When she got to the head of the gangplank she glanced up for a second, panting.

Ryan started, then sat upright. He swung off the seat and ran down the stairs, crossing the deck between the groups huddled under sacks, purloined tarpaulins and other improvised shelters to where she stood indecisively staring about her.

A look of surprise and recognition lit her streaming face and she started to speak, but he brushed it aside. 'Come on!' He took her bag and grabbed her wrist, pulling her after him to

274

the companion ladder. At the head he pushed her up ahead of him into the Wheelhouse and closed the door.

Standing there, her expression a mixture of embarrassment and relief, the thin clinging skin of her dress emphasising every contour and undulation of her body, she was more starkly drawn than if she had been nude. Smooth boneless shoulders that had the satiny gloss of butter, the pouting nipples of big rising breasts chilled and thrusting through the soaking she had taken. A midriff which, expediently, just sufficiently concealed any ghastly angularity of rib bones, and the roundness of heavy thighs burgeoning from long shapely legs!

Her legs were longer than he had realised, and she seemed taller, too, than he had remembered. Maybe five feet nine, or more. Paradoxically, even while he was 'rescuing' her, a jumble of incipient thoughts were running through his mind.

What a Rubens! Except that Rubens had always made them too short, whereas she had the extra height which gave her proportion as well as substance.

He smiled at her reassuringly and made an all-round gesture of introduction. 'Old friend of mine from town ... Miss Russell.'

From the port-side benchseat Ramirez smiled back and nodded. 'Oh, we all know Ida, and her brother. Didn't know you'd changed your name though, Ida?'

'By Deed Poll,' Ryan said. 'I arranged it myself.'

The tall girl smiled nervously. 'Mr Ramirez!!!' She glanced at the Captain and began to edge towards the door. 'Well, thank you, I'll just go and find ...'

Ryan headed her off. 'What? You can't go out there in that.' He glanced across at Ramirez.

'Of course not,' Ramirez said. He winked at the Captain. 'Plenty of room for an old friend of Mr Ryan's, if the Captain don't mind?'

'Kose he don't,' the older women said conclusively before her husband could answer. 'He right pleased to have yo with us, missy.' She patted the seat beside her. 'Yo go dry yo face and hair in de cubicle, honey, nen come and set right here.' She pointed to a narrow door in the corner.

275

'You're all very kind,' the young women said, 'thank you.'

When she had closed the door behind her, Ryan touched the Captain's arm. 'Wouldn't by chance have any cabin accommodation left for the lady, Skipper?' He ignored Ramirez's grin. 'Say about fifty dollars worth, over and above?'

The veteran shifted his cap and scratched the whitish tuft beside his ear but, again, his wife cut in before he could reply. 'Sho' he has, Suh! Kin sleep right here hisself, prob'ly would anyway. He right glad do you frien' a kin'ness, ain't yo, Sam?'

'Well,' he gave a glimpse of teeth that still looked good save for one frontal gap. 'Ah guess it'll be all right ef'n she bunks with yo, Effy? Ain't nowhere else anyway.' Abruptly, as if to stress the shifting of responsibility, he let go with a short ripping burst.

'Kose it'll be all right,' the bulky woman said. She smiled widely. 'What's mo', ah won't have put up with yo stinkin' out de cabin!' She heaved herself upright as the door to the cubicle opened. 'Got yo all fixed, honey. Yo gonna share de Captain's cabin with me. Now yo jus' come right along an' we get you all dried out. Ah reckon we do that fust eh, nen we come back here have some coffee.'

Ida glanced back and forth uncertainly. Freed of the headscarf and loosened, her hair gave her a new and unsuspected appearance that reminded Ryan of a wayback schoolboy crush he had had for Linda Darnell.

She smiled uncertainly. 'Well really ... Ma'am ... Captain. You're very kind but the fact is I don't have a cabin ticket. ...'

'You do now, Ida,' Ramirez said. He waved his cheroot towards Ryan. 'Be surprised the pull these *Inglés* got.'

When the two women had gone, hurrying down the ladder, Ryan got the money from his hip. Every bulky, obtrusive thing counted when you were really hunting, and sooner or later, you always wanted to throw away even the things you *had* to carry. Right now he had about a hundred dollars in cash left over, plus an *Internationale Presse* card, but they would be in town in the morning anyway.

'Thank you, Captain,' he said. 'I'm greatly obliged to you.'

'Plezuh, Suh,' the veteran said. 'Frien' of Juan's here is sho'

276

a frien' of mine, any time.'

Ramirez turned his head. 'How come you already know Ida then, Bwana?'

'On the plane from Miami,' Ryan explained. 'Helped with the bag, gave her a lift into town.'

'I got a notion you'd give her more than that, any time?' Ramirez grinned.

'It's an appealing thought. I'm thinking about it.'

'You and every buck in town,' Ramirez grinned. 'But, I'll tell you one thing, she's really got a mind of her own. No pushover, Ida, believe me.'

'I know that,' Ryan said. He felt a touch of inexplicable annoyance. 'As a matter of fact I helped her fight some of them off. Who wants pushovers anyway?'

'Sho' is a mighty well set-up gel,' the Captain said, 'real set-up! Takes me back when Effy was a woman,' he added pensively. 'Like yo said, Juan, ain't a buck in town wouldn't give his eye tooth.'

'White bucks included,' Ramirez said. 'But none of 'em get to first base.'

Ryan looked enquiringly. 'Present company included, no doubt, Cazador?'

Ramirez chuckled. 'Hell, no. I've got women enough, besides, my wife's a customer of Ida's. Ida runs the fancy end of the Main Street store, dresses and such. That's her brother you met got the *Quinta Penas*, she visits down here once in a while.'

The outer door opened suddenly and Effy came in puffing. The rain had begun to slacken some now, but she could still hardly see through her glasses. 'Goddam rain. That Missy'll be along in a minute.'

She peered up at her husband suddenly. 'By the way, yo didn't tell me yo had a Minister along? Min' yo interdooce me to him, Sam. Looks real nice man he does.'

'Huh?'

'In de S'loon,' she said impatiently. 'Dat venereal ol' genel'-man with de gold testicles in de black coat!'

The Captain stared, then began to chuckle. As his dia-

277

phragm expanded he sounded off again, loud and clear, and the two other men laughed explosively.

Downstairs in the Captain's two-by-four quarters the tall girl stood in her pants and shoes. Sometimes, she didn't wear brassieres, because in the first place, in the really hot hours, they were just extra limp encumbrances. And in the second place she didn't need any figure aids.

Figure un-aids might have been more to the point, she had often thought, because her big eloquent breasts, more than anything, had only ever seemed to give men the idea that she was looking for offers.

Whereas, paradoxically, there had been an instinct in her since puberty that had not only rebelled against the passive notion of winding up with a bunch of half-starved children in one of those God-awful boxwood shanties, but also made her reject the white travelling-salesmen and their transparent drinks-at-the-*Wallace* ideas which she had become so accustomed to.

There were one or two girls at the store who went with white men ... salesmen, logging men in town for the weekend ... and, of course, their assignations were always just deals. The men paid for the steaks and drinks, maybe threw in a charm bracelet or a pair of stockings, and the women paid-off with their bodies. There was no question of it ever leading anywhere.

She had always had these inhibitions. And a deep inferiority complex towards those, unlike the salesmen, whom she regarded as 'quality' white men; such as those who hired Mr Ramirez and were, therefore, always, assuredly rich and important.

But this man, Ryan, though she still felt the same inherent misgivings in his presence, somehow affected her differently.

For one thing there was not only an absence of any suggestion of social inequality about him, but, conversely, he always acted as if it was a privilege to have *her* acquaintance. As if she was the one entitled to dispense any patronage.

It was a novel and disturbing feeling and she found herself

278

increasingly thinking of him, regarding him, in a way that was strangely disquieting.

And he was something to regard, she thought. In features and physique very near to a vague picture she had always carried in her head. Which, the coincidence, was maybe the explanation of the feeling.

The steady drizzle began to falter about an hour after they had been under way, and fifteen minutes later the decks were beginning to steam in the afternoon glare.

Even so, despite the heat, the drinks had stimulated their appetites and, when Ida had returned, the five of them had eaten a meal of turtle soup and tuna, with beans and eggs, that had been as good as Ramirez had predicted.

For a while after the two women had departed, the two men had taken their ease.

But when Ryan had finished off his cigar he swung himself off the bench and went out down the ladder along to the cabin which Ramirez had organised. He stripped off his shirt and gave himself a good smearing of sun oil, then went out again wearing just his cap, glasses and trousers.

There was still no sign of Ida, but right up front, in the prow, he found a coil of hawser and sat down.

A white flurry of gulls squawked and floated over the ship's wake, and one or two took turns to languidly patrol either side of the bows for a while before dropping back.

Ryan lit a cheroot and watched the shore. They were passing another Cay now, about a quarter mile to port, a tangle of brush and mangroves above which a mixed collection of sea birds hovered and planed.

Beyond it, in the far background to the broken line of beaches, a mountain reared out of the green mass of inland jungle. Its summit was engulfed in haze and low cloudbank and its slopes were yellow tinted by the fierce rays which burned through the vapour.

He heard a footfall and turned his head. 'Well, hallo there, Janey.' He got to his feet. 'That was a pretty short siesta.'

She smiled and moved her heeled openwork sandals closer

279

together. 'I just came for some air ... and to thank you for everything ... once again.'

'Please forget it,' Ryan said. 'After all you're already a friend of Juan's and the Captain's, mine also, I hope. Come to that, you might almost say your brother's a friend of mine too.'

'Arturo! You know Arturo?' She moved her head enquiringly, surprised.

'Well, I do now,' he said.

Brother! All you need is higher heels, he thought. *Not another damned thing.*

Aloud he said, 'I was along at your brother's place this morning. That's a nice café he's got there. I really go for those rissoles too.' He gestured to the pile of rope. 'Come and sit down. I'll get another heap.'

For an instant, standing close, she was inexplicably conscious of the fact that he could have lain his chin on her head. The realisation somehow gave her an odd submissive sensation that was new to her, because she was much more accustomed to men of her own height, or, indeed, usually shorter.

When she was seated, he found another hawser coil and set it down beside her. The sun had sunk appreciably now. It still hung midway above the ends of the sea. But it had begun to cast the long golden lances over the water that foretold the gradual approach of twilight, and he suddenly realised that he had been semi-dozing there for quite some time.

He glanced at his watch. 'Five o'clock already! That's opening time where I come from.'

'You're quite a drinking man, Suh?' There was just a smiling diffident suggestion of rebuke in it.

'Now listen, stop calling me "Sir",' he said with mock severity. 'My name's Mark, that's the first thing. As to the question, well, believe it or not, I can take it or leave it alone,' he grinned, 'though mostly, admittedly, I take it. Anyway, you're not a pussyfoot, as I recall?'

'Pussyfoot?'

'Abstainer, teetotaller.'

'Oh, I see, well ... almost. Just sometimes I do.'

280

'Like weddings and celebrations?'

She nodded. 'Uh huh.'

'Well, this is a celebration,' he said. 'I'm celebrating meeting you again for one thing.'

She laughed softly. The edgy feeling had not entirely gone, but her self-consciousness was fading away to a more stirring, stimulating sensation. 'Well, all right. Could I have a Coke then?'

'You could indeed. In fact we'll both have Cokes.'

He got up and went along the deck to the Saloon. When he got back for'ard again with the drinks she half turned around, smiling and arching her back as he laid the tray on the hatch cover. It was quite an involuntary movement, but it stressed her big out-thrust breasts, and, looking down at her, the deep shadow of her cleavage was agonisingly appealing.

He felt the theopathic stirrings deep within him. As perfect as they came in any shade of skin! As luscious as the last peaches of the summer!

He had managed to get Daiquiri, Cokes and ice from the bar. Now he poured out two half-tumblers of Daiquiri, giving one a dash of Coke and topping the other up before spooning a cube into each. She watched him with the trace of a smile, pretending reproach.

'That wasn't the kind of Coke I meant ... Mark.'

'I know but it's the one that tastes best ... Jane. Give it a try.'

She laughed again and reached up. 'All right, then ... Mark, but later you may have to carry me back to Effy.'

'I'll look forward to that all right.' It was just an easy remark, but the way he said it gave her a little queasy feeling that was unfamiliar.

By six o'clock the sunset rays had transformed the water to deep purple. Somebody had set up a crap game on one of the aft hatches, but otherwise everything was quiet and inactive.

'Feeling sleepy now?' Ryan said. 'You look a bit pooped. Do you want to take a real nap for a while?'

'Well, I am a little tired I guess,' she said. 'I suppose it was

281

sitting up so late last night with Arty and his wife, and that big lunch and these Cokes and everything, but it's too stuffy inside.'

'Oh, I didn't mean in the cabin ... you're not going to get away that easily ... right here. Let's see what we can do.' He went back down the deck and when he returned he was carrying two straw paliasses borrowed for a consideration from the forecastle, and two pillows from his own cabin. There was just enough room between the hatch and the rail to take the mattresses side by side.

'There you are then, come and try the bridal suite!'

She knelt down smiling and then stretched out on her back. 'Ooh, that's lovely, you think of everything, Mark.' She turned on to her stomach, laying her cheek on the pillow. Ryan lay down beside her, propping himself on his elbow.

The ship was much closer to land than it had been before, and away on the leeward side the beaches had changed from silver to gold and, in some places, pink. Behind the marginal colour band the high bank of the jungle had become a violet mass and the fading mountain a wash of lighter purple merging into a wake of darkening sky. His gaze returned to the woman beside him, moving over her wide rounded hips and smooth swelling thighs where her dress had ridden higher against the canvas of the paliasse.

'I hear you work in the Main Street store,' he said. 'What's your department then?'

'Oh, I'm in charge of millinery ... I also make dresses to order sometimes.' A whiff of breeze gently billowed the flimsiness of her skirt and for a second he got a further glimpse of long heavy thigh as far as the edge of white panties, before she reached down and smoothed it back.

He said. 'Well, obviously you must prefer it, but it beats me that a girl as beautiful as you should still be single. What's the explanation?'

'Heavens, I'm not beautiful.' She turned her head away to hide her expression. 'For one thing I'm much too big.'

'Beautiful, I said,' Ryan repeated, 'and I come from the branch of a profession dedicated to faces.'

282

For a moment she remained silent, then she said: 'I just don't want to wind up like most of our girls do, that's all.'

'Like downtown in a shanty?'

'Well . . . yes.'

'How about white men?'

'What white men?'

'Well,' for a moment it puzzled him, 'like Juan, say?'

'They're not *proper* white men,' she said artlessly. 'They're different from shanty people, it would be just the same. Mr Ramirez is an . . . an exception. I don't know another man like him.'

'Well how about these proper white men?' He smiled. 'Say like Juan's clients?'

'You're joking, Mark. How could they be interested in the likes of me . . . except maybe for pleasuring themselves.' There was no bitterness or even criticism in it, it was merely an acceptance of fact.

'Am I joking, hell,' he said. '*I'm* very interested.'

By God I'm interested, he thought. It would be out of this world, like drowning in honey.

She gave him a short look which had doubt and enquiry in it as well as some shyness. 'You must be an exception like Mr Ramirez then.'

He put his hand on the back of her knee. It had the smooth velvety texture of a rose and he moved it higher, stroking. For a second she did nothing, then she took his wrist and lifted his hand on to the mattress between them but did not release it.

He smiled to himself. '*Pleasuring*.' That was a Deep South one that had evidently come farther south. Still, it had a certain frank charm, more grace than the usual Western banalities of screwing, stuffing, banging, knocking-up . . . doing it.

He said, 'Don't you like pleasuring then . . . ever?'

'Depends. A little way is all right . . . sometimes.'

'Back to weddings and celebrations again, eh?'

This time she laughed outrightly. 'I think I'd better look out for you, white man.'

'It's not very important, but I think there's a lot of white in you?' Ryan said.

283

'Some.'

'How much? No, let that go, it's out of line,' he said, regretting it.

'No it isn't, I don't mind, if it interests you.' She accepted one of the cork-tipped cigarettes he had got from the Saloon. 'My grandfather was a Mexican man, but our mother was half black and half white, you know ... mulattress?' He nodded. 'Our father, mine and Arturo's, was a sailor, a British sailor.'

'Well, they must have been a handsome assembly,' Ryan said. 'Arturo is a fine looking one too.'

'Thank you.' The pleasure showed in her face at the tribute to Arturo.

'But what are you planning to do then?' he asked a moment later, 'since you're not keen on the caballeros. Stay with the store and let 'em all expire of frustration?'

She laughed again, then let it fade. 'Oh, I save all I can, I have one or two private customers. If I ever get enough I shall open a shop of my own, like Arturo. Maybe even get a house, in time ... a *proper* house ... then I'll be independent, like Arturo.'

Overhead the first star had begun to wink fitfully. Pretty soon now all the heavens would be lit with jewels and scintillating patterns, and the soft prevailing evening breeze had arrived, leavening the fierce heat to a milder warmth.

That's one small enterprise I wouldn't mind financing, he thought. And I wouldn't give a damn about the profit-and-loss account either. Not that she wouldn't make a go of it. She certainly wouldn't have to pay any emaciated sickly-looking scrags to model her stuff if she ever got a wee place of her own.

They fell silent for a while, but in the end she had to ask it. 'Will you be staying long, here in our country I mean?' She made it as casual as she could.

'Until I've got all I want,' he said enigmatically.

'Maybe a week or two more?'

'Oh, hell yes. A month anyway.' He got a fresh cheroot and struck a match on the deck. 'I'm not here just for fun. You might say I'm taking in parts of the scene.' He grinned

284

pointedly. 'And especially people that greatly interest me.'

She pretended to miss the inference. 'Yes, I thought that.'

'Oh?'

'When Effy took me to the cabin,' she explained. 'Mr Ramirez had already told her you were a big writer.'

Ryan chuckled. 'He means big, tall.'

'No he doesn't.'

'All right, I'm a tall writer. So...?'

'Well, I was just thinking ... wondering ...' She fumbled with it a little. 'I don't suppose I'll ever meet a writer again, if I sent mail order would you sign the books when I get them? As a favour?'

He smiled incredulously. 'I'll be damned. You count *that* a favour?'

'Yes.'

'All right then.' He moved over to the rail. 'You do me one.'

'Yes?'

'Stand up and come here.'

She got up, a little wave of expectancy running through her.

'Here.' He waved away her hesitation with a smile and she moved over beside him. He put his hands on her shoulders, turning her round and drawing her close against him. For a long moment he kissed her in the soft curve of her neck and shoulder, gripping her arms. When he raised his head he said softly: 'Listen, it's just that I'd like to buy you a wee present, and I'd like it to be ready for when we get back from up North.'

'What kind of present?' she whispered.

He joined his index fingers at the back of her neck. 'One like so!'

He drew his fingers down over her breasts and joined them again making the imaginary outline of a neckline that would expose that gorgeous cleavage. He put his fingers on her neck again and drew the further imaginary shape of a backless gown which reached down into the curve of her waist. 'Like that!'

'A gown?' she sounded a little breathless.

285

'Yes. A whim, if you like.' He moved his hands higher, gathering up her breasts and titillating the nipples while he kissed her in the same place as before and then all along her shoulder. 'But it's something I must see.'

'On a coloured woman?' There was still a tiny hint of inhibition in it.

'On a beautiful woman,' he said. 'You'd be beautiful if you were black as ink, or sky blue.'

He kissed her ardently then, resolving her lingering innate doubts, bearing down more and more strongly until he could feel her teeth. Then again. There was a faint warm perfume about her like carnations, immensely provocative. But he still held himself in check, because he suddenly knew that there was something more to it than just the tremendous physical urge, that now he cared, too, about not hurting her sensitivities, about not re-erecting this colour barrier thing through disillusionment.

Standing there in the starlight she was not just something to *see*, not just overwhelming temptation. It was a privilege to be there.

She sighed and laid her cheek on his chest for a moment. When she raised her head he kissed her again before she could speak.

'Is that what you really want, Mark? The gown thing, I mean,' softly.

'Yes, but it's just a fancy.' He made a little joke about it. 'Wouldn't make any difference if you wore a sack ... or nothing at all ... not with what you've got.'

For a second she looked quizzical, then her expression relaxed and she laughed. 'I wouldn't *quite* wear a sack to welcome you back.'

Ryan cocked his head, pretending to consider it. 'Oh, I don't know. On second thoughts it might be even more effective ... if it was a very wee sack!'

Ramirez came along the deck towards them and she moved back against the rail. 'Just come along to let you know the Cap's dug up another bottle of your vino, Mark, if you're interested?' the hunter said. 'But I see you've got it pretty

286

cosy right here.' He grinned at the girl. 'You want to look out for this Bwana, Ida. *Es muy vivo.*'

She smiled back. 'Si. *Es muy hombre,* also.'

He laughed. 'Yeh, that too. Big.' He looked out across the water. 'I meant to ask you, what did Arturo say about the raid?'

'Just that two were killed and they have one in the jail,' she told him.

'Had,' he said. 'They've got him down in the hold with a couple of guards. Brought him aboard last night. I've just been down to take a look at him.'

At first, when the Captain had told him, he had thought it better not to advertise his own presence in Punta Quela so soon after the battle. But then he had thought, Aaah, what the hell! When they held the trial even the 'tecos wouldn't have any trouble figuring who had boxed their caper, if they hadn't guessed already, and he had been curious to see which of the *hijos* had survived the bank and fruit company's reception committee. That it had turned out to be the big surly one they had called Tomás, was a great pity, though consistent maybe. The worst bastards always seemed to dodge it when the shooting started.

'What sentence will he get, the *faccioso*?' Ida asked.

Ramirez shrugged. 'They didn't kill any guards, any of our people ... they were on the receiving end ... so they won't hang him. Maybe life, maybe twenty years.' He felt in his pocket and brought out a key. He held it out to her. 'Effy's cabin, in case you might want to go ahead of her, she thought.' He looked down at the mattresses, then at Ryan. 'I think you've got the best idea there, Bwana, I think I'll take one of them on top of the wheelhouse tonight. Well, you know where the stuff is if you run dry.' He turned and started back towards midship.

They would probably have stayed there a good deal longer, but about an hour after Ramirez had come along it began to rain again. He gathered up the mattresses and she went ahead of him to the cabin.

287

The way she walked strongly reminded him of the similarly wide-hipped Somali women. The Masai women were the brazen ones, the tit brandishers, but the Somalis usually gave the more effective performances. They drooped their lids, smiled faintly and swayed their buttocks. He doubted whether she was conscious of it, as the Somalis were, but Ida's hips moved laterally in the same provocative way.

The Skipper's wife was evidently still in the wheelhouse, probably would be for a long time yet. He stepped into the tiny cabin after her and she made no effort to stop him.

It was a pretty hopeless proposition. Just two bunks, one above the other and same narrow width of floor space. With their mutual physiques a man-size four poster would have been none too luxurious.

He put his hands on the smooth boneless ends of her shoulders, kissed her in the nape, then ran his fingers gently back along her velvety skin, and kissed her again.

The kisses and the caresses gave her a kind of roseate feeling which she wanted to extend, not to curtail. She strained back against him, feeling the hard substance against her buttocks.

'You want me to go, Jane?' he said questioningly.

'You know I don't, but I s'pose you'd better.'

She closed her eyes and willed him not to go, and when his hands moved slowly, far too slowly down her back and over her breasts, fondling and caressing her pouting nipples, she began to breathe more deeply.

'There isn't any hurry about Effy,' he said. 'Not that that would matter a damn.' He increased the urgency of fondling and kissing, conscious of her relaxing tension. She stood quite still while he unzipped the back of her dress down on to the swell of her hips and slid it over her shoulders. He let her wriggle it free and then, when she felt the warm hands cosseting her big bare breasts at last, teasing her stark nipples, a wave of weakness went through her. She stood quite still while he pushed the flimsy white pants down over her buttocks and began to stroke her belly, straining until he reached the lips between her legs.

288

Then, as if she could endure no more she flung her arms around his neck and pulled his face lower to meet her parted lips, soft and wet.

'Mark ... you want me now ...'

'Any way.'

For answer she took a cushion from the bunk and dropped it on the floor, then knelt and lowered her head to the pad, offering her hips to him in the oldest female gesture of love and submission.

In the dim light she looked like a gorgeous cream carving, except, moving his hands over her back, gripping the swelling rotundities of her hips, she was the living incarnation of unfeigned feminine bounty, the yielding unsurpassable reality.

11. THE *TROPICAL*

When he followed Ramirez out on deck into the rising yellow, red-flecked glory of the morning, the *Bonito* was already tied up at the stern end. Many passengers had already disembarked, and some were now already as far as a couple of hundred yards along the wharf towards town.

It was funny that there was no sign of Ida, he thought, but then he remembered she had said that she had various urgent chores before going on to her work and, presumably, she had gone with the earlier birds.

From the market a short piece up the river a salty fishy smell came drifting over the morning air. It was not unpleasant but at times, when there was a wisp from the sea, it was blanked out by the sickly sweet smell from a copra boat moored nearby.

There were still three cabs left on the wharf. Two were latecomers who had taken too long sleeping it off and were still touting the groups. The third was the big old roadster with the driver Ryan already knew, Almagro sitting beside him.

At the *Palace* he took a shower and ate a good breakfast,

then went back upstairs to dwell on the two letters which had been lying on his dressing-table.

He knew from the writing whom they were from, of course, and he opened Mark's letter first.

It was four typical pages of disconnected personal and general news scraps; not counting the initial, most important enquiry. 'How are you, Dad?'

It had clearly been laboriously, and conscientiously collated.

Mark wasn't a writing man, wouldn't ever be any kind of professional type ... building dams, mending bulldozers, felling forests, that was his kind of bent. But it seemed as if he would make full-back eventually, and the swimming team, and he would get to Bisley way below the average age. The shooting news didn't surprise him. The boy was bloody mustard ... all parental bias aside ... and he, 'Dad', would take care of the cash-earning side of it when the time came, work out a suitably round hole.

He opened Rennie's letter with a mingled feeling of anticipation and, oddly, a twinge of foreboding, but there was nothing to be conclusively drawn from it one way or another. It was warm, affectionate and in the impersonal passages typically practical. You could hardly call it a romantic missive; in fact it was more like a letter to a favourite brother. But knowing her as he did, it was probably about as indicative as she was likely to be on paper. Not because of any lack of warmth or emotion in her, but because the lyrical written stuff just wasn't in her line of country. Of course, they still had to have their 'Board Meeting' and, for that matter, he still had finally and conclusively to declare himself.

For a moment or two his thoughts turned to those interludes which had occurred since Fiona, since he had been on his own in body if not spirit. Anita, the not-too-sophisticated croupier, Paquita, the delicious morsel of Honduran earthiness, and now this superlatively luscious creature, Jane. He wondered whether knowledge of them would have bothered Rennie. Probably not much. She was pretty adult, and certainly she knew that he had never let Fiona down, which was a fair enough criterion.

For that matter they had all been merely superficial inter-ludes. No, wait a moment, that wasn't a hundred percent. To level with himself, he had to admit that that didn't really go for Ida.

Ida was so sumptuously desirable; so voluptuously appeal-ing in her simplicity that any man could justifiably marry her for her physical self.

She had character, too, and, in her own unassuming way, ambition, as well as intelligence. The right man could prob-ably come as close to complete marital satisfaction with her, certainly in both the fundamental respects of sex and amity, as the odd pair in a hundred ever did.

He got a pad from his case and settled down to write. First, a longish one to Mark, outlining some of the more interesting hunting incidents, and ending with, by implication, some common qualities of great full-backs whom he had played with or against himself.

Next a note to his New York publishers asking them to mail copies of *Six-Five Mannlicher* and *Bwangato* to himself. For Ida. Finally to Rennie, taking some trouble fully to reciprocate her warmth and affection yet, similarly, avoiding any irrevoc-able committal.

As he was finishing it Big Dick appeared at the open door on to the balcony with a note in his hand. It was on behalf of Ramirez, inviting him to eat with his family at the *Wallace* about eight o'clock. The English and the handwriting were good and he smiled at the semi-formal tone of it. Maybe it was a hint that not all the family were bums, because it was signed Consuela Ramirez.

He spent the rest of the day relaxing. A little shopping ... a pair of white high-heeled shoes, a 'birthday' present for Ida ... a swim at the local beach, a few drinks in the bar.

At eight o'clock it was still too hot for more than pants and sandals. But there was the fact of the women, of course. So he dug out the white tropical tuxedo he had hawed about when he had been packing his bag and had finally rolled up and shoved in.

When they got out on the terrace for coffee it soon became

291

clear that Mrs Ramirez was quite anxious to find out if they had a satisfied client. Well, it had been nae sa baad, up to yet, and certainly he had quite a bit of detail in the back of his head, and noted, that ought to make a bit of interesting background stuff in due course.

He told them so, and of his interest in the variety of terrain he had seen. He also paid tribute to Almagro and the other boys, adding a couple of brief African anecdotes illustrative of the kind of things that were liable to happen when you *didn't* have a well-drilled outfit.

Consuela's intercessions were more subjective than her mother's. How did their hunting compare with the African kind though? Was it more, or less demanding, more, or less exciting, satisfying?

He thought about it for a moment, conscious of Ramirez's introversive smile.

He said, 'Well, there isn't any simple answer because they're so entirely different. African hunting is more arduous in some ways, the distances and the footwork, but,' he made a gesture towards Ramirez, 'for me the Cazador's style is more demanding on the nerves. I guess it's like when Mother turns the light out. You don't mind so much if you can see what's coming. I doubt I'd ever get used to your father's way of it,' he added.

Ramirez smiled. 'I'll tell you something, *gatita*,' he said to the girl. 'Here's one guy can hit cats, and he don't run . . . he'd get used to it!'

'Yes, but the explanation of the not-running part is not heroic,' Ryan said. 'It's simply I'm rooted with fear!'

The others laughed and Consuela leaned forward. 'With the *tigrés* it *is* more exciting, then, Señor?'

'No,' Ryan said. 'More scarifying, I'd say, there's a difference. I don't know anything more exciting than when you and a big bull buff are stalking each other, and you both know it; or with a holed-up lion that already has one bullet in him.' He fingered his temple. 'It's hard to explain. With the *tigrés* there's the added element of the dark . . . plus what I call the Snake Thought. . . .'

292

Since they had moved on to the terrace the trio of *mariachis*, the semi-resident musicians, had begun to play. Even when it had still been relatively novel, the approved way of getting more intimately associated with a fancied candidate, he had never been wildly enthusiastic about dancing. And in the atmospheric conditions the notion of energetic rumbas had little appeal. But now they were playing something less boisterous.

He looked across at Consuela, with a smile, 'Would you care to risk the style *Inglés*, Señorita?'

She smiled back. 'But of course, Señor.'

Ryan concentrated. He wasn't all that bad, and once he had gotten his foxtrot adjusted to the time it seemed to go along pretty well. And Consuela made it easier because she floated like swansdown, could have followed a swallow, let alone a sauntering *Inglés*.

When the music ceased, he grinned. 'Well, I'm not quite sure what we were doing . . . I probably invented it . . . but I'd like to do it again sometime?'

She looked up. 'Thank you. I shall also look forward to it . . . and to the fishing, of course, when you return from the Corozoale.'

At about ten o'clock Ramirez put the two women into a cab and Ryan watched their departure with amusement. You had to hand it to them. The way they handled their womenfolk! Maybe Clara was boss, in range of the cooker and the washtub. But outside the home, *los maridos*, the husbands, called the tune, the old traditions prevailed. Wives and daughters, even doted-on daughters called *gatita*, kept their small noses out of men's business and did not raise undue expostulations.

'About this ball you mentioned?' Ryan said when the car had gone.

'Sure thing! Going to take you to a little place on the edge of town, the *Tropical*.'

'Club, cathouse, little-of-this-and-that?'

'Yeh, *just* like that, little of this and that. Kind of varied. Clean though, and the food's good too.'

293

'Sounds useful,' Ryan agreed. 'Let's go.'

In the roadster, the hunter said, 'By the way I appreciate what you told them, Mark. We'll try and make it really pay-off up in the Corozoale.'

'Just give me some daylight then,' Ryan said. 'I just want to *see* some of these overgrown *chuis* in daylight. Ten seconds will do, once in a while, that's all I ask, boy.'

'We just might be able to arrange that up there,' Ramirez said. 'The Caribs don't hunt cat, but they got some semi-trained dogs.' He pinched his nose. 'El Viejo will give us the steers,' he said thoughtfully. 'That *veterano* knows every patch in the Corozoale that holds good cat.'

'The old-timer who works with the gin traps?'

'Yeh,' Ramirez nodded. 'You might find him good book material, eh? I don't know.'

'Could well be,' Ryan said. 'Anyway, now you're talking.'

At the corner of the Plaza, Ramirez called to the driver and pointed, then turned his head. Almagro and the other two boys were waiting by the portico of the City Hall. 'You don't mind if we take the boys along, Mark? I usually give 'em a party between trips.'

'All in favour of it,' Ryan said. 'On me, in fact.'

'Oh, no, I'll take care of this one, Bwana,' the hunter said. 'Don't want no tequila heads in the morning.' He grinned. 'Anyway you're paying for it all right, one way or another.'

The *Tropical* stood a short way back from the beach, some distance beyond the last of the shanties on the town side. From the road it looked like a big wooden barn, but for once the paintwork was in good condition. And, even more surprisingly, by local standards, all the red letters of the neon sign across the façade were functioning.

The sign itself cast a penumbra of pink light on the hard dirt of the road, and from within the mingled sounds of voices and rumba music floated out over the swingflap doors.

They went in like an arrest detail, Tomásco and Almagro in front and Manny bringing up the rear.

Inside, the lighting was amber coloured; not dim but fairly subdued. On either side, raised platforms like elongated dais,

294

ran the length of the place. But midway along, on the left hand side, there was a square pen with a low rail for the three *mariachis* playing piano, guitar and clarinet. White cane tables were scattered about the raised floors and also along one edge of the dance floor opposite the band.

About a couple of dozen couples were dancing, and the rest of the customers were gathered in small groups along the bar at the far end. Two barmen, with sweat-shiny black faces that contrasted with their white singlets, were tending the wide counter which ran the width of the hall and in one corner stairs ran up to a balcony which overlooked the drinkers.

A Spanish-looking woman and a mulatto girl were leaning over the balcony rail desultorily watching the dancers. They both wore party frocks that were very low cut, and it looked as if the breasts of the big mulatto one would lollop forth over the balustrade any minute.

The dancers opened up to make way for Tomásco and Almagro, but they had only got half way along the floor before people began to call out greetings to Ramirez, and it was just like what had happened at the boat at Punta Quela all over again.

A young Negro in a blue singlet and white jeans came out from a corner by the bar. He was carrying a tray and he led them to two tables facing the musicans' pen. There were two men already sitting at one of the tables, but the boy just said something to them and they got up and moved affably along with a nod and a wave to Ramirez as if it was fine to oblige.

'A bottle of *vino Inglés* ... the genuwine stuff mind ... and some cans and fresh orange juice,' Ramirez told the young boy. He turned his head towards the others. 'Also, all the beer they want for the boys, here, and see if they've et.'

'Si, Señor.' The youth wasted no time with it.

On the other side of the floor a half-dozen girls, distinct from the run-of-the-mill customers by virtue of their some-what more sophisticated appearances, sat two to a table next to the band.

Mostly they watched the entrance end for incomers, occa-sionally flashing a professional smile at men lumbered with one of the amateur opposition, and there had been a big stirring when the hunters had arrived. Except for one girl, their interest was now divided between newcomers and the group of hunters. But it was obviously a rule of the house that they were precluded from making direct approaches.

One or two were pretty enough, in shades from coal black to lemon curd, especially one girl who sat on her own occasionally sipping a beer.

The place was barely half full yet, but every now and then people were coming in in ones and twos. A few took tables, but mostly they stood around the bar end where the drinks came ten percent cheaper.

In the corner by the stairs a short wiry man was pressed closely against a woman in a tight-skirted yellow dress who was leaning on the bar. The paleness of her bare back contrasted harshly with the man's heavily negroid colouring, and his small hand, moving over her back, looked like a creeping tarantula. All the time he was importuning her he was stroking and feeling her prominent buttocks, oblivious or unmindful of the sniggers and comments of the adjacent customers. Twice, she stood upright, nearly a head taller than he was, and gave him a lay-off shove. But the next minute he was right back at it again, feeling and stroking while he laid his proposition on the line.

Ramirez saw the mordant half-smile on the Englishman's face and turned, following his glance. At first he didn't get it. He looked back enquiringly.

'The runt,' Ryan said. 'The arseologist.'

Ramirez looked again. 'Oh him. Zambo, the mail man. That sawn-off punk would screw anything on two legs, or four. Some of these days somebody's going to screw him, in a casket.'

He felt a smirk of annoyance, as if the postman's exhibition was a personal affront, and he was on the point of despatching Tomásco to throw the little man out, when the woman in the yellow frock shoved Zambo right away and turned.

Full face she had quite good Spanish features, and at the distance she looked somewhere about her mid-twenties. The

296

small Negro continued to petition her volubly, but despite his persistence he didn't seem to be getting anywhere. She gave him a final flathand gesture of rejection and began to walk over to where the other girls were sitting. After exchanging a word here and there she sat down at the table where the girl on her own was propped on her elbow, staring into her glass with frozen intensity.

Two minutes later Zambo was standing beside them. 'Boss ... Señor Ramirez ...' The small wiry man bent over the hunter's ear and whisped urgently.

Ramirez turned his head and fixed him with a look of irritation. 'Get lost, Zambo, go cut it off. And don't come busting into company again, do you hear me, *enaro*?'

The small man had a long equine face disfigured by a spatule of smallpox craters on one cheek. In his fretting desire he dropped the whispering and spoke more audibly.

'Ah does 'pologise for that, boss, ah really does.' He flashed a preoccupied smile at Ryan. 'But only three bucks, boss, ah got the rest an' she give credit fo' one dollar. Jus' three, boss, ah got to have that big yaller ass.'

Ramirez regarded him with increased annoyance. 'Listen, pest, obscenity.' He grabbed a handful of the Negro's shirt and pulled him close. 'Back of the *Kwikservice* they got a new she-hog, go stick it in that. For free!'

He gave the man a shove which sent him staggering towards the boys and Tomásco, grinning, spun him around and sent him farther along with another hefty push.

Ryan laughed. 'Some hobgoblin. Like something out of Runyon. Horseface Harry.'

'Two-tooled little conch should have them cut off.' Ramirez let the look of irritation fade. 'You want to dance one of the girls or anything, Mark?'

Ryan shook his head. 'No, but you go head if you want.'

'Not drunk enough yet.' A thought struck him. 'You want a room on the balcony ... how d'you fancy these palomas anyway?'

'Oh,' Ryan shrugged. 'So-so. A bit caducous.'

'For Chrissake?'

297

Ryan laughed. 'Going off. Losing the bloom.'

'Well, could be.' He screwed up his eyes and stared across the thickening fug of tobacco smoke. 'Except maybe the two over by?'

There were two men sitting with the girl in the yellow frock and the more petite one now. The men wore straw hats and jeans and there were just four bottles on the table.

'They've already got customers,' Ryan pointed out.

'Hell, those conches don't amount to anything,' Ramirez said. He got to his feet and moved along to the boys' table. In a minute or two Tomásco got down off the dais and went across the floor. He laid his knuckles on their table and spoke to the two women, ignoring the men.

The bigger girl looked across and Ramirez nodded. She smiled, nodding back, then she got up, unceremoniously nudging the other girl, and they followed Tomásco back across the floor leaving the hijacked ones with the extra beer.

'You didn't look happy,' Ramirez said. 'Have a chair.'

Yellow frock smiled. 'Correct. It is nice to join you,' she said in good Spanish.

'Better drinking too,' the hunter said succinctly. 'Here you can have champagne with your beer.' He grinned. 'Even *vino Inglés, rillenos,* too, if you're hungry. Nothing barred.'

'I am Dolores,' the big girl said easily. 'This is Maria. We are from Mexico City.'

'For a short visit only,' the smaller one said quickly, as if it was important. 'A *vacacione,* you understand?'

Her ebony black hair was piled in a cone as high as a Watussi bride's, and she had petite, rather pretty olive features. She could have been twenty but was probably two or three years younger, and there was a certain nervousness about her.

'Oh yes, we understand,' Ramirez said with just a touch of irony in it. 'I am called Juan, and my friend here is Marco. He is *Inglés.*'

'The fare from Mexico City must be quite formidable,' Ryan said. 'I hope all goes well?'

She looked at him with sudden added interest. 'Oh, that is

298

very interesting,' she said irrelevantly, 'that you speak Spanish, I mean. I have never met an *Inglés* before. *Americanos*, but not *Inglés*. . . .'

Ramirez chuckled. 'Watch out for them, Maria,' he said, 'they are more formidable than the fares.'

'You are right about the cost, Señor,' the bigger girl said ruefully. 'Is *gigantesco*.'

Ramirez chuckled again. 'Ah, the practical one. I thought we might get around to cost,' he said in English. He watched their faces, but there was no sign of understanding, and the plump girl looked enquiringly. 'I was wondering why you came here,' the hunter said, reverting to Spanish. 'Since it costs so much?'

'For the *vacacione*, as I said,' the smaller one answered, cutting in quickly again.

'*Ach*, Maria, *conjones* to the *vacacione*!' yellow frock said impatiently, though not unkindly. '*Qué te importa, querida?* These two are not beginners.'

She looked squarely at Ramirez. 'We come here, Señor Cazador, as you will know, because, at home, before the season of the *Americanos*, the competition is very formidable. That is the formidable thing . . . too formidable for some of us who are not as beautiful as Señora Loren and those . . . although,' she made a challenging gesture, 'Maria is more beautiful than some of *them*, no? And because we have to eat!'

Ryan smiled. 'Well said, *muchacha*, that's telling him.' He raised a hand, and when he caught the eye of the boy over by the bar who had served them the drinks, he hooked a thumb.

Ramirez grinned. 'You go for the Sophia here?' he asked in English.

'No,' Ryan said. 'But I like her style, no horsing around.' He leaned back and considered her through the smoke of his cheroot. She might be pushing thirty, but equally, bearing in mind the early, the caducous tendency of all the Latin women, she could be less.

Certainly she was no ugly duckling, and there was nothing wrong with her obtrusive outlines. You could do a lot worse in the Royal Enclosure or Nairobi, he thought, if that wasn't damning her with faint praise.

Nor was she slow on the uptake. 'And, do I pass the inspection, then, Señor?' It was said lightly enough, but there was just a suggestion of underlying anxiety and cynicism in her voice. 'Do I have what you want?'

Ryan parried it. He smiled noncommittally. 'Well, there is just one thing.' He wrinkled his nose and pointed to the silver brooch, the size of an acorn, containing the live incarcerated beetle that was ever so gradually moving across the smooth flesh of her breast.

He got a five-dollar bill from his hip and pushed it across the table, then he reached over and picked the thing off her skin. He dropped it on the floor and crunched it under his heel.

'Sorry, Querida, but I just naturally hate the sight of those *Godawful* bugs! What in the name of God do you wear 'em for?'

For a moment she was taken aback and almost started to expostulate. But then, just as abruptly, she considered and shrugged. This kind of customer was always right, and anyway the bugs cost less than a dollar.

· 'They've all got the bloody things,' Ramirez grinned. 'Feed 'em on sugar.'

'I know,' Ryan said. 'Bloody repulsive.'

'But how *about* Sophia here, though, do you fancy a tumble?' Ramirez asked in English.

'Not that much. Maybe the bug cooled my libido.'

'Uh huh. Well I think I'll give the kitten a roll,' the hunter said. He grinned. 'She deserves a break after all these dime-a-dozen conches. I feel kinda big-hearted.'

In Spanish he said, 'Listen, Dolores, my friend is very tired, and tomorrow we leave early, you understand, but I will entertain Maria for a while.'

The younger girl shot him a brief glance, then at her companion, as if seeking approval, before she dropped her eyes.

'Don't worry about it, kitten,' Ramirez said. 'I've got one like you at home.'

The older woman looked across at Ryan and saw the nega-

300

tive confirmation in his face. For two years now she had been becoming more used to frustration and disillusion, but the dismissal was still a considerable disappointment. Not merely because of the money. The conviction had been growing that with this big clean-looking *Inglés* it would have been less of a chore than for a long time. Perhaps even an interlude, between the clowns and the animals, for pleasurable remembrance.

Just for a moment the disappointment showed in her face, then she gave a little shrug and took out a mirror from her purse.

When she had patted her hair and checked her make-up, so that nobody looking might get the wrong idea about her withdrawal, she rose with a smile that was still friendly, for all the hint of reproach in it.

Ryan put a ten-dollar bill in her hand. She would not normally have hesitated, but this time she did for a moment, then she smiled again and took it.

'*Gracias.*'

Half way across the floor to her former table she seemed to change her mind and turned towards the bar crowd.

'Pity about her ... Dolores,' Ryan said in English. 'Why the hell didn't I have the sense to hunt up Jane in the first place?'

'For Chrissake, why didn't you say,' Ramirez said. 'We could've fixed that.'

'Aaah, forget it. You go ahead with Maria here.'

On his way to the stairs, Ramirez paused for a moment at Almagro's table. He spoke to the younger man for a few seconds, then Almagro got up and began to move through the tables to the door.

Ryan watched him go, waved to the hunter and Maria, and then sat nursing his drink, for maybe half an hour. He felt low. It was a hell of a way to celebrate.

Suddenly he looked over to the entrance, as if his eyes had been drawn in that direction. Almagro had returned, and standing there with him was ... Ida. She was wearing a white dress, with a pair of white shoes ... new shoes ... that gave her that little extra height, and she looked regal.

301

After the heat of indoors, the gentle coolness of the old roadster was like a friend. A luxury worth ten times the cost of hiring the jalopy, self-drive, from Juan's driver. There was a big moon up now, and through shanty town, out across the flats, the beaches were white and the water a silvery sheet tapering away into the ultimate darkness.

They parked the car and walked along to a triangle of palms, the girl walking barefoot, carrying her shoes.

Ryan made a big square of beach towels he had borrowed from Jorge. He lay down on his back, pillowing his head on his arms, and she sat down beside him.

'I am greatly, but *greatly*, in the Cazador's debt,' he said. 'You've really made the night for me.'

Farther along the strand, where the lights from the *Wallace* cast a dim yellow aureole, the faint sound of music was super-imposed on the soughing of the surf. She half turned and looked down at him. 'For me you made the day as well.' She held up the shoes, 'The loveliest "birthday" present I've ever had.' Her teeth were very white and her silhouetted shape was irresistible.

'Less than nothing to your present,' he said. 'You look like a dream.'

'I'm glad you like it.' She smoothed a wrinkle of the gown across her thighs. 'It was quite simple, though I'd barely finished when Almagro came.'

'It's tremendous,' Ryan said. 'You're a genius ... although there is one thing.'

'Yes.'

'I don't see how you get it off.'

She smiled, then laughed outright softly. 'It's easy, but you'll have to find out.'

She stretched down over him and he pulled her close. When the kiss was ended he found the two hooks at the back of her neck and unfastened them. She pushed herself back on her palms, smiling, and the gown slid from her shoulders uncovering her big resolute breasts.

'Is that what you wanted?'

'You're too beautiful to be true.' He fondled them, then

302

kissed the taut nipples that were like rosebuds at the first early pouting; and she closed her eyes, letting the warm pleasure of it steal through her.

Suddenly, compulsively, she bent lower, kissing him passionately. 'Do you want to wait longer, darling?'

She shook her head and got to her feet. Then she turned her back, working the gown down over the swell of her hips. She stepped out of it and folded it over her arm, then she turned again and sank down on to him.

Afterwards, for a little while, they lay facing, side by side, her head pillowed on his arm, while he stroked her warm tactile flesh.

He said, 'Listen, Querida, we won't be back for a week or two, and suddenly it seems like a hell of a long time. Come back to the *Palace* with me tonight.'

'All right.'

'You won't regret it.'

'I know,' she said softly.

He smiled. 'Take a swim before we go then. Fancy it?'

She looked up. 'Without costumes?'

'Sure.'

She sat upright and stared around, as if the idea itself would produce spectators.

Ryan laughed. 'Don't worry about it. Wouldn't matter a damn if we did have an audience.'

'Will you fetch me a towel if someone comes?'

'Cross my heart.'

'All right then.'

He sprinted across the sand, splashed a way, dived and then turned back and stood waiting waist-deep. In a minute or two she followed, panting a little when she reached him. The water was still warm, warmer than an indoor pool and much more regenerating.

When they returned to the trees he gave himself a quick rub down, then slipped on his undershorts and took the second towel to her. He hadn't intended it, but she was so luscious, so voluptuously lovely that it was inevitable. He covered her breasts, cool and satiny-textured like petals, and whispered

303

into the side of her neck. 'Let's not wait for the *Palace*, huh?'

'All right ... Querido.'

She came out on to the balcony and for a short while they leaned on the rail overlooking the cherimoya tree, smoking, and sometimes smelling a waft of the bloom.

He went back into the room and fixed a glass of champagne and a whisky, then he lay down on the bed. He whistled softly and she came in and stood looking down at him for a moment, then she went to turn off the bedside lamp but he said, 'No, leave it on, I want to see you.'

She moved over to the dressing mirror and pouted her lips at her reflection for a moment, but it was just a bit of pretence. A little instinctive play. The white gown and briefs slid to the floor and she bent to take off her shoes but he interrupted again. 'No, wait, keep them on for a moment.'

She half-turned with a smile of enquiry, her wonderful breasts silhouetted. Standing there, just wearing the shoes, she was absolutely incomparable, he thought.

There was no urgency yet, and for a little while they were silent, listening to the cicadas and the frogs. He got his mind off the petting for a minute and gently pinched her thigh.

He said. 'Listen, darling, how much do you need to set up?'

'Set up?'

'In business, for yourself.... Remember you told me about it.'

For a second she was taken aback. She raised her eyebrows, frowning, then she relaxed and began to make a little pushing, undulating movement with her stomach and hips. 'Mark. You want to talk about business *now*?'

'Not for long,' he smiled. 'A couple of minutes.'

'What is it then?'

'How much ... for your own place?'

She made an effort and was silent for a moment. 'With what I have, maybe one thousand dollars.'

God Almighty, Ryan thought. Peanuts! The cost of a term's schooling. He said: 'Well, listen ... *Madame* Jane ...

304

tomorrow *we* are going to open an account for fifteen hundred dollars Honduras, you've got to have a float, girl.'

'Mark.' She reared upon her elbows. 'What is this about?'

'Business. We're going into business, but don't worry, you'll be the managing partner. I'll just be the sleeping partner.' He grinned. 'For you that's the catch, because I'll be that all right.'

For a moment she kept silent. 'Mark. Are you really serious?'

'Damn right I am. Got all kinds of advantages. Business-wise you can't miss. Secondly, it'll give me a stake in the country. Last but not least,' he smiled again. 'I'll have to take a plane out here now and then, won't I?'

She lay still, thinking, trying to absorb it, until he bent over and kissed her breasts. 'What's the matter? You trying to find a way out of the deal? Gyp me out of a good business proposition?'

She said. 'I can't believe it.'

'Well, you'll believe it in the morning, because we're going right around to the bank and get it started.'

'But you're leaving in the morning.'

'Not till we've got this working, that can wait. We'll also have a private account to cover your living expenses for a year. I daresay you'll be making some money before that but meantime you've got to live.'

'Oh, no, I wouldn't need that, Mark.'

'Of course you'll need it. Don't you know most new enterprises fail because they're under-capitalised? And this one isn't going to fail.'

She lay back again and closed her eyes. For a time she was silent, then she said dreamily. 'Mark. Are you buying me?'

The simple sincerity of it was irresistible. He laughed outright. '*What?* For those kind of peanuts? I would if I could, darling, but I'm not Getty and I'd need to be. I haven't got *that* kind of money.' He paused for a moment. 'Why? Would you mind?'

She reached her arms around his neck and whispered against his ear. 'No, I'd be proud.'

305

BOOK FOUR

12. COROZOALE

As they drove north the 'countries' grew more varied and rugged than the southern jungles had been. Belts of *akalche* and semi-swamps of mangrove and palmetto, tangled habitats of water scorpions and land crabs that ran to several pounds— God knew what the crabs preyed on—alternated with courts of tall razor grass ringed by impenetrable boundaries of bamboo.

There were the same profusions of towering big timber as in the south. (Fine woods, for which the demand from a gamut of trades from shipbuilding to choice furniture had once been boundless.) Yet they were, increasingly, moving into another subdivision of geological time, Ryan felt.

The distinctions were not yet sharp, less so, say, than such African contrasts as the Ituri and the Serengeti, or the Highlands and Lowlands of Scotland. But there were more ravines and gorges. Expansive areas of *lavrado*, where sometimes the Savannah stretched in spreading funnels towards horizons of blue hills that, sporadically, boasted mountain peaks.

Occasionally, too, there were tracts of selaginella 'grass' ... which is not grass at all but something between moss and miniature fern a few inches high ... 'meadows', which had maintained their existence by denying the seedlings of both patriarchs and secondary growth through the dense resistance of carpeting which was as thick as fur.

If you took a helicopter over the Aberdares, he thought, you would only see great areas of slewin surmounted by a tabletop of hags. Or, over the Ituri, it would be the ceiling of a vast black-green mass. In the process, in the hinterlands, you would range over game herds the like of which these boys had never dreamed on, true.

But, leaving aside the fauna aspect, if you could plane over this 'country', he speculated, it would really be something to see. Just the panorama of it. Because this was the subtler land, the real *manigua*. The really complex, interacting, organic and faunistic enigma; more intricate than vast sprawling Africa. Over this territory you would look down on a quilt of 'countries', patches which were the distinct habitats of particular species of birds, animals and insects, which even had their own shades of climate, differing from the overall canopy.

He quit dozing over it, pulled himself upright and reached for the fresh wad of cotton waste in the dash to mop his hands and neck.

Ramirez turned his head. 'Coming up for air, then? Well, it was quite a night all right.' He swatted at an errant mosquito with his own rag. These ones in the north were more virulent, they not only carried malaria, but the yellow fever germ which comes from the blood of some monkeys. 'What kept you so long at the bank? I got all the money we'll need, anyway.'

Ryan had already told him the outline of the deal he had made with Ida, now he filled in the details.

A smile spread over the hunter's face as he listened and now and then he chuckled outrightly. 'Well, you're certainly a guy for the fast decisions, Bwana.'

'It wasn't all that fast,' Ryan said drily. 'I began getting notions as soon as I saw her come aboard at Quela.'

Ramirez laughed, 'Really taken, eh? Well, I'll tell you. I think you've got yourself a good proposition. Got sense and class too, Ida. She won't flop.'

'I wouldn't give a damn anyway,' Ryan said. 'Except that she deserves to make out.'

'She'll make out. Probably wind up buying the Store.'

'By the way, thanks for the ball,' Ryan said later. 'One way and another it was a night I'll remember.'

'Had a pretty good time myself,' Ramirez said. 'I wouldn't say the little one was the best lay in town ... she ain't had time yet, but maybe none the worse for that.'

'You can say that again,' Ryan agreed. 'I don't care how many permutations they know, the kind who stop in the middle for more gum are a dead loss. Give me the amateurs with the right qualifications every time.'

Like the way south, but sooner, the dirt road had given way

309

to track long since, and in parts it would have been easy to capsize the truck.

'I like the country,' Ryan said after a while. 'Pretty varied.'

'Yeh. Farther north you go the ruggeder it gets, and with more open pampas, *lavrado*. We're getting into the Sierra country now.' He spat his stub over the side and reached for the fruit. 'Oh, we got mountains all right . . . some.'

'I know,' Ryan said, 'the border country.'

'Yeh. Funny thing about the big ridges,' Ramirez mused. 'The air's cooler, you can see a hell of a lot more and yet they're kind of weirdie. So Goddam still and quiet . . . you ever get that feeling about mountains?'

'No,' Ryan said. 'I like 'em, except they'd be tough going in your climate.'

'Doesn't bother you so much as you'd think,' the hunter said. 'Starts to get cooler pretty fast. Up top you need blankets to sleep.'

'That where you get the mountain cabbage?'

'Yeh, palm celery. Real good.'

Ryan hawked up some of last night's brown taste and got rid of it. He took a peach and bit into it, enjoying the clean sweet flavour. 'You said something earlier about organising some dogs, what kind of mongrels are they?'

'Well, they're mongrels all right. You got that part right. Little brown bastards . . . and they are bastards . . . like short-legged terriers,' Ramirez told him. 'Half tame-dog, half bush-dog. What happens is, every once in a while the Indians come on a litter of bush pups, usually by accident because the burrows take a lot of hunting out. They manage to tame some, and then they cross 'em with what they've got. It works with about one in four.'

'And they hunt well?'

'Yessir! In small packs of about eight or nine. They'll take on any Goddam thing, except a man, maybe. I never heard of 'em turning on a man, but I've seen packs trying to bring down a tapir.'

In the peak heat they stopped at a stream, as they had done on the road south, for a brief siesta and to give the engine a

310

breather. The rill had quite a burble to it and was noticeably cooler than the southern streams had been, despite its long, long journey from the hills across successive tracts of open savannah.

'I was thinking,' Ryan said. 'Might be good policy to start off with a meat hunt for our hosts?'

'Yeh, I had that in mind,' Ramirez said. 'These Caribs take a lot of knowing. Took me ten years . . . and a marriage.'

'Caribs?'

'Well, there are a couple of Mayan villages in the territory, way over west, but where we're going they're Caribs.' He grinned. 'You read up on them, know anything about them? Some people call them Quilembas.'

'I picked up a bit of information,' Ryan said. 'Let me think. Their ancestors were all African slaves who regularly escaped in batches from the logging camps, the same thing happened in Brazil with the sugar plantations and mines. In both cases they pushed very deep into the jungle, far enough to preclude recapture, and set up villages . . . *quilembas*. They were much tougher customers than the native Indians, and they took all the Indian women they wanted, so that, in time, they became a kind of distinct hybrid people. That right?'

'Yeh, that's pretty well right,' Ramirez nodded. 'But you've left out a couple of things. They're the fiery kind . . . some of them are real vicious bastards . . . and they don't like white men. The white-man-hate got handed down, I guess, anyway you have to watch yourself all the time. In the old days they had professional hatchet men. Any white men they got hold of were executed, one of two ways. One was the *corte bananeire*, taking off two heads with one swipe of a machete. The other was the *corte major*. The guy was hung upside down, straddle legged, and sliced down the crotch into two halves.'

'Very anti-social you might say,' Ryan said.

'Yeh. It took me a long time to make real time with 'em. The thing you've got to watch is not taking up with their women. They take four or five wives each, and even nowadays the odd homicide don't bother 'em.'

'Don't worry about that,' Ryan said. 'I'm faithful to Jane.'

311

Ramirez laughed. 'Until a pair of big black tits and a waggly backside pass by, you mean, and some of them have got plenty of both. Besides,' he gave an elbow nudge, 'it's a fact they like big guys.'

Ryan reached out an orange and began to peel it. 'How do you tell the single ones?' he said, deadpan.

The hunter chuckled again. 'They're the ones when nobody slugs you from behind when you're teaching them the *Inglés* methods.'

'I'll keep mine on top for protection then,' Ryan said. 'It's the second best way anyhow. What kind of meat do they get themselves?' he asked when he had finished the orange.

'Mostly armadillo. Hunting, they're not even as good as the Mayans. Armadillo is pretty punk meat, but they're not hard to get. They can burrow faster than you can dig, but once they got one holed-up they flood him out. Some of the Corozoale armadilloes run to three feet long. What with the cats and bush dogs as well, they sure take a beating, but they don't seem to get any scarcer.'

'Just scaly-pork then?'

'Well, they net birds, *powis*, forest hens, macaws. Occasionally they'll get a deer at a drinking hole, and they use the dogs for peccaries. If they turn up a herd they try to get some holed-up under a tree, or some place, then they smoke 'em out and machete 'em as they break for it.'

'That wouldn't go far for a village,' Ryan said. 'They can't get meat all round very often then?'

'No, and with the peccaries they have to watch it. Sometimes the hogs will turn and charge 'em, and just two or three boars will rip strips off them and the dogs.'

'Well, if we get them a load of venison, or a bush cow, that ought to soften 'em up then?' Ryan asked. 'What with you being married to the headman's daughter and all?'

'I'm a widower now,' the hunter said laconically. 'Yellow fever. Also they don't have headmen, kind of a free-for-all council.'

'So. A pantisocracy,' Ryan said. 'Interesting.'

'There you go again.'

'Kind of pure Communism, not the Comintern kind. Governing by all, everybody's really equal.'

'Yeh, that's it.' He grinned. 'Imagine them cruts being ... pantisocrats?'

They reached the store run by the Chinese-Mayan descendant of its founder just before sunset. The trading post was as far as the truck could go. The derelict camp, where the old man lived, was a few miles west, the Carib settlement farther to the north-east.

In the morning it took a little time to sort and divide out the stuff, the tents and the essentials so that each was carrying a fair share in relation to his responsibility. Ramirez, in the lead, bore the smallest pack. But that was fair enough because he was the front man, the insurance, also, shouldering a rifle and carrying a shotgun.

Ryan's share included the ammunition and small gear, plus the Mannlicher and the Luger on his hip. He could have off-loaded some of the ammo on to Tomásco, bringing up the rear, because the big fellow had it easy enough. But he had a thing about ammo, because one time in Africa he had had two misfires which could have been disastrous, on account of the stupidity of the so-called gunbearer.

In the jungle, as always happened at first, the shade was a relief from the bright glare, but in less than half an hour, as the moist overlay began to evaporate, the dark sweat stains began to spread across their backs and under their arms.

All the forenoon, moving in single file, they followed the winding course of a stream which in some of its reaches was almost a river.

Sometimes the *arroyo* passed through dense thickets of bamboo where it was much more expeditious to wade the bed than detour around.

To begin with the wading was not unpleasant, but sometimes the pebbly bed gave way to stretches of soft silt in which you sank to your shins, and every so often they had to labour through clouds of insects hovering over the surface. *Bottlas* flies, mosquitoes and, worst of the insect scourges, the savage

313

cobarra gnats, against which the repellents were never completely effective and had to be constantly renewed.

At midday Ramirez called a halt and they laid out their sodden boots to dry in an open grove where the sun beat down with full uninterrupted force. The jungle seemed to be becoming somewhat sparser now, and nearby they could hear the sound of a waterfall.

An hour later they broke through on to open *lavrado*, and by the time they had half traversed the savannah tract their boots were steaming in the undiffused rays.

About three o'clock in the afternoon they powered through a patch of *akalche* scrub which grew higher than usual, and saw the village.

The huts, of bamboo and thatch, were quite different from the Mayan style. They were shaped and fashioned in a way which proclaimed the people's original West African ancestry, and outside many of them there were ochre-painted gourds and earthenware urns in which fermented the harsh corn liquor called *atole*.

The news of their arrival quickly spread through the village and a mixed crowd began to gather around them. It was obvious that Ramirez was on a good working basis with them, yet at the same time there was no tacit indication of welcome in the attitude of the men. Not overtly hostile, but not friendly either. Questioning.

While the hunter addressed himself to several of the older men, Ryan seated himself on a log and lit a cheroot. Around by the boys stood together in a tight group.

So far as he could judge, the dialect seemed to be an extraordinary mixture, including odd Spanish and English words, which had probably derived from a marriage of African tongues and Mayan, though one or two had a kind of limited pidgin English.

He also remembered, now, that the women were said to have a specific patois of their own, which was 'secret' from the men in the sense that it was only taught to girl children. The men were more heavily built than Masai, but there were certain resemblances, he thought. Few seemed to have any in-

314

clination to smile, but they all had the same mixed air of truculence and arrogance as the *morani*, the Masai bucks.

Not so the women. What Ramirez had meant about them was clear enough. Potential trouble makers!

The cheekier ones strolled back and forth eyeing the hunters, and there was no mistaking the invitation in their eyes and the exaggerated swaying of their buttocks.

Nearly all the younger ones looked as if they were in heat, would have joined you in the bushes at the drop of a hat.

Well, maybe it wasn't surprising at that because, as he now also recalled, the women supposedly outnumbered the men by three or four to one.

Probably they didn't get nearly the attention they could have done with, and at least as far as the surplus of unfavourite wives was concerned, the homicidal tendencies of the husbands would not allow much scope for philandering on the side.

They pitched camp by the small stream which served the village, but sufficiently far from the settlement to ensure that any of the Caribs with pilfering notions would have to cross a stretch of open ground.

An ambience of reflected light from the many open cooking fires had begun to gather over the village now, and as full darkness descended the overcast slowly intensified from soft pink to a more Faustian glow.

The dim shadows of moving people passed between the huts, sometimes momentarily blotting out a winking pane of firelight, and wafts of cooking odours were carried on the torrid wisps of breeze.

The five hunters ate supper in silence. It had been a tiring march and for four of them this interlude of food and relaxation made the best incident of the day. But, unlike the others, it gradually became obvious that Tomãsco had something on his mind.

The first to finish his food, the big fellow had since been moving around the camp in an aimless fretful manner that was quite irreconcilable with his usual style. Occasionally, hands in pockets, he stopped to stare across towards the village, and once or twice he had seemed to be on the point of speaking to

Ramirez.

The hunter watched him sourly. Then suddenly he snapped his fingers and gestured him closer with the leg of *laaba* he was picking at. When the big fellow stood before him, he continued eating for a moment, then looked up. He said, 'Listen to me, boy. I been watching you and you might as well go dip it in the water, because *you* ain't going anywhere. You do, and I'll cut it off . . . you got that, Tomãsco?'

The big Negro shuffled his feet morosely and nodded. 'Sure, boss.'

'Maybe tomorrow I'll make a deal for you,' Ramirez said. 'But there'll be no catting around like last time.' He gestured with the meat in his fingers. 'You got that, *hijo*! You think I've forgotten?'

Tomãsco nodded again. He turned on his heel and went over to the larger tent. He was disgruntled and frustrated, but he had only once crossed his employer before and he knew when the Cazador was not fooling.

Almagro and Manny exchanged grins, and Ryan chuckled. 'What's this? Tom got the ants in his pants or something? Wants into the kypher?'

'That dumb conch!' Ramirez swore. 'Time we were here before he damn near got himself carved up, damn near ruined the whole trip.'

'Couldn't he have married the wench . . . like you?'

'And stayed here altogether? Believe me, he didn't want that.'

'I can imagine,' Ryan said. 'But *you* didn't stay did you?'

'I made a deal with them from the beginning,' the hunter said. 'It cut two ways, suited them well enough.' He leaned over on his elbow. 'Don't get me wrong. You want to take a look around tomorrow, I daresay I can fix it. But the important thing is, you've got to make the deal first, not go screwing around like that dumb bastard did.'

'I already told you I'm faithful to Jane,' Ryan smiled. 'Also, I got close enough to one or two. Boy, they really hum.'

Ramirez laughed. 'You got something there. I used to take mine down the stream for her three-monthly scrape-down be-

316

fore we got into the hay. Used to come up as fresh as a forest lily then!'

In the next several days, hunting the surrounding 'countries' from dawn till sundown, they amassed a big cache of meat and, between gorging themselves, the Caribs were kept busy.

Four big fires, constantly re-stacked with hardwood chips for smoking the meat, were kept going all the time.

Everybody ate as much as they pleased, but, after gralloching, a number of beasts were sewn up in their skins and buried for future consumption.

The rich plentitude of food, with the added surety of full bellies for some time, had a kind of mellowing effect on the attitude of the men. Their language, like Kikuyu, apparently contained no provision for any expressions of gratitude. But there was a noticeable air of toleration, if not full acceptance, of the hunter's presence that had previously been lacking.

Accordingly, after the second successful day, Ramirez had been able to come to terms with the husband of one strapping out-of-favour Iris whose ample charms especially appealed to Tomásco. The woman was equally pleased with the big man's performance, and for Ramirez the deal had other than altruistic advantages. For besides precluding the possibility of any fornicatory fracas, it enabled him to give Manny a turn in the active business of hunting, and Tomásco was assigned, without beefing, to the chores and guardianship of the camp.

As a matter of esprit, similar romantic facilities were also offered to Manny and Almagro. But, save for one time, his inhibitions drowned in a jug of *atole*, when the cookboy eventually accompanied his authorised 'hostess' into the fringe of the *akalche*, neither of them seemed to be taken with the Carib women.

Each day so far they had followed the same pattern of hunting, with the same party of Ryan and Ramirez, Almagro and Manny, with shotguns and four Carib dog-handlers. The dog-handlers each had charge of two mongrels, held on leads until required, and there had been two incidents notably more eventful than the rest.

317

The first had occurred quite early in the morning of the second day. The general plan had been to 'drive' an open area of lavrado that lay east of the village, following a wide semi-circular course that would eventually bring them back towards their approximate starting point somewhere near sundown.

Primarily, Ramirez's tactics had been the same as when they had flushed the first *anta*, in the Parmeque country, except for the new incidence of the dogs. The dogs had impressed Ryan favourably. They were not much to look at, somewhat like scruffy short-legged terriers, but they were very effective hunters. And the basics had been sufficiently thumped into them to ensure that they were not difficult to reassemble after their job had been done.

This time the boys had gone ahead, fan-wise, Almagro and Manny each heading two of the Caribs. At the first several thickets little more than a few brace of forest hens had been flushed. But when the two pincer groups had detoured the sixth island of bush, Almagro had immediately signalled.

From a hundred yards across on the left, Ramirez had whistled and signed, but from the changed note of the dogs' chorusing Ryan had already picked up the message that the grove held something more formidable than birds.

Both men had converged to within forty yards of the heavy brush then, and as the baying of the dogs had risen to a pitch, Ramirez had signalled for the 'terriers' to be released. At once the yapping dogs had begun to circle the thicket, and almost immediately the creature within had disclosed his identity in a long drawn snarl rising to a deep threatening roar. For maybe two or three minutes more, the battle of noise had continued, the hate snarls and warning roars of the cat punctuating and transcending the frenetic yapping of the dogs.

Then Almagro and the others had begun to shout and the added effect of the man sound had ended the stalemate instantaneously.

The *tigré* had exploded from the tall brush, then, like a spotted greyish streak, he had taken a line on Ramirez's side of the thicket and the hunter had promptly swung on him and fired. The big cat's hindquarters had skidded sideways with

318

the force of the bullet, but he had not gone down and, as if befuddled with pain and shock, he had then turned at right angles from his original line, heading for an isolated Mammee tree two hundred yards across the plain.

It had been a lucky turn of events because, although the greater stamina of the trailing pack might eventually have worn him down, bayed him, had he reached the forest belt it would likely have been a long and uncertain business.

As it had been, Ramirez had stood grinning, feeling for his cheroots. 'Well, no hurry now, Bwana, he'll stay up there till we're good and ready,' he had said. Almagro had come up smiling, then, and Ramirez had taken the shotgun from him, handing the younger man his rifle. 'I'll just bring along the insurance, Mark, and you can take this one dude-style any time you like.'

'Looked quite a good cat,' Ryan said. 'Good thing you creased his ass, turned him.'

'Yeh. Just one thing I don't have to tell you, Mark, do I?' the hunter had said as they had begun to walk towards the hullabaloo of roaring and yapping around the Mammee.

'Not if you mean he'll act like a *chui*,' Ryan had said. 'Come for one of us when we get near enough, not the dogs?'

'Yeh, like that. By now he'll have figured out who's really after him.'

At forty yards the big cat, crouched in a fork of the Mammee, had still been mainly taken with the vociferous plague beneath him, spitting and snarling his fury at them. But at thirty yards he had risen, transferring his baleful yellow gaze to the men, and his tail had become more animated.

Then Ryan had dropped to one knee, pushed up the peak of his cap some more and laid the bead on the dark shoulder rosettes, and the heavy thunk of the Mannlicher had abruptly terminated the big feline's snarl like a slammed door.

When they had come to examine him Ramirez's bullet had taken a piece off his flank, but Ryan's had got the heart, cleanly, and the pelt was virtually a hundred percent.

'Good *tigré*, that,' he had said with satisfaction. 'A lot

319

lighter than the *coodoi*, I'd say, slimmer, but damn near as big?'

'Yeh, a young daddy,' the hunter had agreed. 'A stupid one. He'd've been an old daddy he'd have come straight for me when he broke cover.'

Maybe in a year or two he would have built up the bulk that the black one had had. The frame had been there. They didn't have quite the speed of the *chuis*, Ryan had thought, but a good one would see off two leopards, no trouble. Stockier, much heavier quarters, wider, deeper chests and more powerful jaws. Really strong, as well as vicious.

The second, more interesting sequence had transpired three days later. This time they had gone south, skirting the edge of the jungle and through an *akalche* area into what had seemed to be a *callejon*, a deadend, of swampy meadow tracts and big overgrown stagnant ponds.

Even though the Caribs knew the trails and causeways well enough, it was repellent treacherous country, swarming with insect pests. By midday the heat had been monstrous and they had been about to call a halt, when the leading Carib had run on to tracks of unusual interest, pointing excitedly to the spoor with his machete. After he had examined the prints Ramirez had turned with a grin. 'Well, you've still got the luck, Bwana. Buffalo for Chrissake! A loner, but pretty big!' For a few minutes he had thought about it. There had been several aspects to figure, taking into account the hazards and limitations of the terrain.

When he had made his decisions he had called the others around. The Carib who had led would continue, with one dog, the most disciplined one, then Ryan and himself. The others would lie back a hundred yards behind, and make damn sure that they kept the other dogs from sounding off. This he had hammered into them, with threats as well as gestures, until he had been satisfied that the importance of it was understood.

The spoor had been quite fresh, no more than half an hour old, and it had looked as if the buffalo might have just started out to seek a lying-up place, after his midday wallow, which

320

would serve him till sundown.

They had trailed him, then, for more than an hour, and at times the going would have been near impossible had he not been preceding them, forcing through packed walls of young bamboo and groves and tall razor grass.

At last his trail had veered and suddenly, surprisingly, they had broken through on to open *lavrado*. The Indian in the lead had halted at the fringe, staring ahead, then pointed towards a clump of high pampas grass overshadowed by a matopolo tree and Ryan had breathed his relief.

'Thank God for that. If he'd laid up back there in that God-awful stuff it wouldn't have been good, boy. Not if these ones charge?'

'They charge all right,' Ramirez had told him shortly, 'and if he comes we'll give him plenty of room you bet ... a hundred yards between us ... and if he heads for your cover, Mark, for Christ's sake stay down and let him go.'

'Don't worry,' Ryan had said, 'I learned respect of these ones a long time ago!'

When they had verified that they were still well enough down wind of such air current as there had been, they had begun to move slowly forward on either side, leaving Almagro and the others to work round within the fringe of the marsh growth in a wide detour that would bring them up at a point beyond the matopolo.

About fifteen or twenty minutes later Almagro had judged them far enough and they had broken cover, loping forward towards the tree.

It had been inevitable then that the buffalo would catch their scent but, perhaps through a crossing waft, it had happened even before they had loosed the dogs and he had emerged into the open quite suddenly. A massive dun grey bull, still caked with the red mud of the swamps, nose questing, moving his vast hooks to either side.

At once Almagro had called for the dogs to be released and they had begun the shouting.

Slowly, as if incredulous that man or beast possessed the temerity to disturb him, the big bull had begun to move in-

321

stinctively towards the swamp, heading roughly towards the point where Ryan lay screened. Until then he had still only seemed puzzled and suspicious, but when he had begun to quicken his pace Ramirez had fired.

The smack of the bullet, bursting in hide and flesh, had been followed by the bull's prodigious bellow, and in the same instant one of the Caribs had turned in panic running circuitously for the safety of the hunter's guns.

Instantly, then, the bull had charged him, bellowing his rage, oblivious of the dogs yapping at his heels. Berserk, conscious only of the running man, he had gained on the Carib with every stride and Ryan, grunting with concentration, had known for the second time in his life the terrible added responsibility upon him.

He had got the bead where he wanted it and fired just as beast and man had merged unto a single tableau, and the bull's forelegs had crumpled under him. But the buffalo's scimitar stroke had already fractionally preceded the bullet, and when they came up to him the great horn was through the Carib's back and out of his abdomen, skewering the quivering body like a speared fish.

Two days before they left the village Ramirez sent Almagro and Tomãsco on ahead. They were to take the old man bags of meal and a few other perquisites from the store, along with some supplies they had brought for him in the truck.

But primarily it was to warn the old hunter of their coming. For at times, still, when he was working the furthermost of his 'countries', El Viejo spent two or three days in the jungle at a stretch.

Somewhat to Ryan's surprise ... anticipating some kind of ritual or lamentations ... the Caribs had accepted the death of the tracker with a phlegmatic indifference he had formerly associated only with the Zulu and Masai. It had seemed strange at first, since most of their slave ancestors had derived from the voluble and demonstrative West African coastal tribes. But perhaps, he speculated, an infusion of the impassive Mayan philosophy had entered their character in the long process of the evolving banausocracy that had grown out of the merging of the races.

When the three of them came finally through the last of the trees to El Viejo's straggling compound if was near to sundown on the fourth day since the buffalo had spitted the tracker.

A mule stood tethered to the doorless jamb of one of the derelict cabanas from within which came a faint clucking of fowl. The hindquarters of the mule bore long parallel scars on one flank, as if a *tigré* or perhaps a puma, had sometime raked him.

Across from the old huts patches of maize and beans grew in the partial shade of three breadfruit trees, and elsewhere it was evident that the eternal challenge of the jungle scrub had been held in check by burning and the machete.

Tomásco was squatted by the cooking fire before the tent, his back towards them. But the old man had already heard their approach and stood waiting.

With the years his hearing had degenerated little and, trained as it was by long necessity, he could still pick up the dissonant sound of a *tigré*'s grunt at a distance of two arrow flights; distinguish between the rustling of high grass moved by the wind and that of a *tigré* returning, unsuspectingly, to the thicket where she had left her cubs.

It was, of course, one of the reasons why he had survived so long, and he had heard the shot by Ramirez, announcing their coming, twenty minutes earlier, whereas even Almagro had not been sure.

He came towards them smiling, unhurriedly, across the compound. And if his step was measured it was not heavy nor lethargic, but consistent with the muscles of the bare brown calves below his stiff rolled breeks, because he was a Cazador who, in his time, had marched many thousands of miles carrying heavy packs.

He held one arm slightly unnaturally, as if hampered with arthritis, but it did not appear to impede or distress him and Ryan regarded him with interest. From the things which Ramirez had said from time to time, it was assured that the

323

old hunter was of a breed you met but rarely.

Manifestly he was old. Yet his short once-powerful frame was still sturdy. Weathered oak. He was still, indeed, *es muy hombre*!

'*Viva Viejo*,' Ramirez called, grinning. 'That all is well with you, *novicio*?'

'*Amigo ... camarada!*' The old man gripped the younger hunter's shoulders and held him for a moment. His voice, too, was old, low pitched, but not cracked, and with warmth and sincerity in it.

Ramirez turned and spread his hand. 'Another *compradre*, Diego,' he said in Spanish. 'Another hunter ... of big stupid *elefantes*.' He wagged his head pretending derogation of it. 'Still, one of us.'

'*Qué va!*' the old man said. His eyes were china blue, but still unconquered, and the crinkles showed more deeply with his smile. He held out his hand. 'We are all one, Señor, the *estamos copados*, surrounded.'

'It is a privilege to meet you, Cazador,' Ryan said, and meant it.

For a moment or so the old man regarded him in silence. Years ago he had learned with bitterness, from the 'tecos, that it was unwise to trust too soon. Since then he had required proof of any man's sincerity. But his friend of friends, Juan, had called this *Inglés* '*compradre*' and he knew that even in drink Ramirez was not given to meaningless effusions, more the reverse.

'Equally, Señor,' he said. 'You are most welcome.'

'We shall not be staying long, perhaps a week,' Ramirez said, 'hence the newest information will assist us.'

'Of course,' El Viejo said. He dropped his gaze to his feet, hardened and calloused by the scars of thorn and razor grass penetrations of decades.

He had never really understood this business of rich men who wished to kill *tigrés* for pleasure, not profit, or flour or salt. To hunt *antas* without desire for the meat or hide.

It still seemed incongruous to him, though Juan had tried to explain it when he had brought the first of the three previous white men ... *Americanos* who had not spoken Spanish like this *Inglés*, he recalled ... to the Corozoale.

But he was pleased that they should seek his help, and more than gratified for any opportunity to make some small repayment of the debt he owed Juan.

Moreover, the mere fact of it subconsciously renewed his confidence in himself, recalled that, in all honesty, few men and perhaps none, understood *La Hermosura* better than himself.

Across the compound the old woman came from the hut and went slowly, shoulders hunched, to the fire. When she had filled a gourd from the pot hung over the embers she called out, disregarding the strangers, but the old man merely shook his head.

At dawn he had eaten a measure of grey maize and two eggs. But he had no mind for further hot food yet, though perhaps he would take a sliver or two of cold, roasted iguana before he slept.

'How goes it with the birds this time?' Ramirez asked.

'Good,' Viejo said. 'There will be three of the big cages, also one *cajón* of orchids.' He hesitated. 'Perhaps the birds and the orchids will compensate?'

'It has been bad with the cats then?'

'Si.'

'How bad?'

'Since the last time it was all right, at first; well, *medio*. Several *michos*, ocelots, but only one *tigré*. I am sorry.'

Ramirez shrugged. 'Do not worry.' He nodded in emphasis. 'It will make no difference. Am I not a hunter, too, compradre? Do I not know how it goes.'

'It is because I could not work for twenty days,' the old man said simply.

'You were sick?'

'Yes, sick.' He began to peel off his singlet, pulling it over his head with his better arm.

'Christ Almighty!' Ryan said.

The big scars across chest and shoulders were healed now, but still livid. Still painted on the brown of his skin, and paler

325

than the old scar over the joint and bicep of the bad arm.

'Amigo!' Ramirez shook his head from side to side. He grasped the old man's upper arms and peered closer. 'This was a very bad time, the worst of all I think?'

'No,' El Viejo said. He smiled. 'Perhaps the best of all. The time of *El Campeon*.'

The younger man frowned enquiringly. 'You were trying the bow again?' His sympathy and concern were manifest, but there was also reproach in his voice.

'No. It was with the big *trampa*.'

'What!' Ramirez's frown of incredulity deepened. 'How then?'

'The chain broke,' El Viejo said prosaically.

Ramirez swore. 'Cristo Rey!' He punched his palm with mortification. 'Then I should be wearing the scars, camarada, I am to blame.'

'No.' The old man smiled. It gave him a good feeling of warmth that his friend's solicitude went much beyond condolence. But it was because he was his compradre first, before his Patron, that he did not wish him to feel any personal guilt. 'It was El Campeon,' he said. 'His strength!'

Ramirez shook his head to and fro as if he had not heard. 'Christ, forgive me. The chain was faulty.'

'No, not so.' El Viejo gripped the other man's shoulder. 'There was no fault with it, Juan.' He repeated it. 'It was El Campeon, his strength.'

'Even so,' Ramirez said vehemently. 'Hereafter every *trampa* will be doubly tested, by me personally.' He held out his cheroots and when he had lit his own he gestured with it. 'And *you* also will test the chains, compradre, using the mule. And hereafter, also, Diego, you will not take the spear to any big cat, but finish him with small arrows from safe range. Poison him, anything, it will not matter.' He jabbed again with his cheroot. 'You hear me, Diego, *it will not matter* ... I would sooner have all birds and no cats!'

El Viejo smiled again. He felt a reaction that seldom came to him at this time of his life, except sometimes through the small doings of the grandchild and, oddly, for one who had so

326

long earned his bread by primitive unrelenting conflict, there was a surprising element of gentleness in his smile.

'I hear you, Juan,' he said. But within himself he knew that it was doubtful whether he would ever consistently obey.

For one thing you needed three, even four of the small arrows. Which tore the coat. More than that, there was the protraction of the business, the slow dying process!

He had no misplaced sentiment towards the creatures he killed. The harmless, and relatively harmless ones were for food. The *ofensivos* were to help rid the earth. The cats were for living from, and were far more merciless competitors than himself.

But even they, he had always felt, were entitled to the cleanest, swiftest end a conqueror could supply; as he would have wished for himself. Thus, the spear was without honourable alternative.

Oddly, Ramirez seemed to have overlooked the old hunter's name for the beast, but Ryan sensed the significance of it. 'It must have been a very formidable *tigré*,' he said. 'A real *ejemplar*, Señor?'

El Viejo looked at him steadily, reminded. He nodded. 'More than an *ejemplar*. The greatest I have ever killed,' he said simply.

Now Ramirez looked up. 'You mean you brought him *in*, Diego?' he said incredulously.

'Of course,' the old man said. 'To abandon such a one?'

It was the moment now that he had visualised when he had lain stricken beside the great cat, the realisation which had helped him to rise, and rise and go forward again when he had thought he could not. He gestured towards the shack beside the hut, the *almacén*. 'Come.'

He turned, waiting, but Ramirez put a hand on Ryan's arm. 'A moment, Mark, give me five minutes. I'll call you.' He followed the old man across the compound.

In a minute or two El Viejo emerged from the dimness of the hut. He had taken the greatest care in the drying and treating of the skin, giving it twice the usual amount of salting and kneading until now it was just as smooth and glossy as

327

when El Campeon himself had worn it.

He spread the great pelt on the ground and stood back watching the other man's face. 'A *campeon*, Juan?'

Ramirez put his hands on his hips, nodding. 'A campeon, compradre,' he said slowly. His voice rose. 'A campeon of campeons!'

He turned and gripped the old man, returning the embrace which El Viejo had first given. 'But, Diego, again, no more with the spear, you hear me. Not even with chain that would hold two buffaloes!' He shook him gently. 'Not for the skins of fifty such cats . . . you are my friend.'

El Viejo smiled and nodded. The knowledge of the younger man's steadfast regard, understanding, had been a great comfort to him ever since he had first realised it, fortified him against misfortune and bad times. He shifted his feet, not wishing to seem as if he was making too much of this business of the pelt.

'Almagro speaks well of the *Inglés*,' he said, divertingly. 'The *Inglés* has also killed a campeon?'

Ramirez looked up from where he squatted beside the skin. He understood well enough what was in the old man's heart. The battle he must have fought with this great *tigré*, and then the struggle and travail of bringing back the pelt, had probably called for the greatest effort of his life. And in the evening of his time.

To be surpassed, or even equalled now, by a newcomer, with a rifle, would seem an injustice of the cruellest kind.

He smiled and shook his head. 'No, not a campeon. A *coodoi*. A good one, but not a campeon like this.' He got slowly to his feet. 'And now another business, compradre. I plan to take the *Inglés* to the *valle*. It will complete his visit.'

'*Por los pavos*, the turkeys?'

'Partly. A diversion. But it is also a good place for big cat.'

'Truly. Perhaps even better now, for they do not hunt it. . . . Of course,' he shrugged, 'I no longer go . . . they would shoot me.'

'Undoubtedly, and you must never try it. But I still go there

328

myself.'

'Yes, and afterwards they always seem to know.'

'Ah, that is the point,' Ramirez grinned. 'Afterwards! I am always there and gone before they know. I precede their information.'

'But one time they will know before,' El Viejo said soberly. 'That is why I am against it. If you are going there, Juan, it would be better with Almagro, only. Not the *Inglés*.'

Ramirez shrugged. 'Just a diversion, as I said. In that sense I am not going, this time, to twist their noses. Besides, I do not think so. The *Inglés* is no *simplón*.'

'You have full confidence in him? *Genuino?*'

'Yes. He has the same fear we have, but no *panico*, and he kills well. And, yes . . . *genuino*.'

He called across the clearing and waved a hand, pointing down to the wide spotted skin.

Ryan came over carrying his drink. He looked down at the great pelt with a grin, then squatted to examine it more closely.

Bloody great *chuis*, save that the rosettes had no centre spots of course! But bloody formidable. '*Magnifico*,' he said admiringly. '*Magnifico*, Cazador.' The enthusiasm in his voice was wholly genuine, not just because of the scars and his admiration for the old man. The skin really was magnificent.

'We call the place, Diego and I, the *Valle de los Pavos*,' Ramirez said while they ate.

Ryan took another egg and mouthed it whole. 'This is the dicey country we discussed? The strictly illegal stuff?'

The hunter shrugged. 'Just one night?' He let it sink. 'We travel light, get some turkeys, a good cat, maybe two.'

'Don't get me wrong,' Ryan said. 'I'm in favour of it.'

For a moment he watched the darting yellow flames struggling to overcome a fresh application of wood that was giving out some sizzling.

'Let's not start too early though. Have a real breakfast for once and stop this pissing around with bits of fruit and coffee.'

He slapped his stomach. 'All this interminable sweating and

329

no eating or drinking, to speak of, I'm getting like a scarecrow.'

Ramirez laughed. 'Some scarecrow! Well, you can have yourself a whole roast turkey soon, Bwana, and believe me, they're good.'

They entered the jungle at about five in the morning, and for the first three or four hours they followed the caminos that ran nearly enough north-east. Then, close on midday, crossing an *akalche* patch, they saw the first range of hills.

The hills were low, only rising a few hundred yards, but they were both ready for a rest when they reached the top.

Ahead, looking down over secondary timber, the ground ran on flatly for a mile or two, then rose at what looked to be a steeper incline than the first ridge.

This second range was much higher, and at the distance it looked like two lateral bands of colour, like the brush strokes of some gargantuan artist. The lower slopes were washed with the bottle green of big timber, but above them the greenness diffused into a pastel golden shade superimposed with small pustules and striations of blue that were like suspended smoke trails.

It was early afternoon when they reached the foothills and flopped down beneath the duck-blue parasol of a tamarind. Ryan brushed the beads from his face with his forearm and took out the sodden rag of his handkerchief.

'When do we cross the border?'

Deeper within the tamarind grove flocks of crimson macaws and green and yellow parrots were holding their raucous daily conclamation of gossiping and propositioning before scattering about their individual sorties.

'We already have,' Ramirez answered. 'The hills back there, that was it.'

Ryan leant on his elbow and got the flat pint of *White Horse* from his pack. From somewhere nearby he became aware of the gurgling sound of water and he got to his feet again.

When he found it, a tiny rill of mountain water hardly more than a foot wide, he knelt and scooped out a small declivity in

330

the silt, wedging the bottle upright with stones.

Ramirez dug out a package of smoked meat and a second one of hardboiled fowl eggs.

The buffalo meat was dark and rubbery, like biltong, toughened by the smoking, but the flavour was all right and it was satisfying.

They rested longer this time, and then pushed on again for two hours more before stopping again for more than breathers.

Coming up through the tanglier stuff, and then through the shadier twisting avenues of the big hardwoods, the heat seemed fiercer than ever, and the ascent a lot more arduous than any of the Bens back home had ever been.

They made the crest, beyond the successive ridges which had all looked like the crest in the late rays, and for five or ten minutes they lay still, luxuriating in the inaction.

The fine aromatic smell of the forest was all around them and, even sweat-sodden as he was, Ryan began to taste the difference in the atmosphere now. He got a cheroot going and found the taste was nearly as good as when you still had the flavour of the marmalade in your mouth.

When he saw the brown snake with the white line along its head he stiffened and reached for the pistol against his thigh but Ramirez stretched out a hand. 'No, forget it, he's harmless.'

He turned back on to his stomach and began to take some real interest in the panorama of the *valle*. It was worth dwelling on. The coloration, particularly, was impressive. Differing shades of green, browns, blotches of tamarind blue and yellow meadow patches clothed the slopes, and running through the quilt, visible in stretches, was the luminosity of the river.

Ramirez fished in his pack and crawled up beside him on his elbows. He began systematically to scan the valley with the lightweight binoculars he had brought, quartering the ground as you did when you were trying to pick up a parcel of deer. Save for the changing glint of a small waterful way across the valley, a hill burn careering down the slope to join the river, the patchwork lay inert, containing no sign of move-

331

ment, but he persisted for several minutes.

'What's on your mind, two-legged or four-legged stuff?' Ryan asked.

For a moment the hunter continued to study the opposite slopes in silence. 'I'm interested in both,' he said finally.

'I thought you said there were no hunters?'

Ramirez handed him the glasses and felt for his cigarettes. 'They wouldn't be hunters. Here, you have a go.'

'How long will it take to make the river?' Ryan said. He focused the glasses and began to sweep along the banks, covering the open tracts.

'About two hours.' Ramirez drew on his cheroot and blew out a tight stream. 'How about if you fish for our supper while I make camp? Later we'll try for cats, and tomorrow we'll hunt the *pavos*.'

'Suits me,' Ryan said. 'Except what do I fish with, and how are you going to call the cats?'

'I brought some line and hooks,' the hunter said. 'You'll get *lukananis* under the banks . . . it's not a big river. For the cats, how about this?' He drew his knuckles back and forth across his lips and made a little chittering, squealing sound.

Ryan grinned. 'Not bad. Peccary in trouble?'

'Near enough! Not peccary though . . . *acuri*. Of course the gourd's the best, but they'll come for *acuri*.'

They began the descent with Ramirez carrying the twelve-bore and Ryan slinging the Mannlicher. Down through a miscellany of big timber and lesser trees, cohune and monkey-tail palms, festooned with lichens, mountain cabbage and huge feathery tree ferns, and finally out on to a narrow plain of *akalche*.

All the time a white hawk hung overhead, merely shifting his position a hundred yards farther on whenever they drew nearer below, and, on an even higher level, a scattered squadron of vultures kept vigil over the central areas of the valley.

In the forthcoming time of the heavy rains the *akalche* would have been nearly impossible to cross, but now it was still comparatively dried out. At the end of it they came on to a meadow of pale yellow moss, and finally to the river. As

332

Ramirez had said, it was not a big river. About thirty yards wide and, saving for holding pools at intervals, generally running no more than three or four feet deep.

They were prospecting along the bank towards an open stretch when suddenly, approaching a clump of brush, there was a scuffling noise followed by a gabbling alarm call, and three big birds scurried into the open and took off. Involuntarily Ramirez clicked the catch and swung. The first bird plummeted down at a steep angle, but the second, veering from the sound of the shot, wobbled as it got the second barrel and dived down like a landing aircraft. It rolled over on the ground, then picked itself up and began to waddle drunkenly, sometimes falling, towards a patch of fern, squawking and dragging a wing.

The hunter dropped his gun and pack. He overtook the bird just before it reached the foliage. A bunch of tail feathers, loosened with shock, came away in his hand, but he managed to grab the wing.

The first turkey was pretty useful. A cock bird of fourteen or fifteen pounds, handsomely decked in his gleaming greeny-black plumage and long red wattle. The hen gobbler, about half his size, was much less resplendent, tending to plain bronze. The pellets had broken her wing but otherwise she was untouched.

Ramirez shook his head in self-reproach. 'Aaah! Dumb. I shouldn't've done that.'

'All right with me, I mightn't have any luck with the fish,' Ryan said.

'No, it's not that. It would've been smarter to have laid off till tonight.' He began to scan the escarpment across the river, especially the crags near the skyline.

'You mean there could be somebody up there?'

'Yeh. Lookouts ... Indians.' He shrugged. 'Don't worry it's a thousand to one against ... it's a pretty big "country". But it did happen once, with Almagro and me.'

'They tried to take you?'

'Yeh. It must've been just luck because if they'd been waiting for us they wouldn't've had a fire. We didn't spot it until

333

we'd killed a couple of birds . . . they were way along the *valle* . . . then Almagro saw their smoke. After that it was no problem because we had one rifle.'

'You took off?'

'No.' Ramirez grinned. 'We found ourselves a butte back up the hill and let them come to the river. Then we discouraged them . . . they don't like being on the other end and their nearest barracks if half a day from here. When they quit we waited on two days . . . I knew they'd figure we'd run for home . . . then we got ourselves two good cats.'

'Cheeky,' Ryan said. 'But I like it. Anyway, we've got one rifle now.'

Ramirez grinned back. 'Yeh, but we'll keep looking out. What's between me and Cruz now, that *hijo* just might keep a couple of Indians quartered up here. He knows the only thing can ever do him any good is for me to be taken, or have a big accident.'

They chose a site near a bend in the river, at the end of an open stretch in the shady concealment of a small island of cohunes. Ramirez had trussed the live *pavo*, and when he had laid the bird down beside the packs and guns he tapped Ryan's arm and pointed across the river.

'See that big blue rock up there, the one looks like a hook-nosed man? Well, right opposite that, this side, there's a drinking place that's sure fire. We'll set up there tonight, and I'll tie out the bird as well.'

He ferreted in his pack and came up with a flat aluminium reel of eight pounds lines, and small box with a pinch of hooks, eyelets and two or three sinkers. 'There you are, Bwana. Give you till sundown to come up with some fish, after that we'll start roasting the gobbler.'

'Hold on to the bird a while,' Ryan said. He took the reel and the wee box and began to move slowly along until he came to a place where the river widened after a constricted bend and then opened up again, leaving baylets on either side where the water moved more slowly than the main flow.

Here and there along the banks there were small trees that looked like pale green osiers. They had the spring of willow,

334

and he cut out a wand about five feet long and an inch diameter at the thick end. You could have fished handline style, but with the wee makeshift rod it would be easier to cast and, if you got a decent fish, to play him in.

He sat down and bound an eyelet on to the wand just short of the tip with the nylon line, then he threaded on a couple of sinkers a hand's span above the hook. When he had found some deadwood he cut a plug, shaped the bleached white wood to a float like a chunk of a cigar, and looped it on to the line about four feet back from the hook.

It was an inelegant construction, in much the same category as the rural urchin's traditional willow branch and bent pin, except that it was pretty strong, and a few trial casts along the bank confirmed that it worked.

He grinned at his handiwork and then set to turning over stones and digging with his hunting knife at the bank edges until he had a cigarette pack of red and white worms. He was becoming as keen and expectant as a boy now, smiling to himself unconsciously.

The first and second casts fell too near in and he swore, but by the third attempt he had got the feel of it and the sinkers arced out to midstream. He paid out line on free reel and let the float drift along with the sluggish current. Coming opposite to where he squatted the plug bobbed, then disappeared and he struck. For a fraction of an instant he felt the take, then it came away and he swore again.

Obviously it was going to be better to let these ones really mouth it, as with salmon or shark, before you hit them. But they were there all right, and they didn't keep you waiting long. Nothing like uneducated fish for plenty of action.

He reeled in, cast again and this time when the wood disappeared he let it run for a moment or two before he struck. Inside half an hour he had banked three takeable *lukananis*, around two-three pounds apiece, thrown back three smaller ones and killed two *biaras*, wicked-looking useless fish, running to two feet long, which were all big mouth and teeth like oversize *piranha*.

The *lukananis* ought to make an acceptable change, he

335

thought, wrapped in thick leaves and baked in embers; along with the leftover eggs. And they'd cook a sight quicker than the big *pavo*, or even just his breast. And after that there was still a spare half-bottle. No, wait a minute. Better leave that till they'd tried for a cat.

It was fully dusk now and as he returned to the cohunes he could smell the fire which Juan had got going, though he could not see it because the hunter had built a surround of thick brush under the trees on the open side.

Ramirez took the strung fish and held them up, grinning. 'You know, Bwana, you'd make a Cazador at that. You'd live.'

'Cheeky bastard. You bet I'd live,' Ryan said. 'Someday I'm going to take you where they make the jackal stew,' he kissed his knuckles, 'the real goods!'

'I doubt I'd like it there,' the hunter said. 'I'd probably run like hell from the buffs,' he explained.

Ryan grinned back. 'You dassent! Unprofessional conduct ... breaking the rules. Anyway,' he yawned mightily, 'that's enough talk about running, I could sleep for a week.'

'Have a rest when we've eaten, then. Ten o'clock will be soon enough.'

The watering place opposite the big crag with the aquiline profile over on the far ridge was at the bend beyond the one where Ryan had fished. The river ran along the bed of the valley like a silvery artery now, and the slopes on either side were invested with shadow. But a threequarter moon had risen over the skyline of the slope they had first descended, and the opalescent rays produced a reflection on the water that enabled you to make out a fair amount of detail in the vicinities of the banks, once your eyes had accustomed to the wan light.

As they came around the bend a small flotilla of duck took off with a sudden concerted whirring of wings, scurrying low over the surface to plane down again on to the water, perhaps a quarter mile farther downstream, in a sequence of intermittent plops. Nearer at hand something slid into the water with a soft sucking sound and was gone.

The crescented inlet had first been worn out of the bank by

336

successive high-water turbulencies in the times of the rains, and then subsequently piled with silt, smoothed off and hard-baked by the sun, as the water level receded. Geological arrangement, too, had obviously also contributed to the formation of the inlet, for at either end rock piles stood at the water's edge. The basic features of the place were consistent with watering places instinctively chosen by non-carnivorous game of all kinds; the combination of open ground and shallow incline to the water providing a degree of safeguard from ambush attacks by the feline and saurian predators.

Ramirez made across the bare crusted soil of the baylet for the smaller tableau of rocks facing the big flat-topped pyre.

'Pretty good set-up,' Ryan said softly. 'If it's still popular?'

'Don't worry,' Ramirez said. 'You stay here long enough, you'll see specimens of practically everything in the *valle*, that's why I decided to leave the little *pavo* to cook ... we'll have her cold in the morning ... plenty of natural bait ... the cats got to drink too.'

There was room for both men, and to spare, in the snaggle of boulders that had originally been deposited by some stratis-graphical action aeons ago at the edge of the *valle*'s vein, and so had survived the centuries of water erosion that had ground the rest into sand.

Ryan stripped off his bush jacket and laid it along the top of the rock they had chosen. It would absorb any metallic sound and, anyway, you never fired from a barrel resting on a surface as hard as stone or metal.

When they had first arrived the frogs had fallen silent, but now they began to rejoin the chirruping of the cicadas and soon their low gruff chorusing became merged again with the soft murmur of the water.

The first visitors were a quartet of *brockets*, the small bush deer so reminiscent of the diminutive Africa dik-diks. The responsible buck moved slowly forward, delicately pacing the hard mud with his dainty hooves, head moving from side to side, ears flicking, ready for instant flight. His nose quested the air, but what faint current there was came from behind him, carrying the traces of man scent out across the river.

337

Twice he froze, listening, then he gave a small throaty grunt of reassurance, moving forward to the water, and his three charges trotted forward out of the shadows.

For three or four minutes they lapped thirstily, then suddenly the buck raised his head, nose tilted. Maybe some drifting eddy from the ridge had carried back a trace of the man smell over the humid motionless air, or maybe his acute hearing had caught the sound of movement somewhere back in the darkness of the *akalche*.

He voiced his gutteral warning and instantly they wheeled and were gone, bounding away like miniature impala.

More deer came at intervals during the next hour, then a family of peccaries, the boar grunting fitfully and the rank hog smell carrying to the watching men.

Down river an occasional soft splash confirmed the return of foraging *laabas*, or some other of the marsh creatures, to their element of safety. A porcupine came out of the shadows behind the big crag and ran over to the water's edge, the white tips of his barbed quills just discernible in the moonlight. The rodent drank briefly and then began to hunt the fringe of the shallows, but when he heard the heavy resonant footfalls approaching he turned and skittered away in the direction the *brockets* had taken.

The big cow *anta* who had spooked him came lumbering out on to the strand, unhurriedly, with the disregard of caution inherent in a creature largely immune to fear of attack by other beasts. She plodded forward to the edge, her formidable weight imposing imprints which obliterated the light markings of the deer, and dipped her snout into the water. But she had not come to drink so much as bathe, and after a cursory swallow the tapir waded forward to her knees, then plunged and began to swim across the river.

'Okay,' Ryan whispered. 'Let's wrap up the menagerie now and call for cat?'

He glimpsed Ramirez's teeth in the dim light and watched the hunter bunch his knuckles and give the call, sending the weak distess squeal into the darkness and then repeating it. While the hunter called he leaned his forearms on the rock and

338

took a trial squint across the mud flat, and then at another spot higher up. Near the water he could just make out the Mannlicher's foresight, but it would have to be the torch.

They had brought the guntorch instead of the lamps for convenience of packing and he was interested to make the comparison.

Several times more Ramirez called at intervals, but nothing stirred. Ryan started to whisper and to shift his position, then he felt the other man's grip on his arm and froze.

The jaguar came out of the shadows of the big cairn just as the porcupine had done, and moving as slowly as the bush cow had, but contrastingly alert. She seemed similar in size to the big tom they had flushed with the dogs, and in the moonlight she looked handsome and powerful.

For a moment she stook quite still, one ear twitching, staring around her as if seeking the origin of the pain calls, yet, oddly, Ryan had the feeling that it was not the calling that had brought her. Perhaps she had merely come to drink, or was after bigger prey.

She padded over to the water and began to drink, but then, just as his fingers began to firm on the button of the torch, she changed her position and stood listening like the little buck had done.

Ryan had his cheek on the wood now. He was just waiting for her to turn again, or give any indication of taking off, but Ramirez breathed in his ear. 'Wait, she's not going.'

As if to bear him out, the *tigré* moved over to the rocks. She sprang lithely on to a lower boulder, and then a second time on to the top of the crag, as if it was a manoeuvre she was well used to. Now she sank down on to her belly, edging forward until her head and shoulders were silhouetted.

'No hurry,' Ramirez whispered. 'I'll raise her when you're ready.'

Ryan strained his eyes until he was satisfied the bead was just above her, then he tapped the hunter's leg with his foot and drew in a breath. Ramirez whistled shrilly and almost at once the big feline rose, fully silhouetted now.

Ryan pressed the button and brought down the circle of

339

light until he had the bead on the forequarters of the statue. The crash split the oppressive air like lightning ripping through cloud. Up on the crag the jaguar reared on her hind legs, revealing her whole taut outline, then she fell backwards and they heard the thud of her body on the lower rocks.

Ryan knew instinctively that it had been a good one. He grinned. 'I don't think we'll have to scattergun her, boy. I don't think that one's going anywhere.'

'I know it,' Ramirez said. 'Not when they stand on their ass like that.'

13. INCOMMUNICADO

When he heard the shout and the shot it brought him out of his dreaming at once. But for a second or two he was confused, because the sounds had fitted into the chimerical pattern of his waking-reverie about the cat on the rock. Then he saw through the tent flap that it was fully light.

They had sat gabbing and finishing the whisky for quite a time after they had skinned the *tigré*. Now Juan must have got ahead of him and taken a crack at something ... except that, it suddenly occurred to him, the report hadn't come from a shotgun!

He crawled out of the tent and got to his feet.

There was an officer, six *soldados* and an Indian!

The soldiers were dressed in faded threadbare tunics and raggety putttees. The *Teniente*'s tunic was of more recent origin, though the epaulettes and buttons bore the tarnish of neglect, and presently it was fully unbuttoned, displaying the bulge of his stomach above his baggy breeches.

He held an old .45 Colt in his hand, and a faint smell of cordite still lingered on the soft morning air.

Ramirez stood where he had been when the warning shot had come as he had made to go for the guns which he had brought earlier from the tent.

340

The soldiers stood in a circle around the tent, one behind the hunter, staring woodenly at Ramirez, their ancient Springfields held ready against their hips.

'Visitors, Mark,' Ramirez said laconically. 'And us all out of liquor too.'

'I would not joke yet, *ladrón*,' the bulky man said heavily. 'Because if you do not have the *salvoconducto papers* ... as you do not ... you will find that the joke is with you.' His voice had the huskiness of much tequila over many years.

He spat a lick of tobacco juice on to the grass, giving a glimpse of a gold tooth that was new and others that were dulled and stained. His grin was a grimace, humourless. Sour. And the sourness was empiric in him because, ever since he had been promoted to *Teniente* fifteen years ago, life had been an endurance trial.

He had first become soured not only by the hopelessness of any advancement, but also by the omnipresent possibility of dismissal and greater poverty. Soured, additionally, by the scraggy bitch he had married for a dowry that had been myth, and whose vigilance precluded pleasure with women of his own kind, reducing him to the undignified business of compelling Indian girls. Soured, again, by the repeated harryings and cursings of his military and political superiors ... even, several times, before the men ... respecting his frequent failures.

Ryan found his cheroots and held them out. 'All right, Señor Capitan, it is my fault that we did not obtain the *salvoconductos* ... the time factor, you understand ... hence it is my responsibility,' he said easily. He nodded towards Ramirez. 'The Cazador is in my employ. What is the fine?'

The Lieutenant took off his cap and mopped his bald head and his face. They had travelled all night and, even riding most of the way, the Indian leading the mule and the squad trailing behind, the journey to the ridge had been tedious and pestilential. Especially the *ofensivos*, the insects, had been hellish, and the descent into the valley, necessarily on foot lest the mule had betrayed them, had been infernally arduous.

On the other hand he felt borne up by his success, for he had been left in no doubt of Ramirez's importance.

341

He put away his rag of handkerchief and rubbed the bites on his neck and ears.

'Oh, there will be a fine, certainly,' he said heavily. He repeated his previous grimace, attempting sarcasm. 'A sum suitable to your importance, I think. But not for this *ladrón*, he is beyond fines.'

'Why should that be?' Ryan said. 'I already told you he's working for me.' He gestured towards the pelt pegged between two of the cohunes. 'Are you so short of *tigrés*, Señor? Where is the importance of this?' He maintained the conciliatory note,

The grimace faded from the squat man's face.

'The importance is of the law, the importance is that you are merely *ladróns*, *bandidos*,' he snapped.

After all the journey and the effort ... not for the first time to this Godforsaken 'country' ... the implication that the matter was a triviality touched a raw spot. He waved an order with his revolver and a soldier moved behind Ramirez with handcuffs.

'Wait,' Ryan said. 'I find it impossible to believe that we cannot make amicable settlement?' He glanced significantly around. 'And, of course, it is understood that there would be adequate additional expenses.'

The fat man stared. The fact that in this case he dared not contemplate any such practical arrangement only increased his inner sense of frustration and persecution.

'Do you understand yet?' he said stridently. 'He is under arrest ... you are both under arrest.'

'Don't upset the *Teniente*, Mark,' Ramirez said sardonically. 'With all these witnesses he has to think of Cruz.'

The Lieutenant swung round, his mouth drawn into a crescent of anger. It was not only that this man had been the origin of past humiliations, he could not rid himself of a feeling of inequality with both the hunter and this rich *Inglés*. And there was, too, the fact of the men. His command.

Suddenly, explosively, he hit Ramirez angrily across the face, back and forth. '*Ladrón* ...'

The hunter staggered back. 'You shouldn't have done that, *chino*,' he said sibilantly, quietly. 'I'll remember that one, *chino.*'

The reference to his baldness ... *chino*, curly ... was like an added goad to the glowering man. A nerve began to pulsate beneath his eye, almost as if he was winking, and his fingers opened and closed. He transferred his grip on the pistol in his hand to the barrel and started towards the fettered man.

'You do that and I'll bloody crucify you, policeman!' Ryan said harshly.

The anger and the venom in his voice made the other man check. Somehow the imperiousness of it reminded him of higher authority, reminded him that this *Inglés*, though he made no difference to the substance of his orders, offered a certain complication.

He turned and glared. He was still consumed, but he experienced an unfamiliar quirk of misgiving for a moment.

'What, you threaten *me, Ignorante*? Do you not know that I could execute this *ladrón* now? *Here?* He tried to resist arrest, he has fired on us before ... !'

Ramirez sensed the reservation in his voice. 'And ordinarily you might rate a bonus for the execution,' he said. 'From Cruz! But not this time, eh, *Teniente*? This time Cruz would remove your *cojones* for such a blunder ... before a neutral witness.'

The Lieutenant hesitated, resentment and doubt as well as frustration showed in his face. Any mention of the name of El Jefe Politico in this matter, he remembered, was rigorously to be avoided. He bit at his lip, fretfully, deciding to ignore the hunter's taunt, and glared balefully at Ryan.

'You consider yourself in a position to threaten me, then, *extrangero*?'

'Not threaten ... warn,' Ryan said coldly. He held out his British Press pass, and the other of the Association Internationale de la Presse.

'So, a *periodista*. This makes a difference?' He spat his unconcern on the grass.

'A *periodista politico*,' Ryan lied. 'And *your* Jefe Politico will explain to you that it makes a great deal of difference.'

He gave it all the enigmatical implication that he could.

343

The bulky man hesitated. He became conscious of the twitch beneath his eye again. 'Move,' he said angrily. 'Enough time has been wasted.'

He nodded to the corporal who had handcuffed Ramirez and the man came forward with a second pair of handcuffs.

'Wait,' Ryan said. He swore. 'Do you expect us to march like that? I suggest you chain us together, *Teniente*. In the name of Catholic decency, of course ... and international journalism,' he added acidly.

For a moment they stared at each other in stony silence. Then the Lieutenant spat again and nodded grudgingly to the corporal. The soldier took out a key and made the adjustment, shackling their wrists together.

When they came to the place, much farther along the valley, where the Indian had chosen to ford the river, the *Teniente* climbed on to the back of one of the *soldados* and another of the men waded beside them, steadying his comrade.

In places the water rose waist high. When it lapped his boots the Lieutenant swore, but the Indian had known his business and it would have been hard to find a flatter, shallower place.

The Mayan leading, they moved steadily through the *akalche* belt and then began to climb the far slopes in a straggly file, the corporal and two others at the rear of the column.

The pace so far was easy enough, and with periodic halts. The Lieutenant rarely travelled other than by mule, and he was in no condition for forced marching through rough country.

For a while more they walked in silence, then, suddenly, Ramirez said awkwardly, 'Some bloody *tonto* I turned out to be, Mark, I don't know what ...'

'Aaah, forget it,' Ryan interposed. He turned his head. 'You think they can really hold us?'

'Not you,' Ramirez said. 'They won't want you around anyway. But it might take a week ... the formalities.'

'How about you?'

Ramirez grimaced. 'Oh, they can hold me ... period! Till

344

they've softened me up, or till they arrange for me to "escape". It will depend on the proposition.'

Ryan frowned incredulously. It still seemed incongruous. Bizarre. 'Look, I know what you told me, but Christ almighty, man, this isn't the eighteenth century.'

'It is *here*,' Ramirez said with unusual emphasis. 'Like Mexican eighteenth century, believe me.'

'How about Cruz?' Ryan said after a pause.

'We won't see Cruz. Cruz will be missing. Taking a vacation in Mexico or someplace. This is the only chance he'll ever get. He'll be missing all right.'

Up ahead the Lieutenant stopped again. He fished for his sodden bandana and bawled pettishly at the Indian to halt.

Ryan raised his free hand. '*Por favor, El Teniente* ... to smoke?'

The sweating heavy-set man stared for a moment then nodded curtly. He seated himself on a boulder and felt for his own cigarillos. He had been unsuccessfully searching in his mind for an excuse to teach this *Inglés* a lesson, preferably one which would allow rifle butts. *Qué te importa*, the *Inglés*, anyway? Still, a *periodista*! It would be better to be cautious, to curb himself, at least until he had the other one behind bars.

His thoughts turned back to the *ladrón*, Ramirez. It was obvious from the importance which had been set upon the man's capture, not to mention the castigations he, an officer, had suffered for the previous failures, that there was more behind it than illegal hunting operations. That El Jefe Politico was concerned with something beside enforcement of the penal laws, some kind of personal vendetta. Not that he cared a centavo for that aspect, save that he could see little prospect of any reward in it for himself . . . for all his own tedious trouble and discomfort. Reward would no doubt be forthcoming from Cruz but, he thought morosely, it was not likely that any of it would extend beyond the pockets of El Jefe Policia, his own direct superior.

As he stubbed his cigarette on the rock, he had a thought. It was only a mean trivial thing but he had still been unable to

345

think of a pretext for real punishment. He went back a few steps and reached peremptorily for the cheroots in Ryan's shirt pocket. As he guessed, they were much superior to the cheap yellow cigarettes he was accustomed to.

'No more. Confiscated!' He put the pack in his pocket.

About twenty minutes later they reached the crest of the ridge. The Lieutenant found a rock and sat down on it, breathing heavily. The others stood around waiting while the guide went for the mule they had tethered farther along the summit.

When the Indian returned with the beast, the Lieutenant got the leather *bota* looped around the rifle scabbard against the mule's side and gave himself three long squirts of tequila. Then he lit one of Ryan's cheroots and signed to the Indian.

The Mayan knelt down on all fours and the fat man mounted the mule, using the Indian's bare back as a step. He raised his hand and they got roughly into file and began to march across the undulating summit area of hags and rocks, the Indian leading the mule but moving at a quicker pace than formerly.

The sun was coming up to full force now, and when they had descended the other side to the flat and crossed a stretch of *akalche* it was a great relief to enter the shade of the big trees.

'Listen,' Ryan said softly. 'We'll give it two days. If I haven't got any sense out of them by then we bust out!' He didn't think they could overhear him, but he spoke in English because it had become clear that none of the others understood it.

Ramirez smiled. 'I had a similar kind of notion,' he said. 'Except it will just be me, Mark, not us.'

'Forget it.'

'No.' The hunter shook his head. 'You're really a good guy, Bwana. But let's not be stupid. *You* don't need to take any chances ... they got to spring *you* sooner or later. If *I* can bust out ... before they let me bust out ... I can lose these *hijos*!'

'Forget it I said,' Ryan insisted. 'What do you take me for?'

For a time the camino they were following allowed the

346

Lieutenant to continue mounted, though sometimes he had to lie flat on the mule's neck to avoid the groping tendrils and drooping tangles of lianas. But in the afternoon the Indian took them along a trail where, frequently, the archway of the forest was simply too low and he was obliged, cursing, to dismount and walk.

Surprisingly, when they came finally out of the trees the town bridge was only four or five hundred yards ahead.

The cortège straggled wearily along the burnt dirt track, the men dragging their feet in the red dust, guns slung haphazardly. The Indian had been ordered back to the rear now and the Lieutenant headed them himself as a matter of prestige.

He turned in the saddle to bark an order and they made the tedious effort to achieve a more military appearance, straightening up and shifting their slings.

The town sweltered sulkily in the excoriating heat. Inevitably, as he bitterly reminded himself, it seemed largely unconscious of the Lieutenant's triumphal return, deserted, as it always seemed to be when he was successful.

Only a few fowl, ineffectually hunting the dust of the street, and a handful of barefooted children gave sign of life, though dark wondering eyes peered from behind some of the shutters of the crumbling adobe houses.

Otherwise the only witnesses to their coming seemed to be the three peónes sitting patiently on the wooden bench before the Station.

They had been awaiting the return of Authority all day, and if they were not called by the time the Angelus was rung they would go home, returning next morning to go before the *Teniente* and pay their fines, or the instalment of a previous fine, or, in extremity, to offer the mitigating consideration of a daughter prepared to share the Lieutenant's bed. What else with no money or hope?

A *soldado* came forward and hitched the mule to the rail outside the low whitewashed building which was the *cuartel* and the jail. The Lieutenant dismounted heavily and the three peasants rose respectfully, doffing their hats.

347

One of them, more venturesome, murmured something in a low voice and another hopefully shuffled his feet, but the *Teniente* ignored their presence.

He turned and waved away the small silent throng of children, then gestured irritably to the corporal. The soldier completed the dispersal of the urchins, and jerked his rifle for the prisoners to precede him inside.

The room within was square and sparsely furnished, as austere as a railway waiting room. At one end a wooden bench, for miscreants and supplicants, ran along one flaking wall. At the other end the seat of justice, an old rolled-top desk, faced it.

The desk was copiously marked with circular stains and cigarette burns, and beside it, presumably for visitors of importance, there was an easy chair of plaited henequen.

On the wall behind the desk there was a faded picture of the Nativity clipped from a magazine, and above it a carved Cross. Clips of dusty papers and notices hung from nails on one side of the Mercy emblem, and on the other, bitterly, a poster of a wanted peón with a frozen expression and puzzled, staring eyes, was pasted to the wall.

The Lieutenant stripped off his tunic and threw it on to the bench. He undid the top three buttons of his shirt and went over to a door in the corner by the desk. He flung it open and shouted, waiting a brief moment, then shouting again more impatiently. In a minute or two a man in a dirty white singlet appeared in the door of the men's quarters across the courtyard. He was not one of those from the arrest detail, but he wore the regulation trousers and puttees.

'Beer. *Immediatamente*. Then food!'

'*Con su permiso, Teniente*,' Ryan said. He laid a note on the desk. 'We would like to join you, adding a bottle of tequila ... in the name of civilised justice, of course.'

The fat man stared back resentfully. Such assurance on the part of the prisoner was incredible, infuriating.

On the other hand it also gave him a slight feeling of unease ... and he saw that there was enough for two bottles. He hesitated, then went to the open door and called to the soldier

348

again, augmenting his order.

One of the men from the squad came in from the street with the rifle and the shotgun which they had taken from the hunters. He laid the guns on the bench, also Ryan's pistol and holster.

The Lieutenant picked up the five-dollar bill and moved over to the bench. He pinched his nose with his stubby nico-tined fingers. It was in his mind to confiscate whatever money they carried before his Chief returned.

The *Inglés*, at least, was probably carrying a large sum, and it was foregone that El Jefe would find a way of confiscation.

He, the mere instrument, would be lucky to wind up with one of the guns.

He pulled at his lip indecisively, but then, reluctantly, he remembered the added complication in the case ... Cruz. ... It was quite maddening but he dared not risk any major indiscretion with the *Inglés*, lest, for some reason beyond him, it embarrassed their plans for the *ladrón*, Ramirez.

As the orderly came in from the courtyard he made an abrupt gesture to the corporal waiting by the street door and jerked his head.

'All right, put them away ... *las jualas*.'

'A private word with you first, Capitan,' Ryan said. '*Por favor*.'

The Lieutenant paused. He had the feeling that there was some kind of derisive intent in the Englishman's periodical misrepresentation of his proper rank. He nodded shortly to the corporal. 'Take away the criminal first.'

When they had left he sat down at the desk and poured himself a glass of tequila.

'Well?'

'With your permission.' Ryan reached for the bottle. He poured out a second glass of tequila, downed it and took one of the beers.

He said, 'Where is El Jefe Politico ... Señor Cruz ... Capitan?'

The Lieutenant glowered. He would dearly have liked to have had this one strung up and himself taken the knout of

349

caiman hide to him ... his own invention ... but his instinct still counselled constraint.

'That is something to you? You are a personal friend no doubt?'

'No, but it will be to you,' Ryan said acidly, 'because I am acquainted with some of higher station.' He nodded slightly, affirmatively, to lend emphasis to the bluff.

The Lieutenant experienced a slight sensation of confusion. For a moment he wondered whether there might have been some misunderstanding of his instructions respecting the *Inglés*, or between Cruz and his Chief.

'Unavailable,' he said brusquely. 'Also irrelevant. Señor Cruz is not of the Policia.'

'Well, then, where is *your* Jefe?' Ryan said. 'El Jefe Policia.'

'*Cristo!* I warn you not to provoke me further with these nonsenses.' The feeling that, fantastically, he himself was being interrogated made him almost shout. Then he remembered what he had forgotten to make clear at the outset. 'They are both abroad, but,' he thumped the desk, 'irrelevant. I am the law here, *Inglés*!'

'That is what I wished to establish,' Ryan said easily. He put another note on the table. 'Let us have another drink and I will explain.' He shook a cheroot from the pack, his own pack, which lay on the desk. '*Con su permiso!*' he said ironically.

When he was lit, he spread a hand. 'Since you are solely in authority surely there is no need of delays of complications?'

'Complications?'

'Let us be practical, Captain,' Ryan said flatly. 'If we do not return soon a lot of things will start to happen for which,' he made a gesture of deprecation, 'you will have to take the responsibility.'

The Lieutenant sat upright, a bead of sweat ran down the channel of his jowl. His colour mounted. 'So, you dare to threaten me again? By Cristo, I teach you ...'

Ryan released the rage which had been mounting in him. The forced march like a felon! The bombastic malevolence of this two-bit no-account sawn-off ersatz Gauleiter, acting God in a burnt-up backwater that God had forgotten!

350

'No, I will teach you,' he thundered. 'Shut up, SHUT UP AND LISTEN!'

It was in English, spontaneously, but the force of the outburst took the other man by surprise, choking the threats in his throat. For a moment they stared at each other in silent animosity, then, like an anticlimax, a man entered from the courtyard.

The soldado gave a slovenly salute and shuffled across the room. 'El Teniente ... the three waiting outside ... permission to leave ... ?'

The Lieutenant waved him away exasperatedly. 'Si, si. Mañana, mañana.' When the soldier had gone he raised a threatening finger. 'This is the last time, periodista, politico or not, the last time I warn you. Now come to the point of it,' he snapped vehemently, 'I have no more patience.'

'There are two points to it,' Ryan said, lowering his voice. 'First, I am already overdue to return to my country, hence if we can settle this matter now one would be correspondingly appreciative, you understand?'

'Oh, yes I understand,' the Lieutenant said mordaciously. He helped himself to a cheroot. 'But I am in no hurry ... and your inconveniences are irrelevant ... what is the other point?'

'You made it yourself ... that you are the Authority. So what need of delay? I will pay the fines, plus appropriate recompense for your personal co-operation in expediting the matter ...'

'So.' The Lieutenant twisted his lips in his mirthless grimace. 'The bribe offer again.' His frustration heightened the spite in his voice.

'Not at all, merely a business expedience. Nada por nada. If I am delayed it will cost me more,' Ryan said levelly. 'One has business assignments.'

'So simple, eh? Do you think ...' the fat man started, but again Ryan interrupted.

'Say one thousand?' he said bluntly. 'For each, I mean.'

The Lieutenant closed his mouth. The sum was impressive. Even half of one half of it was more money than he had ever

351

handled in his life. The thought begot another in his mind. Clearly, they did not really want the *Inglés*. In fact they might even commend him for promptly disposing of the complication of the *Inglés* on his own initiative. And if he told them that he had imposed a fine of five hundred dollars that would be entirely credible.

'You have that sum, two thousand dollars?' he said sententiously, incredulously.

'Of course not,' Ryan said. 'But it raises no problem.' He could almost smell the man's cupidity in the sweating atmosphere now. 'You have the *teléfono*?'

'Si.'

'You call the bank yourself then. I speak to them in your presence. We have had a business transaction. They confirm to you that the money will be deposited in your name. Then we send a letter, also enclosing a specimen of your signature. That is all, except that the letter should be sent by messenger and would request them to telephone you verifying that the transfer had been made.'

'But how. . . .'

A third time Ryan interrupted him. 'You arrange for yourself an *absentio* ... two-three days ... then you draw the money. Bank business is strictly confidential,' he shrugged. 'How you adjust the business . . .' he shrugged.

The Lieutenant pulled at his lip in silence. He poured himself another drink. A conflict of thoughts was going through his overburdened head. There would bound to be some snag, some risk, but he could not see where. Five hundred dollars! Maybe he could chisel *seven* hundred out of it, tell them he had settled a fine of three hundred on the *Inglés*. *Cristo!* He would need to give this much thought, though one thing was quite clear.

'So far as you are concerned, an *extrangero*, I will consider,' he said finally. 'But for the *ladrón*, Ramirez, it is out of the question, of course.'

Ryan felt a stab of angry disgust. 'By what reckoning is that, the offence is the same?' He made it sound as if he was merely puzzled rather than unduly concerned.

352

'No. He is many times an offender, and with him there are other things also,' the bulky man said, vaguely. 'He will be dealt with ... tried, that is ... by El Jefe personally. That is the order.'

'So. You have arrested him before? You have evidence of previous offences?' Ryan persisted ingenuously.

'What is evidence?' the Lieutenant said petulantly. 'We *know*.' He jabbed with his cheroot. 'Why do *you* make so much of him?'

Because of his own monocentric attitude to life there was some genuine curiosity in the question.

Ryan shrugged. 'Merely that one feels a certain responsibility, you understand. He was in my employ, and it was I who requested that we hunt the *pavos*.'

'An unfortunate request,' the Lieutenant said, deriving some pleasure from it. He gave a glimpse of his mordant grimace. 'Expensive!'

Ryan ignored it. 'When do the Excellencies return?'

'Perhaps four-five days, a week. El Jefe has business in Gualitza.'

Oh, yes, the pig has business all right, he thought sourly. Profitable grafting business with his friends of the *Aduana*, the Customs Department. Most pleasureable business with the ladies of *La Festivo*, and the other houses of joy for which the pay of a *Teniente* did not allow.

Except, he suddenly thought, if this business could be efficiently carried through!

The idea was almost as attractive as the possibilities it offered. He poured out another drink, and this time for Ryan also.

'I would suggest that you come to an early decision then,' Ryan said shortly, 'in our mutual interests?'

The Lieutenant nodded without replying. He went to the door into the courtyard and shouted. When the corporal came in he jerked his head to the adjacent door. 'Take away the prisoner!'

There were only two cells in the cuartel itself, each with two

353

wooden bunks and straw paliasses. The others faced the men's quarters in the courtyard.

Apparently they were to be kept apart for some reason, though it seemed pointless because there was a grating in each for ventilation from the courtyard, and one set high in the dividing wall, which made it easy enough to talk anyway.

In the room outside the barred doors of the cells there was an iron camp bed, a rusting metal locker, a chair and a small table with an oil lamp.

On the walls there were several pictures of women that looked as if they had come from old cheesecake magazines. One bore the superimposed crayoned representation of a man's genitals, suspended over a recumbent starlet in two or three beads and a *cache-sexe*.

Elsewhere on the peeling plaster there were other crude examples of erotica, and one or two sycophantic slogans ... *Viva El Jefe ... Viva lo Regimiento* ... presumably laboriously scrawled by successive men on station duty.

'They wouldn't have any drinkable stuff in this town?' Ryan asked as the corporal opened the door of the second cell.

'Tequila,' Ramirez said shortly. He had more ponderable thoughts.

'All right, we'll have to settle for tequila then.' He got a note from his pocket and held it out to the corporal. 'Two bottles of tequila and beer, amigo? Cheroots also ... the best.'

The man stared at him in astonishment. He had never known a prisoner like this one. Often, in his time, they had brought in Indians volubly berserk on *atole*, but otherwise he had known only peóns, like his own parents, silent and cast down. A rare one had pretended defiance maybe, but none indifference.

'It's all right,' Ryan told him. 'Auténtico. El Teniente will agree and the money left over is for yourself.'

The corporal looked doubtfully at the bill and went through to check with the Lieutenant.

'You must have got through to *chino*,' Ramirez said when the man had gone. 'What passed with him?'

354

'Nothing any real use. You seem to have been right about everything, including that Señor Cruz and the Police Chief are unavailable. I don't think this bastard is going to be any good,' Ryan said. 'I think we are going to have to do it without him.'

He began briefly to recount his talk with the Lieutenant, leaving out the Policeman's flat rejection of any consideration for Ramirez, and he had almost finished when the corporal returned. The soldier still had an air of incomprehension, but he had the liquor and when he had given Ramirez his share he unlocked the other cell and handed Ryan a box containing two or three sheets of notepaper, a steel pen and ink.

When he had gone again Ramirez tapped the wall under the grating. 'Listen, Mark, like I told you, they'll *have* to spring you. Don't pay that bastard a dime.'

'It won't arise, we shall be leaving tomorrow night ... together,' Ryan said softly.

When the other man did not reply he went on. 'No good trying it tonight, too soon. They've got to have confidence in us, and we've got to observe the routine.'

'You got an idea already?'

'Sort of,' Ryan said. 'Have yourself a couple of drinks while I think about it.'

Standing on the lower bunk he could see out into the courtyard through the grating. The low adobe building that seemed to be the men's dormitory ran along one side. Opposite, there were two half-door stables, and two urinals. The lavatories had square unglazed windows for observation of the occupants, and looked like confession boxes. A heap of straw, dyed orange with urine, was piled against the side of the horse-boxes and the door of one of the lavatories sagged half-open on a single hinge.

Three or four pigeons were prospecting the yard and the straw, and two vultures stared down superciliously from the thatch of the stables. Farther along, the lethargic notes of a guitar floated out from a far window of the dormitory on to the exhausted air of gathering twilight.

About eight o'clock a *soldado* entered with a tray. Two

355

bowls of black beans and two tin cups of maize coffee.

Ryan swung off the lower bunk. 'What's this?'

The man stared woodenly. '*Comida*.'

'What! You call that supper? Go tell the Lieutenant we are men ... hungry ... not pigeons.' He waved a hand authoritatively. 'Some eggs, meat ... chicken, or iguana. ...' He rattled the coins in his pocket. 'We will pay for it.'

The soldier looked at him blankly. 'El Teniente is not here.'

'The corporal then,' Ryan said testily. Through the open door to the outer office he could hear someone moving.

The soldier frowned with amazement. He noticed the beer and tequila in the cell. It was unheard of, of course, but it was obvious that this prisoner must be of much importance, or rich. He put down the tray and went out.

'You've got them baffled,' Ramirez said. 'They'll think you're a *millionario*.' Ryan sat down on the bunk and poured some more of the luke warm beer. 'I hope so, that's part of the notion.'

Half an hour later the soldier returned with some drumsticks of chicken and hardboiled eggs. This time the corporal accompanied him. He waited while Ryan paid the man in the greasy singlet, then he said: 'You have a letter for El Teniente?'

Ryan shook his head. 'Not yet. Later. When we have eaten.'

When they had gone out Ramirez tapped the bars with his mug. 'You are going to buy that *hijo* then?'

Ryan stretched up closer to the grating. 'No. I shall write the letter, but don't worry, they won't get far with the signature I shall give it,' he said softly.

While they were eating, the corporal came in again carrying a bowl of soup and tortillas. He put the tray on the table and went to fetch coffee. 'We are getting a guard then?' Ryan said. 'I was hoping for that.'

'The *chino* will be out celebrating.'

'Keep your voice down. Watch it.'

'No, it's all right ... no English.'

'How do you know?'

'I can tell,' Ramirez said. 'Try him yourself.'

356

The corporal returned with a mug. He sat down without looking at either of the prisoners and began to eat. Eventually, when he had finished, he took off his boots and lay down on the bed with a yellow magazine and one of the lime yellow cigarettes that stank like smouldering dung.

Ryan went over to the bars. 'Have a drink, friend?' He repeated it and the corporal turned his head, but there was no understanding in his expression. He changed into Spanish and held up the bottle. 'Have a drink, amigo?'

The soldier stared then grinned. He didn't have any gold teeth, or fillings, and one of his uppers was missing. He got up and came over.

'Can we get another bottle when this is finished?'

For a moment he considered. 'Si.'

'All right, have as much as you want then. Finish it.' Ryan spoke over his shoulder in English. 'Get into the conversation, Juan. Let's get friendly. You can ask him if it will be all right for a bottle tomorrow night.'

Ramirez took up his cue and after a few minutes he led him round to it. They were fortunate, the corporal told them. For the next two nights he himself would still be on guard. He accepted a cheroot and went back to the bed, but after he had taken a third half-mug of tequila the magazine fell on his chest and he began to snore.

'*Cristo*, they can't even handle their own brew,' Ryan said.

'They don't get to see it but once in a month, when they get a buck,' Ramirez explained. 'The rest is this Yuca beer . . . the kids could drink it.'

'I like the sound of that,' Ryan said. 'Tomorrow night we shall all have a bottle of tequila to ourselves I believe, say about ten o'clock.' He paused. 'You hear me, Juan?'

'Yes.'

'Just so long as El Teniente doesn't elect himself in, join the party.'

'I'll keep my fingers crossed,' Ramirez said shortly, meaning it.

He lay down on the bunk and lit a cheroot. Give it two days more and the old man and Almagro would have figured what

357

had happened. But there was nothing they could do. Cruz would stay in the background, of course. Unavailable. Indefinitely. Until he had made a deal. And he had a pretty good idea what kind of a deal it would be. Probably including Consuela.

And there was the other, more final possibility. Because he had to face the fact that for Cruz the better proposition would be his permanent removal. He could understand that, to Ryan, as to Clara, the idea of it was unreal. But, ironically, the realism of it was buried in their unreality. Cruz would not blink an eyelid.

Here, where El Jefe was undisputed, they could get away with murder, and did. All the time. Cooked-up 'escape' attempts, a hired pistolero, any of half a dozen 'jungle mishaps' for which there would be no difficulty of corroborative testimony. If anybody was interested.

His attention was attracted by a buzzing sound. The *avispa* had come in through the grating and blundered into the web that the owner had draped across a corner of the ceiling. The spider ran out from his concealment, then stopped short. He was bigger than the wasp, but he recognised the identity of his adversary and the formidable jaws and darting sting gave him pause. The wasp made a powerful effort, biting and beating with his wings. He broke through the mesh, recovered himself and began to cruise angrily around until at last he found the outside grating.

They woke soon after dawn to the baying of dogs. In the night the bugs in the straw had given some account of themselves and he wondered whether any of the soldiers had had the sense to bring in the pouch of repellents and salves which had been in his kit, but the corporal's bed was empty.

Outside in the courtyard there were some signs of torpid activity. A soldier came out of the lavatory and slouched across the yard, braces dangling to his flapping unfastened puttees. Farther along from the horse-boxes two Indians had brought out the dogs from a shed and were fixing rope exercise leads to their collars. Both the dogs were savage-looking

358

brutes, reddish coloured, about the size of Alsatians but with heads shaped like mastiffs. Of no breed that Ryan recognised, perhaps some kind of mongrels from the same litter.

He spoke through the grating. 'How about those ugly looking bastards, Juan, have you seen them?'

'You mean the dogs?' Ramirez said. He did not get up.

'Yes. They guard dogs?'

'No.'

'For deer?' He heard Ramirez's short laugh.

'Men! Any peón or Indian they're looking for.'

Ryan watched the Indians lead the dogs away. The brutes were big enough to kill a woman, he judged, or maybe a scared man.

'How are you feeling, Juan?' he said.

'Fretful. I can't stand being caged.'

'Don't let it get you,' Ryan said. 'I don't think we'll be spending another night here.'

There was no sign of the Lieutenant and the corporal himself took the morning parade. It was held outside the Station. A daily show of force by means of which the town was reminded of Authority's eternal presence.

Afterwards, still in his semi-permanent uniform of dirty singlet and breeches, a yellow cigarette dangling from his downturned mouth, the orderly brought mugs of grey coffee and some eggs, and again the corporal accompanied him.

He sat down on the bed until the cook had gone. 'You have the letter for El Teniente?'

'Yes,' Ryan said. 'But isn't he here?'

'*Licencia*. On leave until tomorrow.' He grinned sardonically. 'He is resting, meanwhile he wishes to consider. I am to send it to him.'

'All right,' Ryan said. Obviously the fat man was still suspicious, or jittery about it and wished to cogitate some more before arranging the telephone call. Or maybe he figured to play it closer. Get a messenger away sharp, by mule or canoe, and enclosing a covering note from himself specifying when and where the bank should telephone them. Perhaps some

359

place more private than the station or the Ayuntamientos' office. He sealed the letter in a blank envelope and passed it through the bars.

He had written it in Spanish, with a signature that did not resemble his own, so that the manager of the bank would surely smell a rat even if some conplication arose and it reached the bank before they were able to make the break.

He saw the corporal cross the yard and five minutes later a *soldado* led out the mule from the second horse-box and rode away.

The day dragged on interminably, and as the heat rose to peak the stench from the slop pails increased until finally, in response to Ryan's shouts, the buckets were removed. Again it was the orderly who grudgingly undertook the chore, but he took the money and later he returned with beer and more cheroots.

'How will he send the letter?' Ryan said. 'Mule?'

'More likely dory. One of his own *hijos* and two Indian paddlers. They can make a pace ... could deliver it by midday tomorrow.'

'Sounds like the thing for us? By dory, I mean.'

'No,' Ramirez said. 'No good. They got a launch here some place ... the *policía* ... it's a heap, but they'd still overtake us. We make the trees, I can lose them. By dory we'd just be targets.'

'That's how we'll go then,' Ryan said. 'By the trees.'

As the day wore on they spoke less frequently. He could sense Ramirez's tension, sometimes hear him pacing the few steps back and forth, but there was nothing much to discuss now and nothing to do but wait.

In the late afternoon Ramirez reached up and tapped the wall with his mug. For some time he had been lying on the top bunk studying the brooding sky, occasionally sniffing the torrefied air drifting in through the outer grating.

'Mark.' He kept his voice low.

'Uh huh?'

'I think we got some luck coming. Look at the sky.'

Ryan got up on the bunk. There was a certain overcast far

360

off above the western horizon, but otherwise it was cobalt and inert. 'I don't get you.'

'There's a storm coming,' Ramirez said. 'Maybe a big one.'

'You think so?'

'I'm damn sure. I hope to Christ it breaks tonight.'

The men had got the idea of the profit in it now, and about eight o'clock a soldier brought in two slabs of iguana and some fruit. An hour afterwards the corporal came in carrying his supper as before.

When he was through eating he pushed away the tin plate and looked around with a half-grin of expectancy. 'You want tequila?'

'Not me, I still got some,' Ramirez said. He held up the bottle, showing an inch or so in the bottom. 'How about you, Mark?'

'Nor here,' Ryan said offhandedly. 'Maybe later. Besides it is too expensive.' I hope that whets your drinking appetite, he thought.

The corporal's expression showed some frustration. He had been counting on the kind of 'bucket' that rarely came his way and he felt cheated.

'Maybe I make them lower the price this time,' he said hopefully.

Ryan pretended to consider. He called out loudly, maintaining the note of indifference. 'What do you say, Juan? You want a bottle?'

For a moment Ramirez kept silent. 'Aaah! *Pues nada*, there is nothing else to do, certainly,' he said. 'All right, agreed. I will pay this time. Three bottles then.'

The corporal grinned. 'Si, si. Three bottles.'

He went over to the hunter's cell and took the money. There was no prospect of the *Teniente*'s return before tomorrow's assembly for he knew, with envy, where he had gone.

Now and then, outside in the courtyard, flurries of wind slapped the awry lavatory door against the jamb and dark banks rode across the rising moon. Another hour dragged by.

At first the corporal had taken two half-mug slugs within ten minutes or so, but then he had stretched out on the bed

361

with another of the *Teniente*'s magazines, merely taking an occasional sip from the bottle on the floor beside him.

Ryan shifted on to his elbow. 'I do not think our amigo cares much for the tequila, Juan,' he called in Spanish. 'I am almost through with this one.'

'Me also,' Ramirez answered. 'Maybe it is too strong for him.'

'Ah, so. Too strong, of course!'

The corporal turned his head, frowning.

Ryan held up his bottle. He had poured most of it into the pail, leaving only a minimum. He grinned. 'Too strong for you eh, *amigo*?'

The soldier stared. *Cristo!* What drinkers. Yet clearly not drunk. He had a feeling that this was some kind of joke at his expense, but even if not intended it was insulting.

'*Disparate*, nonsense, foreigners! Gomez,' he tapped his chest, 'sometimes he drink two, three bottles, like that.' He snapped his fingers in heavy emphasis. The thickness was in his voice, though he was not yet drunk.

Ryan shrugged. '*Qué va!* Let us finish these then and get three more while we can, since there will be none tomorrow.'

The corporal stared back uncomprehendingly. '*Cómo que nó?* What is this of tomorrow?'

'I shall be released,' Ryan said assertively. 'You remember the letter. When they get the letter it will be ordered at once, from the Capital. With the teléfono.'

'Beyond doubt,' Ramirez said conclusively. 'Immediately. The Señor is of great importance.'

The corporal looked from one to the other, his lower lip drooped open. It was probably true. Certainly El Teniente had despatched Lopera with the letter at once, and by canoe, the quickest way. He had never known such urgency displayed before. Clearly it would only be sense to make sure of another bottle. He sat up on the bed and refilled his mug. 'All right, I get three more.'

He got up, but Ryan said. 'Wait, amigo ... *por favor*. You will be some time in the taberna, eh?' He winked. 'Give me the book and the light while you are gone?' There were other

362

alternatives if this failed, but the man wasn't going to be awake much longer. He rolled on to his side, yawning, and felt for the money in his hip pocket.

The corporal swayed slightly, collecting his wits. Well, it would not matter. In fact after this the *Inglés* could keep the magazine because when he returned from the taberna across the street, he, Gomez, would sleep. And if he did not grant the favour the *Inglés* might withhold the money.

He handed the magazine through the bars and went through into the outer office for the keys. When he returned he picked up the lamp from the table by the bed and drew the Lieutenant's .45 from the holster on the wall. Nobody had ever fired it except the Lieutenant, but it was available for anybody on night duty.

He went over to the cell, changing over the gun to his left hand, holding the lamp and dangling the revolver by the barrel while he turned the key.

Ryan lay on his back, one arm behind his head. He belched and held out the money. 'Over there under the window, amigo.'

The corporal put the lamp on the floor and straightened up. As he turned Ryan gave him a tremendous round arm chop on the side of the jaw which carried all his weight from the waist up.

In the next cell Ramirez heard the heavy slap of it, but the only other sound was the thud of the gun on the floor as the corporal's knees buckled. Ryan caught him as he fell and bundled him on to the bunk, then turned for the gun and the keys hanging in the door. As soon as he had released Ramirez he checked the gun. Ironically it was not loaded.

'Wait,' he stared softly towards the office door, but Ramirez hissed. 'Christ, not the street.'

'Of course not.' He edged the door open a crack. There was another oil lamp burning on the Lieutenant's desk. He saw his own belt with the Luger and the knife hanging on the wall beside the desk and in two strides he had it.

Ramirez peered through the slit of the door into the yard. The sound of a guitar came from the dormitory and the light

363

from the windows cast two dim pools on the cobbles. He turned his head and hooked his arm. 'Come on. Clear.'

'A second.' Ryan twisted the glass funnel off the lamp. He slopped the kerosene on the floor and all around the desk, then laid the naked burner in it.

They sidled swiftly through the door and closed it. For a moment they stood still, pressed against the wall. Then they bent low and ran along the yard on tiptoe in the shadow of the horse-boxes. The whole business from the slugging of the corporal could not have taken five minutes.

At the end of the yard they were into the outer darkness, but the low houses of the street were silhouetted against the night sky and there was a path which ran along the backs of them towards the river.

The force of the wind had increased now. It came in violent gusts which were growing more frequent all the time. Up ahead, as they got closer, the structure of the bridge and the dark sheen of the water were just discernible in the intermittent moonlight.

They were past the end of the street now and there was an open stretch. They sprinted it and crossed the bridge, bent low against the fencing rail. On the other side they slid down the side and halted for a moment in the deeper shadow of the piles, panting a bit now because they had run non-stop from the yard.

The small blobs of light in the town, dim cataracted eyes of oil lamps, were still few and far between. But where the station was, a glimmering had begun to develop like the yellow glow of a bonfire and shouts began to carry faintly back over the wind.

Ryan stared over his shoulder. 'Christ. It's taken all right! With this wind it'll go like a bomb.'

He had a momentary vision of the Lieutenant being dragged from his bed, maybe in the midst of a session, to observe the catastrophe ... and then to contemplate the calamity that was coming to him personally on the return of El Jefe and Cruz. Despite the tension in him he grinned vengefully. 'That'll hold the bastards for a while!'

364

'Yes, it was a good idea,' Ramirez said tersely. 'But it won't hold *chino* for long. He'll come after us with everything he can raise ... his balls depend on it.'

Ryan fastened the gun belt he had been carrying and they began to run again, only more steadily now, settling to a pace that was within their full capabilities.

14. SURVIVAL

The rain began when they were still a couple of hundred yards short of the black mass of the jungle. It came from behind them, blotting out the receding yellow dolls-eyes of the town and the redder light of the fire, marching over them like waves of hail, the heavy drops peppering the ground and the foliage.

Already the smaller trees of the fringe were beginning to lash and strain, and overhead the lightning puctuated the increasing artillery barrage with forked stabs.

They entered the jungle at random, weaving deeply into the twisting avenues of the big timber to escape the downpour, but after a time even the vaulted roofs began to let through in places, like parasols rent with pellets.

For about an hour the tempest raged, churning the ground in the glades, ripping and tearing at the seams of the forest. Then suddenly, abruptly, the rain ceased, and as they got farther away the orchestrations of the storm began to fade like dying drum beats.

They had settled to a steady walking pace now and Ramirez began to search for a camino which suited him, but it was nearing three o'clock before he was satisfied. For an hour or more they followed the deer path, then he halted again.

'Okay, we'll take a rest. No sense going farther till I'm surer.'

They found a dry spot beneath the great uncinate roots of a towering fig that was almost like an arbour, and stretched

365

themselves on the starved moss.

A few yards away a fallen giant, victim of some bygone thunderhead, its roots exposed like the tentacles of a monstrous squid, had left a ceiling gap that was open to the stars. But elsewhere, all round, the jungle was dank and sullen as if implicit with disaster.

The first spurious energy had been expended now and both men were glad of the pause, though neither could have slept.

Ramirez slumped on his elbow. He could feel the muscles quivering in his legs, and the reaction was not wholly due to fatigue. He was also conscious of an emotional strain, and there was an urge in him to press on, but all his professional instincts insisted that it might be folly yet before he could properly figure their bearings and position.

After a while he sat up. There were still four cheroots left in his tin, and they sat side by side, smoking, waiting for the warmth and the light.

The sun rose finally, lethargically, as if sardonically inclined to delay the heat required to dispel the clamminess of clothes still not dried out by body heat. Everywhere the sodden foliage gleamed with wetness, and grey streaks of mist rose knee-high from the forest floor.

They crossed a small open glade of squelching, beaten moss and picked up another camino. The trail wound on for half a mile, then ended abruptly at a stream. The bank of the watering place was scuffed bare with the spoor of a variety of creatures, and some of the deeper imprints still held tiny puddles of water from the storm.

Ramirez studied the flow of the water, then glanced in the direction of the sun. He moved around looking for light gaps in the overhead, double-checking with the prevailing trend of the treetops, then suddenly he swore. 'Goddammit to hell, we've been making near due south.' He pointed at an angle to the stream. 'The *valle* is there ... a good thing we laid up here.'

'Aaah, what's the difference?' Ryan said. 'The main idea was to get lost first wasn't it?'

'Yes, but we've lost a lot of start.'

366

'I don't see that,' Ryan said. 'They won't have an idea where we're heading.'

Ramirez shook his head. 'I wish you were right. But they know we've got to go by the *valle*—and we have.'

'Why? What for? The hell with the valley, let's just keep ploughing south.'

Ramirez shook his head again. He made a gesture of rejection with his palm. 'No good. Man, that would take us a *week*,' he said conclusively. 'For one thing, I don't know that "country". We'd have to prospect, break trail, maybe make big detours, and we'd have to eat, sleep . . . and the longer we take the more chance they got.'

'So what?' Ryan said. 'They'd have to eat, too, wouldn't they? Christ, we can out-march those bums.'

'We can't out-march their *Indians*,' Ramirez said flatly. 'Because they know the "country". Once they'd figured the line we were heading they could get ahead of us.'

'What?' Ryan said incredulously. It seemed ludicrous. 'You mean to tell me they'd find us in all this?'

'Look,' Ramirez said. 'I never really travelled that "country", but I know this about it. Going south you got to cross a big range, and I mean big, and before you come to it there's miles of open *lavrado*. Sooner or later, from the ridge, they'd spot us a mile away . . . because there's only two passes.' He spat vehemently. 'They'd wait for us in the passes, likely with dogs, that's what I mean.'

Ryan's mouth curled. 'I don't think we need to worry so much about those Indian runts, or dogs,' he said. 'You've forgotten. We're not naked you know.' He tapped the knife and the Luger on his belt. 'I don't say I can shoot cigarettes out of your mouth, but I can hit Indians all right . . . or dogs.'

Despite his preoccupation, Ramirez smiled. 'Look, Mark, you did bloody good back there. The gun too . . . I'd have missed out on that . . . but leave me handle it from here. Believe me we *got* to go for the *valle*.'

The jungle was becoming more audible now, activated by the mounting sun. A macaw called harshly, and at intervals the screech of a howler transcended the soft rising hum of the

367

insects in the glades.

In twenty minutes they were warm, and by the time they had broken through on to a camino suiting the general direction they needed, the sweat was issuing on their chests and in their armpits. Soon their shirts began to stick and then steam.

Ramirez checked again at the first opportinuty with the living compass of a tree fern.

The deer path took them a good way before it began consistently to veer away east and they were forced to break trail again. They were into the heavy jungle now, tangled and matted with creepers and lianas, bamboo groves that had to be detoured, and there were no more caminos.

Near to noon they came on to the tiny trickle of a stream that was not much larger than a field drain, and drank, but there was still no sign of any let-up in the density of the going.

Ryan drew his forearm across his face and rubbed his palms on his trousers. 'You still happy, boy? We don't seem to be getting any place?'

Ramirez watched the water. He studied the vegetation along the rill then turned on his elbow and glanced up towards where the direct rays made a vaguely lighter patch in the nave of the jungle.

'No, it's all right. We lost a lot of ground, but we've got to hit the *valle* soon.' He pointed to the stream. 'I'll lay you fifty the arroyo takes us to the river.'

'Well, let's hope it's soon, I reckon we should have crossed that river a while ago?'

'Don't tell me,' Ramirez said. He was still conscious of a feeling of self-disgust at having blundered, and he was acutely aware that the sun was gaining on them.

They got going again, following the course of the stream directly where they could, and coming back to it when they had to skirt around tracts through which it would have taken an hour to make a hundred yards.

As they slogged on a suspicion of doubt began to intensify in Ryan's mind, for the jungle seemed utterly boundless.

He was not dismayed but, increasingly, the feeling grew that Ramirez's calculations and prediction about the stream

368

had gone awry. That despite the previous evidences he had had of the hunter's ability to read the vast mazes of the manigua they were now simply blundering ahead blindly. Indiscriminately.

But just as he was on the point of bluntly voicing his thoughts he became aware that the light was increasing. At first it was barely perceptible, but soon there was no doubt of it.

Involuntarily Ramirez increased his pace, unmindful of the fatigue in his legs, until he was twenty yards ahead, then he halted at the fringe of the trees. At first, coming up behind, Ryan thought that they had merely broken through on to a glade that was larger than usual, the source of the improved light. But when he reached Ramirez's side Ryan saw that they had at last really reached the end of the big wilderness.

The clearing had been gouged out of the jungle by hurricane, as if, perhaps only for a few minutes, some monumental circular saw had sliced into the frieze of the trees on its eccentric course. The dead trees, some sundered, some uprooted, were strewn at all angles and beyond them the land fell away in a long increasing gradient.

Ryan put a hand on the other man's shoulder. He blew out a long breath. 'At bloody last, eh?'

Before them the vast elongated quilt of the valley stretched out on either side to the limit of the naked eye, the wavering vein of the river directly below. There was no doubt that it *was* the valley, and yet, somehow, its contours, and the outline of the escarpment on the other side, seemed different.

'How far did you say it ran?' Ryan said. 'The full length, I mean.'

'Say twenty-thirty miles!'

'We're a bloody long way from the place we camped then?'

'No. Not so far,' Ramirez said. 'Look.' He pointed at a tangential angle across the rift. 'Follow the skyline. See that break like an axe-head, that's the pass we came through. We could've done a lot worse.'

As the crow flew it looked about five miles, Ryan thought.

'Well, you're not a bad jungle pilot, I'll give you that.'

369

'Not this time,' Ramirez said disgustedly. 'I sure loused it up this time.'

'What're you talking about, man? We made it, didn't we? Two or three hours we'll be through that pass.'

'Yeh ... If they're not there waiting for us. I sure gave 'em enough time.'

'Aaah, balls!' Ryan said. 'You did bloody well, boy, and no little brown runts or any of *chino*'s army are going to stop us now.'

Ramirez got the last cheroot from his tin and broke it in two. 'We could wait for dark,' he said reflectively. 'But if we're still ahead it would be crazy to give them all that time. Wouldn't help a lot either ... be a full moon tonight. What do you say?'

'I say we're still ahead,' Ryan said. 'I say let's go ... besides I'm getting hungry.'

'Hungry?' It sounded absurd. Irrelevant.

'Sure, hungry. I could eat a turtle raw right now.'

Ramirez grinned. All along his primal urge had been to get up and go, but now something of the other man's mood conveyed itself to him. 'How many rounds you got for that popgun?'

Ryan glanced down at his belt. 'About twenty, plus the magazine.'

'Okay. We don't use them on *hijos*, we'll eat roast *laaba* tonight ... our side the border.' The other man's confidence had begun to supplement his own.

Ryan grinned back. 'Attaboy. You've got a deal there.'

'I hope your eyesight's in good shape,' the hunter said. 'Because there could be a dozen Indian lookouts strung out along that ridge and their eyesight's pretty good. Remember that all the time, and move like you're stalking buff.'

For ten minutes more they scanned the slopes below them, and those across the valley, but there was only a white hawk hanging above the bottom land of the river, moving every few minutes to a further section, and they began the descent.

Except in some places where the brush grew sparse and stunted, or where a court of selaginella moss had formed, and

370

they had to bellycrawl, the scrub gave cover for a man bent double. But the strong light of the sun was identifying them now and the crouching snail-pace travelling was more exhausting than struggling through the tortuous stuff of the jungle, so that at intervals they lay flat, heads on forearms, resting their aching backs, resisting the natural urge to spring up and go headlong for the river.

They lay listening again and peering again, the sweat coursing down their necks and faces, conscious of the big silence against which the occasional call of a bird and the low thrumming of the insects were puny things that emphasised rather than disturbed the brooding yellow overall quiet.

They had made about half the distance to the river now, on a line that, roughly, ran directly from the clearing far behind them. But now Ramirez began to move across the slope at an angle heading towards a bend of the river where two converging white patches suggested a linkage of boulders.

About half an hour later they reached the place and halted, lying side by side in the last edge of cover before the open strip of bank.

Ramirez pursed his lips. The aspect of the water gave him a twinge of anxiety. It looked formidable. A different proposition now from the relatively placid river they had crossed two days before. Forbidding.

The current had quickened to three times its normal pace and the water was dark, thickly opaque with the colouring of chunks of earth and other debris sloughed and gouged from the banks. In midstream a big flat-topped rock rose just above the surface, and the quivering semi-circle of white spume piled against it left no doubt of the drag power in the water. But it was not only the much increased hazard of the current. It was obviously much deeper now, the water risen above the normal confinements of the banks.

'Not so good, eh?' Ryan said. 'No kid stuff now.'

'No. The *valle* must've got the full force of the storm.'

'You think we should scout the bank for a better place?'

The hunter shook his head, 'No . . . could take all day . . . we haven't got that time.'

371

'What kind of a swimmer are you?'

'The not-so-good kind. You?'

'All right,' Ryan said. 'I'll go first then. See if I can make it wading. If I can, you can, there isn't much difference between us.' He pointed. 'We'll start well this side of the rock so you can go for it if you have to.'

He looped the gun belt twice around his neck so that the holster hung high on his chest, and they crawled forward to the edge.

The water was surprisingly cold, mountain water, augmented by many hill burns that would not begin to absorb the sun's heat fully until the main turbulence had subsided.

He began to move out into the current, arms raised, and suddenly the recollection of the tapir calf incident flashed across his mind. I hope to Christ this river doesn't hold any of the big bastards, he thought. Anaconda! It was unlikely because the *fangosos* mostly habited the lakes and the big rivers, but the remembrance made him press ahead.

He halted for a moment, bracing himself against the flow, and glanced back over his shoulder. Ramirez hadn't waited, he was ten yards behind him, moving tangentially towards the rock, the water swirling and buffeting around his waist.

Ryan stumbled on. The water rose to his chest. It had a menacing insidious strength now, as if the passive sluggardly force it normally was had been transformed into an active malignant enemy, but he forced on past midstream, leaning against the current, and the heavy drag began to lessen.

The water level subsided to nearer his waist. He halted and looked back again. Ramirez was almost abreast of the rock at armpit depth. He called out. 'Hug the rock, Juan, take a breather, you're nearly through the worst.'

He turned again, splashing forward, and in the instant that he had begun to drag himself out on to the bank he heard the baying, the report and then the whinging passage of the bullet over his head.

Another bullet slapped into the mud beside him as he bellied forward. He rolled over and over until he was into a tangle of reed and osiers then scrambled to his knees. He saw

372

the blue puffs when they transferred their fire to the target of the man in the water.

They were a good way back up from the slope behind them on a crag, a butte which jutted from the face of the hillside, two soldiers and an Indian.

A bullet pinged and ricochetted off the flat rock, then another, raising a grey puff of fragments. He called urgently. 'Come on, come on, *keep going*, Juan!'

Ramirez had his back against the rock. He was semi-crouched now so that the water was lapping his chin. He raised his head. 'Run, Mark. Go on, run for the trees.'

Ryan ignored it, raging. 'For Christ's sake come ahead. *COME!*'

He could not understand why Ramirez did not seem to realise the vital urgency. Aside from the fact that he was giving them time to get the range dead right, they could come closer firing alternately. And they were trying all right.

It went through his head that there would undoubtedly be a big bounty on both of them now ... money, promotion, probably both. Nor was it likely to depend on recapture alive. With his own future hanging in the balance the Lieutenant would be way past any such conditions now.

The accuracy of their fire was improving, chipping the rock, sending slapping spurts nearer to the head of the man in the water every time now.

Ryan shouted again, anger and entreaty filling his voice. Ramirez gathered himself. Paradoxically, it was the water far more than the shots that he apprehended, drowning was the one thing he had always feared. He nerved himself and plunged forward.

Ryan made a swift estimate of the parabola to the scout party on the crag. The range was way beyond the effective capacity of the Luger, but the pistol had a crack to it which an unversed ear would take for a rifle, and if he could drop a couple of falling slugs in their vicinity it might give them indecision. He gave them two deliberate calculated rounds, then three in a quick burst like automatic fire.

Ramirez was fighting towards the bank, twice his head went

373

under and came up again.

'Come on, boy, *come on*!' Ryan shouted. He fired two more high trajectory rounds, then, as the gasping coughing man neared the bank, he ran forward. He grabbed the hunter's outstretched wrists and wrenched him powerfully from the water, his great strength surcharged with urgency.

He felt a stinging sensation like an electric shock in his thigh, but he never heeded it. The shots were coming in rapid alternation now, merely the time of returning bolts between them, but more wildly as if in desperation. Then, as he strained, he heard the distinctive slappety-thud sound he dreaded and ... Oh Christ ... again.

He heard Ramirez's indrawn gasps but the sounds only goaded him. He got his hands under the hunter's armpits and dragged him swiftly into the cover of the osiers.

Ramirez lay prone, face down. A shock spasm ran through him and he was panting from the effort and the water he had taken. There was a spreading patch on his left arm and the limb looked shattered. But the stain which filled Ryan with anxiety and cold hate was below the right shoulder blade.

'How is it, boy? They really clobbered you?' Involuntarily he almost whispered it, urgently.

Ramirez turned his head in the grass. There was blood at the corner of his mouth, and his voice was staccato, breathless. 'Give me ... minute.' He let his head fall flat again, feeling the burning pain, wanting to retch.

'Sure, sure. Wait till your breath comes.'

Ryan turned on to his elbows and peered through the tracery of the osier branches, replacing the shells he had fired from his belt.

It was only Juan who worried him now, not the 'tecos. For them his feeling had changed in a stroke from contempt and dislike to lethal hatred. He wished passionately that they would come ahead. Would just try it. Because one thing for sure was that no one would get as far as the rock!

He brought his mind back to the impasse situation. The trio across the river were obviously a lookout patrol. Spotters. Probably there were others spread along the valley who might have heard the firing. It was essential to get moving as soon as they possibly could.

'How is it, Juan?' he said again, urgently. 'Got to get you to a place where I can patch you up, boy.'

'Yeh.' Ramirez struggled to his knees.

'No. Get on my back,' Ryan said. 'Make it faster that way.' He lay flat on his stomach while the stricken man dragged himself on to his back.

'Get an arm round my neck, get a hold on me.'

'Yeh.'

It was about fifty yards to the first of the trees. He forced himself up, then rose to a half bent position. He took a firm hold on the other man's wrist and began to run, weaving as he went. The sortie seemed to have taken them by surprise. Only two shots ploughed past them as he ran, then they were into the first shadows.

He kept right on into the heavy cover for another fifty yards or so before he set the wounded man down, carefully as he could, lowering himself flat.

When he had him seated with his back against a tree he knelt beside him and got his knife. He was about to cut off the hunter's sleeve at the shoulder when he remembered. Christ, no. The insects!

Later they would have to run the gauntlet of the *cobarras*, and all the bloody rest of them, augmented, too, by the added inducement of the blood smell.

He rolled the sleeve carefully back over the tomato blotch above the elbow, then he cut off his own sleeve at the elbow and made a twice-around bandage with it, securing it above and below with two strips torn from his bandana.

For a few seconds he listened, but there was nothing except the renewed baying from somewhere across the far side of the river.

'On to your belly again, Juan. Easy, boy.'

He helped him down on to his stomach and began to ease up the sodden shirt over the red patch. Ramirez gave a little hiss, then he closed his eyes and kept quiet.

Ryan made a pad of the remains of his bandana. The handkerchief was still soaking from the river and he began to sponge and dab at the patch as gently as he could. When he could see the extent and exact locality of the wound he felt slightly relieved.

Thank Christ it had been a hardnose slug! The blood was pulsing out, but slowly, not violently, trickling down the muscular creases under the shoulder blade. His knowledge of human anatomy was pretty sketchy; with all the variety of creatures he had gralloched he knew much more about animal structures in fact.

Maybe it had missed the lung, gone into muscle. It seemed low enough to have missed. He raked back in his memory, trying to remember long-ago schoolboy charts showing the extent of the lung cavities.

The frothy trickle of blood in the corner of Juan's mouth was what worried him most. It was not extensive, but by animal comparisons it looked like lung blood, and if it was, if his lung was punctured, then sooner, more than later, he was through.

On the other hand, he reassured himself, although his breathing sounded stertorous, he was not coughing now, and there were no sudden gushings such as he would have expected.

He bent over him. 'It's not bad, boy. Not bad. You got yourself a couple of real hurty holes but they'll dry up. Just got to make sure our 'teco friends haven't got any more ideas, then we'll go home. Nice and easy.' He helped him back to a sitting position against the tree.

Ramirez heard the words, though not with normal clarity.

His senses were dulled, his mind half preoccupied with the pain in his side, his arm too. But, once again, the strength of the other man's personality and the typical confidence in his voice ... feigned though it was, this time, had he known it ... refurbished his resolve. Came through like a stiff drink when you badly needed one.

He smiled briefly, then he noticed the stain on Ryan's thigh. 'They get you too ... Mark?'

Ryan glanced down at his leg. Paradoxically, he had for-

376

gotten about it, as you forgot about socks and wallops in the heat of a football ruck. The bullet had grazed his thigh, but it was only a surface nick and his blood had always coagulated quickly.

'Nothing. Just a scratch, I'm a hundred percent.'

He put up his hand and both men listened.

The sound of the dog seemed nearer, more pronounced. Maybe they were down at the river now.

'I ain't going to be much use to you, Mark,' Ramirez said breathlessly. 'Maybe you should take off . . . you could make it alone.'

'Don't talk bloody rubbish,' Ryan said.

He felt a deep and special anger about the dog. The very concept of hunting human beings with dogs had always seemed to him the ultimate degradation. Nazi stuff, even though it was conceived centuries before Himmler's swine had hunted Jewish children with half-savage Alsatians that were like starving wolves.

His mouth hardened. Well, come right ahead, dog, he thought. I promise you this is one time you are not going to indulge yourself . . . tearing up some child, savaging some poor sod of a peón, ripping the throat of a wounded man, dog! This is one time when you are going to get the bloody worst of it, dog, I promise you that.'

He checked the Luger and cocked it. Then he squatted. 'Juan. Can you handle the pistol?'

Ramirez nodded. He took it in his good hand.

'Listen,' Ryan said, 'the dog will come first, probably in a few minutes now. Then the Indian I expect . . . just afterwards . . . then the 'tecos, say ten minutes later, or maybe not at all. That is how I figure it.'

'Yeh.' Ramirez nodded again. Above the pain he felt very tired. Drawn. Perhaps it was how you felt when you were going to die. He fought off the drowsy light-headed feeling. Nobody was going to die . . . yet; and this man, Ryan, had four beasts on his hands. He, Ramirez, must help, scale down the odds, hold on.

'If the dog gets past me,' Ryan said. 'Try and pump it into

377

him.'

He lifted the seated man farther around the bole of the tree until, just his shoulder projecting, he could see back down through the trees the way they had come. Then he went back down the slope a little way and moved in behind the massive column of a nargusta to wait.

The big hound was baying as he came. The fresh spoor was ridiculously easy for him, even without the sporadic spatterings of blood.

As soon as he saw him weaving up through the trees, Ryan stepped out. In the light the great dog looked sepia colour and even more the shape of a mastiff. He was running easily, but when he saw the man he came full out, raggety black lips drawn back from yellow fangs. He was very confident, used to fugitives who cowered, or ran screaming at the sight of his savage slavering mask, and the blood lust was coursing through him.

Ryan stood braced, unconsciously grinning with fury, head drawn back a little, hands held like talons. The dark shape launched high for his throat and Ryan took him, as once, years before, he had taken a leopardess returning to her cubs. Even the cat, coming like a projectile, had not knocked him down and the dog did not even stagger him.

His powerful fingers caught and dug into the rough hair of the creature's neck and he bore him down, paws scrabbling at his chest and thighs. He got his full weight on top of the writhing struggling animal, pinning him down, and the instant he had a full handful of skin and throat beneath the snarling muzzle he took the knife.

Bastard . . . bastard . . . bastard. Three times he drove it into the beast with all the force of his arm, continuing to bear down until he heard the rattle. He could have strangled the brute, he knew, but it would have taken longer, and even as he started to rise from the twitching body he heard a sound and wheeled.

The Indian was barely a dozen yards away on his right, grimacing with shock or enmity. He had the bow in his hand and was reaching for the arrows on his back when Ramirez shot him twice. The first bullet took him between the shoulder

378

blades, and the second in the chest as he spun.

The hunter was on his feet, the smoking pistol dangling against the tree. He leaned his head against the bole, the beads of effort forming on his brow, mouthing against the pain running through him. When the paroxysm had slackened he slid down to his former posture and put his head back against the tree.

Ryan dropped to his knees beside him. He spoke urgently. 'Juan! Listen, Juan, it's only the 'tecos now. They've got to come soon ... ten minutes ... or not at all, they've got something to think about now, boy. Can you hang on with the pistol?'

Ramirez opened his eyes again. Oddly, as it seemed to him, his arm was the worst punishment. The hurt in his back and side had become a duller burning sensation, it ached unceasingly but it was bearable. The more excruciating spasms came from the smallest movements of his arm.

'Okay ... Bwana.'

'You think you can still handle the gun?'

'Yeh ... but ... you better have it.'

'No, listen. If they come close together give them the lot, the magazine, from close. If they're spread out I'll get one and you can cover me.' He took the pistol and replaced the two rounds from his belt. 'You might nail him at that.'

Ramirez made a semblance of a smile. 'Got the *hijo*!'

'You did, boy. You really did,' Ryan said. He nodded, forcing a grin of encouragement. 'Just a mite longer.'

He got to his feet and went back to where the dog lay. He lifted the carcase and flung it farther down the path the animal had taken, then he took up his position again against the big nargusta.

It was even money whether the *soldados* would come, he thought. Damn sure that those ones wouldn't relish crossing the river, unless perhaps the Indian had known an easier place. It probably depended on what reward they had been offered. Or what penalty they would have to suffer for quitting.

More than anything, the thought of Juan tormented him. He was in a pretty bad way. At best it was going to be touch and

379

go. Time was going to be the essence, he felt, and all his instincts were for them to get the hell out of it. Put some distance between them and the river, and get him laid up somewhere to rest till the worst of the heat had passed.

But it was essential to establish whether the bastards were going to keep after them. They could not take the chance of being overtaken and jumped, hampered as he was going to be.

He glanced at his watch. Over ten minutes had passed since he had returned to the tree, without any further sound or sign. Maybe they had quit. Certainly the disappearance of the dog and the Indian would have literally put the fear of death into them, he fancied. They would have heard the shots all right, and they'd know that in this dim light their old bolt action guns didn't offer any advantage, less in fact that the rapid automatic action of the Luger.

Frettingly, he gave it another five minutes, but there was still nothing, and he was about to rejoin Ramirez when he heard the snap of dead wood. And then the sound of someone brushing through scrub, someone lacking the stealth of a forest creature or a practised hunter.

The soldier came hesitantly through a small patch of filtered sunlight, his rifle thrust forward from the waist, peering to left and right, straining his eyes against the gloom and shadow of the trees. He was alone, yet maybe not alone. From somewhere farther down the slope, to the right, Ryan caught another sound.

He crouched, edging gradually around the great bole of the tree keeping himself out of line. He heard the man's hiss of surprise and apprehension as he came to the dog. For two or three minutes there was silence ... evidently the evidence of possible lurking death had shaken him ... then the rustling footfalls came on again, more trepidly.

Ryan held the knife, blade poised upwards. He had already decided to risk his aim and count on Ramirez, not much higher up the slope, if he missed. He let the man pass, move three-four yards higher, then he threw the knife with pent force and sprang forward.

380

The knife took the *soldado* in his upper arm, his scream echoing through the twisting labyrinth of the trees, and the muzzle of his gun sagged from his palsied hand. He half wheeled as Ryan covered the several yards between them, then the big man was on him. The rifle fell from his hand as Ryan smashed him down and dropped on top of him. He started to yell but the cry was strangled in his throat.

The inexorable berserk thoughts flashed through Ryan's mind.

You tried to kill us, when we were in the water ... to mutilate us ... maybe you have killed him, but you'll never know. ...

The soldier's sallow face grew purple and his eyes bulged, but his frantic flailings and writhings were futile. As futile as the hopeless struggles of a rat gripped by a tumbler eagle against the power of the wrists squeezing out his life.

Ryan got to his feet, and as he did so Ramirez fired, then twice more. Ryan bent low and ran for deeper cover.

The second soldier had arrived just a few minutes after his comrade. He had thought the fugitives to be unarmed until Ryan had fired back from the reeds, and ever since then he had wanted no more part of it. He had never faced return fire before, only terrified peónes, and he was a very scared man now.

When they had reached the river he had argued passionately against attempting further pursuit, stressing that going after men with a gun, in the gloom of the forest, was madness. Suicide. But, urged by the thought of the reward, his companion had insisted, threatening to report any dereliction, and maintaining that the Indian or the dog would get one man or the other. That they had only to follow at safe distance.

The had made the crossing at a place much lower down stream than the flat rock, and when they had returned to it he had counselled that they should not keep closely together, which had made sense and, more pertinently, had enabled him to hang back behind the older man, as he had intended.

The sound of his comrade's scream had shocked him badly, and now, just as he had come upon the body, staring up at him

381

like a crazy man with bulging eyes and protruding tongue, Ramirez had opened fire.

Two of the shots, missing him narrowly, had completed his total demoralisation. Now he ran blindly for the river, convinced that certain death lay behind him.

Ryan dropped to his knees beside the hunter.

He was breathing hard, but more with excitement than exertion. 'We've done it, boy. Paralysed 'em.' He jerked his head. 'That one won't come again, nor cross the river till it falls, I fancy. Plenty of time now.'

Ramirez wiped his face with his good hand and made a grimace. 'Maybe not so much time, Mark,' he said tonelessly. A scalding wave of nausea ran through him.

'Aaah, balls! You lost a peck of blood, boy, that's all.'

'Listen, Juan,' he made it as convincing as he knew, 'it didn't get the lung. Too low. If it had you'd have been finished before this. We get this bleeding dried up, you'll make it all right.'

It wasn't wholly propaganda, because the red wetness at the corner of his mouth didn't seem any worse, but in himself he only gave it part credence.

'The worst thing ... is the arm,' Ramirez said sibilantly, almost self-reproachfully. He looked at it disparagingly, as if it had betrayed them. Even the smallest movement made the bone ends grate, transmitting stabs of pain that made him suck in his breath.

Ryan nodded. 'Yes, yes of course. We'll have to get that fixed, boy.'

He took his knife and began to hunt around for suitable strong light branches. In a short time he had what he wanted. Now ... binding? He frowned, then he remembered the dead man.

He went back to the corpse and began to unwind the length of *cordel* around the soldier's waist, and with which, the Indian leading no doubt, they had probably made the crossing. He had no compunction about handling the body, as he might have had if they had genuinely attempted recapture. Bloody *fisi*, hyena, who preyed on the maimed, the defenceless and

382

their own kind! Bastards who had it coming if any did.

The shirt would do for bandage strips. He turned the corpse over with his foot and tore it off. Surprisingly, the man had a flat leather *bota* under it, looped over his shoulder. *Mescal.* Bloody awful stuff, raw, but alcohol nevertheless. Lucky.

When he returned to Ramirez he dowsed the hunter's bandages with the spirit, also the smarting abrasion on his own thigh. He unspliced a length of the *cordel* into strands the thickness of string, re-bandaged the arm and fixed the splints, taking pains over it until it was as rigid as he could make it.

'How is it now, boy?' He got to his feet.

'Better for that,' Ramirez said. He leaned his head back against the tree. The fixing had been hellish painful, but the immobilising of the fractured parts had helped. 'Could you . . . make . . . sling for it?'

'Sure. But it'll have to come off if I have to hump you any time.'

Despite the nausea feeling, Ramirez smiled. 'You think . . . could heft me?'

'I thought I told you,' Ryan said. 'I humped an African once, on and off, for a sight farther than we're going.'

'Did he . . . make it?'

'Sure, he made it,' Ryan said. '*Es muy yesca.* Plenty of spunk. You remember that.' He turned the leather flask over in his hands, considering. About stomach wounds he knew, but about lungs nothing. He held out the *bota.*

'I don't know, but just a wee dram . . . see if it hurts.'

Ramirez took a small sip, then another. It burned, but it seemed only the normal burning of any fiery spirit. He spluttered slightly, but there was no coughing fit.

Ryan smiled. 'Okay, then, take a real dram, but nice and easy.' He jerked his head. 'Soon as you want we'll try it some more, you making your own pace . . . also nice and easy.'

Ramirez nodded. He took another pull and then they began the long grinding march up through the trees.

For an hour they wove slowly up the slope, halting each time the hunter was obliged to lean his chest and brow against a tree waiting for the nausea to pass.

383

All the time so far he had made it alone, but now he became obliged to accept the other man's help. He hung his good arm around the taller man's neck and Ryan gripped his wrist so that he could rest more of his weight and steady himself whenever he needed to.

They were proceeding in shorter spells now, stopping every hundred yards or so, and then every fifty yards.

The next time that it happened, Ryan decided on a longer halt. He helped the wounded man to settle in the shade of a Mammee and sat down beside him.

When they had approached the tree a number of macaws and surly-faced howler monkeys had raucously departed and there was a small scattering of fallen apples on the ground. He gathered two or three and laid them beside the resting man.

'Going to hunt around a little, Juan,' he said.

The prone man did not reply. He was lying with his head pillowed on his sound arm, and his eyes were closed. The red patch on his back was shining wet, but it did not seem to be generating more blood.

Ryan swished away the flies and covered the place with the remains of the soldier's shirt. I hope to Christ it's just exhaustion ... sleeping ... not coma, he thought.

He got to his feet and began to scout across the slope. Quite soon he found a small grove of half-grown coco palms bordering a clearing, and managed to shake down some of the nuts. They were greenish but the milk was acceptable enough, and cool.

When they had first descended the ridge to the valley there had been a sparse scattering of little spruits that wound down to the river, he recalled, but it took him a lot longer, perhaps fifteen minutes more, to find one of the rills now.

It was even smaller than the one they had followed earlier, the other side, but the water was good. He smashed one of the nuts with a rock, gouged out the flesh and lay flat, scooping the water up until he had drunk his fill. If he had had some other container there might have been some sense in retaining the remainder of the *mescal*, but water was going to be more to the

384

point. He gave the *bota* a good flushing out and then filled it.

Ramirez looked as if he had not moved. His breathing was legato now, not heavily drawn, as you would expect from an exhausted man, yet his sleeping looked natural. For a quarter hour more, making most of an hour since they had come to the Mammee, he let him lie. But the light was almost gone now, and there was the nagging thought that he might finally have lapsed into a coma.

He took the hunter's wrist, gently squeezing the pulse and shaking it. 'Come on, boy ... come on.'

After a minute or two Ramirez groaned and his eyelids flickered. For a second he stared back blankly and the vacancy of his expression gave Ryan a twinge of unease before the light of recognition showed in his eyes. 'Mark!'

'Yes. Come on, boy, let's get you sitting. Got some water for you.' He helped him upright and gave him the *bota*.

The hunter drank about half of the flask, greedily, then he checked and held it out. 'Sorry ... yours.'

'No, go ahead, finish it,' Ryan said. 'I'll go fill it again.' He reached for his knife and pierced the three fresh nuts he had brought back with him. 'Sup these as well while I'm gone.'

When he returned from the burn again he was relieved to see that the hunter was still sitting and awake. He offered him the *bota* again, but Ramirez shook his head. 'No ... save it.' He gazed up the slope. The light had almost gone now. 'Let's try it some more ... better at night.'

Except for the stiffness in his arm and the vicious stabs when he moved it, and the deep-down burning in his side, the sharp edges of pain seemed duller, and he felt that he had recovered a little from the effort of the march.

'You reckon you can go another piece? Rested up enough?' Ryan said.

He nodded.

'All right. But take it easy, don't force it, boy. Stop every time you want, I think the bleeding is drying up ... we don't want to louse that up.'

In the next hour they made several more stops and now,

385

again, they were down to intervals of fifty yards. Then, at last, the trees began to thin out and the Pass loomed ahead of them.

It ran upwards like a shallow twisting chasm, and even though the light was gone and the moon not yet risen, they could make out the beginning of it, shrouded in heavy shadow, from the bluffs on either side, that distinguished it from the lighter substance of the face, and the vague silhouette of its ending at the skyline.

'Take a good rest now, Juan, sleep if you want, we can afford it,' Ryan said. He unscrewed the cap of the flask and held it out.

Ramirez sat hunched, breathing deeply through his nose. For a moment he seemed not to have heard, then he straightened up. 'No.' He spoke jerkily. 'Moon coming ... go far as we can before heat comes up ... give me ten minutes.'

Forty minutes later they made the head of the Pass in three slogging, dragging stages that, for the stricken man, were dreadfully punitive.

He lay now where he had slumped, in the lee of a crag, face down, head pillowed on his uninjured arm.

He was utterly and completely spent.

Occasionally a tremor passed through his body, but presently the pain in him became submerged in the depths of his dreadful weariness. His breathing became less laboured and he slept.

Near the head of the Pass, where it swept in a great bend that ran almost parallel with the crest before it turned again, they had taken to a smaller defile leading more directly to the summit, and the ground before them now was wide open. The moon, lustrously clear, as Ramirez had predicted, was fully risen now, and in the bright silver light the terrain stretched away flatly to where the next descent began.

It was like the high veld, Ryan thought, except that it had a spectral, lunar look. Here and there scattered outcrops of ashen grey rock produced impenetrable black pools of shadow on the side of the crags shielded from the wan rays, but everywhere else the ground was washed with light.

You could have seen a man approaching from two, maybe

386

three hundred yards, and once as he watched, forearms rested on the rock, a *tigré* crossed just a stone's throw ahead, on its way to the Pass and the low ground of the *valle*. The big cat gave him no qualms, save the thought of what might have happened had he come on the wounded sleeping man alone, but he drew the Luger and checked the magazine just the same.

For the better part of an hour, it seemed, Ramirez lay still. Then, turning, he jarred his splintered arm and the pain of it entered his mind. He opened his eyes and Ryan bent to help him to a sitting position.

Again, as he had done before, he stared dazedly about him for a moment or two like a man striving for consciousness.

Ryan squatted beside him. There was not much left in the *bota*, but he gave him a drink, then damped a corner of his bandana and dabbed the hunter's burning brow.

'How's it coming, boy. You had yourself a good sleep there.'

The other man did not reply. He sat still, his unhurt shoulder slumped against the rock, his chin on his chest. Both wounds were throbbing, and he knew, felt, that he was still losing blood, though the wet patches looked no worse. Until now his mind had been concentrated on the desperately serious effort of the marches from the river, with avoiding the worst jars, husbanding his breathing. But now an inexorable feeling of foreboding began to settle on him.

He was a man who loved life, but he was not afraid of death and there was no panic in him. As with El Viejo, the omnipresent possibility of death had been a major hazard of his calling for most of his manhood, and, like the old man, it was more the place and manner of it than the thing itself which concerned him. There was great grief in it of course. But you did not *fear* sleep. Only that it was better in a clean quiet place. Like here, above all the jungles he had ranged.

He began to consider it, dispassionately, speculating how much farther he could go before he could go no farther. Whether it would be better to stay, wait out his time in the cool pure air of the hills and not lie, ultimately, in the foetid mire of the *akalche* and the crabs.

387

But then, as he was on the point of voicing his decision, Ryan's voice came through, resolute, insistent, as if he had read him telepathically.

'I thought the river would be the worst, boy,' the Englishman said. 'But it wasn't. *This* was the worst, and you've licked it.'

He paused, awaiting a flicker of response, and when none came he went on persistently: 'Downhill now, boy, nice and steady!' He put the note of confidence and optimism in it, even though it was partly spurious.

Ramirez looked up, brushing the mistiness from his eyes. 'Another one yet, Mark, another ridge ... I couldn't make it, Bwana,' he said. His voice was low, but quite calm, with a note of finality in it.

Ryan pretended exasperation. 'Aaah! How many times do I have to tell you? You're not alone. *We'll* make it.' He dismissed the roughness from his voice but it was still authoritative. 'You think we're going to throw it away after what you've done?'

Despite the unreason for it, even the suspicion that the other man might not really believe it himself, there was a force in it that got through to him. It was as if an unspoken pact had been agreed between them, a contract which imposed the mutual obligation of maximum endeavour, and maybe a little more.

'I wouldn't want to finish in the *akalche*.'

'I promise you,' Ryan said. The cool intermittent breezes which at first had been so welcome had settled now to a consistency of coldness, rippling the grass and even stirring the sparse islands of knee-high scrub.

He bottoned his shirt front higher. 'Listen, Juan. I had an uncle once, a sergeant, machine-gunner, called James Ryan. They gave his wife and kids his postumous V.C. He could have let the Krauts through and they would likely have saved him, but he didn't. He kept on holding them up. He was minus an arm and a foot. The citation said he "continued to fire his gun until he died" ... *that was at the end of the second day*.'

'*Es muy yesca!*'

388

'You could say that.'

Ramirez smiled wearily. 'Let's go, Bwana.'

'*Es muy yesca*, Cazador,' Ryan said.

The table top of the escarpment had looked no more than the extent of a couple of fields, but it took a lot longer. Skirting the banks and pitholes of the hags, detouring the scattered thickets of waist-high brush. At the end of it Ramirez sank to his knees against a peat mound, his thighs were quivering with fatigue.

'There ... drink left, Mark?' The words came between convulsive inhalations.

'Sure, boy. Only a mouthful, but we'll find a burn going down.'

It might have been twenty minutes or a half hour later that they started again in the full brilliance of the moon. They went even more slowly now, the brush and the secondary growth whipping and tugging at their legs, but later, within the trees, it became easier, starkly contrasting with the crucifying climb up through the trees from the river.

Halting, making a stretch, they came to the end of the timber and the beginning of the *akalche* flat in the first streaks of the false dawn.

Almost at once Ramirez slept again, while the other man hunted across the fringe of the slope for one of the rills that later, in the approaching time of the sustained rains, would transform the flat land into full swamp and drive the land crabs on to the slopes.

This time he had to search for half a mile, his anxiety quickening, before the croaking of frogs gave him the clue. He scraped a hole in the bed sufficient to submerge the *bota* and then, remembering the *akalche* to come, he drank his fill, and more, before he refilled the wineskin.

When he returned Ramirez looked not to have moved a muscle, except that his lips were parted. Occasionally, he murmured, unintelligibly, save that once, quite distinctly, he said 'Clara', and moved his head as if in refusal.

Ryan settled beside him. He hunched on his elbow watching the gradual misty emergence of the skyline of the second ridge

389

way out across the *akalche*, the lesser ridge.

Christ, the *lesser* ridge! For the torn and afflicted man beside him it might as lief have been the murderously exhausting *Meall* barrier back home, for the suffering man would never make it on his feet.

The sunrise made a striking diurnal bridge which arced the undulating outline of the ridge, investing the slopes with a tricoloured hodden of yellow, green and purple. But he knew that the glory of it was ephemeral. Satirical. A gimcrack mechanism of the tyranny to come. And the urge to get going fretted him.

But even while he was still wondering whether to rouse him, the hunter stirred and turned, groaning as the pain fangs and the stiffness bit deeper.

'You want to stay longer, Juan?'

Ramirez stared out towards the ridge, screwing up his eyes against the brightness. Under the beard growth his face was pale and drawn. 'No ... try make some distance ... the *akalche* ... before the big heat.'

They began to cross the *akalche*, the hunter hanging heavily on the taller man's shoulder, in the same fashion of ever shortening stretches, and to the sentinel vultures planing overhead the manner of their labouring crawl was manifestly portentous.

It was like a dreadful race against the mounting yellow enemy overhead, and against the substance of Ramirez's last reserves.

Several times he almost fell, his breath coming in sobbing gasps, but they came to the end at last, and Ryan marvelled at the tormented man's immense resolve. He helped him to the small shade pool of a tamarind and held the *bota* to his parched lips; then he lay down himself. He put out of his mind the thought of the searing climb to come, and tried to sleep, to gird himself for the big effort. The supreme test.

Perhaps an hour later he got to his feet and went forward for a short distance, a hundred yards or so, prospecting the way and seeking for a rill. He had almost returned when he saw with amazement that Ramirez was on his feet, swaying,

390

trying to follow. The hunter took two or three more steps, but it was no use. He called out hoarsely as Ryan ran to him, catching him as he pitched forward.

He laid him down, carefully, apprehensively, and listened for his heartbeats. They seemed strong enough, fitful but not irresolute.

Well, this is it, Ryan! The last adversity that had had to come. *Get stuck-in, Ryan!* Time's what counts now, not when it suits. *Move!*

As gently as he could, fearing a haemorrhage, he got the groaning, whimpering man on to his shoulder and began to slog upwards through the trees. At first he lurched, but then he fell into the tempo of it.

He made three hundred yards, and told himself he could have gone farther if he hadn't come on to this rill; that he dared not ignore it lest he should not find another. He laid Ramirez down nearby and crawled the few yards forward on hands and knees.

An elongated cloud of *pequenos* hung over the driblet and he slashed at the dancing overspread savagely, dispersing the flies long enough to fill the *bota*.

While he drank he studied the hunter's bandages again. The patch on his back had not spread and did not seem to be freshly weeping, but there was a steady drip from his arm and, looking back, he could see the stains at intervals of a few steps apart. Maybe it would dry up if he could avoid jarring him. He soaked both bandages with water, refilled the flask and got the unconscious man on to his shoulder again.

He made four more grinding forays.

Crossing the first *akalche*, his shirt had almost dried on his back, the sun's heat gaining on the rate of his own perspiration, but now it was wholly sodden and the sustenance in the limpid air grew less. The sweat rolling down his face kept blinding him, filling his eyes, and continually he had to shake his head to avoid blundering. Each time that he paused to lean against a tree, chest heaving, sucking for breath, it was a great temptation to relieve himself of his burden even for five minutes. But the effort of setting him down and lifting him

391

again would have been uneconomic, even despite the respites.

He began to force upwards again, and now he tried to help himself with a stratagem, a *ruse-de-guerre* with which men had fought pain, even preserved their sanity, in extremities of war and suffering, since the dawn of human intellect, concentrating his thoughts on inner visions that diverted his mind from the agony of the treadmill. Mark ... Renate ... *Greenacres...*!

Eight, or perhaps ten halts later, he came on trembling legs to another stream. It ran transversely across his path and, ironically, unburdened, he could have crossed it with a runing jump. But it was cut deeply into the hillside, steeply banked, and it might as well have been thrice the width.

He laid Ramirez down beside it, and for a moment he sat hunched, contemplating the obstacle dully, listening to the synchronised pounding of his heart and convulsive breathing. Curiously, he had no compelling urge to scramble forward and drink at once. Oblivious of the mosquitoes and the bottlas flies attacking the glistening wet surfaces of his neck and arms, he was wondering how he had got this far. Whether the uncontrollable twitching of his limbs was the manifestation of conclusive exhaustion. Whether he was done.

After a few minutes he crawled forward and lowered himself into the water. Surprisingly it rose to his waist. He bent and drank, and drank. Then he went to his knees and immersed himself completely, and again. It was lukewarm, yet indescribably allaying, and gradually he felt a semblance of revival that was more mental than physical. He wanted, now, just to drag himself on to the bank and sleep, but practical sense demanded that he should get over this obstacle first.

Still standing in the water he got his arms under the legs and back of the unconscious man and lifted him across on to the other bank. Ramirez groaned, but he gave no other sign, nor even when his face was dabbed with the rag and his bandages re-soaked, dislodging the living pads of flies.

Ryan stood looking down at him, letting the ache of the lifting effort fade from the sinews of his biceps. The arm wound seemed to have ceased dripping, but now the other was suppurating blood again, oozing from the edge of the cloth and forming trickles. He covered both places with his sodden rags, then he lay down, burying his face in the moss, and slept.

He lay motionless beside Ramirez for some misty nebulous time that could have been half an hour or infinity. He had lost all sense of time and position in the great effort of the climb, but when he woke, the jagged alarm cry of a macaw piercing his consciousness, it was still light.

A stone's-cast to his right, as he now saw, there was a break in the trees, a small rocky enclave bare of growth save for a few parched tufts of moss. He went over to it. At one point you could just see the river, back down through the trees in the bottom of the valley. But, much more pertinently, the summit of the ridge was fully visible. The sun, redder now, hung at half-height above the highest peak along the crest, tinging the edges of the cloud with blood, and it came to him that he had made three-quarters of the ascent.

The realisation surprised him and then, slowly, it began to act upon his self-confidence, seeping back morale, hardening his resolve. He returned to the stream and began to steep Ramirez's bandages afresh and to sponge his brow. Suddenly under the sensation of the water, the prostrate man stirred and mumbled. Then his eyes opened.

'Drink. . . .'

While he gave it to him in mouthfuls, Ryan forced a grin. 'We've nearly made it boy . . . nearly to the top.'

Ramirez considered the words. It was as though he had flickers of understanding, though the look of delirium was in his eyes, but he had no idea how long they had been travelling or where they were.

'Where . . . top?'

'Top of the last ridge, the *Border* ridge,' Ryan said with hoarse emphasis.

Ramirez stared, trying to think. 'Only half way . . . half.'

Ryan felt a spasm of anger and resentment. 'Aaah, you're wandering. We're nearly over the *ridges*, it's the ridges that count, man, don't you understand that?' His voice tailed off as he realised the other man's incomprehension.

Ramirez frowned. He held out a hand for the *bota* and poured the water over his face. He was trying to force himself back to full consciousness, to consider it substantively. It came to him finally that he was still the man responsible. And he was going to die. And he was terribly, unbearably tired. And he did not want to move any more.

He said. 'Leave ... here, Mark ... go for ... boys ... do as I say.'

Ryan said nothing. There was some element of sense in it. But he knew instinctively, conclusively, that if he did Ramirez would be dead when they returned. More than that. That he might not even die in peace. A defenceless man, sodden with blood. *Tigré*, puma, wild dogs, snake, even transient peccaries could take him as he was.

He waited until the other man's head fell back again. Then, after a few minutes more of rest, he got him on to his shoulder and started on the slogging agony of the climb again, thrashing and staggering upwards, conscious only of his feet and the ground immediately before him

Three hours and seven stages later, heart bursting, lungs dragging for oxygen, his vision a bloody blur, Mark Ryan made the crest in the last rays of twilight!

He lay where he had slumped. As yet he was beyond sleep, as if inoculated with a drug that preserved his consciousness. Obliged him to lie, listening to his own sawing breathing, feeling the trembling of his limbs, the twitching of nerve ends, the singing in his ears, and denying him the great reward of oblivion.

It was near to midnight when he woke in the fullness of the moon. His whole body ached, and though he was cold now his thirst was prodigious. He reached for the *bota*, then thought of the other man and moved closer to him, Ramirez seemed wholly comatose now. His face and neck were covered with bites and swellings and he realised that his own were the same.

The idea of searching for water was exorbitant, and it was unlikely that Ramirez would wake now. Or ever? He drank half the flask, enough to relieve the parched condition of his throat. They would have to take the chance of hitting a hill burn on the way down.

On the way down!

Even the idea of repetition was an anguish. He shook his head and knuckled the mistiness from his eyes. After the sleep he had had, maybe the ache and the stiffness were no more than the soreness after the first day of the season on the Bens, would pass when he was moving again? He began systematically to rub his limbs and flex his aching overtaxed muscles.

Ramirez gave a little moan as he got him up, but before they had made fifty yards his mumblings tailed off and he was unconscious again.

He moved very carefully now, more slowly than he could have gone, because it would have been very easy to stumble, even to break into a staggering run in the steeper places, and a fall would have been final, certain haemorrhages.

His arms were leaden, and the muscles of his thighs and calves quivered with strain. But incredibly, after a time the sharper convulsions of rigidly unyielding sinews began to relax a little, as he had hoped, giving way to the duller, more familiar feeling of pure weariness that, paradoxically, held a measure of relief.

He made the descent through the lesser timber and secondary growth of the east face with five halts.

It had been immensely, incomparably less punitive than any of the crucifixions from the river, but it had taken a lot longer than he anticipated. Still, he had done it.

They were over the big divide, whatever else might befall, the Border was behind them. The fact of it leavened his brooding contemplation of the battle still ahead a little. Now, above all, he had to husband his last resources, avoid mistakes, conserve every grain of strength left in him, plan and discipline the effort.

He decided to give himself fifteen minutes' respite and took off his watch. The unbreakable face had survived, and though the dial was a white blur, obfuscated by the salt of his own sweat, it still worked, and he prised it open with his knife and wiped it clean.

When the quarter-hour was passed, the first faint flail-and-ball semblance of the morning-star had risen in the sky.

There was, as he recollected, two miles of *akalche* flat before the real jungle. The thought of the jungle, for all its tenuous hazards, was like the promise of a refuge from the naked oppression of the sun, if only he could reach it.

He began to drive forward again like a ponderous machine, a clockwork figure. Each time he went on to his limit, till he felt that he was going to fall, because there were no trees to help him, and because he had to minimise the awful sapping efforts of laying down and lifting his burden. And each time, after the terrain lay finally exposed in the wash of hard yellow light, he subsequently rose on his knees, brushing his eyes, waiting for the black-green horizon mirage of the jungle to loom out of the sweat mist.

For this was one mirage that wasn't, and, surely to Christ, it was getting nearer!

It was still far short of peak heat yet, but already, now, the sun was lighting on his eyes and chest like a spotlight focused on a stage performer. He gritted his teeth, his face working with the racking strain of lifting again, and went on. Sank, and rose again, repeating it.

He was like a man in a dream now, hardly conscious of his bodily agony, obsessed, driven, by a concept from which Ramirez was excluded ... was irrelevant to. By some obscure mental clonus if had become a grim, highly personal contest between himself and the *akalche*.

Even more than the instinct of self-preservation the illusion kept him lumbering forward conpulsively, sometimes now wasting the effort of breathing to curse the land out loud.

Almost without knowing it, in the mid-forenoon, he reached the end of the *akalche* and lurched blindly into the dark haven of the jungle's fringe, the blazing, conquered glare behind him.

For some indeterminate time he lay still, sucking for oxygen, envying Ramirez's condition of stupor, his own mind wavering on the borderline, then suddenly he slept.

For two or three minutes when he woke his brain could

396

barely assimilate the confused medley of thoughts running through his mind. And then, suddenly, he became conscious of a vague feeling of guilt, until he saw from the position of the sun that it was only noon.

He took the flask and moved up to the sprawled figure lying deeper within the shade of the matopolo tree. The hunter's breathing was almost imperceptible, and even the heavy swarthiness of his beard could not disguise the pallor of his skin. He was just alive.

At first he felt only surprise at the fact of it. Increasingly he began to wonder whether, with death so near now, further endeavour would simply be a criminal futility that would destroy his own chances.

It was the seeming futility that weighed most heavily. The problem of the jungle did not scare him . . . if he was going to be alone. Alone, he could last for a week if necessary. He had enough rounds for food, the jungle fauna had to drink, he even had matches. Sooner or later, alone, his strength recovered, he could make it, whether by the sun, or the stars, or by what he had learned from Ramirez.

But then, as his head cleared, the moral and the obligatory considerations returned and he felt a sense of shame.

Once more he damped Ramirez's bandages, wetted his mouth and brow, and drank the last of the brackish water himself. He nerved himself for the lift, got the limp body on to his shoulders and moved off into the trees.

He had to find a *camino* now, and then water.

Within a short space he was streaming with sweat again, breathing heavily, but now at least there were trees. He did not need to lay Ramirez down. And, as yet, in this initial tract, there were few tangled barriers of lianas and no hellish thickets of bamboo.

But at the fourth time of halting he was still working blindly, and sometimes, almost literally, from the swellings around his eyes.

Then, as he began to feel the first twinges of anxiety, he came on to a *camino*. He set down his burden, and when he had rested a while he began to cast around, working in widen-

397

ing circles, searching for the fern.

The first two clumps he found were abortive, though they had seemed identical to the vital species. But the third time he was lucky.

He took his bearings from the yellow compass of the plant, and confirmed the prevailing directional trend of the treetops with it. The deer path was not directly on course, but it would serve until it led to water.

The trail made better going than before, but he was down to mere stretches of a hundred yards or so before he hit the watering place. He gave himself fifteen or twenty minutes before he began to plod again. Now he was into heavy jungle, and when at last he broke through on to another *camino* he was more spent than at any time since he had left the *akalche*.

All through the afternoon, twice re-checking with the fern, he drove on at irregular intervals, staggering, lurching, sometimes making a mere fifty yards, sometimes three times as far where the green walls rose straighter.

But there was no sign!

He could not estimate the miles he had travelled, how far remained, and the dreadful uncertainty of it tormented him.

He came around a bend, a dim archway of the *camino*, and a sound brought him to a swaying halt. With his free hand he wiped the sweat mist from his eyes and peered ahead. Then, as realisation dawned, he rolled Ramirez from his shoulder and tugged the pistol from his hip.

The spiralled bundle on the trail looked like a coil of rope, save that it was alive. Light brown, with dark brown markings outlined in white, the thickness of a man's wrist. The bushmaster hissed again, and raised its flat evil head to the chest height of a man with a sinuous spiralling movement.

This was the one that came ahead nine times out of ten, and there was no question of waiting or attempting any detour now.

As the head sank again, preparatory to attack, Ryan began to fire. He saw two shots plough the ground beside the gathering coil, then the snake came. He kept firing and then, suddenly, within a few feet of him, rising again now for the strike,

398

the liquid glide was halted and the reptile began to lash.

Jesus! He waited, then, carefully, resting the barrel on his forearm, he fired until a bullet smashed the creature's head.

He stood still, shaking with hatred and relief, refilling the magazine of the Luger from his belt with a hand that, now, trembled uncontrollably. It was a minute or two before he remembered Ramirez ... the heavy fall. The hunter lay inert in a twisted heap, and the wound in his back was suppurating freely.

Ryan dropped to his knees beside him. His face was lined with bitterness and he wanted to yell his grief and hate. Even the bird calls had seemingly taken on a malevolent mocking note.

After a while he remembered dimly that where you found these kinds of snakes there were often more than one. He got to his feet and started away, then stopped and turned. He knew it was futile, dangerous to delay here. But he could not leave him.

He plumbed the last drops of his resources, lifted the still form once more and went slowly forward again until he could go no farther.

He lowered the stricken man for the last time and pitched beside him. But even the oblivion he pleaded was withheld from him. The lousy, God-cursed, bastarding jungle had won after all! He dragged the pistol from his holster and began to fire until the magazine was finished.

Irrationally, as he began to sink, he murmured a word ... *Fiona*. And then, strangely, it was as if there was someone calling, lifting him, and he opened his eyes again, There was a shape, an oval shape floating above him. It drew away and then returned, became more detailed. He strove to disinter remembrance, and then it came.

El Viejo!

399

15. REQUIEM

He saw the dust cloud of the car as it entered the last rutted stretch of track to the store. When it appeared, he had been on the point of firing a couple of practice rounds at the vultures on the top of the chicken hut which the Chinese had over the way. But now he put the Luger away and got up from the boardwalk, resting his hand on the jamb of the porch.

As the car came nearer he saw that Almagro sat beside the driver. The two women in the back of the car wore black and their faces were partly hidden by the veils over their heads. The man who sat beside the elder woman wore a white linen suit, but he had a black tie.

Even though there had been no alternative to the deception, cruel deception, of the older woman, and while she herself would not yet fully understand, he had been certain that he could count upon Consuela's co-operation because she was very intelligent; would know that what he had instructed was necessary and important. Also, because the letter which he had sent to her by Almagro, two nights previously, had been carefully written and emphatically explicit.

Nevertheless, he had not been sure that the man would come. Although there were several good reasons why, he had figured, it was more than a probability. Accordingly, the fact of the man in the white suit gave him great satisfaction.

Ironically, he had been very near the camp when El Viejo had heard his shots, and he had written the letter immediately he had sufficiently recovered.

Almagro and Tomásco had driven all night in the truck. The young hunter had also impressed upon Consuela that she must delay for two days, then Tomásco had returned at once with the driver of the Buick and another man.

The second man had remained all day before returning to the Capital.

The car drew up a few yards from the store, its tyres churning the red dust, and Almagro got out and opened a rear door.

400

Ryan nodded to each of the women and gestured to where Tomásco stood by the door.

The man in the car glanced about him, then he got out and made to follow but Ryan grasped his sleeve. 'Not you, Jefe. Later!'

'Where is the priest?' the squat man said sharply. He frowned.

'Later,' Ryan said curtly.

The Ayuntamiento stared. It astonished him that the *Inglés* should still be here, had not returned to the Capital.

After he had learned of the escape he had been beside himself, and the Jefe Policia and the Teniente had felt the full measure of his rage.

Thus, when the message had come, he had hardly been able to believe that the business had so conclusively succeeded after all.

His response had been immediate, and politic. In itself an indication of his deep solicitude.

There had been no difficulty in explaining how the tragic catastrophe had happened during his Mexican absence. Not to Clara. She had, he knew, always opposed Ramirez's dislike and deplored his refusals.

Equally, she had never understood her husband's substance, just as she had never lost her inner dread of returning to the poverty from which he had lifted her. She was prostrate now, but of course it would pass.

He had only now to continue playing the eminent kinsman, *guardián*, with a minimum of adroitness.

There might still be a little difficulty with Consuela, but, in these new circumstances ... and even with her, the fact that she had sent the radio message had seemed to be a good augury.

That part, the dessert, would come, and probably soon enough, when he had control of Ramirez's affairs. Which was the real, the practical reward he stood to gain. But the presence of the *Inglés* gave him a vague quirk of unease.

On the occasion that he had first seen him, sitting in the dining-room of the *Wallace* taberna, he had not closely

401

observed him. But now, studying the powerful substance of him, he was prepared to give credence to the Teniente's story that this periodista *must* have carried Ramirez from the Border.

He tried to pull away his sleeve. 'What is this? Of what concern to you?' he said with assumed hauteur.

'Oh, of much personal concern,' Ryan said evenly. 'Also, we have some things to discuss, Jefe, you and I. A preliminary.'

He jerked his head. His face was expressionless, yet the look in his eyes gave the other man a further sensation of disquiet.

'This way, Jefe.' He grasped the stout man's arm.

The Ayuntamiento tried to pull away again, but Ryan tightened his grip, jerking him forward unceremoniously.

'*This way, pequeño!*'

His tone had changed now, allowing no refusal. 'First ... something for you to see.' He jerked his head again. 'Then we will discuss the business while the ladies are attending to theirs.' He led him around the side of the store before releasing his hold.

At the back of the place there was a window hung with mosquito netting.

'This of the priest,' Ryan said. 'Well, oddly, we do not seem to need one now.' He drew back a fold of the netting and hooked his thumb. 'See for yourself, Jefe.'

The swarthy olive-skinned man hesitated, frowning. He was conscious of a leaden feeling in his belly. 'What is this then . . . ?'

Ryan moved closer. He shoved the other man roughly towards the window.

'Look for yourself, I said. *Take a good look, Jefe.*'

Despite the sudden premonitive feeling of apprehension that ran through him, the thick-set man craned forward.

Inside, the women stood one on either side of the Chinaman's iron bed. The elder one was weeping uncontrollably, yet at the same time smiling through her tears.

Ramirez lay half reclined, the sunrays from the window dappling his shirt.

402

One of his arms, heavily bandaged, was much shorter than the other, terminating near the elbow. His face was very pale and drawn, but his voice was strong and even.

He stared past Cruz and raised his single hand to Ryan.

'Ah, Mark, give the Ayuntamiento a drink before you explain our business with him,' he said with savage humour.

The staring man drew back from the window, his face working with confusion and unbelief.

'Dios . . . not dead then. . . .'

Immediately he tried to recover himself. '*Acción de gracias!*' He made the formal observation in a hoarse mutter.

Ryan laughed harshly. 'Indeed. *Mucho acción.*'

He jerked his head. 'This way, Jefe. We will discuss it.' He gave the shorter man a shove. '*Move.*'

The Ayuntamiento began to bluster, but he could not disguise the unease in his voice. 'What is the meaning of it . . . why were we not told?'

Ryan grinned bleakly. 'You might have been reluctant to accept my invitation.'

They were walking towards the car now, but Cruz halted abruptly. 'Enough of this farce,' he said shortly. He tried to make it authoritative.

'You . . . *extranjero* . . . you do not understand who I am.' Hate and anger reared between them like a coiling viper.

'Farce?' Ryan said softly. He considered him as if he was seeing him for the first time. The round heavily jowled face, the flat tawny eyes, the wide mouth beneath the black moustache. This was the fugging bastard who had tried to have them killed, *and he was still arrogant.*

'Farce?' He moved closer and shook his head. 'Oh no! A certain humour in it, but no farce.' He slapped the stout man savagely, viciously, back and forth across the face, followed his staggering, and sent him down with a sudden huge blow.

The prone man cried out with the pain in his face. He got to his knees in the dust and suddenly his hand darted inside his jacket, but Ryan stretched him flat on his face with a heavy kick between his broad buttocks. He bent down and ripped the pistol from under the white jacket.

'So. You wanted to try it *again*, Jefe?' he said softly. He dragged him to his feet by the throat of his shirt and sent him down again with another piledriver.

The pistol was a flat Biretta. He emptied the magazine and pocketed the shells, then he threw it in the dirt. 'Pick it up, Jefe, you are going to need it. I shall return the slugs later.'

Cruz lay in the dust.

'Get up,' Ryan said. He waited a moment then raised his foot. '*On your feet!*' The battered man dragged himself up. Blood streamed from his nose and mouth on to his white lapels and shirt.

'Now about the ... farce,' Ryan said.

He got a cheroot from his shirt pocket and lit it, watching the battered man contemptuously. 'Which is not so much a farce as a *peripeteia*, a reversal of circumstances.'

He took a draw and let the swaying man wait. 'We are going to play a game, Jefe, you and I, and an old acquaintance of yours, El Viejo.

'It will be somewhat like a game the *Inglés* play, called hare-and-hounds, only it will be more serious for you because you will only have your popgun and I shall have a rifle. I have not yet explained it to the old man, but you may be sure that he will approve it.'

The bloody-faced man stared back, uncomprehending. His lower lip was twitching and he was oblivious of the large black fly on his chin seeking the blood.

'We are going to see the old man now,' Ryan said. 'And tonight we shall take you a good distance on your way. Into the jungle. *We* shall return, then, but you will stay, Jefe. In the morning we shall begin the hunt ... which will give you even more start than we had with your *soldados*.'

He laughed. 'I hope your jungle craft is good, Jefe, because you might make circles for a month if it is not, if we changed our minds. You don't look much of a hare, but you might surprise youself ... make the *akalche*.'

He paused for a moment to let it penetrate. 'You'll get your gun, too ... in case you hit a bushmaster before I hit you.'

The frightened man turned suddenly and ran. Ryan let him

404

go. It was like the last desperation run of a *mako* against the hook. Tomãsco stood leaning against the door of the store and Almagro squatted beside him, but they did nothing. The driver of the Buick was nowhere to be seen.

The desperate man went for the car, but when he saw there was no key he wheeled and ran for the trees. Over across the track from the Post a great matopolo presided over a grove of tamarinds which protruded from the edge of the jungle like a promontory.

Cruz passed the feathery blue trees and halted at the fringe of the jungle, hesitating. He was about to run again when a sound rent the stagnant air like the passage of an angry bee.

The arrow transfixed the frantic man with a soft sucking sound like wet sailcloth torn by a gust, and his scream rose, then ended in a sobbing gasp. He looked down at his stomach open-mouthed, and grasped the shaft. For a few yards he staggered aimlessly feeling the ripping pain and the hot bubbling blood in his mouth, then he crumpled, the blood pulsing from his middle and where the arrowhead protruded from his back.

Just for an instant Ryan sensed movement in the corner of his eye. He caught a tiny motion, like the flick of a deer's head, within the heavy dappled shadow of the tamarinds.

All three men began to walk over to the edge of the jungle. Ryan looked down at the crumpled heap of white and crimson with interest. Previously he had never fully realised the shattering force of a big arrow, and the power of it greatly impressed him.

When he saw him coming, the old man put down his machete and called to the woman to prepare maize coffee for the visitor.

'I have come to tell you that we are leaving tomorrow,' Ryan offered.

'*Gracias, Señor,*' El Viejo said slowly. 'I will be at the *tienda.*'

Ryan held out his cheroots, and for a few moments they smoked in silence until the old woman came from the fire with the gourds.

405

'However, that is not the only reason I came,' Ryan said. 'A personal thing.' He drew in and exhaled. 'I wished to say that it was a privilege to meet you, Cazador.'

The old man regarded him steadily, but when he saw that the other man was sincere his blue eyes crinkled. 'That you may come again. Señor?'

'It is quite certain,' Ryan said. He smiled. 'Though not to hunt *los pavos*.'

They were silent for a moment then El Viejo said, 'He was an evil man. *Malo*. Without courage or compassion.'

'Yes. A *fisi*,' Ryan said. 'Hyena. They have the villainy of your *fangosos* and the cowardice of the *suassorans*.'

'*Si*,' the old man said simply, reflectively. 'And he would have destroyed a good man.' He looked up. 'Even two good men.'

For a few moments more they remained silent, drinking the coffee.

'You say it was a big arrow?' El Viejo said.

Ryan nodded. 'An arrow for *tigré*, I would say.' He paused for an instant. 'But I saw the Indian, too, as did Almagro.'

'So?'

Ryan looked into the old blue eyes, his lips formed into the trace of a smile. 'Yes, beyond question a Carib. We shall testify to it in the Capital.'

After a while the old man said. 'Do you think he will hunt again ... Juan?'

'It is not sure,' Ryan said. 'Maybe ... this of the arm, you understand.'

'Ah, *si*,' El Viejo said. He glanced down at his bad arm critically. 'At least I have him all. Even at times, now, he can pull the great bow again.'

Ryan smiled again, and for a second something passed between them. 'Of a certainty,' he said. He got to his feet and held out his hand. 'Viva Ramirez!'

CONCLUSION

Ryan rested his heels on the rail of the terrace and watched the sea while he waited. From within the open doors, on the bar counter, the radio said 'Jerusalem has been bombed again....'

I hope to Christ the little fellows paralyse the bastards, he thought, and remembered that ten years before he had printed the prophecy that if it ever came to it they would.

When he had heard enough the bartender turned off the radio and put on a real vintage record... '... *but Eadie had kerlass with a capital Kaaay* ...'

Ryan picked up the *Daily Mail*, left by an incoming Scottish thread salesman, and began to re-read the piece by the paper's Commonwealth Correspondent.

FEARS GROW OF HONDURAS SELL-OUT. Rumours of such a deal provoked violent rioting ... last year, and fears of a 'sell-out' have now been revived ... by the London talks.... The colony is likely to quickly lose its distinct identity ... as opposed to Latin American characteristics....

Jesus Christ! Was there no end to the crawling, jellyfish performances of a crew by whom, as a Briton, he had never felt more misrepresented?

Before he had left home, the world, by courtesy of television, had witnessed a former Labour Minister abasing himself before the tin Sword of Islam. Before that President who presided over more total envy, indolence, inefficiency, dirt, disease, corruption and open sewers than elsewhere in the world. The one who was prepared to risk world war for personal aggrandisement! And before that Britons had contemplated the spectacle of their pious 'brothers' ... ears smarting from the cuffs of the French Anglophobe ... fingering rumps reddened by the kicks of the bankrupt Spanish Pharaoh. Now this ... *fears of a sell-out* ... *revived*....

Three days had passed since their return to the Capital. Yesterday he had completed the affidavit which, with the testi-

407

monies of Almagro and Tomásco, took care of Cruz's demise-by-misadventure, and tomorrow he was leaving.

The phonograph changed wheezily to another classic 'oldie' as she came out on to the terrace. '*Do not forsake me*,' *Oh my Darling . . .*'

He got up and pulled her chair closer to his own.

'Well, you never got your fishing after all, Mark,' Ida said. 'I'm . . . sad about that.'

'I'm sad about more than that,' he said. 'But you needn't be. I'll be back when Juan is well enough mended.' He smiled. 'Apart from the fishing, I've got some pretty special interests in the place one way and another now, haven't I?'

But it's a good thing in a way, he thought. There was a problem to be resolved, or rather a decision to be made, and he had always been a man who could not abide postponements, horsing around. Among the letters that had been waiting for him there had been four which counted. Two from Mark and two from Renny.

It was the second one from Renny that had raised the problem. Clearly she had made *her* decision. And yet, despite the warmth and affection, there was no really unequivocal declaration. '. . . *Mark, dear, please don't think I'm stalling, still less that I haven't been thinking and thinking and thinking—every day. But it is a very big, very special thing, isn't it, and you're so far away, and I'm not a writer, darling. I can't tell you here what I want to tell you. Not nearly well enough. . . .*'

Well maybe, woman-like, the atmosphere and the prompting of conversation were inportant to her. It was understandable, natural enough.

But he wasn't going to think about it now. He would begin the process of making his own decision when he was aboard the old Dakota in the morning, because right now he was far from sure about it.

Ida made an effort to introduce a more impersonal note. 'Mark, I don't think you're going to lose your money. It's going well . . . the shop, I mean.'

He smiled. 'Hell, not *shop*, darling. Salon, or something like that, you're an *haute-couturière* now . . . *Madame* Ida! And

408

of course it isn't. You've only got to go around town looking like that, and they'll come running!'

They had eaten dinner at nine o'clock, some time ago, and now the moon was fully risen. There were no other people on the terrace, but he said: 'Let's have another wee one and then go for our swim. It's kind of crowded here.'

She laughed softly. 'All right then.'

He looked over his shoulder and called through the open doors to Paco. 'Hey, Paco. More coffee and two more benedictines!'

When the boy had come and padded away again she took out her cigarettes and, reaching towards the table, dropped her matches. She got up before he could move and bent down. Her dress was a white material with a black-and-red floral design. It clung to her like a sheath, outlining the mould of her hips, and, as she leant over, it rode to the top of her seamed stockings.

Maravilloso was the word, he thought, not just ... beautiful.

When they had finished their drinks they went down on to the sand and walked right along until they came to the place of the three palms, and spread out their beach towels there.

She had a costume this time, of two pieces, like a *bikini*, and when she stretched beside him, lying face down, he began to caress her from her neck to her feet, sometimes kissing her neck and shoulders, and the backs of her thighs, and the soft valley in the middle of her back.

After a while he unfastened the breast hook of her costume and slid the lower half of it down over her feet. He moved his hand over and over her wide buttocks and between her legs until she felt that she could wait no longer and turned on to her back. But he still continued to kiss and fondle her big purposeful breasts and her legs. For some minutes.

She opened her eyes. 'Mark. Are you tired?'

'A little.' He was about as tired as a stallion full of brandy-mash.

'Let me do it then ... besides I don't want to wait any longer.'

'All right.'

409

He lay back while she got to her knees. She slid the trunks from his hips and climbed on to him, moving down until they were wholly joined, his hands spread over her hips.

When at last she had finally melted into fulfilment, she sank down on to him, savouring the quiescent, ebbing pleasure in her big heavy breasts. For a few minutes he held her, stroking her and kissing her shoulder.

'Darling. You're a *melodía* ... you must have invented it.'

She said, 'Mark. Please tell me truly. Will you really come again?'

'So help me God,' Ryan said. 'Of course, and *of course*.' He smiled. 'Not only you, my love ... Every year, or more often, I shall fish with Ramirez.'

She stared down, searchingly. Her eyes were moistened.

She said, 'Viva Ramirez!'

It was the morning after he had got back to *Greenacres*. He could have phoned. Even have driven over to *Donach* there and then. It had only been about nine o'clock. But he had still had that feeling of uncertainty in him. Novel; unwelcomely so. Disconcerting. And an abstruse, uncharacteristic inclination to delay the issue, sleep on it. For all the clarification that would produce as, subconsciously, he knew damn well!

He had a good breakfast, and then he carried the spare phone through to the work-room and plugged it in.

For a second or two he thought, conscious of the quickening sensation within him. Then he dialled and after a brief intercession he heard The Voice. It sounded a shade more evanescent, breathless, than usual. But every bit as effective.

He said: 'Good morning, Voice ... it's that man again.'

'Mark ... darling ... you're back?'

'Last night,' he said. 'Right here on the old patch.'

'Oh that's *wonderful* ... *marvellous*. Did you, are you ... ?'

'Whoa, now, whoa. Hold everything. Can I come over?'

'Please!' There was a second of silence, then she began again. 'How'd it go then ... are you well ... was it ... ?'

But again he interposed. 'Fine. Fine to everything. Only let me get moving, huh?'

'Oh, yes, of course.'

'How about if we run out some place for lunch?'

'No, no, *here*, of course.'

'You mean in the Board Room?' he said, succeeding in making it light.

There was another instant of pause, then: 'Yes. Yes, that too.'

Down along the road from the house the glistened flint chips blinked in the cold sunlight, and the air had the crisp tang of first frosts.

Big Henry ... he was in the north field now ... leisurely turned his head, his breaths making steamy puffs like transitory protests against his solitary state. In back beyond him a gentle salted wind rustled the pines and a solitary peregrine hung like a dark fleck on the blue background canvas over the treetops.

The green acres rolled down to the brighter blue of the sea, bisected at intervals by the autumnal red-gold bands of the beech hedges. It was a kaleidoscope you could never forget, of course. But there were others. And why couldn't you have the best of both worlds, he thought?

Whoever had contributed that saying had been one of the half-cocked Godfearing Brethren all right. Mao certainly had it. 'Thoughts' and all, notwithstanding. Every no-account Sword of Islam bum from Casablanca to Cairo had it; set up in droves. Like the South American Gauleiters, and their less obvious counterparts of the Western world did, from the Senators and Governors to the Cabinet Ministers and the assembly-line T.U. dummies.

He swung in at the west gates and, in his preoccupation, almost ran down a peacock, the bird accelerating from its stately meandering to an undignified scuttle, squawking its fright and dissatisfaction as it went.

He saw her immediately he came around the curve of the 'Tulip', standing outside the house, and as soon as he was out of the car she came forward to be folded and kissed.

Tallish, handsome, smiling the smile that was perfect in its tiny imperfection, elegant in a dark green suit now, rather than

411

the kind of jodhpurs and turtle neck stuff she usually wore on ordinary mornings.

They went inside, arms around each other's backs.

'Now, then, you coffee-brown-Bwana-N'Kosi man, tell me all about it! Was it all you expected, did you get all you wanted?'

Ryan smiled back from the couch before the amber glow of sitka logs. 'That and more. Made a couple or three good friends I'm pleased about too.'

For a time they continued, but then, once the prologue was done, they came to the crux of it.

'Well ... forgive me for rushing you, dear,' he said finally. 'But you know how I am, and I've got that old practical feeling coming on....'

For a moment she was silent, looking down at her cigarette. Then she said softly: 'Oh, Mark, I've had a bad time with it ... if that's any consolation ... but ... it's like you said. I'm, well, I'm wedded to the place ...'

He tapped his ash into the stirrup tray on the arm, watching it disintegrate. 'And that's not quite all, really, is it?' he said, equally quietly.

'No. Not quite all.'

'The chemistry is lacking a bit ... insufficient?'

She felt a pang of mingled contrition and something that was indefinable, uncertain. 'Oh Mark, I do love you, dear, but ...'

He smiled: 'But like a brother, maybe?'

She got up and came over to the couch. Then she bent down, taking his face in her hands. 'Yes, in a way ... dear, dear brother.'

He put his arm around her, drawing her close, and returned her kiss. He could feel the agitation, sense the self-condemnation in her.

'Please don't hate me, Mark.'

He gave her a little squeeze. 'It's all right, dear, don't worry about it. It's *all right*!'

'But don't hate me.'

'God in heaven,' he said. 'Hate *you*? You just got yourself a

412

devoted, but *devoted* brother, dear.' He smiled down at her. 'Devoted nephew, too ... we hope.'

'Yes, yes, yes ... for ever,' she said.

For a little while longer they watched the fire, silently, until the small clock on the mantel sounded the hour in its restrained tinkly voice. Then he said: 'Let's take a run over to White Crags ... have ourselves a couple of aperitifs before lunch?'

'All right, that would be nice.'

Even before she went for her things, from the moment she had said 'in a way', in fact, he had been aware of a strange lightened sensation that he still hadn't fully analysed.

He picked up the newspaper on the end of the couch, consciously seeking distraction. Trying to still his mind. Enoch Powell had been handing it right back to the soulful-faced, virtue-sodden Brethren again. Reminding them of the hard economic facts about poor old arse-out John Bull, everybody's sugar-daddy. Oddly enough the politician had passed ahead of him through the same alumni portals as himself.

He got up and went out of the house for the car. And then at last it hit him squarely, and he knew, feeling now a kind of guilt in the knowledge, why he was not downcast, why the guilt feeling was overborne by one of release.

She had not yet returned when he went back indoors and he strolled over to the record player and pressed the button. '... *They heard the breeze in the trees* ...'

Just about now, he thought, if he had it figured right, the first evening wisps would be stirring the fronds of the three palms just along a little piece from the *Wallace*.

There was a lot of unarguable commonsense in what old Enoch had said. But, just the same, he was going to have to put up with one more immigrant now. Well, for say half of every year from here on, anyway ... not that *she'd* be any added charge on the State. On the way home he would stop off at the airport cable office.

He began mentally to phrase the message. Carefully. Because it would have to be entirely clear that he meant it for *Aye*. And entirely imperious, too, brooking no argument, nor a

413

day longer delay than it took to hire a locum for the 'salon'!

He stared critically into the mirror over the mantel, and all of a sudden his right eye winked back at him. Indirectly, irrelevantly, it reminded him of something he had been going to do for long enough. Tomorrow he would call the Insurance folks. Cover the hazard of his trade which had become important again.

Well, there had been a lady called Mistinguette, who had insured her legs for a million dollars! And he still had to do the *Kodiaks*. Ten footers of mean and upright Alaskan fury who came running, not waiting for you start anything, and, they said, took three softnose bigger than .375 to stop, even when you were shooting right.

So that old scrunched-up eye, the important one, ought to be worth looking out for. It stared right back, cold-blue over the practiced wrinkles of frequent concentration, and, involuntarily, it winked again.

Give or take a year or two it still ought to be thirty years good enough to nail the Oncomers, or spot a running marlin.

He began to whistle. Extraordinary how a whole horizon of prospects could suddenly change, regain full lustre, just on a phrase. All that ... all the fishing too.... How right Ida had been ... the two words said everything. Suddenly, he shouted them aloud: 'VIVA, RAMIREZ!'

A SELECTION OF FINE READING AVAILABLE IN CORGI BOOKS

Novels

☐ 552 08651 7	THE HAND-REARED BOY	*Brian W. Aldiss*	25p
☐ 552 08889 7	CALIFORNIA GENERATION	*Jacqueline Briskin*	50p
☐ 552 07938 3	THE NAKED LUNCH	*William Burroughs*	37½p
☐ 552 08849 8	THE GLASS VIRGIN	*Catherine Cookson*	40p
☐ 552 08793 9	THE PRETTY BOYS	*Simon Cooper*	35p
☐ 552 08440 9	THE ANDROMEDA STRAIN	*Michael Crichton*	35p
☐ 552 08868 4	I KNEW DAISY SMUTEN	*ed. Hunter Davies*	40p
☐ 552 08125 6	CATCH-22	*Joseph Heller*	35p
☐ 552 08652 5	THY DAUGHTER'S NAKEDNESS	*Myron S. Kauffmann*	62½p
☐ 552 08872 2	LADY BLANCHE FARM	*Frances Parkinson Keyes*	25p
☐ 552 08850 1	FOR INFAMOUS CONDUCT	*Derek Lambert*	40p
☐ 552 08833 1	HOW FAR TO BETHLEHEM?	*Norah Lofts*	35p
☐ 552 08888 9	REQUIEM FOR IDOLS	*Norah Lofts*	25p
☐ 552 08817 X	A FIG FOR VIRTUE	*Nan Maynard*	30p
☐ 552 08791 2	HAWAII	*James A. Michener*	75p
☐ 552 08867 6	THE COLLECTION	*Paulo Montano*	40p
☐ 552 08124 8	LOLITA	*Vladimir Nabokov*	35p
☐ 552 08853 6	THE MONKEY PULLED HIS HAIR	*Frank Norman*	30p
☐ 552 08630 4	PRETTY MAIDS ALL IN A ROW	*Francis Pollini*	40p
☐ 552 07954 5	RUN FOR THE TREES	*James S. Rand*	35p
☐ 552 08887 0	VIVA RAMIREZ!	*James S. Rand*	40p
☐ 552 08891 9	THE BALLAD OF THE BELSTONE FOX	*David Rook*	30p
☐ 552 08597 9	PORTNOY'S COMPLAINT	*Philip Roth*	40p
☐ 552 08712 2	UHURU	*Robert Ruark*	50p
☐ 552 08814 5	SOMETHING OF VALUE	*Robert Ruark*	40p
☐ 552 08794 7	BANEFUL SORCERIES	*Joan Sanders*	35p
☐ 552 08852 8	SCANDAL'S CHILD	*Edmund Schiddel*	40p
☐ 552 08372 0	LAST EXIT TO BROOKLYN	*Hubert Selby Jr*	50p
☐ 552 07807 7	VALLEY OF THE DOLLS	*Jacqueline Susann*	40p
☐ 552 08523 5	THE LOVE MACHINE	*Jacqueline Susann*	40p
☐ 552 08217 1	THE CARETAKERS	*Dariel Telfer*	35p
☐ 552 08091 8	TOPAZ	*Leon Uris*	40p
☐ 552 08384 4	EXODUS	*Leon Uris*	40p
☐ 552 08073 X	THE PRACTICE	*Stanley Winchester*	40p
☐ 552 08481 6	FOREVER AMBER Vol. 1	*Kathleen Winsor*	35p
☐ 552 08482 4	FOREVER AMBER Vol. 2	*Kathleen Winsor*	35p
☐ 552 08483 2	THE LOVERS	*Kathleen Winsor*	35p

War

☐ 552 08738 6	THE BARREN BEACHES OF HELL	*Boyd Cochrell*	35p
☐ 552 08874 9	SS GENERAL	*Sven Hassel*	35p
☐ 552 08779 3	ASSIGNMENT: GESTAPO	*Sven Hassel*	35p
☐ 552 08855 2	THE WILLING FLESH	*Willi Heinrich*	35p
☐ 552 08873 0	THE DOOMSDAY SQUAD	*Clark Howard*	25p
☐ 552 08621 5	MEDICAL BLOCK: BUCHENWALD (illustrated)	*Walter Poller*	35p
☐ 552 08757 2	DEFEAT INTO VICTORY	*Field-Marshal Sir William Slim*	40p
☐ 552 08892 7	THE FORTRESS	*Raleigh Trevelyan*	25p
☐ 552 08893 5	THE ENEMY	*Wirt Williams*	30p
☐ 552 08798 X	VIMY! (illustrated)	*Herbert Fairlie Wood*	30p

Romance

☐ 552 08842 0	EDINBURGH EXCURSION	*Lucilla Andrews*	25p
☐ 552 08878 1	NURSE IN THE SUN	*Sheila Brandon*	25p
☐ 552 08784 X	THE DUTIFUL TRADITION	*Kate Norway*	25p
☐ 552 08859 5	THE ROUNDABOUT	*Yvonne Tobitt*	25p
☐ 552 08897 8	IF YOU SPEAK LOVE	*Jean Ure*	25p

Science Fiction

☐ 552 08785 8	I SING THE BODY ELECTRIC	*Ray Bradbury*	35p
☐ 552 08879 X	NEW WRITINGS IN SF-20	*ed. John Carnell*	25p
☐ 552 08804 8	THE AGE OF THE PUSSYFOOT	*Frederik Pohl*	25p
☐ 552 08860 9	VENUS PLUS X	*Theodore Sturgean*	25p

General

☐ 552 98789 1 **INVESTING IN MAPS** (illustrated) *Roger Baynton-Williams* 125p
☐ 552 08768 8 **SEX MANNERS FOR OLDER TEENAGERS** (illustrated)
Robert Chartham 30p
☐ 552 07950 2 **SEXUAL BEHAVIOUR** *Dr. Eustace Chesser* 25p
☐ 552 08805 6 **WHO DO YOU THINK YOU ARE?** *Dr. Eustace Chesser* 25p
☐ 552 98572 4 **NEE DE LA VAGUE** (illustrated) *Lucien Clergue* 105p
☐ 552 08745 9 **MAGIC AND MYSTERY IN TIBET** *Alexandra David-Neel* 35p
☐ 552 08800 5 **CHARIOTS OF THE GODS?** (illustrated) *Erich von Daniken* 35p
☐ 552 08861 7 **THE AUTOBIOGRAPHY OF A SUPER TRAMP**
W. H. Davies 40p
☐ 552 08677 0 **ON THE EDGE OF THE ETHERIC** *Arthur Findlay* 30p
☐ 552 07400 4 **MY LIFE AND LOVES** *Frank Harris* 65p
☐ 552 98748 4 **MAKING LOVE** (Photographs) *Walter Hartford* 85p
☐ 552 08362 3 **A DOCTOR SPEAKS ON SEXUAL EXPRESSION**
IN MARRIAGE (illustrated) *Donald W. Hastings, M.D.* 50p
☐ 552 98247 4 **THE HISTORY OF THE NUDE IN PHOTOGRAPHY**
(illustrated) *Peter Lacey and Anthony La Rotonda* 125p
☐ 552 98345 4 **THE ARTIST AND THE NUDE** (illustrated) 105p
☐ 552 98862 6 **INVESTING IN GEORGIAN GLASS** (illustrated)
Ward Lloyd 125p
☐ 552 08069 1 **THE OTHER VICTORIANS** *Steven Marcus* 50p
☐ 553 08664 9 **THE HUMAN ZOO** *Desmond Morris* 35p
☐ 552 08162 0 **THE NAKED APE** *Desmond Morris* 30p
☐ 552 08765 3 **THE HERMIT** *T. Lobsang Rampa* 30p
☐ 552 08880 3 **THE THIRTEENTH CANDLE** *T. Lobsang Rampa* 35p
☐ 552 08630 4 **BRUCE TEGNER'S COMPLETE BOOK OF**
KARATE (illustrated) *Bruce Tegner* 40p
☐ 552 98479 5 **MADEMOISELLE 1 + 1** (illustrated)
Marcel Veronese and Jean-Claude Peretz 105p
☐ 552 08807 2 **BIRTH CONTROL NOW AND TOMORROW** *Clive Wood* 30p

Western

☐ 552 08532 4 **BLOOD BROTHER** *Elliott Arnold* 40p
☐ 552 08907 9 **SUDDEN: TROUBLESHOOTER** *Frederick H. Christian* 25p
☐ 552 08841 2 **BAD HOMBRE** *J. T. Edson* 25p
☐ 552 08895 1 **GO BACK TO HELL** No. 65 *J. T. Edson* 25p
☐ 552 08840 4 **UNDER THE SWEETWATER RIM** *Louis L'Amour* 25p
☐ 552 08896 X **HOW THE WEST WAS WON** *Louis L'Amour* 30p
☐ 552 08857 9 **REVENGE** No. 11 *Louis Masterson* 20p
☐ 552 08858 7 **STORM OVER SONORA** No. 12 *Louis Masterson* 20p
☐ 552 08906 0 **SUDDEN: MARSHAL OF LAWLESS** *Oliver Strange* 25p

Crime

☐ 552 08826 9 **MURDER WITH MUSHROOMS** *John Creasey* 25p
☐ 552 08875 7 **THE TWISTED WIRE** *Richard Falkirk* 25p
☐ 552 08809 9 **MADRIGAL** *John Gardner* 25p
☐ 552 07780 7 **DEAD MARCH IN THREE KEYS** *Norah Lofts* 25p
☐ 552 08604 1 **RED FILE FOR CALLAN** *James Mitchell* 25p
☐ 552 08839 0 **TOUCHFEATHER TOO** *Jimmy Sangster* 25p
☐ 552 08894 3 **DUCA AND THE MILAN MURDERS** *Giorgio Scerbanenco* 30p
☐ 552 08758 0 **SURVIVAL . . . ZERO!** *Mickey Spillane* 25p

All these books are available at your bookshop or newsagent: or can be ordered direct from the publisher. Just tick the titles you want and fill in the form below.

CORGI BOOKS, Cash Sales Department, P.O. Box 11, Falmouth, Cornwall.
Please send cheque or postal order. No currency, and allow 5p per book to cover the cost of postage and packing in the U.K., and overseas.

NAME ....

ADDRESS ....

(FEB. 72) ....